Praise for
The Last of the Appl

'What a cracker of a debut! A beautiful story of family and orchards, of secrets and love and forgiveness' —Victoria Purman, author of *The Women's Pages* and *The Land Girls*

'Mary-Lou Stephens has crafted a taut family drama set against a backdrop of environmental and political upheaval. The crisp prose sparkles and the characters stay with you long after the story ends. A wonderful debut' —Lauren Chater, author of *Gulliver's Wife* and *The Lace Weaver*

'This beautifully told story, starting in the late 1960s Tasmania in the midst of a catastrophic firestorm, explores how change – whether wrought by disaster, transforming social mores or politics – impacts upon individuals, families and communities. Following the lives of two orchardist families across the years, it has such emotional heft and a huge heart. Timeless yet also telling an achingly familiar story to us here and now, this is an unforgettable tale of love and loss, triumph and tragedy, featuring flawed, resilient and courageous characters who will linger in your heart and mind long after the last page' — Karen Brooks, author of *The Good Wife of Bath* and *The Darkest Shore*

'*The Last of the Apple Blossom* is a love letter to Tasmania's Huon Valley and a testament to the resilience of the human spirit. Mary-Lou Stephens writes evocatively about family secrets, love, sacrifice, and finding the courage to rise again after devastating loss. An engrossing and poignant story, beautifully told' —Christine Wells, author of *Sisters of the Resistance* and *The Juliet Code*

'I have long been a fan of Mary-Lou's writing, which is always evocative and compelling. What a wonderful story this is, set at such a poignant moment in Tasmania's history. I loved it' — Josephine Moon, author of *The Jam Queens* and *The Cake Maker's Wish*

'An epic story of love, friendship, secrets and betrayal, and the woman who fought sexist tradition to retain the family orchard. Set in the aftermath of the disastrous 1967 Black Tuesday fires that devastated Tasmania and the thriving apple industry, *The Last of the Apple Blossom* will uplift, and keep you guessing, until the very last page' —Jodie Miller, author of *What Does it Feel Like Being Born?*

Mary-Lou Stephens was born in Tasmania, studied acting at The Victorian College of the Arts and played in bands in Melbourne, Hobart and Sydney. Eventually she got a proper job – in radio, where she was a presenter and music director, first with commercial radio and then with the ABC.

She received rave reviews for her memoir *Sex, Drugs and Meditation* (2013), the true story of how meditation changed her life, saved her job and helped her find a husband.

Mary-Lou has worked and played all over Australia and now lives on the Sunshine Coast with her husband and a hive of killer native bees.

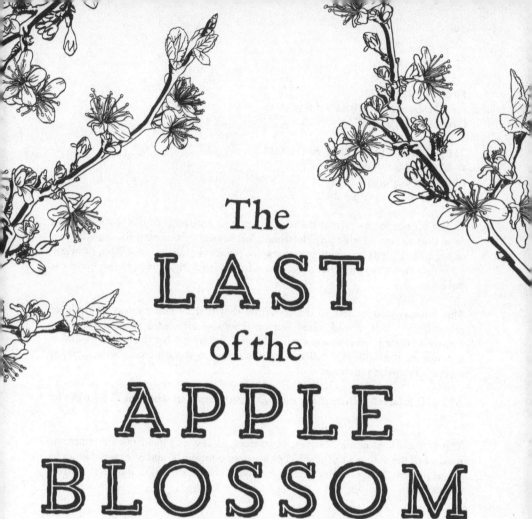

The
LAST
of the
APPLE
BLOSSOM

Mary-Lou Stephens

FICTION
HQ

First Published 2021
First Australian Paperback Edition 2021
ISBN 9781867226437

Published by
HQ Fiction
An imprint of Harlequin Enterprises (Australia) Pty Limited (ABN 47 001 180 918),
a subsidiary of HarperCollins Publishers Australia Pty Limited (ABN 36 009 913 517)
Level 13, 201 Elizabeth St
SYDNEY NSW 2000
AUSTRALIA

® and TM (apart from those relating to FSC®) are trademarks of Harlequin
Enterprises (Australia) Pty Limited or its corporate affiliates. Trademarks indicated
with ® are registered in Australia, New Zealand and in other countries.

A catalogue record for this book is available from the National Library of Australia
www.librariesaustralia.nla.gov.au

Printed and bound in Australia by McPherson's Printing Group

MIX
Paper from
responsible sources
FSC
www.fsc.org
FSC® C001695

For the orchardists, it wasn't for nothing.

1

Hobart, 7 February 1967

Catherine

Catherine thought the beach would be safe, with its slim arc of sand and the cool water just beyond. The children would splash like shimmering fish, darting through the soothing mix of salt and fresh water of the Derwent Estuary. They'd get through this day together, playing and laughing in the shallow water.

She was wrong.

It was obvious almost as soon as she left the frightened occupants of her classroom under the care of Miss Downie. In the playground the wind was fierce, whipping her with leaves and grit. Catherine put a hand up to protect her eyes and leant into the hot blast as she struggled across the melting bitumen of the forecourt. The smoke was thick and heavy, assaulting her throat and lungs with a brutal thuggishness. She pushed her way towards the gate leading to Nutgrove Beach.

'Where're you going?' Tim made his way across the playground towards her, his head bowed against the wind.

'To see if the beach is an option.'

'I'm coming with you. Stay close.'

Catherine nodded. Tim was the school's part-time gardener and handyman – a young man of surf-bleached hair and sea-blue eyes, who had, on this strangest of days, taken on the unlikely role of protector for the teachers and children who fretted inside the school's red-brick walls. The lane between the school and the beach, usually a delightful sandy path with tree-fringed fences, had become an eerie gateway to hell. Stumbling through the haze and heat they reached what had once been friendly shores. Today the hot, relentless north-westerlies blasted it into a howling sandstorm. Catherine almost cried out against the razor-like cuts of sand biting into her skin. The water was darkly ominous and shifted restlessly under a sky black with the smoke of a hundred fires that ringed the city. On any other day the Hobart docks would be visible from where she stood, a mere two suburbs away, but today the unnerving darkness obliterated any sense of place or familiarity.

Tim reached for her hand as they made their way back, and she grasped his gratefully, half-blinded by the acrid air. Crossing the deserted playground, her heart thudded against her ribs, from lack of oxygen or from her growing concern she wasn't sure. Tim squeezed her hand as they pushed through the main door of the school into the relative calm of the foyer.

'Don't worry,' he said. 'We'll be okay.'

Catherine wanted to believe him but her instincts told her otherwise. She'd grown up with the ever-present threat of bushfire. It was the scent of her summers in the Huon Valley, surrounded by rows of apple trees, cow paddocks and the bush – eucalyptus, banksia, wattle and black sheoak – all ready to burst into flames with just an errant spark or an ill-considered burn-off. But here in beachside suburbia, among the prunus and agapanthus, neat houses and concrete pavements, the threat was dangerously out of place. Catherine dropped Tim's hand with a despairing shake of her head. Would they be okay? Sandy Bay Infant School was only one row of houses back from Nutgrove Beach. She'd thought it would be enough to save them. Now she wasn't sure.

In the bathroom she peeled off her sweat-soaked slip and stockings. A bare-legged young teacher would usually have the mothers' tongues wagging, but today she doubted anyone would notice. Splashing her face and underarms with water, Catherine pushed down her feelings of unease. She smoothed her cotton dress, knowing she needed to look composed and confident when she stood in front of her pupils. They'd arrived for their first day of Grade One this morning nervous and excited, with brand-new exercise books and freshly sharpened pencils at the ready. Now they were too hot to think or care. The sky was frightening, the air didn't smell right and it hurt to breathe. They wanted their mothers, and even though more than one of them would call her 'mummy' in the coming year, Catherine knew that she was not an adequate substitute.

'Andrew, can you make sure all the windows are tightly closed?' she asked one of the three Andrews in her class. 'And Sarah, help Philip pull down all the blinds, please? The darker it is in here the cooler we'll feel.' Catherine knew this wasn't necessarily true, but she needed to reassure the children, and the huge red sun outside the windows was working against all her efforts. She bent down and touched the floor. The linoleum was only slightly cooler than the air but it was enough. If the smoke got worse the floor was the safest place. The air down low would stay breathable for longer.

3

'I have an idea,' Catherine said to the heat-flushed faces in front of her. 'Boys, take off your shirts. And girls, if you want to, you can take off your uniforms.' The school dresses were made of nylon – easy care for busy mums but the worst thing to wear in this debilitating heat. 'We're going to lie on the floor where it's cooler.' There were a number of confused frowns. Catherine laughed lightly, straining to keep a hint of optimism in her voice. 'It's just too hot to do anything else.'

Slow, hot minutes ticked by. The children lay listlessly on the floor. The wail of yet another siren racing down Sandy Bay Road echoed along the corridor. It had been the constant soundtrack to the day. Catherine's mind raced with it. How many fire engines were there in Hobart? How many police cars and how many ambulances? More importantly, would there be enough?

Miss Downie knocked gently on the open classroom door and beckoned Catherine into the corridor. 'I've just heard from the Education Department.' Miss Downie kept her voice low to prevent the children from hearing. 'We're to send the students home. I'll ring as many parents as I can while the lines are still up.'

'While the lines are up?' Catherine swallowed her rising sense of panic.

'Telephone poles are burning. Phone lines are down in the outer suburbs.' Miss Downie closed her eyes for a moment. When she opened them again, the look of determination and strength Catherine was accustomed to was back. 'I see you brought your car to school today.'

Catherine nodded. When her grandmother had died last year Catherine had inherited her old but well-maintained Hillman Minx. She'd never have been able to afford a car otherwise. The school was less than a ten-minute walk from her rented garden flat, but this morning she'd decided to drive. In this heat, she'd have been a red-faced mess by the time she arrived in the classroom if she hadn't. Not that it mattered now. There was sweat in every crevice of her body, even without her stockings and slip.

'Good,' Miss Downie said. 'I want you to take the students who live on Mount Nelson to Mrs Dunlop's house. Tracey Dunlop and Andrew Wells from your class, Deborah Mitford from Grade Two and Cecily Fletcher in Kindergarten.'

Catherine knew Mount Nelson well. It was a popular suburb just up the hill from Sandy Bay with beautiful views of Hobart and the Derwent. But it was also surrounded by bush.

'Are you sure?' Catherine asked.

Even in this heat Miss Downie's frown was withering, reminding Catherine that she'd always be intimidated by her. 'Yes. Take the children to Nelson Road. It's the last safe house on the mountain.'

2

Huon Valley, 7 February 1967
Annie

Annie had seen fire before. Every summer, the smell of burning eucalypts filled the air. Flames raced through the grass in the paddocks and plumes of smoke from bushfires rose above the hills over the river behind Port Huon. Most fires were easily contained. Sometimes one would threaten property, and a call would go out for volunteers to man hoses, buckets and bags. But in the years she'd lived here, nearly a decade now, she'd never experienced anything like this. The north-westerlies were blasting the orchard with dust and leaves, pushing the bitter smoke into every corner of the house. She'd been forced to close the windows and stuff wet towels under the doors. The air inside was stifling, almost suffocating, but it was better than more smoke coming into the house.

Annie prayed the precautions her husband, Dave, had put in place would be enough to keep them safe. Mark, a friend from Dave's

6

school days who was staying in the old house with his family, had helped as well. They'd taken the ute out hours ago to open the gates so the cattle could escape if the paddock caught fire and to check the upper block where the apple trees grew close to the bush. One ember and the dry open forest with its ground layer of grasses and shrubs would go up like a tinderbox. Her eyes flicked yet again to the kitchen clock. They should be back by now.

Her youngest sons started whinging again, Scott toddling around wearing only his nappy and Greg, who was almost toilet-trained, in his bathers. Mark's son Charlie, nearly the same age as Greg, had stopped playing with a Matchbox car, a hand-me-down from one of her many boys, to stare forlornly at nothing. His quietness worried her, but she wasn't surprised given what he'd gone through. Only little Angela was unfussed by the crushing heat. She lay calmly in her bassinet, staring at the ceiling with serene newborn eyes. Annie could hardly pull herself away from her tiny, perfect face. What a blessing after five boys.

This morning she'd waved goodbye to the school bus with her three eldest on board, relieved the summer holidays were finally over. Now she was worried. Surely the school would be in touch if there were any problems in Cygnet?

Greg stomped up, red-faced and cranky. 'Too hot,' he said, pointing to his bathers. 'Swimming?'

The idea had crossed Annie's mind but she'd dismissed it. The river wasn't far, but in this heat, with these winds, still an impossible journey. Their best bet was to stay in the house where there were other ways of keeping the boys cool.

'Yes, a swim,' she said. 'In the bath.' Dave had asked her to fill the tub before he left. If the fires came it would be faster to scoop water out of the tub than fill buckets from a tap. She didn't want to think about that, or pay any attention to the churning in her stomach. The children were her focus. Annie stripped off Scott's nappy, helped Greg out of his bathers and plonked her boys in the bath.

'Charlie,' she called out. 'There's room for you too.'

His face peeked around the doorway. Mark's son looked so much like his father. The boy slipped off his shorts and waited for Annie to lift him into the bath. Her boys had accepted Charlie as one of their own. They were used to being surrounded by brothers, what was one more? But Charlie came from a different world and she sensed his hesitation. She splashed Charlie gently. 'See, isn't this better? Much cooler.' He nodded. Not much of a talker, this one, but it was a relief to have a quieter boy around.

Annie filled the bathroom basin with water, lifted Angela from the bassinet and unwrapped her nappy. While the boys played in the bath, Annie trickled cool water over her.

'What a beautiful girl.' Annie bent down to kiss the small, soft forehead. The sweet smell of her baby filled her nostrils, dispelling the rough, smoke-tinged air just for a moment. Annie stroked the fine down on her daughter's head. 'The things we'll do together. The times we'll have.'

The tin roof rattled loudly in a fierce gust of wind. Thank God Dave had cleaned the gutters two days ago when the fire danger had risen to extreme. Last winter had been unseasonably wet, followed by an early spring and then the driest summer for more than seventy years. All the growth from the rains was now tinder dry, ready to burst into flames at the slightest provocation.

Her husband knew his way around fire, having grown up here in the valley. He respected and feared it. Only this morning Dave had sworn under his breath, so the children wouldn't hear, about the idiots still burning off and the firebugs up Mount Wellington who'd been caught but let off with only a warning and whose fires still burnt. The practice of letting fires in the bush just burn themselves out was a particular bugbear. 'Burn themselves out?' he'd muttered. 'As if that's going to happen in these conditions.'

Before they'd left, he and Mark had hosed down the house and set sprinklers on the browned-off grass around the house. He'd blocked the downpipes and flooded the roof gutters with water. They'd also filled the orchard sprayer with water and left it close to the house and filled as many buckets as they could find. Dave had a couple of knapsack pumps in the ute to put out fires on their property and in case he was called to fight other fires in the area. He was a good man; thoughtful, generous and capable. A pang of fear stabbed her heart at the thought of him out there battling the heat and flames. She couldn't – no, she wouldn't – lose him now, not after everything they'd been through together.

They'd first met on a day very different to this one. On the fifteenth of September 1957 the heavens had opened and dumped a record amount of rain on Hobart. Annie was in her last year at an all-girls private school. After staying late to swot for her final exams, she'd made a run for the bus, but it went sailing past. She was left bedraggled and soaked to the skin. A ute pulled up and a young man at the wheel asked if she wanted a lift. Even though his appearance was one of clean-scrubbed honesty and she'd wanted desperately to say yes, she'd had to refuse. What would her parents say? What would her friends think? The school would definitely disapprove. He drove away, and her heart sank. She was disappointed he'd given up so easily, but to her joy he hadn't gone far. She'd watched as he parked just outside the bus zone and came running back with an umbrella, offering to stay with her until the next bus arrived. He introduced himself as Dave Pearson and told her he was from the Huon Valley. Dave had taken a drive around the town while waiting to pick up his father. She'd laughed – in such pouring rain! He'd laughed too and admitted to thinking it was a stupid thing to do – until he'd seen Annie, clearly in need of rescuing. He'd seemed genuinely open and friendly, and his umbrella was a godsend. It had helped that he was tall and good looking, but she'd learnt not to trust those attributes. Some of the boys she met at school dances were handsome, but vain with it. They were from rich families, like hers, and tended to be condescending and often mean. She saw none of those traits in Dave. Their conversation flowed with warmth and laughter as the rain pelted down around them.

They were together for just a few minutes on that September day but within that time a connection formed which had surprised them both. That was ten years ago. Before they were married there'd been a time she was terrified he would abandon her, but he'd remained, steadfast and true. It was her parents who'd disappeared from her life.

The wind was fiercer now, the roar of it like a train rushing past. The darkness was almost complete, the smoke blocking out the sun. Annie flicked the light switch but nothing happened. Singing gently to Angela, she picked her up from the basin, holding her baby's wet skin close to her own. 'Sweet little baby, don't you cry,' she crooned. 'I'll keep you safe from the fire in the sky.' Annie walked slowly into the lounge room, suppressing the growing anxiety gnawing at her stomach, and tried the light switch there. Nothing. In the kitchen she picked up the phone. No dial tone. She took a steadying breath. She had to stay calm, for the children.

'Mummy,' Greg called out to her from the bathroom. 'Mummy?' There was a tremor in his voice. The tears would start soon.

3

Catherine

The children were quiet on the drive towards Nelson Road, their wide eyes taking in the eerie orange sky raining black ashes around them, the emergency vehicles racing by and the trees bent over double in the gale-force wind. The sun was mesmerising, a dirty red ball ten times its usual size. None of it felt real. It was some strange dream or a horrible nightmare. How would it end? Catherine lifted her chin in determination. She would not allow her thoughts to take her there.

Inside the last safe house on the mountain, the lounge room was full of children, playing or listening to a story one of the mothers was reading from a picture book. Usually the view from this room would be a stunning vista over Sandy Bay, down to the Derwent and across to the Eastern Shore, but today the large windows presented nothing but a vague shifting view through the pall of blackening smoke. Catherine settled the children and went into the kitchen

11

where a group of women huddled fretfully around the radio. All of them had homes further up the mountain and husbands battling to protect those homes with nothing but garden hoses and wet gunny sacks. Would these women have houses or husbands to go home to at the end of this terrible day?

Mrs Dunlop stood behind the laminated kitchen counter busying herself with a pot of tea and plates of homemade biscuits. Wisps of hair had escaped from the bun at the nape of her neck, and she had the look of a woman who'd known hardship but nothing as bad as this. Catherine cleared her throat. 'Mrs Dunlop, I'm Tracey's teacher, Catherine Turner.'

Mrs Dunlop smiled but it didn't reach the worry in her eyes. 'Yes, of course. Thank you for bringing her home – and the other children.' She raised her hands to indicate the hubbub in the lounge room and kitchen. 'I couldn't get away. My husband ...' She paused and tucked a wayward strand of hair behind her ear. 'He has the car.' Her eyes flicked towards the mountain.

A muffled cry came from one of the women at the kitchen table. 'What is it?' Catherine asked.

'The fire's reached Waterworks Road. Houses are burning in Proctors Road and at Taroona.'

Catherine bit back a gasp. Proctors Road was just the other side of Mount Nelson and Taroona was the next suburb down the river from Sandy Bay. The fire was all around them, and getting closer.

'We're surrounded,' another of the women whispered, her eyes fearful.

Mrs Dunlop placed cups of tea in front of them. 'Stay calm. We're here to take care of the children. And turn the radio off. It's only upsetting you.'

Rather than turning it off, the women huddled closer to the radio in a tight knot. The constant stream of updates might be grim, but the spell it wove was strong. There was a need to know what was going on, even if it forebode disaster.

Mrs Dunlop shrugged, too hot and anxious to fight that battle. She turned to Catherine. 'Do you need to stay? You're more than welcome.'

'Thank you, but I have to report back to the school.' Her thoughts raced to Miss Downie and any of the children who might still be there. If Taroona could burn surely nowhere was safe.

The Hillman's headlights did little to cut through the smoke as Catherine drove back along Sandy Bay Road. Her hands gripped the steering wheel hard, turning her knuckles deathly white. Thankfully the road was wide since it was impossible to tell if a vehicle was coming the other way until it was right in front of her. She pulled into the small car park. Tim's station wagon wasn't there. He might be taking some of the children home or perhaps he'd left the school to its fate. A small twinge of disappointment surprised her. Tim was a cliché in some ways and an enigma in others. His part-time job at the school was a means to an end. He lived to surf. More often than not there was a mattress in the back of his station wagon and a few supplies, plus a surfboard strapped to the roof racks. As soon as his work was done he'd set off on one of his surfing adventures up the east coast or, if the conditions were right, braving the wild waves of the west. Sometimes, when she was on playground duty and he was in the yard, he'd talk to her about weather and winds, water and tides. In turn she'd tell him about spring apple blossom, long twilight summers and crisp autumn mornings just right for the harvest. Nature was their common ground, although his was salty and shifting while hers was firm and fertile.

Inside the school the air was heavy and eerily silent. Every window was shut tight and all the blinds pulled down. Catherine found Miss

Downie in her office, her usually perfectly coifed hair ruffled and a sheen of sweat on her brow.

'Are all the children safely home?' Catherine asked.

'Home, yes, or in other people's homes. Safe?' Miss Downie's frown deepened. She motioned to Catherine to sit in the chair opposite. 'The fire has surrounded Hobart. It's also widespread down the Channel and in the Huon Valley.'

Catherine felt the trepidation growing inside her. Her home was safe – her parents, her brother, the orchard. Weren't they?

'I'm afraid the fire has jumped the Huon. The fire front is moving so rapidly not even a river can stop it.'

'What? Where has it jumped the river?' At Huonville the river was narrow but further down the valley, where their orchard nestled on its banks, the water was over a mile wide.

Miss Downie stretched out a hand as if to comfort Catherine then hesitated; her fingers stranded in mid-air. 'Wattle Grove.'

The shock hit Catherine like a blow. But fire didn't discriminate, she knew that. It couldn't be held back by the force of love or righteousness. She stood, her knees shaky, and grabbed the back of the chair for support. 'I have to go.'

Miss Downie stood to face her. 'You can't. The roads are closed. Mount Wellington is on fire, as is the Channel. There's no way through. The safest place is here. Even if the fire comes this far you can take shelter at the beach—'

'The beach is a sandstorm. There's no protection there.'

'There are some coves, facing south. Even Long Beach would provide a form of refuge.'

It was true. Long Beach was close, just around the corner, and with its jetty and pontoon anchored off the beach it offered many places for the desperate to cling to. Catherine shook her

14

head. A frantic buzzing hummed in her brain and she couldn't dislodge it. 'No.'

'Please, reconsider.'

Catherine backed towards the door, shaking her head. Every other thought had been obliterated. The only words she could hear were the ones that kept repeating in her mind. She had to get to Wattle Grove. She had to get home.

In the car park, her chin tucked down against the gritty wind and ashes, she faltered, but only for a second. Her little brother needed her. Her parents. The orchard. A spare pair of hands at a pump, on a hose, or even with a bucket could make all the difference.

Tim's car appeared out of the smoke like a phantom. He jumped out and was at her side in a moment.

'What's happening?'

'All the children have been evacuated. I'm going home.'

He frowned. 'Home? Which one?'

Catherine paused. She had only one. Much as she loved the little garden flat she rented during the school year, it would never be home. She reached to open her car door.

Tim placed his hand on hers. 'Where are you going?'

Catherine wrenched her hand away, and pushed back against the threat of tears. 'Wattle Grove is on fire.'

'You can't go down the Huon. No way.'

'So I keep hearing. I don't care. I'm going.' Her teeth grated tight with tension. She had to be as fierce as this fire. Fiercer.

'Not in your car. Let's take mine. And we'll need gear from the workshop if we're going to have any chance of getting through this. Come on.'

'We?'

He turned back, his voice strong against the wind. 'I'm not letting you go into that firestorm on your own.' He put up a hand to stop the objection forming on her lips. 'No way. So come and help me.'

Catherine paused but only for a moment. She could see sense in what he said. His Holden was more robust than her small car and if there was anything in the workshop that could help get through a fire, it was a bonus. Every minute she hesitated was a minute wasted. She shielded her eyes against a hot gust of ash and followed him.

4

7 February 1967

Annie

'Why is it so dark, Mummy?' Greg asked. 'Is it bedtime? We haven't had tea.'

Annie smoothed his wet hair. 'It's a funny old day, isn't it?' She kept her voice light, hoping he wouldn't hear the tremor in it. 'The clouds are black today but there's no rain. We could do with some rain, couldn't we?' She dipped her hand in the bathwater, lifted it up above his head and let it sprinkle on him in big heavy drops. 'Rain like this. Wouldn't it be wonderful?'

Greg giggled. 'I'm going to make it rain on Scott.' He scooped up some water and poured it onto his little brother's head. 'It's raining, it's pouring, it's raining, it's pouring.' He was yet to master the rest of the nursery rhyme.

Angela lay on a towel on the floor, gurgling with delight every time a drop of water from the boy's antics landed on her naked skin. Annie closed her eyes for a moment. 'Please, God,' she whispered.

17

'Help me keep them safe. And if I can't …' She stopped. She didn't want to think about the alternative, let alone voice her concerns to a God she wasn't sure existed. In Hobart she'd gone to church with her parents every week, but that was another life. When she'd first come to the valley she'd attended church with Dave every week but after the birth of her third, a whole Sunday morning spent organising and transporting her brood, then trying to keep them quiet in a church not designed for noisy, squirming boys, seemed like a waste of time and energy when there was so much work to do. Still, if there was ever a time for prayer it was now.

Above the screaming wind, Annie heard her husband's voice, calling her name. Her body slumped, the relief incredible. He was home. Everything would be all right. Dave would protect them.

'I'm in the bathroom.' She staggered to her feet, weakened by the hours of staying strong for the boys.

Dave pulled open the door and she fell into his arms, clinging to his blackened, sweat-stained body.

'It's okay,' he whispered in her ear. 'I'm here. Sorry I've been gone so long. We drove the tractor and the ute into the middle of the biggest block in the orchard and had to walk back. Hopefully they'll be safe there. The truck and the crawler are behind the house. If the garage goes up and the fuel bowsers with it, we'd lose them all.'

Annie pulled back and looked into his eyes, so blue against the grime and soot covering his skin. 'The school? Our boys?'

'Hang on a sec.' Dave knelt down beside the bath and gave his youngest boys a hug.

'Yuck, Daddy. You're all dirty.' Greg rubbed at the grime on his father's face with hands too small to make much difference. Scott scooped up water and splashed his dad, trying to help.

'You little scamps.' Dave smiled. He ruffled Charlie's hair. 'Your dad's busy at the moment but he'll come and see you as soon as he can.'

Charlie nodded.

Dave stood and took Annie's arm. 'Now, I just need to talk to Mummy for a sec.'

They edged out into the hallway. Annie left the bathroom door open a little to keep an eye on Angela. Dave took her hands. 'Are you all okay?'

She nodded, not wanting to speak in case her voice revealed the fear churning inside her.

'The school is safe. Looks as though Cygnet is going to be all right at this stage.'

Annie let out a small groan. Despite the heat, Dave put his arms around her and she nestled into his chest. 'Thank God,' she whispered.

'Listen.' He held her elbows and pulled away slightly to look into her eyes. 'The fire has jumped the river. The scrub beside the lower orchard is burning and it's headed this way.'

Annie's throat seized up. The lower orchard was just on the other side of the house. 'Can we make a run for it? Get the kids in the car and go?'

Dave shook his head. 'Too late for that.' He kissed her forehead. 'I love you. Always will.' He tilted her chin up and kissed her lightly on the lips. 'Remember, whatever happens, we will be together.' He took a step away from her, his face heavy with a sorrow she'd never seen before. 'Mark's in the yard with the hose. I'll take over so he can see Charlie for a moment.'

Annie tried to speak but had no words. Mark might be saying goodbye to his son.

19

'We've set the sprayer on the house.' Dave's voice held a quiet determination. 'We've got enough water for now. But I'm not going to lie to you—'

'You never have.'

'It's not good. I've never seen anything like this. But we're prepared. We have a fighting chance.'

Annie met his eyes, desperately holding back her tears.

He kissed her once more, and was gone.

5

7 February 1967

Catherine

Barricades and a policeman made a clear statement at the roadblock on Davey Street, barring access to Huon Road. Lines of stationary cars filled the street as people milled around in the wind and smoke trying to find out if they'd be able to get to their homes. Catherine was reassured by the assortment of gear she and Tim had piled in the back of the station wagon – an axe, containers of water, gardening gloves, bolt cutters, a hacksaw, two woollen blankets soaked with water, and a chainsaw.

'Should we try?'

Tim shook his head. 'Nah. There's no getting through here.'

'Let's try Strickland Avenue. We can get onto Huon Road from there. We'll have to go up Cascade Road.' There was no way Catherine was giving up at the first hurdle.

Tim nodded, his mouth set in a determined line as he turned the car around.

They cut across the suburban streets of South Hobart where weatherboard and brick houses shifted like spectres through the ashen gloom. The sky grew ever-darker with the sun a dull, apocalyptic red. Crawling along Cascade Road in thickening smoke, the only other cars they saw were abandoned, many with doors left open. Catherine checked her watch. On a good day the drive to Wattle Grove would take at least an hour and a half along the winding and treacherous roads. Today was not a good day. Anxiety rose in her chest. How long would it take them to reach her home? To reach her little brother? Shadowy figures staggered past – a woman clutching a photo album to her chest, a young man carrying a record player, and two men carting a couch onto the footpath. Another man appeared out of the dense air, waving them down. Tim slowed to a stop and wound down his window. The wind blasted through the car like a furnace.

'You can't go any further,' the man said. 'Be mad if you did.'

'We have to,' Catherine said. She touched Tim's shoulder in a small insistent plea.

'You going to try and stop us, mate?' Tim asked.

'Look, all I know is I was trying to get home and the police stopped me. They were barricading the road but got called somewhere else. They asked me to redirect traffic, to stop people from going any further.'

Catherine's voice was barely more than a whimper. 'Please.'

'Appreciate what you're doing, mate,' Tim said. 'But we're gonna give it a go.'

The man shrugged. 'The Brewery is about to go. Fern Tree too. Hell, the whole of Mount Wellington is on fire. You want to die, it's up to you. I've done my bit.' He stepped back, clearly hoping they'd turn around. Instead Tim drove forward.

It was a mistake. They'd hardly made it to Strickland Avenue before they were surrounded by burning houses and gardens. Wild tongues of fire shot out from the side of the road. An explosion blasted through the roar of the wind as a gum tree succumbed to the heat. Burning bark and twigs flew past. The smoke was choking, and visibility almost zero.

'We have to go back.' Catherine shook her head in frustration. 'That man was right. There's no chance we can get through this.'

'You sure?'

'There's another way. The Channel Highway.'

'Okay.' Tim put the car in reverse. There was a shudder, and the engine stopped. He frowned, turning the key in the ignition. Nothing.

'What's wrong?'

'The heat. It's probably evaporating the petrol before it gets to the engine.'

'Is that even possible?' Nothing about this day made sense.

'Just need to get down the road a bit, away from this.'

Catherine looked out at 'this' – walls of smoke tinged with red.

'Slide into the driver's seat,' Tim said. 'I'm going to push.'

She grabbed at his hand. 'You can't go out there.'

'We can't stay here. We have to move.'

Tim struggled to open the car door against the force of the gale. She gasped as the choking smoke poured into the car, scouring her throat and lungs.

He reached into his pocket and passed Catherine a handkerchief. 'It's clean.' In spite of everything, he grinned at her. 'Honest.'

She took it from him, wet it and wrapped the cotton over her nose and mouth. 'What about you?' Her voice was muffled.

Tim pulled out an old rag. 'This'll do me.'

Catherine poured some water on what once was an old T-shirt from the look of it, and handed it back to him.

A burning twig flew into the car, landing on Tim's leg. Catherine flicked it off and threw the last of the bottle's contents on the ember.

'Good idea.' He picked up a couple of the other bottles and poured the water over himself. 'While I push, keep trying to start the car, okay?'

Before she could object, he was out of the car. Catherine slid behind the wheel, made sure the car was in reverse and released the handbrake. She looked in the rear-view mirror but the hot, dense mist obliterated everything.

The back door swung open. Searing wind blasted through the car again. 'The metal's too hot,' Tim said. 'I need gloves.'

He moved around to the front of the car and pushed. The car began to move slowly, back down the road. Catherine turned the ignition. Nothing. She watched Tim straining against the car, his eyes streaming from the smoke. A burning leaf flew into his hair and to her horror she saw it catch alight. Didn't he realise? In this heat who could tell what was air, what was skin, what was fire? She yelled out, 'Your hair!'

Tim must have heard. He ripped the damp rag off his face and smothered his head with it.

'This is crazy,' Catherine muttered. 'And it's my fault.' She turned the ignition again. The engine spluttered, and her heart jumped with it. Then it cut out again. She slammed her hands against the steering wheel. The smoke turned orange. There had been flashes of vermillion and ochre before, but now the hue was steadier and closer. The roar of the wind was augmented by another sound, fiercer and stronger. 'We're not going to die here. We are not.' She turned the key and pumped the accelerator. 'Start, you cow. Start now!' Nothing. They were stuck. Trapped.

Catherine heard it before she saw it – a wall of flame above the car, 60 feet high, massive and terrifying. Her mind froze in fear for a moment, before her racing heart kicked her brain back into motion. She yanked on the handbrake, grabbed the damp blankets from the back seat and jumped out of the car.

'Get down,' she yelled at Tim, pulling him onto the ground as she threw the blankets over them.

The wall of fire crested and crashed, spitting out fireballs as it hit the verge on the other side of the road. Then it was gone – moving on to create more chaos and destruction. The stench of scorched, wet wool assaulted her nostrils, but she welcomed it. It meant they were alive. Catherine shook with fear and relief. She leant into Tim's body as they huddled together, hot and stinking and, miraculously, still breathing.

Tim's voice was low, and soft. 'I think you just saved my life.'

'More likely almost killed you.' Fire was unpredictable and they may not be as lucky next time. 'Let's get out of here.'

'I'm going to give Erica Jane one more go. If she doesn't start we'd be better off making a run for it.'

'Erica Jane?'

'Yeah.' His smile pushed through the layers of pain and exhaustion. 'Erica Jane, the EJ Holden. She's been on some wild rides with me and come up trumps, but this ...'

He stopped, and Catherine understood. It was indescribable.

They eased back into the car, still wrapped in the blankets. It was stifling, but at least they were protected from the fiery embers, dropping from above like rain. Tim muttered some words Catherine couldn't hear, a prayer perhaps, as he placed his hands on the steering wheel. The soot on his forehead ran dark tears of sweat into his eyes. Slowly, almost reverently, he turned the ignition. The engine caught, and turned, and kept turning.

Tim didn't hesitate. He rammed his foot on the accelerator and reversed.

They retreated through the ghostly, deserted streets towards Sandy Bay. Catherine directed Tim to her flat in a daze. She needed a change of clothes and a chance to think. This urgency to get home to the orchard, to the valley, to her little brother had nearly got them killed. Catherine prided herself on being reliable and clear-headed, but her actions today had been anything but. It was as if forces greater than herself were at play, not only externally but internally. The buzzing was still in her head; the impulse to go home had not abated, despite all they'd gone through. When they arrived, Tim followed her past Mrs Sampson's front door and down the path beside the house towards the garden flat. It wasn't until they were inside – her single bed up against the wall near the wardrobe, the kitchenette, the small couch and coffee table – that she realised her mistake. 'You can't be here.'

'What do you mean?'

'My landlady, Mrs Sampson, doesn't allow male visitors.'

'Far out! Is she stuck back in the 1950s?'

'I guess so.' Catherine's parents had been concerned about her living in the city on her own and had vetted Mrs Sampson thoroughly. Catherine hadn't minded. In many ways she was still a country girl. And that's where she needed to be right now, home, in the valley.

'I don't care. And I don't think she will either, not today. I'm not leaving. We're gonna get through this together.'

Catherine turned towards the sink in the pretence of pouring a glass of water. Her hands were shaking. The physical shock of their narrow escape still resonated through her body. The memory of the massive wall of flame was still vivid. She couldn't risk Tim's life again. Catherine turned again to face him, leaning against the sink for support. The scorched patch of hair on Tim's head, the burns on his hands and his smoke-reddened eyes made her determination to go on alone even stronger. 'I'm going to keep going, but I'm taking the Hillman—'

Tim tried to object but she stopped him. 'Long Beach is probably the safest place – even in this wind; you could go there. But I'm going to try to get to Wattle Grove. My little brother ...' Her voice faltered. She was frustrated by its betrayal. 'I have to get home.'

He stepped closer. 'You saved my life.'

She shook her head, annoyed with herself, with him, with everything. 'I put your life in danger. I could have got you killed.'

His voice was gentle. 'You didn't force me to go with you. It was my choice. And I'm choosing to do it again. You're not going out there again without me.'

Catherine steadied herself against the sink. His gaze was intense and compelling. He was an idiot for wanting to come, but despite her reservations, gratitude welled inside her. She didn't have to do this alone. 'Okay.'

'All right then.' He smiled. 'But first, do you think I could have a shower without your landlady completely freaking out? I gotta wash the crap out of my eyes and get some Savlon on these burns.'

'Oh, gosh.' That was the first thing she should have done: help patch up some of the damage she'd caused him. 'Yes, of course.' Mrs Sampson must be out, otherwise she would have been knocking on Catherine's door by now. Catherine hoped she was safe, or as safe as anyone could be with a fire raging out of control in the suburbs of Hobart.

'Through here?' He nodded towards the only internal door.

'There's a clean towel on the shelf. The Savlon's in the drawer under the basin.'

'Won't be long.'

While Tim was in the shower, she stood at the kitchen sink washing her face and arms, sloughing away the soot and cinders. The water from the cold tap was almost hot. The heat of this day was relentless. Catherine flicked on the radio, listening through the whine of the wind for the latest reports, none of them good; the Channel was a fiery crucible, Snug was gone, Kettering, Oyster Cove, Woodbridge and Margate, the list went on. And in the Huon? She listened keenly for any mention of Wattle Grove, or of Cygnet – half hoping, half fearing. Her little brother, her home, her parents, the orchard, her best friend Annie on the neighbouring orchard – all the things she loved were there. What was left?

The rattle of the plumbing stopped. Tim must be out of the shower. Quickly, she changed into jeans, a long-sleeved woollen shirt and her sturdy Blundstone boots. She'd be even hotter, but better protected from embers and burning debris. Back at the sink, she filled more bottles and jars with water.

Tim emerged from the bathroom, shirtless, with his hair still dripping. Catherine averted her eyes. It was one thing to see men in their bathers at the beach, but a half-naked man in her flat was another thing altogether. Her mother, let alone Mrs Sampson, would be horrified.

'Just gonna grab a cleanish shirt out of my car,' he said. 'Hey, you should have a shower too. It'll help.'

Catherine frowned at her hands, the couch, anything to avoid looking at Tim's naked chest. She could never have a shower, be naked, knowing he was so close. A blush rose up her chest and neck, flaming her cheeks. She turned back towards the sink and fussed with the jars of water to hide her embarrassment. 'We need to get back on the road.'

'Yeah, and we will. Reckon we should hang tight for a little while though. I'll check the wind, see what she's doing, and we'll take it from there.'

She knew he was right: the sky was black and fierce, blasting her flat with ash, but the pressure in her head still pounded at her temples. 'I really need to get home. Peter needs me.'

'Peter?'

'My little brother.'

'Oh, right, yeah. How old is he?'

Catherine chewed her bottom lip. 'He turned eighteen last year.' She knew it sounded silly, calling Peter her little brother. There were no other siblings – just the two of them, growing up together on the orchard. As she was older by almost five years, she'd always been protective of him. And now he was in the worst possible danger.

'Right, I gotcha. And he'll always be your little brother.'

Catherine didn't trust herself to speak. Tim got it. He understood.

'We're just gonna take a breather then set out again. Reckon we might've seen the worst of it. Hopefully this wind'll drop and the fire has to burn itself out at some point.'

Catherine took a deep breath to steady her aching heart, the buzzing in her head.

'It'll be okay. We'll get you home to your little brother.' Tim's voice was reassuring.

Catherine dared herself to look at him – his tanned torso, those lean brown arms, his gentle smile. She'd almost got him killed and yet he was still willing to help her. And there was no denying she had a better chance of getting to Wattle Grove with him than without him. She would wait, but not for long. 'Okay.'

The Channel Highway was closed and barricaded at Kingston. Power lines were down and fallen trees across the road. Even if they breached the barricade they wouldn't get far. Catherine directed Tim to the back roads that would take them through Sandfly, her one remaining hope of a way home. The wind had dropped slightly and changed direction, which might be enough to slow the fire front, if not stop it. It felt as if the temperature had dropped as well. Could the worst of this day be over? As they drove through the back country, the landscape was almost unrecognisable. What was once the drab green of eucalyptus and scrub was nothing but blackness and ashes. The only colour was from the orange glow of slowly burning tree stumps. The fire had raged through here, taking everything in its path, and moved on. The remains of a house appeared as they rounded a corner. Only the chimney was left standing, the rest a smouldering pile of rubble and twisted metal. Catherine's heart contracted to a painful hard nub. Is this what she'd see when she finally arrived home? If they could even get there.

Her mind was brought sharply back to the present as Tim slammed on the brakes. A fallen tree, broken and blackened, blocked the road.

'This is where you're glad you let me tag along.' Tim opened the back of the station wagon, pulling on gardening gloves and grabbing the chainsaw. 'There's another pair of gloves. I'll need a hand getting the pieces off the road. We'll use the crowbar to lever them away.'

Catherine worked by his side, the physical labour helping to calm her tension. The massive red sun halved and disappeared below the horizon as they rolled the last of the broken tree off the road. Catherine leant against the car, exhausted and sweaty, watching the scorched landscape around them seethe and glow as the remaining light faded. Embers fluttered through the air like malicious fireflies. The charred trees shifted and shimmered, looking like Christmas lights in a cruel mockery of the day when new life was celebrated. The earth heaved with constantly shifting mounds of fiery ash.

A different kind of light sliced the growing darkness. Headlights. A ute slowed and came to a stop.

'G'day.' A man stepped out and walked towards them. 'How in hell did you get here? Where did you come from?'

'Hobart,' Catherine said.

'Can't believe you made it this far. Most people headed the other way.'

Catherine heard the inference. He thought they were reckless idiots who should have stayed in Hobart. 'I have family down this way. I've got to get to them.'

'Well, it's bloody lucky we've been working along this road.' He nodded towards his colleague in the ute. 'Cleared some fallen power poles and a tree ahead, so you should get through.' He saw the logs they'd hauled to the side of the road. 'Thanks for doing this one. Saved us some time.'

'You trying to get back to town?' Tim asked.

'We're from the Hydro. Just helping clear the roads for now. The hard work starts tomorrow, assuming the fires have burnt out by then.'

The Hydro Electric Commission supplied power to the state. Restoring electricity to the area would be an enormous undertaking with so many poles down.

'Where are you headed?' the Hydro man asked.

'Into Cygnet and then Wattle Grove,' Catherine said.

'Cygnet's okay, well, most of it. The brigade did a good job and lots of open pasture helped. But Wattle Grove ...' He sucked his teeth. 'That's where the fire jumped the Huon. It took the full brunt—'

'Yeah, thanks, mate.' Tim stepped in and slapped him on the shoulder. 'It's great we can get through. Much appreciated. We'd better be on our way.'

31

'Righto.' The man frowned. 'Good luck. It's been a hell of a day.'

Catherine clenched her jaw, trying not to dwell on the Hydro man's words as Tim drove in silence past more ruined homes glowing with the remains of their destruction. The stench of burnt flesh, most likely sheep and cows, overwhelmed the pervasive smell of smoke and burnt vegetation. Catherine swallowed repeatedly to suppress the nausea that rose in her throat. Finally they reached the small township of Cygnet, nestled between the narrow waters of Kangaroo Bay off the Huon River and the rolling hills behind. The Hydro man was right – apart from some properties on the outskirts, the town appeared to be untouched by the fire. Catherine was surprised to see the Four Square supermarket still open this late in the evening. Old Mr Varian had kept his chemist shop open too. A few people had gathered on the footpath. Catherine glimpsed their faces as she and Tim drove by. Blackened by ash and crumpled with fatigue, they were unrecognisable to her. Over the hill towards the Huon River and Wattle Grove, Catherine's anxiety increased as a new odour assaulted her senses. Burnt apples. She pointed the way and they turned onto the dirt road that led to the river and home. The gate to her parents' house hung loose and open in an ominous sign. She peered through the windscreen, anxiously searching for the familiar lights of home, but saw only darkness. Of course, she reasoned, the power was off, there would be no light. And then, in the shifting glow of a dying fire, she saw it. A stab of pain pierced her heart. The house she'd grown up in, reduced to rubble. The only recognisable feature was the chimney, standing stubbornly amid the destruction.

'My little brother.' Catherine said it aloud, unconsciously. 'My parents.' The panic rose, constricting her lungs and her throat. 'Drive a bit further,' she whispered, barely able to speak.

Tim drove past the house, past where the packing shed should have been, the garage and the sprayer shed. With a growing horror Catherine realised they were all gone. Finally, she spotted a glow that wasn't embers, but the yellow light of a hurricane lamp at her grandmother's old cottage. A sign of life. 'Oh, thank God,' she whispered. Catherine jumped out of the car and ran up the path. On the verandah her parents slumped on the wicker chairs. They hardly looked up as she rushed up the few steps towards them.

She wrapped her arms around her mother and wept. 'You're okay. Thank God.'

Her mother didn't respond. Catherine pulled away, confused. She looked into her mother's face and saw the rivulets of dried sweat and tears on soot-stained skin, the vacant eyes. 'Mum?'

She turned to her father. 'Dad? What is it?'

Her father formed his lips into the shape of a word then shook his head, saying nothing. What Catherine saw in his weather-beaten, blackened face frightened her. He'd always been so strong, but here was a man she didn't recognise. The house was gone, the sheds, the equipment, but there was something else, something beyond this material world. The realisation slammed into her, knocking the breath from her body.

'Dad? Where's Peter?'

6

8 February 1967
Catherine

Catherine woke with a start after a restless, broken sleep. Everything hurt. Her eyes and throat felt as though they'd been scoured with steel wool. At first she was confused. The tongue-and-groove walls of the poky room were unfamiliar, and why was she wearing nothing but her undies and a filthy woollen shirt? She heard a muffled sob from an adjacent room and the memories came crashing back, raw and intense. Peter was dead, that much she knew, but how? Last night her parents had been too traumatised and exhausted to explain. Catherine pulled on her blackened jeans and boots, bracing herself to face what she dreaded most.

In the kitchen she avoided looking out the window and instead searched for tea and sugar. Even without milk she knew her mother would benefit from a strong cup of tea. She ached to be able to offer her even a scrap of solace. The cupboards were bare of food, the old tea tin completely empty. She remembered how she'd helped her mother clean out the cottage after her grandmother had died last year, leaving nothing edible for the marauding ants, mice and possums. There was a kettle, but without electricity they'd have to use the old wood stove for boiling water and cooking. The thought of flames, even securely contained within the firebox, was too much to endure. She took a dusty glass from the cupboard and filled it with warm, rusty water from the tap. The sediment swirled in the glass. Is this all she had to offer her mother?

Gently she knocked on the bedroom door. 'Mum? Dad? Can I come in?'

There was no answer, only a long, low moan. Catherine opened the door and waited while her eyes adjusted to the gloom. Her mother lay, curled in a tight ball, on the bed. Her father was not there.

'Mum? Do you want some water?' Catherine sat tentatively beside her mother. She placed the glass on the bedside table.

Her mother shook her head, keeping her eyes closed tight. Her face and clothes were still grimy from the fires. She wrapped her arms around herself and rocked slightly from side to side. 'My baby,' she murmured. 'My beautiful boy.' A shudder racked her body and a low guttural sound escaped her mouth.

Catherine reached out a hand to comfort her, but her mother flinched at her touch. Catherine put her hands in her lap, feeling useless. 'Mum, I'm so sorry. I'm sorry I wasn't here.' Could she have done anything to help? She'd never know.

'It was just me and Peter.' Her voice was jagged and hoarse from crying. 'My boy.'

Catherine couldn't bear to see her mother so broken, the woman she'd loved and looked up to for longer than she could remember. Her mother had always been the glue that kept the family and household together. But now she was unravelling and Catherine felt as helpless as a child.

'I thought I was going to die,' her mother moaned. 'I wish I had. Why wasn't it me instead of Peter?'

Peter had grown up slowly and quietly, like a walnut tree taking years to fruit. Strange to think that at eighteen he was taller than their father and strong from working hard in the orchard. He was blond and blue-eyed like Catherine, but with slightly crooked front teeth. Not that it ever stopped him from smiling his wonderful, heartwarming smile. When he was little she'd loved pushing him around in the pram and playing with him for hours as if he were a doll. She looked out for him in the packing shed too – always fussing over him, to the amusement of her mother and the other women. When she started going to school she would rush home to tell him all about her day. And when it was time for him to join her at Cygnet Primary, she'd kept an eye out for him, protecting him from any perceived or real dangers. But when he'd really needed her, she was miles away.

Catherine squeezed her eyes tight. She longed to crawl onto the bed beside her mother and give way to her grief, but her father was outside somewhere, dealing with the wreckage of their lives. 'I'll be back soon, Mum.' She went to stroke her mother's matted hair but she rolled away and began to sob once more. Catherine stood. She couldn't avoid what awaited outside any longer.

It was worse in the light. Catherine's despondency grew as she walked past row after row of blackened apple trees. The wooden props used to support their heavy limbs still smouldered and the smell of burnt fruit lay heavy in the air. Only a week ago she'd picked some Gravensteins from the home orchard to take to Mrs Sampson back in Hobart. The Gravensteins were useless for export, since they didn't keep, but her mother loved them for cooking, as did Mrs Sampson. Now those trees were blackened skeletons, the fruit withered and dead.

She found her father by the remains of the house with his twenty-two rifle cradled in his arms and a hard, bitter frown on his face. Peter's dog sat nearby, his golden fur completely blackened with soot.

'Dad?'

He shifted the barrel towards Benno. 'The bloody dog deserves to die.'

'What? Why?' Benno had been Peter's tenth birthday present. He'd named the puppy after his favourite cricketer but hadn't quite got the spelling right. Peter and Benno had been inseparable. Until now.

'The dog should be dead. Peter should be alive.' Her father coughed, a spasm racking his body. He wiped a blistered hand across his reddened eyes. The layer of grime and ash on his face accentuated every wrinkle, every line of sweat and tears.

'What happened?'

'I was fighting a fire at Lymington with some other volunteers. Saved another man's house and lost my own.' He hung his head. 'Your mum and brother did the best they could but—'

Catherine wanted to know, but couldn't bear to hear it.

'Peter couldn't find his precious dog.' Her father's voice was like a snarl. 'The house was on fire. Your mother tried to stop him. Tried to go in after him. But the heat, the flames, it was impossible ... She saw the roof collapse and knew he was gone.'

'Oh, Dad.' It broke her heart to see him so defeated. And her mother? No wonder she was shattered after the horror she'd seen. Catherine gently touched his shoulder, but he shrugged her off. 'Come on, Dad. Hasn't there been enough death? I understand how you feel, but don't you think—'

'No.' Her father spoke through gritted teeth. 'I'm done with thinking.'

Catherine knew if her father had wanted Benno dead he'd have shot him by now. But she had to tread carefully. 'Peter loved Benno. Do you really want to destroy something he loved?'

Her father shifted his stance, but said nothing.

Catherine thought for a moment, desperate to find a solution. There was one possibility. 'What if I promise you'll never have to see Benno again?'

'Never?'

Catherine saw the softening around his eyes and sensed his weakening resolve. 'Never.'

His nod was barely perceptible.

Gently, Catherine took the gun from his grasp.

Catherine walked slowly along the dusty road towards Annie's house, past the ruined orchard. Smoke rose in slow curls from felled fence posts. Benno padded beside her. She'd tied a piece of rope to the dog's collar since his lead, like everything else, was lost in the fire. Benno hadn't wanted to leave the ruins of their home. Peter – she stumbled, almost falling – Peter's body was still in there. What would happen now? Would an ambulance come? Too late for that. The police, then. Someone had to take the remains of her brother. Catherine put one foot in front of the other, willing herself to keep going when all she longed to do was collapse to the ground and howl in despair. Benno whined softly, as if reading her thoughts.

Tim had slept in the back of his EJ. He'd offered to come with her, but Catherine had told him no. If he wanted to help, she was sure there was something he could do, like going to the Four Square for supplies.

The easy ten-minute walk to the Pearsons' was one she'd done hundreds of times before, but this morning, with legs as heavy as her heart, it felt like an endless journey. The necessity of finding a new home for Benno, along with the thought of seeing her best friend, kept her trudging forward. Annie had arrived in Wattle Grove ten years ago, on the arm of Catherine's handsome neighbour, Dave Pearson. Annie was only a few years older than her, but was much more mature – a woman compared to Catherine, who was still a young girl in so many ways. Catherine was thirteen at the time and Annie eighteen, but already married, and pregnant. She seemed so sophisticated and worldly, having grown up in Hobart with wealthy parents. Catherine thought Annie looked like Princess Margaret with her crown of dark waves and had always been jealous, since her own hair was straight and tawny blonde. When they'd first met, Catherine was shy, even intimidated, but Annie had put her at ease. They'd become unlikely friends. At first her parents had disapproved – Annie was a fallen woman, Dave had been forced into a shotgun wedding – but once they realised how devoted the couple were to each other, they'd relented. It helped that Annie had regularly attended church, for a while at least. Over the years their friendship had grown. Annie became the sister Catherine had never had, someone to share her first crush with, and her first heartbreak. As Catherine grew into a young woman she found herself seeking Annie's advice, more than her mother's. Her mother's counsel was always the same: be a good Christian girl and keep yourself nice. When Catherine's first period arrived, her mother handed her a belt and some sanitary pads in a brown paper bag. It was Annie who'd had to explain how to use them and what was happening to her body. 'Let me be a warning to you,' she'd laughed. Those friendly warnings continued through the years as Annie became mother to five boys. Catherine was honoured when Annie asked her to be godmother to Scott, her youngest. And now there was another baby on the way with Annie due next month. During the school holidays, which she always spent helping out around the orchard, Catherine loved catching up with Annie. She'd bring a slice or biscuits fresh from her mother's kitchen to bribe the boys so she could chat with her oldest friend without being interrupted, if only for a while. This pregnancy had been unusually hard for Annie. Catherine had helped out when she could, even if it was just doing the washing up, or baking a pudding for the boys, but towards the end of the holidays Dave had apologetically turned her away, saying Annie needed rest. When Catherine had called in to say goodbye before heading back to Hobart to prepare for the start of the school year, Annie's locked front door had baffled her. No one in the valley ever locked their houses, or their cars. Dave eventually came to the door looking wretched and apologised. Annie's difficulties with the pregnancy were worse, he'd said, and she wasn't up to seeing anybody. Now Catherine feared she might never see Annie again.

An uneasy feeling made Catherine pause. She turned slowly, her eyes blurring across the charred orchard, to focus on the river below, the blackened hills across the water and in the distance the Hartz mountains shimmering through the smoky haze. Standing perfectly still, she held her breath and listened. An unearthly silence. Chattering wrens and finches would usually be busy flitting here and there. And where were the magpies? Her mother had told her that magpies lived as long as thirty years, staying in the same place, often with the same mate. Catherine had loved the magpies' song ever since. But now there were no songs, or magpies. No birds at all.

She quickened her pace up the slight incline, Benno panting beside her, and rounded the bend, steeling herself against the possibility of Annie and Dave's house being reduced to nothing but a shell. A sudden lightness flooded through her when the large weatherboard house came into view, still standing on its brick foundations. The fence was burnt, and the house scorched, but by some miracle still intact. At the front door, the sound of Annie's boys inside, their footsteps pounding across wooden floorboards, was a welcome reassurance. She went to knock, but the door opened before she had the chance. Michael, the oldest boy, stood there grinning.

'We've got the day off school today,' he announced. 'I helped put fires out yesterday. With a hose.'

'Me too.' Eric was the second oldest. He pushed his brother out of the way. 'I helped too.'

'Yeah, but you didn't have a hose.'

'I had a bucket.'

Michael made a *pfft* sound with his lips, dismissing his younger brother. 'I helped save the house—'

'Did not. Dad had already saved it by the time we got home from school,' Eric interrupted. 'But other stuff burnt down. Lots.'

Catherine steadied herself against the door frame at the unexpected onslaught. The boys were happy, even gleeful. To them, it was all a big adventure. They still had a home, and presumably parents, given their joyfulness, but she was having difficulty with their excitement. It was as if the fire was on a par with a trip to the Hobart Show.

Eric crouched down and slapped his knees. 'You've brought Benno. Here Benno, here boy.' Benno gave a small wag of his tail. 'Gosh, he's dirty. So much soot on him. There's ash everywhere.' Eric stretched out his arms to indicate the entire valley.

'Eric? Michael? Who's at the door?' Dave called from inside the house.

'It's Cath-er-ine,' Eric sang out.

'Dork.' Michael elbowed him in the ribs.

Dave appeared at the door. 'Come in, come in.' There was a tea towel over his shoulder and a bottle of milk in his hand. His face was grey with swirls of soot, as if he'd tried to wash with dirty water, and his eyes were bloodshot. 'We're having breakfast. Weet-Bix all round, with lots of milk before it goes off. No power. I'll fire up the generator when I get a chance. That's if I can get any fuel. Have you eaten?' He spotted the dog, panting patiently at the end of his makeshift lead and frowned. 'Why have you brought Benno?'

Catherine took a breath, but it stuck in her throat. All she could do was shake her head.

'Oh, God, Catherine. Are your folks all right? And Peter?' Dave's face was stricken. 'It was such a hell of a day yesterday. I didn't have a chance to check on them. Come on in.' He took her by the arm and led her into the house.

'Can we take Benno outside to play?' Eric asked.

Catherine nodded. 'If it's okay with your dad.'

Dave hesitated for a moment. 'All right.' He turned to the boys, his expression serious. 'Make sure you wash your hands after you pat him. And don't go near your grandparents' old place. Not till I get there.'

'The old house burnt down,' Michael said, proudly.

'And the old packing shed too,' Eric butted in, not to be outdone. 'And the cool store.'

'I'm sorry,' Catherine said, although she didn't know why. The boys seemed thrilled. She loosened the rope from Benno's collar. 'Off you go.' She gave him a brief pat on his filthy back and tried not to cry.

Michael and Eric ran off into the yard with Benno loping along beside them. Dave shut the door. 'I know they weren't born in tents, but honestly.' He shrugged. 'Come on, I'll make us a cup of tea.'

As they passed the lounge room she noticed a man asleep on the couch, his body curled protectively around a young child. Annie had mentioned a friend of Dave's had come to stay in Dave's parents' old house with his family, but with Catherine's work in the orchard and Annie's difficulties with the pregnancy, they'd never met. Could this be him?

Dave sat her down at the kitchen table between Paul and Greg, who were shovelling soggy Weet-Bix into their mouths, and little Scott who was mushing his breakfast onto his high chair. Dave filled a billy with water from a bucket and lit a camping stove on the kitchen bench. Catherine put her head in her hands, leaning heavily on the kitchen table. Crumbs and grains of sugar pressed into her elbows. The babble of the children floated past her ears. All the little things of life Peter would never experience again, as simple as breakfast, and all the big things – like a wife and children.

Dave put a cup of tea in front of her along with a bowl of Weet-Bix. 'You look as though you need a bit of a feed. I've put lots of sugar in your tea, it'll help.' He sat down next to her. 'What's happened? Why have you brought Benno here?'

Catherine shook her head, unable to speak.

'Are your mum and dad okay?'

She nodded.

'Thank God. And Peter?'

Catherine wanted to tell him but the words wouldn't come. Her tongue lay thick and useless in her mouth.

'I'll get Annie.'

She sat staring blindly into her tea. The boys chattered around her but their voices were distant and muffled as if she were at the bottom of a deep well.

A gentle hand touched her shoulder. Annie looked down at her, but she was different, changed somehow. Her face, usually ruddy from exertion and tanned from a life mainly spent outdoors, was a pale, ghostlike image of the woman she knew. The voluminous nightie she wore hung from sharp collar bones, reinforcing the ghostly appearance. Annie pulled up a chair and put her arms around Catherine.

'Oh, Annie,' Catherine sobbed, the tears coming at last.

'There, there,' she soothed, as if Catherine were one of her children. 'There, there.'

'Why is Catherine crying, Mummy?' asked one of the boys.

'She's sad, that's why.'

'Is that why you cried all the time, Mummy?'

Annie stood. 'Let's go into the bedroom. It'll be a little more private, if we're lucky.'

Catherine stumbled after her, relieved to be with her dear friend. Of anyone, Annie would truly understand the depths of her grief, knowing how close she was to her brother. If it was at all possible, it was here she'd find the comfort she so desperately needed.

Annie opened the door to the main bedroom and gently closed it behind them. The curtains were drawn and the room was warm and dark. 'Catherine,' Annie said.

Catherine took a breath, willing herself to speak the words that hurt more than any words had a right to.

Annie touched her arm. 'I have a little surprise,' she said, with such intensity that Catherine was momentarily startled. She led Catherine, almost reverently, to the other side of the double bed. There, lying on pink sheets, in a bassinet covered with frills, was a baby. She was a tiny thing, no more than days old. Annie bent over the bassinet and gently lifted her up. She turned proudly to Catherine, presenting the baby as if she were a prize. 'This is Angela.'

Catherine was overwhelmed by a tumble of emotions. She was hoping to unburden her grief, to sob in Annie's arms – a brief moment of comfort amid the trauma her life had become. Dave would have told Annie that Catherine's parents were okay, but she didn't know about Peter. She hadn't asked what had happened nor talked about their own battles with the fire, which had clearly come so close. Instead Catherine was being shown a baby. Perhaps this was Annie's way of consoling her, demonstrating that everything was going to be all right – even though their world was burnt and ravaged, new life had prevailed and would always do so. It was true, the baby was a miracle in a way, and a blessing after Annie had had such a tough time with the pregnancy. And Catherine knew how long Annie had longed for a baby girl. With a strength of will, Catherine pushed aside her grief and forced a smile. 'Oh, Annie. I'm so happy for you. She's perfect.' She reached out to stroke one of Angela's tiny fingers. 'But isn't she a bit early? I thought you weren't due till next month.'

Annie snatched Angela away from Catherine's touch. 'She's mine. My little angel.' She shielded the baby with her body. 'I might have got my dates slightly wrong. Not everyone is as organised as you.'

Catherine felt as though she'd been slapped. She staggered to the bed and sat down. It was so stuffy in here. The room was closing in on her. Peter was dead. Her home was gone. The orchard in ruins. But Annie had a new baby. A girl. Grief and joy. Death and life. Nothing stable. Nothing to hold on to. Her world was a swirling vortex. Then blackness descended.

7

8 February 1967

Mark

The wall of flames towered over him, wild and ferocious. The blistering heat singed the hairs on his arms. The smoke was like a savage animal, clawing at his eyes and throat. He couldn't breathe, he couldn't see.

'Charlie?' His voice was swallowed up by the thick, roaring air. Panic hit him hard in the chest. His son. Where was his son? 'Charlie!'

'Daddy?' The voice was distant, small and fragile. 'Daddy.' Closer now, the touch of small fingers on his cheek.

Mark opened his eyes. His boy lay in the crook of his arm, patting his cheek with clammy fingers. Mark hugged him to his chest. 'Charlie. Thank God.' He smelt the smoke in his son's hair and the memory of yesterday broke through the remnants of his dream. Fire racing through the scrub, the winds whipping it into a fury. He and Dave with hoses, buckets and wet sacks, attacking every ember. The fence catching fire, the prayers he muttered into the flaming heat and smoke. His son was inside the house he was battling to protect. If Charlie died, it was Mark's fault. The blame was on his shoulders. Not Lara's. Not this time.

'Bad dream, Daddy?' Charlie asked. Mark's heart swelled with love. His boy giving comfort, as Mark had comforted Charlie so many times.

Mark held him closer still. 'Everything's all right. Everything's fine.'

Charlie giggled. 'You're squashing me.'

Mark rolled onto his back and lifted Charlie above him. 'Better?'

Charlie chortled. 'I'm an aeroplane.'

Mark's arms ached with the effort. Every muscle and sinew screamed a reminder of the battle he and Dave had fought yesterday. He'd marvelled at his friend's resourcefulness, at the preparations Dave had made before they'd left to check the rest of the property, and the calmness he'd shown while the fire roared around them. Dave was the reason they were all alive today. Although their survival was miraculous, even during the worst of it in his heart Mark knew that Dave would get them through. His friend had been his rock over the past few years. Through all the confusion and frustration with Lara there had been no one else he could turn to. Dave's generosity and understanding were the reason Mark had brought Lara and Charlie to the valley a month ago. How could any of them have known it would turn out like this?

Even though Mark was sore and battered, he knew the real work, the heartbreaking grind, would begin today and stretch into the days to come. Thankfully the new packing shed was still intact. Dave was so proud of that shed. The orchard crawler – a strange beast, part tractor and part tank with caterpillar treads instead of tyres – was fine. The fate of the tractor and the ute were yet to be determined.

Dave's station wagon was okay, but Mark had no idea where his car was. Lara had taken it and she could be anywhere.

'I'm hungry,' Charlie said, wriggling off Mark's chest and sliding to the floor. Mark winced as his son grasped his arm on the way down. He'd put some antiseptic cream on the burns last night and Annie had wrapped a bandage round his forearm. There'd be no lasting damage, and more importantly his hands were untouched, thanks to the thick gloves Dave had tossed his way before they'd started fighting the flames. His hands were his life. Or had been.

'Let's see what's on the menu for breakfast then.' Dinner last night had been Vegemite sandwiches, given the lack of electricity. Mark shifted his weary body off the couch. He and Charlie were lucky to have somewhere to sleep, now the old house was gone. But they couldn't camp out in the lounge room forever. The house was already too small for Dave's big family. When Lara came back, which she always did, they'd say their farewells. In the meantime he'd make himself useful. God knows there was plenty of work to be done.

Charlie reached for his hand as they walked down the hallway towards the kitchen and the noise of young boys, the clatter of bowls and plates, with Dave's gentle murmurs providing the steady bassline. Dave's boys had accepted Charlie into their clan without a moment's hesitation, but the rough-and-tumble of country boys was foreign to him. In Melbourne Charlie had lived a strange half-life with a mother who often forgot he existed. And now Lara was gone, Charlie had no anchor at all except the hand he was holding.

In the kitchen, Dave and Mark greeted each other with the weary smiles of survivors. 'Get some Weet-Bix into you,' Dave said. He chucked Charlie under the chin. 'You too, mate.'

Charlie dipped his head and pulled away. Dave shrugged and put a bowl in front of him. 'Dig in.' He turned to Mark. 'You up for a tour of the property? See if there's anything left to harvest?'

'Sure.' Mark marvelled at his friend. Years of work might have been destroyed in one day, but his tone was calm.

'Plus I want to check on my neighbours, the Turners. Their orchard is a lot smaller and was right in the line of the main fire front. Copped it pretty bad, I reckon. Their daughter, Catherine, is here now, with Annie. She said her parents are okay, but she turned up with her brother's dog. Something's wrong there, for sure.'

'Is the doggy hurt, Daddy?' Paul, Dave's six-year-old, had finished his breakfast, the remains of it clinging to the corners of his mouth.

'Ah, no, son.' An expression Mark couldn't decipher crossed Dave's face. 'The dog's fine. In fact he's out the back playing with your big brothers. You wanna join them?'

Paul didn't hesitate. His chair scraped across the linoleum as he hurried out through the back door.

'Me too, Daddy?' Greg always wanted to be with his brothers.

'Sure, off you go. Just be careful though.'

In his highchair, Scott began to grizzle. He was missing out, as usual. 'Yeah, I know,' Dave said to him. 'Life's tough. But you know what? It will get better just before it gets really, really tough again. Now, finish your breakfast, if you can scrape it off your highchair.'

Scott let out a wail, picked up a handful of mushed Weet-Bix and threw it on the floor.

'That's enough of that,' Dave said.

'No, no, no!' Scott's voice raised in volume with each word as he threw more of the mush on the floor.

'Dave?' Annie called from the bedroom. 'I need some help in here.'

'Always the way.' Dave sighed. He turned to Mark. 'Mate, can you find out what Annie needs? I'll take care of this little menace.' He winked at his son.

'Sure.'

Annie stood in the doorway to the main bedroom. 'It's Catherine, our neighbour,' Annie said, frowning at him. 'She's fainted. Can you get me a damp washer, if we have any clean water left?'

'There's water in the kitchen, in a bucket. Is she okay?'

'Yeah. But she's not the kind of girl to faint.'

Mark stepped into the room where Catherine lay on the bed. At least she'd had the good sense to land somewhere soft. Her face was stained with smoke and tears and sweat. Her clothes were filthy. Clearly she'd been close to the fire front and had no time, or water, to wash. Probably no clothes to change into either. 'What's happened to her? And her family? Dave was worried about them being close to where the fire jumped the river.'

'She didn't say. Can you get the washer or not? I don't want to leave Angela.'

Mark bit his lip and turned away. He found a washer in the bathroom. In the kitchen Dave was scraping Weet-Bix off the floor while Scott hiccupped after the exertion of his tantrum. 'Everything okay?'

'Your neighbour's fainted.' Mark dipped the washer into the bucket of water. 'I'll give this to Annie.' He headed back down the hall.

Annie was next to the window with the baby in her arms. 'Can you help Catherine? Angela needs me.'

Mark clenched his jaw and nodded, not trusting himself to speak. He knelt beside Catherine and wiped the washer over her forehead, leaving a pale track across her face. She murmured something. A name? Reaching underneath her with his undamaged arm he gently edged her up so he could squeeze water down her back. Her eyes snapped open, wide and frightened.

'Peter?' Her voice was a whisper.

'It's okay.' Mark kept his voice low and soothing.

She stared at him, her deep blue eyes close to his and so unlike Lara's. His wife's eyes were wild and extraordinary, a stormy sea of hidden dangers. These eyes were clear, but filled with sadness.

'Everything's all right,' he reassured her.

'No.' Catherine slowly shook her head. 'It's not. And it never will be again.'

8

9 February 1967

Catherine

It was a strange and morbid procession that made its way to the ruins of the house. The police had the grim job of searching through houses for bodies, while the Army provided the transport. The officer in charge told Catherine and her father that Peter's remains would be taken to Forensic Pathology, as a matter of protocol, and then released to the funeral director of their choice.

Her father gave one brief nod and walked a couple of steps away, his shoulders hunched.

'How long—' Catherine swallowed, the lump in her throat making speaking an effort. 'How long will it take?'

The policeman sighed. He was a stranger to her, one of many who'd been assigned this unpleasant duty. 'Hopefully, within the week.'

'A week? But why? We know who he is. And how he died.' It seemed cruel to string out the agony for both her and her parents.

The policeman avoided her eyes. 'The forensic department has been rather busy.'

'How busy?'

'Over fifty cases so far.'

Catherine knew the fire had been widespread and horrendous, but so many dead? It was incomprehensible. Then the full weight of the policeman's words hit her. 'So far?'

'The toll continues to rise.'

She nodded mutely, unable to think of a response.

Catherine could hardly bear to watch as the men, alongside her father, sorted methodically through the wreckage, shifting sheets of tin and searching through the piles of rubble. What would they find? A few bones? A skull? Her mother was right to hide from it. For the past two days she'd stayed in the stuffy bedroom with the curtains closed, shutting out the scorched reality of what their lives had become. Early this morning Catherine had heard her weeping through the thin wall separating her bedroom from her parents'. Her father's voice had been soothing but the sobs continued. Later Catherine had tried to talk to her, but her mother was too traumatised to be reached. Instead Catherine had sat at her bedside, hoping her presence would be a form of comfort. Sometimes Catherine had murmured reassuring words, platitudes that fell like lies from her tongue. Other times she'd just sat and shed silent tears, heavy with the weight of grief as her mother sobbed beside her. If tears could water this parched land, the pastures and orchards would bloom back to life overnight.

'Here,' one of the policemen called.

Her father, his jaw held tight, moved towards him. Together they lifted a charred lump while two others brought a stretcher. Was that Peter? The bile rose in Catherine's throat as she struggled to stop herself from vomiting. A strange sensation crept through her body, as if the earth beneath her feet was cracking wide open.

After the men had gone, Catherine found Tim at what was left of the packing shed. He was, she realised, respectfully staying out of the way of the morbid proceedings. His clothes and skin were black with ash. She watched as he shifted some debris aside, his arms strong and lean from surfing. 'Hey,' she called out softly, not trusting her voice.

Tim turned, wiping the sweat from his forehead with a gloved hand, leaving a black smudge across his brow. 'Hey,' he answered, matching the softness in her voice. Today was not a day for loud noises, or sudden movements.

'You're still here.' Parts of yesterday were still a blur. After coming back from Annie's, she'd seen a tall, blond young man following her father around, helping put out spot fires and dousing the smoking ruins of the house. For a moment she'd thought he was Peter.

He made his way through the rubble towards her. 'Reckon I'll stick around for as long as you need, or till you get sick of me. Whatever comes first.'

'Thanks.' Tim's kindness was a balm. The tightness in her chest shifted slightly. 'But you're going to need a change of clothes at some stage.'

'You too.' His crooked grin was a flash of white against tanned and grimy skin.

Catherine wiped her hands down her filthy jeans and shrugged. 'I can always borrow some clothes from Annie or Mum, but you,' she smiled back at him, 'you'd look pretty funny in my dad's clothes.' The attempt at lightness ended up sounding strained as it hit her. The only clothes her dad had were the ones he was wearing. Same with her mother. Everything they owned and everything they loved was in the burnt ruin of their home, including Peter.

Tim stayed silent. Waiting. She appreciated the time to get her thoughts in order. 'The, ah, the funeral won't be for another week or so.' The words were like jagged little rocks in her mouth. 'I need to go back to town and pick up my car.' She paused. 'I have a few things I need to do.'

Tim searched her face with piercing blue eyes. 'You're going to quit your job, aren't you? And move back here.'

'I can't stay in Hobart, not now.'

'But you love your job. And the school.'

She dropped her head. It hadn't always been that way. 'When I was young all I wanted to do was work in this orchard. At first Dad was great, he'd take me along on the tractor while he was ploughing and spraying. He taught me how to prune, and all about black spot and codling moth.'

'What happened?'

'It was the year Nathalie Norris was crowned the Apple Queen at the Apple Festival. She ran a successful orchard just over the river. I was so excited I told Dad everything I'd do when I ran our orchard.' Catherine was aware of the tension in her voice. Her father's rebuke still stung even after all these years.

'Didn't go well?'

Catherine shook her head. He'd told her straight out to forget it. Peter would take over the orchard and that was that. Shocked and disappointed, she'd turned to her mother, but she'd only agreed with him. As long as there was a man around, he would always be in charge. Nathalie Norris was an exception. She was the only one in her family available to run their orchard and yes, she did it well, but she had no husband and no children of her own. Was that what

Catherine wanted? To be a childless spinster? Her mother didn't think so. Catherine would get married and have children one day. 'Peter was supposed to take over the orchard.' She pressed her hand against her heart, still beating despite the pain.

'So, teaching then.' Tim's voice was gentle, urging her on.

'Well, first Mum suggested I marry the Fletcher boy, then I could run his packing shed during the season.' Catherine tried to smile but it was more of a grimace.

'Not your scene?'

Catherine couldn't believe she was telling Tim this, but there was an odd comfort in it. The only other person she'd ever talked to about it was Annie, over many tear-filled teenage rants. 'When it became clear I wasn't interested, Mum and Dad sat me down for a talk. I could get a job at the cannery or the evaporating factory in Franklin. Because I was doing well in school, nursing was mentioned, but Mum thought I'd make a good teacher.' Catherine suspected her mother hoped being around young children would make her daughter yearn for children of her own sooner rather than later. Her father was keen on the teaching idea too. It was clear he wanted to get her focus off the orchard and onto a career of her own. They were both pleased when she was accepted into the teaching course and with the scholarship that went with it.

'For what it's worth, Miss Downie reckons you're a good teacher.'

'She does?' Catherine had been glad to land the job at Sandy Bay Infant School after two years of teaching in the country, even though Miss Downie terrified her. 'She told you that?'

Tim smiled. 'I gotta toe the line around her, like everybody else, but sometimes she lets her guard down and says something nice.'

'I think she said something nice to me once too.' Catherine had only taught there for a year, but during that time she'd come to admire Miss Downie and the way she ran the school. Everything had been going so well. Her garden flat, the beach, the walk to school, the students, the school itself – she enjoyed every aspect of her life. Tim was right, she had grown to love her job and the little school by the Derwent. But that was before. Catherine squinted at the sky, avoiding his eyes. 'Everything has changed.'

Tim's sigh was slow and heavy. 'I'll give you a lift. I need to get back too. There'll be a stack of work to do at the school.'

They were silent for most of the long drive to Hobart. Words seemed empty in the midst of such devastation. Catherine had seen photos of bombed cities from World War II, and of the horrors of Hiroshima. These were the only comparisons she could make. North of Huonville the outline of Sleeping Beauty stood stark against the sky. Catherine usually delighted in the view of Collins Bonnet and Trestle Mountain forming the head and body of the mythical Beauty. As a child she had thought it was magical. But today there was no delight, no magic. Sleeping Beauty was not sleeping. She was dead, like everything else. Mile after mile of blackened paddocks, charred and bloated sheep and cattle, gutted houses with only the chimneys standing, and burnt-out cars. Catherine found it hard to breathe – her hands were clenched and her shoulders tight with tension.

Tim turned to her, his eyes full of concern, then returned his attention to the road. 'Yeah,' he said. 'It's full on.'

Catherine appreciated he didn't try to reassure her. How could he? How could anyone? His gentle understanding was enough to ease her anxiety. She pushed away the thought that she'd have to drive back through all of this again and next time she'd be on her own.

As they got closer to Hobart, the suburbs lined up like rows of broken teeth. Here a ravaged house, the despairing owners sifting through the wreckage, then right next door a weatherboard home completely untouched. There were many stories of fire razing homes to the ground while the adjacent house remained unscathed. Her family had experienced it, with their home gone while the fire skipped over her grandmother's cottage. It made no sense to Catherine. Was it God's will that some should lose everything and others nothing at all? That some should die while others lived?

After what felt like an eternity, Tim dropped her off at the school. He leant over the bench seat and gently touched her arm. 'This isn't the last you'll see of me, Miss Turner. No matter what you say, you saved my life. Only a fool would let an angel slip away. Besides, I promised your old man I'd come down and help, so we'll be seeing each other again real soon.'

Catherine couldn't stop a tear from escaping. The future was uncertain, her little brother was dead, but this unexpected ally had accompanied her through hell and considered her an angel. It felt like a blessing in this desert of ash. 'Okay,' was all she could whisper.

Catherine's car was covered with the blackened debris of the fire. She slipped into the driver's seat, holding her breath as she willed it to start. She wasn't ready to face Miss Downie yet. First things first, she thought, as the Hillman spluttered into life.

Mrs Sampson burst into sobs as soon as she answered her front door. Wrapping Catherine in a bosomy hug she said she'd been worried sick, truly sick, about her. Her landlady released Catherine from her damp embrace. 'Oh dear, look at you. Filthy. And I am too now. Oh, but I couldn't help but hug you. I honestly thought you were dead. It was a dreadful day, wasn't it, dear? Dreadful. The smoke! I couldn't breathe. The sky was orange and oh the sun!' She looked skyward. 'A big red giant.'

She led Catherine to the kitchen. 'I was visiting my sister in South Hobart. She assured me everything would be all right,' she continued. 'She said we were safe. Bushfires belong in the bush, so she said.' Mrs Sampson hurrumphed as she put the kettle on to boil and spooned tea into her much-used aluminium teapot. 'Well, she was wrong, wasn't she? We were lucky to escape with our lives.' Mrs Sampson lowered her voice as a solemn expression settled on her features. 'Not everyone was so fortunate though. Have you heard? So many dead.' She was breathless with the drama of it. 'Those poor souls. May they rest in peace.'

Catherine's heart lurched, but she said nothing. Much as she longed to pour out her overwhelming sorrow, she knew there were some, like her landlady, who would turn Peter's death into a drama of their own. She needed time to grow a membrane over her grief. Fortunately Mrs Sampson didn't expect Catherine to talk. She was more than willing to do enough for both of them.

'But whoever would have thought that a bushfire, a *bush*fire, would come right into Hobart. It was only a wind change that saved the city, you know. We could've all been burnt. All of us pushed into the sea. Like those poor people in Snug. Huddled in the water, some with babes in arms. For hours they were stuck there. And when it was safe to come out of the water, there was nothing left. No houses, no school. All burnt.'

The kettle boiled and Mrs Sampson made the tea, gathering milk, sugar, and rock cakes from the biscuit tin, all the while keeping up her commentary.

'People running everywhere, trying to save their precious possessions, their pets, their cars. Absolute bedlam! They even let the prisoners out to fight the fire. Criminals! Let them out, just like that. Never asked us if we were happy about it. But I have to say, they did their bit. Of course there are stories about looters, trying to steal whatever they could. Now those people should be locked up and never let out.'

Mrs Sampson sat down at the kitchen table and poured the tea. 'I really did think you were dead, you know, or worse. I've heard the stories of those poor people in hospital. Some very badly burnt.' She lowered her voice again. 'Some of them not expected to make it.'

Catherine closed her eyes briefly, trying to control her emotions, then distracted herself from thinking about Peter by loading her tea with sugar and choosing the biggest rock cake from the pile. She took a sip from her steaming cup. Usually she didn't take sugar, but Dave had been right, the sweetness helped.

'Did you hear?' Mrs Sampson didn't let up. 'The Prime Minister is here. Flew back specially from New Zealand. Harold Holt himself, having a look at all the damage. He's gone down your way too. You might have passed him on the road. I think he'll get a surprise. Those mainlanders have no idea what we went through. I'm so glad you're all right.' She patted Catherine's hand. 'Very dirty, but all right. Were you fighting the fire too? I've heard about children right in the thick of it, trying to put fires out with branches and watering cans. Kiddies! It's not right, I tell you. But people did get desperate. A travesty all round. Still, here you are, safe and sound. Everything tickety-boo at the orchard then?'

Catherine took a breath and steeled herself. 'Actually, the family home is gone and a lot of the orchard, plus the packing shed, the tractor and all our equipment.' Her voice wavered – she couldn't bear to dwell on the most important thing they'd lost. She pushed on before Mrs Sampson could interrupt. 'My grandmother's cottage is still standing, but apart from that there's not much left. I'm sorry, Mrs Sampson, I'll have to vacate your flat. I'll pay to the end of the month, of course, but I need to move back home. As I'm sure you can understand, there's a lot of work to do. I am sorry to leave you in the lurch, but it's such a pretty little flat, I'm sure you won't have any trouble finding a new tenant.' She tried to smile but failed, succeeding merely in holding back her tears.

Mrs Sampson surprised Catherine by expressing a 'hah' of relief. 'That's the best news I've heard all day.'

'I beg your pardon?'

'Oh, not about your home and everything. No, that's dreadful. My sister's house survived but her friend was burnt out and has nowhere to go. She could stay at the camp the Army set up in Brighton, very well organised it sounds like, too. There'll be close to 500 people living there, you know. So many people without a home to go to or friends or family to stay with. Oh, but they'll have everything provided for them, including toys for the littlies and all meals prepared by Army cooks. Sounds like a holiday to me. But my sister's friend wants to stay closer to town and her friends. I guess it's bad enough losing your house, let alone be surrounded by strangers who've all had their places burnt down too. Anyhow, I saw it as my Christian duty to take her and her kiddies in.' She lowered her voice. 'The husband took off a while ago. Another woman.' Mrs Sampson nodded in a conspiratorial way. 'But we don't talk about that.' She herself was a widow with no children and never a whiff of scandal. 'The trouble is, there's not enough room here for all her children. The two youngest can bunk together but there's the oldest, a boy.' Mrs Sampson sniffed. 'The garden flat will be perfect for him. Everybody will be a lot happier. Including you.' Mrs Sampson patted Catherine's hand again. 'You'll be back in the country with all that space and fresh air, not cooped up here with three children and a deserted wife.'

Catherine was left with the distinct impression that Mrs Sampson had taken in this unfortunate family not only for the altruistic value it bestowed upon her within her social circle, but also for the extra gossip she could extract from the situation. Ungraciously she found herself hoping Mrs Sampson would take a trip out to the country one day and see the truth of all that 'space and fresh air'.

'Where is this unfortunate family now?' Catherine asked.

'You've heard about all the appeals for clothing and food and such? Well, the response has been so enormous they've had to move all the donations to the Princes Wharf. Can you imagine? The entire pier is chockablock. My sister has taken them there to get some clothes. Toys for the kids and food too, canned mainly, but also butter and flour and suchlike. I've asked them to bring back what they can. Those children eat a lot. But they have everything at the wharf. You should go. Clothes, shoes, blankets, kitchenware – anything you need.'

There were sheets and blankets as well as crockery at her grandmother's cottage but little else. Her parents needed clothes and her father needed new boots – his only pair had been ruined fighting the fires. Tim had stocked the cupboards with bread, cheese, jam, sugar and tea, for which she and her father were grateful, but her mother hadn't eaten a bite. Catherine knew she'd need to rustle up something more substantial and also try to tempt her mother with some soup, but the power was still out and the wood stove remained too daunting. Even a cup of tea had been beyond her. 'Do they have portable stoves? Those small gas-fired ones?'

Mrs Sampson's face lit up. 'Oh yes, I've definitely heard it mentioned. Because people have no power and they've got to cook on something.'

Catherine thanked Mrs Sampson and excused herself. She had a lot of packing to do as well as a trip to Princes Wharf. She opened the door to her garden flat for the last time, taking in all her little treasures on the window sills, the tea set neatly arranged next to her electric kettle, and the cushions she'd made out of the latest fabric from Silk and Textiles. There was so much she'd enjoyed about her life in Hobart; this flat, her friends, the vibrancy of the dances and cafes, and the children she nurtured as a teacher. She slumped in a chair and closed her eyes. Much as she loved the orchard, was she ready to say goodbye to all of this?

A memory of Peter came into her mind. They were young, running through the orchard in springtime, the air alive with apple blossom and bees. The scent was intoxicating, sweet with the promise of the fruit to come. Peter had stopped and turned to her, his eyes bright and smiling. 'Every winter when I was little, I used to think the trees had died,' he'd said. 'They look so sad without their leaves. It made me sad too. Now I know they're not dead at all, just waiting to come back to life. New life, every spring.' He'd spun around in a circle. 'This is heaven, Cat. Heaven.'

Catherine rubbed the ache in her chest, right above her heart. 'I promise you, little brother, the orchard will bloom again. I promise it'll be just like heaven once again.'

9

15 February 1967

Annie

Annie stood cradling Angela in her arms, rocking gently from side to side, as she watched the men. She'd never imagined seeing this – the Army working on the property. But here they were, shovelling rubble and carting away the twisted metal of the coolroom. She was glad Dave's father wasn't around to see it. Keith had built the coolroom, with its double-frame weatherboards, vapour seals and wood chips for insulation. Not many properties had cool storage, but the Pearsons' orchard was large enough to make it worthwhile. She missed Keith, who'd been a steadying presence during the furore of her hastily arranged wedding to Dave. He, and Dave's mother Dorothy, had loved her with as much fervour as her own parents had rejected her.

The shriek of grinding metal made Annie wince. She was glad to see the buckled roofing iron go. A decent gust of wind could pick it up and the sharp edges do any amount of damage. Yesterday the

Army boys had dealt with the old house, knocking down the chimney and removing anything that could be a threat. Mark had poked through the ashes, but all he'd found were a few lumps of metal that might have been anything; Charlie's toys, taps, cutlery. The fierce heat had melted them all. Miraculously, two of the old pickers' huts were left standing. Mark had cleaned up the larger one and he and Charlie had moved in. Annie was glad to have her lounge room back, but she wondered how much longer Mark planned to stay – it had been five weeks now, surely he'd return to Melbourne soon. With the shortage of labour because of the fires, Dave needed an extra pair of hands, it was true, but with them came another boy, meaning two more mouths to feed. A wry smile flickered across her lips. She hoped Mark would be gone by next month, but if he stayed on he'd have to help with the picking. It would be interesting to see how the city boy, with his long hair and dark brooding eyes, would cope, day after day.

Annie headed back to the house where yet another load of washing waited for her. The old washing machine was a workhorse but needed constant attention, and the hand wringer, while effective, was laborious. She wondered why she bothered. The smell of burnt apples, dead livestock and charred eucalypts hung like a shroud over the entire valley, tainting the washing on the line. It was impossible to get anything clean – the fine dusting of soot was never ending. Having three boys at school made her days a little easier. Not all children in the area had returned to school after the fires, with many families now homeless. She knew her family was fortunate, but today, soot-smudged and weary, unable to keep anything clean let alone herself, she didn't feel it. In the backyard her two youngest boys played with Charlie and Benno. The sight of the charred orchard behind the house still shocked her. Death had come so close. The upper orchard had copped the worst of it. Dave had summed it up: 'Nothing worth salvaging there.'

Their other blocks had fared better. The fire had burnt only the outer rows of trees. In the middle of the orchard, where not one blade of grass was allowed to grow, the trees were largely untouched. Dave had done the right thing leaving the tractor and ute there. A lot of the fruit was badly damaged, only good for factory fruit or juicing. It remained to be seen, as the season continued, how much of the crop would qualify for the domestic market, let alone for export where the real money was. No matter the outcome, Annie would be in the shed as she'd been for the last nine seasons, packing and supervising. She smoothed Angela's downy head.

'Not the life I'd imagined for myself, my little angel. And my parents certainly didn't either. But don't worry, whatever you choose to do, and whatever so-called mistakes you might make, I will never disown you.' She glanced over at Charlie – such a quiet child, despite the wildness of his mother, Lara. She stroked Angela's cheek. 'And I will never abandon you.'

The crunch of car wheels on the gravel of the driveway caused Annie to frown. The men were in Huonville. Dave was sorting out the insurance and Mark was hoping to get help from the police to find Lara. Good luck with that. The coppers were run off their feet right now without looking for runaway wives. As far as Annie was concerned Lara had done them all a favour by disappearing. Before she and Mark had arrived from Melbourne, Annie already knew all about Lara. For the last few years, since Charlie had been born, Dave had been a constant support for Mark, who'd been worried and confused about Lara's behaviour. Mark thought that with Dave being a father so many times over, he might have some insight or advice. None of Mark's other friends had children, which was no surprise to Annie. They weren't the kind to settle down. After every phone call, Dave would tell her what a hard time Mark was having with Lara. She could barely look after herself, let alone their child.

Dave had felt hopeless to help but did what he could, even if it was only to lend an ear. When Mark was at his wit's end, Dave, being the generous soul that he was, suggested his friend bring his family to stay with him and Annie for a while, to help get them on an even keel. Annie huffed. Look how that had turned out.

Annie found a late-model Holden parked in the driveway, and two smartly dressed women standing beside it.

'Good morning.' One woman walked towards Annie in high-heeled shoes, her hand extended. 'I'm Mrs Carter from St Barnaby's Women's Auxiliary, and this is Mrs Worthington.' The other woman nodded her head. 'We're doing a tour of affected properties and providing whatever aid we can. We're aware that many people in outlying areas can't make it to the distribution centres in Hobart, so we're coming to you.'

Annie shook the offered hand. It was soft, with the faint scent of lavender soap. 'Mrs Pearson.' She usually introduced herself as Annie Pearson but these women preferred formality. 'The Salvation Army have set up a centre in Huonville, so we have most of the necessities.'

Mrs Carter shook her head daintily. 'We only deal in quality goods. All new. Nothing second-hand, or shop soiled.'

Annie was confused. Was this woman offering help, or trying to sell something? Either way, her manner was condescending. 'We're happy with the goods we've been given, and very grateful.'

Mrs Worthington stepped forward. 'What a lovely house,' she said, casting an eye over the weatherboard structure. 'And how wonderful to see it unscathed.'

'Yes, a bit of scorching round the side but that's it. My husband had precautions in place.'

'But not so fortunate with the other dwelling and outbuildings, I hear.' Mrs Carter raised a perfectly plucked eyebrow.

Who'd been talking to this woman, Annie wondered. Someone in Cygnet? If gossip was currency they'd all be rich. Or maybe it had been Dave, when he was looking into the many forms of government relief.

'And what a lovely baby.' Mrs Worthington crooned over Angela. 'She's so tiny. How old is she? Barely weeks, from the look of her.'

Annie took a step back. She didn't want these women near Angela. Why were they here, with their lipstick and fashionable clothes? Both of them so clean. What Annie wouldn't give for a long shower. She hadn't washed her hair in over a week. These impeccably dressed women were a reminder of a time long gone. Annie missed her life in Hobart sometimes, especially when the kids were noisy and the work was endless. As if he'd read her thoughts Scott started wailing in the backyard.

'Thanks for dropping by,' Annie said with a tight smile. 'But we're fine. The Salvos, Red Cross and St Vincent de Paul have all been to visit. Honestly, it's a full-time job talking to you lot.'

Mrs Carter's mouth turned down in a faint frown. 'There isn't anything you need?' She looked Annie up and down, making her acutely aware of her old and grubby housecoat.

Scott's cries increased in volume. 'Mummy!'

Annie looked Mrs Carter in the eye. 'I need to see what's wrong with my son and feed my daughter. I need good soaking rain. I need the power and telephone back on. And workers for the harvest. Are either of you any good at grading or packing?'

Mrs Carter stiffened. As she opened her mouth to reply, the other woman laid a calming hand on her arm. 'We understand.' Mrs Worthington's voice was low and smooth. 'It's a trying time for everyone. Please be assured we're here to help if you do discover you need anything, anything at all. Except perhaps packers.' Her laugh was tight. 'I'm afraid we'd be more of a hindrance in that regard.

But wait, we might have something.' She delved into the boxes in the back of the car. 'Here we are. Just the thing.' It was a small teddy bear in a pink tutu. 'I think a certain little girl might like this, don't you?'

Annie accepted the bear. Angela deserved it.

'Mummy,' wailed Scott again. Benno began to bark and Annie was struck with a terrifying thought. 'I must go. There might be snakes. The fire's driven them out of their usual places and they're looking for water.'

'Oh my.' Mrs Worthington backed away. 'We'd best be going.' The women hastily seated themselves in the car, shutting the doors firmly. Mrs Carter wound down her window, but only halfway. 'Remember,' she said. 'We have nice dresses, *new*, and in this season's style. Donated by the finest boutiques. We might even have one in your size.' And with a wave of her hand they were gone.

Annie muttered a word she didn't want Angela to hear, even if she couldn't understand it. Some things about her upbringing she didn't miss, like those women; judgemental and disapproving. In fact, Mrs Carter reminded her a little too much of her own mother.

'Right,' Annie said, too busy to let a snobby stranger get under her skin for long. 'Let's see what your brother is screaming about.'

10

15 February 1967

Catherine

Her father surveyed the ruined trees. 'We worked so hard. Me, my father and my grandfather. Through rough times and more than a few bloody disasters. But this fire,' he paused, looking down at his bandaged fingers, 'it's knocked something out of me.'

Catherine felt the pain in his words. She watched the river, beyond what was left of the orchard. The reflection of the fire-ravaged bank on the opposite shore shimmered in the grey waters of the Huon, too far to swim but close enough for a strong man to row on a calm day. The blaze had jumped it as if it were a puddle. 'What will happen to the trees, Dad? Are any salvageable?'

His sigh carried the weight of many failed harvests. 'Possibly. Someone from the Ag Department will help me decide, once they've finished with all the dead stock. Horrible business. And now there's the lack of feed for the cattle and sheep that managed to survive. Apple trees are down the list in importance.'

Catherine knew supplies of hay from the north were meagre and the rains still hadn't come. Tim was taking lawn clippings from the school to the Queen's Domain on Saturday for Operation Grass Clippings. Many in Hobart were doing the same. The clippings were for farmers to use as feed for their stock. Catherine was amazed there was enough grass left anywhere for the scheme to be a success. Everything around her was black.

Her father frowned at the orchard. 'The first four rows haven't survived, and need to be grubbed out. Most of the remaining trees will have to be chopped back at least. Even if they pull through, those ones will be unreliable croppers. I think we'll have to rework the lot with new grafts. Best not to make them struggle. A stressed tree is an unhappy tree—'

'And an unhappy tree brings pests and diseases.' Catherine completed his sentence. 'Yes, I know.' She remembered well her father's lessons from when she was younger, before Peter had taken her place in the orchard. She'd never resented Peter – he hadn't had a choice either. Their father's attitude was cut and dried – men ran the orchard, a woman's place was in the packing shed, and that's where Catherine had spent every harvest, first as a baby nestled in an apple box, then in one of the big wooden bins with the other toddlers. From the age of six she was standing on a box beside her mother, copying her as she packed. Catherine could do it in her sleep. Take an apple in one hand and a square of tissue paper in the other, place the apple nose down into the middle of the paper, twist the apple around and then pack it on its side in the box. Two-handed packing was preferable to grab packing, her mother explained, because you could see the blemishes. Catherine was astounded by how fast all the women were, their hands flying over the fruit, wrapping them neatly and filling the wooden boxes with such speed. At first, her apples with their scrunched tissue paper and lopsided efforts were given a special box all of their own. Even so, her mother was proud. 'Good work, Catherine,' she'd say. 'You've been a big help.'

'Could be for the best,' her father said.

'What?' Catherine was startled from her reminiscences.

'Markets are changing. There isn't the demand for some of the crop any more. Granny Smiths and Golden Delicious will always do well, but we needed to grub out some of the older varieties anyway. Red Delicious are the way to go, and we need more of them.'

'Ugh.' Catherine hated Red Delicious. They were like vain, handsome men – great to look at but under the skin lay nothing but disappointment.

'I know. No good for cooking, or eating. But the research station reckons they have some beaut new varietals. Plus we're making inroads into the Asian market and they love them. England will take anything, so ...' He shrugged. 'It makes sense.'

'As long as we always have some Cox's for home use. And a Lady in the Snow.'

'We'll always have a Lady; your mother loves them too. But the business is changing. Costs keep going up and there's a lot more competition out there. We have to keep ahead of the game and if we can't, then at least keep up with it.'

Catherine had a lot to learn if she was going to help run the orchard now her brother was gone. The changes had been rapid and the irrigation system was one of them. During the recent summer holidays she'd watched Peter and her father lugging the irrigation pipes around. It was hard, constant work and she'd been happy to stay out of it. Now it would be her instead of Peter bending her back to the task – but that could wait. The irrigation system was a wreck like everything else.

'Are we going to have to pick all the ruined fruit?' she asked.

'If we can avoid it we will. There's no point bothering with the trees that'll be bulldozed. Most of the other trees are scorched. Even in the centre of the orchard there are patches where the fire rolled over the top and randomly touched down.'

Her father's jaw clenched, a small muscle twitching with tension. Was he thinking about her mother, alone in the middle of the orchard, with fire all around her, after watching their home explode in a fireball with her son trapped inside? She'd fled, fire licking at her heels and raging over her head through the canopy of the trees. In all that smoke she'd found Petunia in the middle of the orchard. Their house cow had instinctively sought the safest place. The same couldn't be said for the chickens. There was still no sign of them. For all his talk about the ruined trees being for the best, Catherine knew her father was deeply heartbroken over the loss of his son, anxious about his wife's emotional state and worried for the future of the orchard. It was too much for either of them to bear on their own. Together though, if he'd let her, they might pull through.

'Hopefully some fruit will be salvageable. We should get a premium price for them at the evaporating factory. The fire's done half the work for them already.'

Catherine smiled at his attempt at humour. The evaporating factory paid very little at the best of times, but at least it was better than anything they'd get for juicing.

He cleared his throat. 'If we do end up doing any picking, I'm sure your fella would be keen to help.'

'Who?'

'Young Tim.'

Catherine felt herself reddening. 'He's not my boyfriend, Dad.'

'Really? He said you knocked him off his feet.'

'He told you that?' Catherine spluttered. 'He didn't mean what you think. We were caught in the fire, with a wall of flames coming at us. I had to do something.'

'It's okay. He told me what happened. You probably saved his life.'

'But it was my fault.' A shudder ran up her spine. 'I can't bear to think of him telling people I saved him when I almost got him killed.'

He waved her concerns away. 'His hair is a bit long for my liking, but he's a decent bloke, I reckon.'

Catherine raised an eyebrow but said nothing. Tim's hair barely touched his collar. In one of their schoolyard chats he'd bemoaned the fact that Miss Downie was always policing the length of his hair.

'You could do worse,' her father continued. 'He's been a great help. Couldn't have been much fun, mucking in all day and then sleeping in his car. And he's keen to come back on his days off. As I see it there can only be one reason for it.'

Catherine wasn't sure how she felt about Tim. Their casual acquaintance had turned into something deeper when they were thrown together, literally, in the inferno of Strickland Avenue. He'd been such a support to her on that horrible day, she doubted she could have got through it without him. She'd had boyfriends before, but nothing serious. It was only last year that the marriage bar had been abolished, but women still had to leave their careers if they became pregnant. In the end it was simpler to stay single. Not that it was an issue for her any more. Last week Catherine had resigned from the Education Department. She hadn't told her parents yet. That was a discussion for another day.

'There's too much work to do to even think about a boyfriend.' Catherine changed the subject. 'How can we pick apples without a tractor to lug the bins?' The tractor was a write-off, the chassis congealed, its metal fused in the furnace of the fire.

'Insurance will cover it. And we're in no hurry. Even if any of the apples are worth picking, they won't be worth exporting. The factories won't care if the apples have been left on the trees too long.'

Their heads turned towards the sound of a car coming up the rutted driveway. Catherine was surprised by the flutter in her stomach at the thought it might be Tim. Did she have feelings for him after all? But the car was a blue Holden sedan so new not even the dust could mask the shine of the duco. It pulled up in front of the cottage and two women alighted, both wearing bright dresses in the latest fashion, one a yellow floral and the other a red polka dot.

'Hello,' the woman in yellow said. 'I'm Mrs Carter and this is Mrs Worthington.'

11

17 February 1967

Catherine

Catherine couldn't help but hope that Peter's funeral would be sparsely attended. It wasn't out of lack of love for her brother, but concern for her mother. Judith hadn't left the bedroom since the fires ten days ago. The constant crying had eased to fitful sobs, but the thought of leaving the cottage to face people, no matter how sympathetic, was overwhelming to her.

At least Catherine had thought to ask the women from the Women's Auxiliary if they could provide a simple black dress for her mother. Mrs Worthington and Mrs Carter had returned within days with a beautifully cut dress in her mother's size plus a few other items. It had been difficult persuading her mother to wear the dress and taken a good half hour to coax her outside and into the car on yet another stifling summer's day.

As they reached the church, Catherine baulked at the number of people who'd come to pay their respects. She knew she should be pleased her brother was so well regarded, but helping her mother past the crowded pews was an effort of pure endurance. Every face turned as they shuffled past, many of them already dabbing at tears and nodding in sympathy. Her mother acknowledged no one. She kept her eyes downcast and clung to Catherine with a strength surprising in a woman who'd barely eaten or slept for over a week. Catherine guided her mother to the front of the church where a pew was reserved for them.

Her father was one of the pallbearers, along with Dave and four of Peter's friends. Catherine watched the young men as they set down the coffin in front of the altar. They were strong and healthy, 'strapping lads' as her father would say. Each of them would've helped fight the fires and each one of them was still alive. She could imagine their mothers silently thanking their lucky stars, while her mother sat, almost catatonic, shutting everything out.

Her father joined them, sitting on the other side of her mother, to shield her as best they could from concerned but curious eyes. Dave sat in the pew behind, where Annie cradled a sleeping Angela. Their older boys were at school and the younger ones at home in the care of Dave's friend, Mark. 'A funeral's no place for a child,' Annie had said. Catherine had agreed at the time, but now wondered if a few noisy boys might not serve as a much-needed distraction. She stared at the coffin with its brass handles and splay of limp flowers on the lid. Was her brother really in that box, or what was left of him? She'd seen the charred lump pulled from the debris of the house. How could one so full of life and love be reduced to such an awful thing? She bit her lip, willing the pain to come. Anything to stop her mind delving into dark places. She must remember Peter the way he'd been, joyful and alive. Catherine scrabbled in her handbag for a handkerchief. She should have brought more than one.

The service flowed around them in the steady patterns of ritual. Her father gave one of the readings, his voice a monotone and his face a rigid mask. With a sinking heart Catherine made her way to the lectern when it was her turn. She wished she'd never agreed to do the other reading. The Bible lay open in front of her while the rector regarded her with sympathy and encouragement. She tried to focus on the words and began.

'The reading is taken from Ecclesiastes, Chapter Three, verses one to four.' She paused and took a breath.

To every thing there is a season, and a time to every purpose under the heavens:
A time to be born, and a time to die—

Her voice wavered. The Byrds had had a massive hit a couple of years ago with a song based on these words. Peter had bought the record with his pocket money and played it endlessly.

A time to plant, a time to reap that which is planted ...

Every word reminded her of her brother. As kids they'd been given small plots beside the vegetable garden where they could grow whatever they wanted. Peter had planted potatoes and carrots while Catherine grew sweet peas and fragrant roses; Peace with its pink-tinged yellow petals and the vigorous pink blooms of the Queen Elizabeth. They'd tended their gardens all through their teenage years, although Catherine's had fallen into neglect while she was away studying and then teaching. When Peter realised, he took care of her roses as well. Everything he touched had thrived. Now there was nothing left of their gardens except ashes. Was Peter tending another garden in another place? Oh God, she hoped so.

A sob escaped from deep within her. She gripped the lectern and stared at the Bible, willing herself to continue even as her tears blurred the words. She sensed the congregation holding their breath, waiting for her to crumble. She looked desperately towards her father, but he was holding her mother and both their heads were bowed. A movement from the pew behind them caught her eye. Dave. He came and stood beside her, inclining his head towards the Bible in a gesture of permission. She nodded and he began to recite.

> A *time to kill, and a time to heal;*
> *a time to break down, and a time to build up,*
> A *time to weep, and a time to laugh;*
> *a time to mourn, and a time to dance.*

He smiled at her with compassion. Dave had known Peter all his life, and being ten years older had been like a big brother to him. In years to come he and Peter would have worked their neighbouring orchards, sharing tips and ideas, borrowing equipment, and celebrating or commiserating at the end of each season as their fathers had done before them. Peter's loss reverberated throughout the valley in ways Catherine hadn't considered.

Dave turned back to the congregation. 'Thus endeth the lesson.' He took her arm in his, guiding her back to her place before he returned to his seat.

Catherine was numb to the proceedings as the service continued, until the organ played the introduction to the final hymn. Her father left her mother in her care and took his place by the coffin with the other pallbearers. Together they carried her brother out of the church to the strains of Peter's favourite hymn: 'All Things Bright and Beautiful'.

Outside, in the forecourt, mourners milled around, talking in low voices. Catherine noticed Annie. Despite the circumstances she seemed deeply content, even happy, as she presented Angela to anyone who took an interest. Dave watched, his face creased in a frown, no doubt thinking it was the wrong time and place for such a display.

The procession moved to the cemetery. Catherine had hoped Peter would be buried in the orchard. She knew he would've wanted to be part of the earth and the trees themselves, forever in the place he called heaven. But her father wouldn't allow it. 'Think of your mother,' he'd said. 'To bury him here would be a constant reminder.' Reminder or not, Catherine doubted her mother would ever forget. None of them would. As Peter's coffin was lowered into the ground her mother's knees buckled. The cry that came from her was almost animal-like, a guttural wail of grief. Catherine and her father struggled to keep her upright, her body heavy with the agony of grief and both of them weak from their own.

By the time the graveside ceremony was over it was clear that attending the wake in the church hall would be too much for her. Catherine ushered her mother towards the car before any other mourners had a chance to approach. Her father stayed on alone to represent the family.

Once they were out of Cygnet, away from the cemetery, her mother began to speak in a low monotone. 'I never thought it would be Peter, never. Your father, yes, but not Peter.' She looked straight ahead as the road wound out before them. 'You were a baby when he was away fighting the Japanese. I was always terrified I'd lose him. But he came home safe to me. Unlike so many others. Some of them never returned and others left part of themselves over there – a limb, or an eye, or their minds.'

Catherine listened in silence. This was the most her mother had said since that awful day.

'I was always grateful, to have him and two healthy children. It would've been greedy to ask for anything more.' She turned to Catherine. 'Was I greedy? Did I want too much? So many husbands never came back, but I had everything I ever wanted.' She began to cry.

'Oh, Mum. You weren't greedy. You never have been.' Catherine's mother had worked hard for the little they had. It wasn't a life of luxury, but it was a good life. Until now.

'I should have stopped him. I should've.'

'There wasn't anything you could've done.' If Catherine had been there, could she have prevented Peter from going into the house? The ache in her heart sharpened. She'd never know.

'All creatures great and small.' Her mother repeated the words from the hymn. 'He cared more about that dog than he did for his own life.'

'He loved Benno.'

'And you. He thought the world of you. Why did you have to go filling his head with ideas?'

Catherine gripped the wheel tighter. She knew what was coming. The idea was never hers, but what did that matter now?

'Your father will never tell you this, but the last words he had with Peter were angry ones. He'll never forgive himself. What a pair we are, your dad and me. So many regrets.' She began to cry again, jagged sobs that wrenched at Catherine's heart with guilt as well as grief.

Peter had first told her of his dream of being a vet when he was sixteen. He was so intent on it she couldn't help but get swept up in his fervour. It made sense for him to have a career saving the lives of the animals he loved so much. He'd planned to live at the orchard and work as a vet in the valley. 'The best of both worlds,' he'd said. Most boys his age were leaving school to help on the family orchard or farm by then. Peter had convinced their mother, who could never deny him anything, to let him stay on at school, much to their father's annoyance. Catherine had helped Peter choose the matric subjects he needed to get into veterinary college, but when they'd discovered he'd have to go to Melbourne to study and the costs were prohibitive, Catherine had thought he'd give up. Instead, over the past two years, Peter's resolve had grown. He'd surpassed himself at school and was confident his grades would get him an offer at the veterinary college. Their grandmother had left them both a small amount of money when she'd died last year and Catherine had immediately given her share to Peter along with money she'd saved from her wages. She'd assured Peter that if he got into the college he didn't have to worry about the orchard because she'd come back to Wattle Grove and work alongside their father.

The letter had arrived only weeks earlier, before Catherine went back to Hobart for the start of the new school year. Peter had not only been accepted, but he'd also won a scholarship. However, at the age of eighteen, it'd be almost three years until he could make his own decisions. He needed his parents' permission. Over the years Peter had tried to broach the subject with their father, but he'd always dismissed the idea. Peter was conflicted and considered deferring until he turned twenty-one. Catherine had suggested he try talking to their father again, now that Peter's dream was a reality.

And now she knew the outcome of that conversation. Angry words. And her mother blamed her.

12

March 1967
Catherine

Usually in March the pressure was constant. Orchards couldn't survive on second-grade fruit. Apples had to be harvested at exactly the right time, when their sugar levels were perfect for the lucrative export market. But this year there was no urgency at the Turners' orchard. Instead Catherine's father had begun grubbing out the badly burnt trees, leaving them to lie in gnarled, black windrows. There was plenty of damaged fruit from the other orchards in the valley to supply the factories. The Turners' apples would stay on the trees, until the wind blew them off, or the possums and birds ate them.

Tim came down to the valley to help out when he could, often staying overnight in his car. Catherine had been surprised at first, that he'd kept his word to her father. And even more surprised that her father accepted someone like Tim courting his daughter. He was as far from the respectable church-going country boy her father wanted for her as imaginable. In any other circumstances a 'long-haired' surfer would be totally unacceptable, but Tim put a lot of effort into winning over her father, knowing he wouldn't have a chance of being with her otherwise. She found herself looking forward to his visits. Often they'd go walking together by the river. He'd always bring up the fact that she'd saved his life and was his angel, and she would shush him and ask him about the surf instead. Catherine listened to his tales of waves and salt water with wonder – it was like a foreign language to her. But when he talked about his work at the school she was strangely detached. It had only been a month, but already her life in Hobart felt like a dim memory. So much had changed since then. When Tim took her hand one afternoon while they walked, she didn't resist. But when he tried to kiss her, she turned her head. It didn't feel right when there was still so much grief in her heart.

'It's okay,' he said. 'I'll wait.'

The pall of despair around the cottage weighed as heavy as the smoke on that awful day and Catherine was guiltily relieved when Annie asked her to help with the packing. Her father encouraged her to go. She sensed he'd be happier with her out of his sight. No more had been said about the argument he'd had with Peter. Her mother barely spoke and her father hadn't brought it up. Catherine had been glad to avoid the topic. She was grateful for the opportunity to escape to the bustle of the packing shed where her body could swing into the familiar movements it knew so well, leaving no time for thinking. When she was studying and then teaching, she'd always come down on the weekends to pitch in at the family orchard. Arriving on a Friday after work as the autumn twilight stretched into evening, their packing shed would be a frenzy of activity with her mother at the helm. Picking might stop with the light but the packing continued. Catherine would slip into the routine and work into the night. On Saturday mornings the packing started again at eight and didn't ease up until nine in the evening. Sundays were for church and housework. Catherine would return to Hobart, tired but happy to have been part of the ongoing operations at the orchard.

Her mother would joke that Catherine had the perfect job, with the first school term ending about the same time as the harvest. Catherine missed out on most of the work, but was home in time for the end-of-season parties. Her mother, like most wives of orchardists, was in charge of the packing shed – on her feet all day and most of the night, bending over the bins, packing, as well as doing all the organising and supervising. She was too exhausted to attend any events. In return Catherine joked that her job was to represent her mother at the parties, onerous as the task might be.

That was back when her mother still laughed. Catherine despaired she ever would again.

Despite wanting to be there, Catherine's stomach trembled with nerves when she arrived at Annie and Dave's packing shed. She was used to her family's smaller shed, with its wooden floor and old pallet truck. The size of the Pearsons' orchard justified them being set up for bulk handling, with a concrete floor, strong enough to support the forklift and the loads it carried, and a massive grader running the entire length of the shed. So much sound and movement compared to the last month of slow, heavy days on her family's orchard.

'Morning, Catherine.' Annie slipped an arm around her shoulders in a quick squeeze. Her voice dropped as she murmured in Catherine's ear, 'You'll be okay, but if you need a break at any time, just let me know.'

'Thanks.' Apart from Tim, Annie was the only person Catherine could talk to about her anguish over Peter's death, a subject she never dared raise with her parents. There were many evenings when she'd cried on Annie's shoulder after the children had gone to bed. She knew she could depend on her friend to keep an understanding eye out for her in the busyness of the packing shed. Catherine sought out any familiar faces. She knew a few women from church, but none of the packers Annie employed were as young as Catherine. Not that it mattered; any friendships from her school days had lapsed after her move to Hobart.

Annie led her over to one of the rotary bins. 'You're here between Liz and Deb. Two of the best packers in the valley.'

The two women beamed at Annie's praise. They were both middle-aged, with worn faces and a comfortable layer of padding around their middles.

'This is Catherine,' Annie said.

Liz's face fell. 'Catherine Turner? I'm so sorry about your brother.'

'So awful,' Deb added.

'Thanks.' Catherine looked away, unable to say more.

'Right, girls,' Annie said, putting an end to the conversation. 'We've got apples to pack.'

Catherine took her place at the grader as the apples began rolling off the conveyer belt into the bin beside her. She was pleased to be packing into the familiar wooden boxes this morning. They reminded her of a simpler, happier time. Sadly, the apple boxes, with their brightly coloured labels, were being phased out for cardboard cartons. She traced her fingers across the painted hills, stylised river and bright red apples of the Pearsons' label. Catherine's grandmother had designed the labels for their family orchard, with a spray of pink apple blossom and the name *Turner* proudly displayed across a bright blue sky. All of them were ashes now. A dull pain throbbed in her heart. With everything that had happened, and the changes in the industry, she might never see those beautiful labels again.

The cardboard cartons were lighter and more time-efficient – individual cells for each apple meant the apples no longer needed to be wrapped in small squares of paper. However, some of the European countries continued to order their apples in the wooden cases and Catherine's two-handed packing skills were still useful. The repetition of the task was soothing; the feel of the apples under her fingers, wrapping them in tissue paper and the careful placement into the boxes. There was a sense of accomplishment as each box was finished and whisked away. Catherine knew she would suffer aching hands and legs later, along with the physical exhaustion, but welcomed it. Her hope was when she finally crawled into bed at night, she'd sleep deeply and not wake in the early hours to the sound of her mother's sobs.

There might have been many changes in the packing shed but the chatter of the women stayed the same; the gossip, digs at their husbands, and boasts alternated with complaints about their children. This year, however, there was a new flavour to the words that flowed around Catherine.

'When the Cascade Brewery got burnt out I thought my hubby was going to cry. But it's back. He reckons it doesn't taste the same though.'

'That's because it's not. They're selling Carlton in a Cascade can.'

'What?'

'Yeah, it's true. Until they're up and running again, Carlton is supplying them with Melbourne beer.'

'Blasphemy, that's what it is. I'm not going to tell my hubby. That'd be the last straw.'

'How come people who didn't have their places insured get a free house? The government's rewarding shirkers. What about the hard-working people who kept paying their insurance anyway? What do they get?'

'Our insurance payout won't cover what we've lost. So, what does the government do? Offer us a loan, with interest! Where's the fairness in that?'

'Did you hear, the Governor's Fire Relief Fund has got to over three million dollars. Three million!'

'They reckon it might go as high as five million after the television appeal.'

'Where's the money going? We could all use some of it around here. The McPhersons are selling up. That's the third family I know of who are leaving the valley.'

'But selling to who?'

'Hah. There're some nasty characters skulking around trying to buy land cheap. Parasites. Should be a law against it.'

'Talking about parasites, what about the bloody rubberneckers coming to gawk at the burnt-out houses?'

'I don't mind if they're only gawking. The ones doing the looting are the problem. Stripping the houses of copper wiring and pipes.'

'See 'em off with a twenty-two or a shotgun. That'd do the trick.'

'Ooh, wait up. Here comes Dave's mate. Still no word about his wife.'

'She must have run off with another man. That's the only explanation.'

'Wish she'd run off with mine. Be welcome to him.'

The women guffawed and Catherine glanced up. Her stomach twisted in shock. She knew that face. She'd seen it in magazines. But more than that, she'd seen it up close and in real life. After fainting at Annie's place, Catherine's impressions of that day were jumbled. She had a vague memory of a man with a calming voice. Later Annie had told her he was Dave's friend Mark, staying with them from Melbourne. Whenever she'd visited Annie since then, Mark had either been out working in the orchard with Dave or in his temporary home, one of the pickers' huts, with his son. Catherine had been relieved, not wishing to revisit the embarrassment and trauma of that day. But now, watching him, it came back to her in sharp relief. A wave of emotion and confusion crashed over her. How could this be? Dave's friend was Mark Davis, the lead guitarist for The Scene, one of Australia's most successful bands. Why had Annie never mentioned this fact? And how was it even possible? The Scene had gone to the UK months ago. What on earth was Mark Davis doing here?

The other women took a break, but Catherine kept her head down and carried on working. She didn't want to join the others. They'd talk about the fire, and Peter, and offer their condolences. She couldn't face it. Everything was too raw. But when she sensed Mark approaching, she stopped wrapping apples and slipped out the side door. What could she say to the stranger who'd cradled her in his arms and woken her from her faint, especially now she knew that the stranger was none other than the famous Mark Davis?

13

March 1967

Mark

Not even lunchtime yet and his shoulders ached, his arms were sore and his back was throbbing. Mark reached up and picked yet another apple. He'd been doing this for weeks but his body still objected. And no wonder. Stretching, reaching, grasping, plucking, twisting, up and down ladders, filling the canvas bag that hung down his front, carrying it to one of the wooden bins and finally emptying the haul. Then doing it again and again. Dave hadn't trusted him with the Golden Delicious, which were harder to pick and bruised easily. Instead Mark was picking Jonathans, day after day. It was surprising he still enjoyed the taste of them, sweet but with a bit of a tang. Charlie liked them because they were smaller than most apples, a better fit for little hands and small teeth.

Over a month had passed since the day they'd dubbed Black Tuesday, but still no word from Lara. None of Mark's friends in Melbourne had heard from her and their return ticket on the *Princess of Tasmania* hadn't been used, so she must still be in Tasmania somewhere. And here he was, picking apples, waiting. Like all the other times she'd run off, he was sure she'd return, behaving as if nothing had happened. Then it would start again – blaming him for everything, demanding a divorce and insisting he have custody of Charlie because it was her turn to be free. It was true he'd spent too long away from his son. The band's touring schedule had been punishing and even when he was home the number of gigs they did every week was crazy. Yet playing in a band was seen by others, including Lara, as an exciting, glamorous life. Honestly, he'd rather be picking apples in a fire-ravaged valley than be back on the road.

He stretched his back, shifted the canvas bag and twisted another Jonathan off the tree. When he'd started picking, being surrounded by other people for the first time in weeks, he'd been worried he'd get hassled. But as Dave had explained, *Go-Set* never made it to Cygnet and not many people had televisions around here, so no one gave two hoots about The Scene. He'd been right.

Most of the pickers stayed in the orchard at lunchtime with a sandwich and a thermos of tea, but Mark always headed back to the packing shed. Often, by the time he got there he could only stay for fifteen minutes, but he never missed lunch with Charlie. A Vegemite sandwich and orange cordial tasted great as long as he was with his son. The men who worked in the shed – driving the forklift, wiring the apple boxes and lugging them onto pallets, or working the grader – sat on upturned boxes outside the big wooden doors, smoking and yarning, their faces weather-beaten and hands work-worn. In the age-old Australian tradition, the men kept to their space while the women had lunch inside with the children. Usually Charlie came running as soon as Mark appeared, but today there was no sign of him. Mark sought out Annie and found her in the centre of the group with Angela, as always, clasped in her arms.

'Have you heard the news?' Annie's eyes were bright. 'Prince Philip is making a special visit. Today.'

'What – here?' Mark looked around the dusty shed; full wooden boxes were stacked on pallets near the door, the grader silent for the moment, the boxes yet to be packed, and the open bins of rejected apples, ruined by the fire or black with sunburn. The scent of warm apples, overpowering and cloying, almost drowned out the smoky aroma that still persisted weeks after the fires. But where were the Union Jacks and the red, white and blue streamers? People generally went to a great deal of effort whenever a royal turned up.

'No, silly.' Annie's laugh was girlish. 'He's going down the Channel though, after he's had a look around the worst of Hobart.'

'Strickland Avenue,' one of the other women said. 'He'll definitely go there.'

'He'll be in the general area,' Annie added. 'Snug, for sure.'

'Right.' Mark gave a tight smile. Snug was miles away.

'Such a shame,' another of the packers said. 'Almost completely wiped out. He's visiting Camp Snug, the temporary village they've set up until the homes can be rebuilt.'

Mark knew about Camp Snug. It had become world famous. 'Have you seen Charlie?' he asked Annie.

'Such a quiet boy.' It was a woman with red hair and faded blue eyes. 'Wish my boys were more like him. Gawd, they're a rowdy bunch.'

'Where is he?'

'He's fine,' Annie said. 'He was a bit upset, so Catherine's having lunch with him outside. Round the side of the shed, I think.'

'She's good with the littlies,' the red-haired woman said. 'A teacher up in Hobart, but she's staying close to home for a while after ... well, you know.'

'Yeah.' He'd seen Catherine every day in the packing shed, but only from a distance, her fair hair tied back in a ponytail and her sad eyes fixed on the monotonous job in front of her. Dave had told him what happened. Mark wanted to say something to her, but what? 'Hi, I'm the guy who dribbled cold water down your back when you fainted. Sorry about your brother.' Not a good idea. Anyway, when he'd tried to talk to her she'd avoided him, so he'd let it be.

'Thanks.' Mark headed back out into the unrelenting sunshine. He'd seen more daylight these past few weeks than in the last ten years.

They were sitting in the shade of the shed, with their heads almost touching, her fair hair a stark contrast to his son's. Her voice was assured and gentle. Charlie said something that made her laugh, a sound Mark hadn't heard before. In the throng of chatting women, Catherine was always quiet, and so full of sorrow. She leant towards the boy and began to tickle him. Charlie retaliated and then both of them were giggling and squirming, finding the ticklish spots and trying to avoid each other's fingers. It struck Mark that he'd never once seen his wife and Charlie play together.

Charlie struggled to his feet, and spotted Mark. 'Daddy!' His short legs broke into a run.

Catherine's face changed. It was if a wall came down behind her eyes. She ducked her head to brush the dust from her clothes. When she looked up, her expression was a polite mask. 'Hi,' she said.

Charlie pulled at Mark's hand. 'Come and meet Cat. She's not really a cat but she said I can call her that. Only me though. No one else is allowed to. She said I'm special.'

'Charlie was having a bit of trouble with my name,' Catherine explained. 'It has a few too many syllables.'

'And I'm a little mouse,' Charlie said. 'So Cat has to chase me.' He began to run towards the trees, laughing. 'You can't catch me.'

'Oh, I think I can.' Catherine pretended to try but let him keep just out of her grasp as they wove between the trees. Charlie stumbled to the ground in his gleeful haste and his face crumpled. Mark rushed to pick him up as Catherine stood back, chewing her lip.

'Sorry,' she said. 'I should know better than to get him overexcited. It's just—' She stopped. The sorrow was back in her eyes.

'It's okay,' Mark said. 'No harm done.' He hugged Charlie to his chest. 'You're a good boy.' Charlie mumbled something into Mark's shirt. Mark tilted him back a little. 'What's that?'

'I'm not a boy. I'm a mouse.' And there was his cheeky grin, the grin that never failed to melt Mark's heart.

'A mouse who hasn't finished his lunch,' Catherine said. 'And I guess you haven't even started yours,' she said to Mark.

'No. It's in the shed. I'll get it.'

'Don't bother. We've got enough to share and goodness knows there are plenty of apples.' Her smile was tight, as if she was making an effort. She hadn't been like that with Charlie.

They settled themselves in the shade and Catherine handed Mark her sandwich. 'You don't want it?' he asked.

'I had a big morning tea.'

Mark sensed she was lying but didn't pursue it. He was famished, and the devilled ham sandwich hit the spot. Charlie nibbled at the remains of his Vegemite sandwich while Catherine sat in silence, gazing at the trees.

Mark washed down the last of the sandwich with a mouthful of orange cordial and stroked his son's hair. 'I've been told this little mouse was upset today.'

'Nope.' Charlie shook his head.

'Ah,' Mark said. 'Then maybe it was Charlie who wasn't happy.'

He stuck out his bottom lip but said nothing.

'I think it's time you had a nap,' Catherine said. 'All mice need a little sleep in the afternoon.'

Charlie's mouth trembled. 'I don't want to go back in the shed.'

'Then you don't have to.' Catherine's voice was soothing. 'I've heard little mice often sleep outside under trees, curled up nice and safe. Would you like to do that?'

His face brightened. 'Yes.'

Catherine stood up and reached for his hand. 'Let's find you the perfect spot then.' Charlie held her hand as they picked a shady tree and piled some leaves into a soft mound. After a few words Mark couldn't hear, Charlie curled up and closed his eyes. Catherine walked back with a pensive expression. She sat down and leant back against the shed wall. 'He thought you weren't coming.' She kept her eyes on Charlie, not looking at Mark. 'The other children all have their mothers, which makes him the odd one out. Then today you were late.'

'We're working in the northern orchard and it's a bit of a hike. I'd have run all the way if I'd known.'

'He's a very quiet child. Withdrawn even.' Catherine spoke softly so Charlie couldn't hear. 'Is he usually, or is it because he misses his mother?'

'He wasn't quiet or withdrawn with you.' Mark was caught off guard. No one had talked to him about Charlie this way before.

'Ah, but I'm a cat and he's a mouse. That's different. I'm talking about with other children. What's he usually like with his friends, back in Melbourne?'

So, she knew he was from Melbourne. He wondered what else she knew. A familiar tension tightened his jaw. He'd been lucky so far, but Catherine was much younger than the other workers and until recently she'd been living in Hobart. He'd play it cool. 'I'm not sure.'

'You don't know?'

Mark shrugged defensively. Charlie was a quiet kid. Lara had liked that about him at least. Now this pretty school teacher was telling him it was a problem. 'He never spent much time with other children. His mother ...' He paused. 'Lara has some unusual views.'

'Such as?'

'She expects Charlie to do what she does. He doesn't play with other kids.' Mark clasped his hands around his knees, hugging them close to his body. He didn't dare tell Catherine everything. 'I wasn't home enough to have much say in it.'

Catherine turned towards him. 'Annie mentioned you and Dave are old friends from school and that you came down here for a holiday. It seems an odd choice though, staying on an orchard miles from anywhere.'

A holiday. So that's how Annie described it. If Catherine had heard the story from Dave, it would have painted a different picture. Dave had been Mark's steadfast friend since they were twelve years old. At boarding school, when it became clear that Mark's globe-trotting parents hardly ever returned for holidays, celebrations or birthdays, Dave began inviting him to stay at the orchard. They formed a bond that distance and fame had never tarnished. When Mark started making a name for himself on the mainland he'd send Dave newspaper and magazine clippings, and later the 45s his band released. Dave, proud father that he was, would reply with photos of his boys and letters full of their latest antics. Part of Mark had envied Dave's life – steady, reliable, surrounded by family and with a sense of belonging within a community, none of which he'd ever known. He rubbed the pad of his thumb across his fingertips, feeling the hardness there. 'We needed to get away.'

'Oh, right. Well, I can understand that.'

'You can?'

'Your life, the band ...' She hesitated and her cheeks flamed. 'I can't even imagine.'

'Right.' So Catherine did know.

'Don't worry. I won't tell the newspapers.' Her shy smile was genuine. 'And Annie has never said anything about it, so clearly she's not the slightest bit impressed.'

'You're right about that. Dave's grateful to have me helping out, but I think Annie would prefer it if I packed up and left.' He tried to keep the bitterness out of his voice. 'Not that I've got much left to pack.'

'Of course. You were in Dave's parents' old house. Did you save anything?'

'My son and my guitar. The two most precious things in my life.' He looked over at Charlie, sleeping in the nest of leaves. 'I won't always be able to make it in time for lunch.' He let out a slow breath. 'Would you mind, I mean, if it's not too much bother, could you take care of Charlie for me, just until I can get here? You have a way with him.'

Catherine nodded, her lips curving into a near-smile. 'I think I can manage that.'

14

Late May 1967
Annie

Begrudgingly Annie had to admit that, after a shaky start, Mark had pulled his weight as a picker. All new pickers were sore, stiff and slow, until they got the hang of it. By the end of the season Mark had managed to pick a respectable four bins a day. But now the harvest was over, surely it was time for him to leave. His wife still hadn't returned and there was no guarantee she would. It had been almost four months. Tasmania was a small island. Lara would have found her way back by now if she'd wanted to. It was likely she'd hooked up with another bloke, that was all there was to it. If Annie had her way, she'd be waving goodbye to Mark, today. Dave felt differently. Warily she'd watched his friendship with Mark deepen even more over the months and when she protested, he kept insisting he needed Mark around. Sure, after the fire Dave had needed another man to help out, but now things were settling down there was no reason for Mark to stay. He should cut his losses and get back to Melbourne and his real life, if 'real' was the word to describe what he did. Playing guitar to screaming teenage girls wasn't a fitting occupation for a grown man. She'd need to have another talk with Dave.

But right now, Annie had a party to plan and it had to be the best one yet. The months since the fire had been hard, with precious little to celebrate. A real shindig would be a tonic for the gloom that had settled on the blackened fields. With the lack of work and ongoing drought, families continued to leave the district. She'd been lucky to pull a packing team together and was grateful Catherine had been crazy enough to throw in her teaching job and move back to the valley. Catherine was a good worker, often continuing through her breaks. Annie could understand her reticence to socialise with the other women. They were forever going on about the fire and the growing death toll. Only one thing had made Catherine smile in the past months. She'd really taken a shine to Mark's boy, Charlie. He was coming out of his shell now, thanks to Catherine. Annie didn't approve of the growing friendship between Mark and Catherine though. There was only trouble down that road.

Annie shifted Angela on her hip as she stirred the pot of stewed apple. The steam fogged up the windows and scented the kitchen with cloves and cinnamon. She never got tired of the smell. It was the aroma of home to her now. Gently she put Angela in her bassinet on the kitchen table, tucking her up under a pink quilt. 'You're such a good girl,' she whispered. Not like her boys, always cawing about something like little crows, from the day they were born.

Dave barged into the kitchen from the backyard, leaving the screen door banging in his wake and letting in a blast of ice-cold air. The rains still hadn't arrived and as the bright days grew colder the air was as sharp as mountain water.

'For heaven's sake, close the door and do it gently,' Annie said. 'You'll startle Angela and wake the boys. It's rare for Greg to have an afternoon nap these days. God knows what I'll do when he won't go down at all.'

'Sorry, love.' Dave closed the door firmly but quietly. 'I just saw Jack Turner. Thought it was time to talk about the packing shed idea, among other things.'

Annie took in her husband's expression. 'Didn't go well then?'

'Stubborn old bastard.'

'What happened?'

'I told him we're going to grub out the upper orchard.'

'Uh huh.' They'd agreed it made sense. The upper block had fared the worst, being so close to the bush. It was harder to irrigate because of the steep slope where the water tended to wash the topsoil away if they weren't careful. And Annie always worried when Dave was up there ploughing or spraying, even with the crawler. Those things could tip over just as easily as a tractor in the wrong circumstances. 'What did he think about your plan to go with fat cattle instead?' They'd always run a few cattle and it would be simple to expand the herd. It was getting harder to make money out of apples. At least this way, if prices kept dropping and expenses kept rising, they'd have something to tide them over.

'He thought it was a good idea. He's planning to do some rationalising himself and get rid of the less popular varieties.'

'So, what's the problem?' She turned the hotplate off. The apples would keep cooking under their own heat.

Dave sat down heavily at the kitchen table. 'I told him we're going to buy the Fletchers' orchard.'

'And? What did he say?' The Fletchers' place would almost double their forty acres. They had the capacity in the new packing shed to handle the extra fruit from the viable trees. The rest they'd grub out for more cattle, once the drought broke.

Dave looked up at her with a hurt expression on his face. 'He accused me of profiteering. Taking advantage of other people's calamities, he called it. I was gobsmacked.'

'But we're offering a fair price. Market value.'

'Yeah, he scoffed at that. Told me the market had plummeted and I knew it.'

Annie was concerned. They'd always had a good relationship with Catherine's family. 'We're doing the Fletchers a favour. They want to get out, and we're offering them a way.'

'You and I know that, darl, but Jack Turner sees it differently. And you know what he's like. Always thinks he's right and everybody else is wrong.'

'Did you get a chance to talk about him using our packing shed?'

'Yeah, but he'd already got his back up. He knows it makes sense and it's what the Ag Department wants, rationalisation of the industry and all that bureaucratic mumbo jumbo, but he still wants his own packing shed.' Dave threw up his hands in frustration. 'Maybe he thinks I'll price gouge him on the agreement, who knows. But the man's hardly going to need a packing shed until the new trees start bearing. The block he's managed to save won't yield much. I was just trying to help out.'

'I know.' Annie started scrubbing potatoes at the sink. They were old and soft. Good produce was hard to get with the drought and the aftermath of the fire. It was time to get their veggie garden going again, now the harvest was done. The boys could help. And she wanted some new chooks. She missed those girls with their endless clucking and fresh eggs. Poor darlings. All of them gone in the fire.

Dave was silent, staring at his callused hands. Annie frowned at him. 'Something else is wrong. Come on, spit it out.'

Dave huffed out a long breath.

'Come on. What is it?'

'I might have put my foot in it.'

'Really? Not one of those big, booted, farming feet of yours? Surely not.' Annie's voice was gentle and teasing. He'd just shut down if she was pushy.

'We were talking about insurance, grants and loans for rebuilding, the endless to and fro we've all been going through.'

Annie had heard little else lately. The government had been generous in some respects, but frustratingly dense in others, especially when it came to primary producers.

'And how they won't replace houses unless it's the principal place of residence.'

'Yes,' Annie said in a slow encouraging way. This was a particular bugbear of her husband's. His parents' old place wasn't eligible for a replacement grant. When Michael, as the oldest son, took over the running of the orchard, the house would have been his, to raise a family of his own.

Dave looked like one of their boys when they were in trouble. 'I said he was luckier than us. He still has the cottage and'll get a brand-new house with all the mod cons while we're stuck with this draughty place that's way too small and no money to rebuild the old house.'

'Oh.' Annie understood.

'Soon as I saw his face I realised what an idiot I was.' He shook his head. 'Of course he'd rather have Peter than a new house.'

'He said that?'

'He didn't need to.'

'Right.' Annie turned back to the sink. There wasn't anything she could add. He'd done wrong. He was sorry. 'I guess Jack and Judith won't be coming to the party then.'

'Sorry, darl. I know how much it means to you.'

'It's not just for me, it's for everyone. We all need cheering up.' She turned back towards him. 'You know what I was thinking? Live music would be good. Do you think Mark might play some guitar, give us a song or two?'

'I don't think so. He left Melbourne to get away from all that.'

'Yeah, but he has to get back to his own life at some point.'

'I guess. But until then I'm glad of his help. Doesn't look like Ben will be coming back.'

'No?' Ben was their permanent worker, up until the fire. Like so many others he'd moved up to town and was building houses. Construction was booming given so many homes had burnt to the ground. There was talk of having to bring builders over from New Zealand.

Dave shook his head. 'He's got more work than he can handle and it'll be going on for a while.'

'Well, we should hire someone else who knows about orchards. When *is* Mark going back to Melbourne?'

'He can't leave, you know that.'

'Surely he's still not hoping his wife'll come back? Not here to the orchard?'

Dave stood up and walked over to her. 'Come on, Annie. You know why he's still here.'

Annie shook off his hand that rested on her shoulder and began peeling another potato. 'I was thinking I might invite my parents to the party.'

Dave rocked back on his heels. 'Your parents?'

'I'm sure they tried to call, after the fire and everything. They would've been worried. But the lines were down for so long. They would've wanted to know we were safe.'

Dave's voice was cautious. 'Even after what they said to you last time you saw them?'

Annie continued peeling the potato, gouging into it to remove an eye. She still remembered the look on her father's face when she'd told him she was pregnant. Annie had never seen such viciousness or hatred. The words he spoke were spiteful things, full of loathing. He'd insisted she leave his house that minute. She'd had no time to pack – all her clothes, jewellery and books were left behind. Later she'd tried calling her mother, but she would never come to the phone. One day the housekeeper told Annie her mother insisted she had no daughter, that she was dead to her now. But still Annie held out hope. 'Water under the bridge.' Annie's laugh was little more than a grunt. 'If only there was. This drought!'

'Darl, I don't think it's a good idea. You'll get your hopes up ...'

'I wrote to them, you know. About Angela.'

'I thought we'd agreed you wouldn't.' Dave's voice was strained.

'Just because they've never written back in the past.' Annie had written to them after the birth of every one of her sons. She'd sent them Christmas cards every year. They'd never responded. 'But a granddaughter. How could they resist?' Annie found a large blemish on the potato and picked up a paring knife to cut it away.

Dave sighed. 'I didn't see a letter from them.'

'I just thought, now especially, they'd want to visit. You know, to see how we're getting on after the fires and meet their granddaughter. Once they see Angela, they'll fall in love with her. I know they will.'

'Oh, darling.' Gently Dave removed the small knife and the mangled potato from her hands. He turned Annie to face him and put his arms around her. 'I'm so sorry. I'm sorry they never wrote back. I'm sorry for all the hurt they caused. But I don't think anything's going to change that.'

'A girl. A beautiful, perfect baby girl.' Annie's voice trembled.

'I know, my darling. I know.' Dave's body was strong, a safe harbour. Annie felt herself letting go, dissolving into him. Only then did the tears fall.

15

Late May 1967

Catherine

'Come on, Mum. You've got those beautiful dresses from the Women's Auxiliary. Either one of them would be just the thing for Annie's party.'

'How can you think of going to a party?' Her mother closed the bedroom door firmly, leaving Catherine on the outside, as usual. Her mother had only recently started attending church again, but even then never stayed for the morning tea afterwards. Mostly she huddled in her bedroom, where there was no view of the orchard or the ruins of the family home. Now the weather was closing in, Catherine had bought some yarn and suggested they knit together during the cold evenings, hoping to find a way to connect, but her mother refused. The magazines Catherine gave her went unread, the latest news from Cygnet ignored. Everything Catherine tried ended in the same way, with her being shut out.

Catherine retreated to the kitchen. Her father sat at the table, frowning at piles of receipts, bills and forms. 'I don't suppose there's any chance you'll come to the party tonight, Dad.'

'After what Dave said?' her father growled. 'Not likely.'

Catherine wasn't surprised. Dave's comment had been out of character, but still hurtful. She sat down beside her father. 'What are you doing?' Now the harvest was over, Catherine wanted to get up to speed with everything in the orchard, including the paperwork.

'Insurance will cover the fences, sheds and machinery.' Her father pointed his pen at a sheaf of invoices. 'But there are a lot of other outlays. The Fire Victim's Welfare Organisation helped me apply for money from the Governor's Fire Relief Fund. And I can try the Returned Servicemen's League fund too, being a member and all. Then there's Apex and the Lions Club. Makes a lot of forms to fill out.'

'And what about these?' Catherine indicated a separate pile of papers.

'They're bills I can't pay. Orchard expenses. Usually the harvest would cover them but ...' He spread his hands out on the table. 'Thankfully the government is taking care of them.'

'So, how are we looking? The orchard, I mean.'

The phone rang. Her father rose to answer it. 'Catherine, it's for you. It's your beau.'

Catherine felt herself redden. She pulled a face at her dad and took the receiver from his grasp. At least his harmless teasing brought a rare smile to his face. He gave her a wink before joining her mother in their bedroom, giving Catherine a semblance of privacy.

'Hi, Tim,' she said, her face still flushed.

'Hello, Angel. You'd better save every dance for me tonight at this party.'

Catherine smiled. Tim had been vague about whether he'd be able to make it tonight or not. 'You can come?'

'Might be a bit late, but yeah.'

A flutter of excitement stirred in her stomach. She'd been worried she'd feel awkward at the party. Annie would be hectic, making sure everyone had a good time, and Dave busy manning the bar and drinking with his mates. But now Tim would be there. She wouldn't be a wallflower after all. She said goodbye with a smile.

Her father came back into the kitchen. 'Tim's going to the party tonight then?'

'Yes.'

'Good. He'll take care of you.' He sat down at the table. 'We haven't seen so much of him lately.' He left the inference hanging in the air.

Catherine chewed her bottom lip. Over the past months Tim's visits had dropped away. The lure of the surf had proved too strong. Instead he had invited her along with him to the wild beaches he loved. He'd hoped she'd be like the other girlfriends, waiting on the shore, admiring their men doing battle with the waves. She'd gone a few times, but sitting on the beach doing nothing seemed a waste of time when there was so much to do in the orchard. He'd also hoped she'd be like the other girlfriends in other ways. She knew what went on behind the dunes or in the cars, but the thought of it made her uncomfortable. She liked kissing Tim, but as soon as his hands started straying she would squirm away. She'd been brought up knowing that kind of thing before marriage was a sin, and as much as she liked Tim and as much as he kept insisting she was his angel, love had never been mentioned, let alone marriage. Sometimes she wondered if she was hopelessly old-fashioned; the world was changing so fast, but here in the valley it was if time stood still.

Annie, as always, had been her sounding board. 'Sex, with the right person, is wonderful.' Annie's eyes had misted over, making Catherine fidget with embarrassment. 'If you're worried about ending up like me, you could go on the Pill,' she'd suggested. 'You'd have to go to Hobart to find a doctor willing to prescribe it to an unmarried woman. It's expensive and I've heard the side effects can be bad, but for peace of mind it might be worth it. The question is, is Tim the right person?'

It was a question Catherine hadn't been able to answer. She knew how enamoured Annie and Dave were with each other, even after all their years together. She wanted a love like that. Would she ever find it with Tim? So far, he'd been patient, but she wondered how much longer it would last. On the weekends when he didn't come down to the valley he always made sure he called her on Sunday night when STD calls were cheap. He'd tell her stories about the sea and she'd chat about the orchard, her parents, the valley and the packing shed. She'd even told him about Charlie, their lunches together and the games they played, but Tim had become sullen. She never mentioned Charlie again.

'Is he still working at the school?' her father asked.

'Yeah.' Tim had told her he'd rather be with her, or surfing, but he needed the money. Plus the job helped keep him fit for surfing.

'And what about you? They've been very generous, giving you all this time off, but isn't it time you went back?'

Catherine held her breath. She'd been dreading this conversation. 'I'm not going back.'

Her father's face froze in a frown.

'I resigned.'

'What?'

'I couldn't stay in Hobart, not after the fire. I need to be here. I have to help you get the orchard up and running, now that Peter ...'

'Catherine.' Her father spoke slowly. 'You know there's no money in this orchard. There won't be for years. The insurance will help get us through, but even so, we mightn't survive.'

'I can chip in. I've saved the money Annie paid me.'

'Packing's a job wives do for a bit of extra shopping money. It'll never replace a teaching wage.'

'But I can be more use here than in Hobart. There's so much to do.'

'Men's work.'

'We can't afford to hire a man and we don't need to. I can do most of it. I've spent years hoeing around the trees. I can prune and graft. And help with the spraying and ploughing.'

Her father pressed his lips together and shook his head slowly. 'Peter told me you planned to take on the orchard if he became a vet.'

Now it came. The accusations. She'd been wrong to hope his argument with Peter had been forgotten or put aside in favour of more pressing problems. 'It wasn't like that.'

Her father's face closed in, dark with anger. 'What was it like then? You pit my own son against me, and after he's gone you throw in your teaching job, come back to the orchard and expect to take over the place?'

Catherine gasped with the shock of his words. How could he think of her in such a way? Tears pricked her eyes but she refused to cry. She took a breath and tried to slow her racing heart. Being a vet might have been Peter's idea, but her parents couldn't forgive her for supporting him in his dream. It was easier for them to blame her than Peter. She was the difficult daughter who wouldn't get married and have children, who had the crazy idea of running the orchard one day just because she was the oldest child. And Peter? He was the perfect son and always would be. Even so, it wasn't all her fault. 'He tried to talk to you about it but—'

'It was never going to happen.' Her father shut down her protestations. 'You made it worse by giving him false hope. Filling his head with pipe dreams. Telling him you'd run this place and he could be a vet. As if either of those things were going to happen. He knew he'd take over the orchard from me, like I did from my father and he did from my grandfather. Do you really think you can take Peter's place?'

'No, Dad. Never. But let me help. Please.'

'You really want to help?'

She nodded, desperate for both him and her mother to forgive her. There'd been too much pain, for all of them.

'It'll be years before the orchard is productive. In the meantime we need some form of income. The best thing you can do is to go back to teaching. You can work in the orchard during holidays and weekends but that's it.'

Disappointment dropped like a stone. She'd hoped she and her father would work side by side to bring the orchard back to life, but clearly it wasn't what he wanted. A heaviness enveloped her. 'It'll be tough finding a teaching job at this time of year. I can start looking but there mightn't be anything until next year. In the meantime, I can help you rework the trees.' Catherine was determined to keep her promise to Peter. The orchard would be heaven again, no matter what it took.

His expression softened but was still stern. 'A good government job. There's security there. Not like the land. That's where you're the best use to the orchard – teaching.'

His meaning was clear. Her money was good enough to keep the orchard running, but she was not good enough to run it.

The packing shed was jumping by the time Catherine arrived. Annie hadn't been able to hire a band but she'd come up with a brilliant solution – a jukebox filled not only with the latest hits, but singles from the fifties too, catering for all age groups. Kids, mums and dads laughed while attempting their own versions of the twist. Soft drinks and cans of Cascade beer nestled in tubs of ice and the supper table was laden with plates of sandwiches, homemade biscuits and slices. Two of Annie's boys, along with a couple of boys around their own age, sidled up to the food and filled their pocket with biscuits. 'Hey,' Annie yelled. 'I saw that. Leave the food alone.' The boys ran out of the shed with their haul, laughing.

'Great party,' Catherine said to her friend.

Annie beamed, Angela on her hip. 'Isn't it? So many people have turned up. We all need a bit of fun after what we've been through.'

'Sure do.' She was glad of the distraction of a party after the conversation with her father. Catherine watched the dancing crowd. Annie was right, most of them had suffered some form of hardship.

'What's your poison?' Dave was standing by the tubs of cold drinks.

'I'll have a creaming soda.' It was for the kids but she was in the mood for something fizzy.

'Whatever the lady desires.' He fished out a bottle of soft drink, flipping off the lid with a bottle opener.

Catherine bobbed her head in thanks and took a stroll around the shed. It was astounding what a few streamers, balloons and coloured lights could do. The boxes and pallets had been cleared out, along with Dave's precious forklift. Wooden bulk bins served as tables and apple boxes as stools. The grader still dominated the space, but no one was paying it any attention tonight. The smell of cigarette smoke and perfume was strong but the underlying scent of apples persisted. Catherine stood near the far wall, comfortable in the knowledge that she wouldn't be on her own for long. The other women's faces would turn towards her in envy once Tim was by her side. A handsome stranger was always cause for interest.

Close by, a group of women sat huddled on upturned apple boxes, drinking and laughing. Catherine recognised some of them from the packing shed. She should have put in an effort to make friends during the harvest, but she'd been too sad at first, then spent every lunch break with Charlie. Now she wasn't sure whether to approach them or not.

'Cat.' The decision was made for her with the arrival of an enthusiastic young boy. He was so different from when they'd first met with his solemn face, his serious brown eyes, and his determined struggle to say her name. When she'd suggested he call her Cat, she'd taken herself by surprise. Her little brother had been a quiet, solemn child too. He'd had trouble pronouncing her name and called her Cat. Peter was the only one allowed to, until Charlie.

'Little Mouse.' She squatted down to his level, easy to do when she was wearing her packing shed clothes of shorts or dungarees, not so much in a dress with a hemline above the knee. 'Are you having fun?'

'I had a fizzy drink.'

'I have one too.' Catherine lifted her bottle of creaming soda.

'There he is.' Mark stood above her, smiling. 'I had to chase this little scamp clear across the room. Soon as he saw you there was no stopping him.'

'Are you hungry? Let's get a sandwich before Annie's boys eat them all.' Catherine stood, taking one of Charlie's hands while Mark took the other. Before they could make it to the supper table

Charlie broke away to join the dancers. He jigged up and down on the spot, beaming.

'He's a tad excited,' Catherine said with a laugh.

'I think he has the right idea.' Mark took the soft drink from her hand, placing it on a nearby apple bin. 'Shall we join him?' He gestured in the direction of the makeshift dance floor.

Catherine hesitated. Surely Tim hadn't been serious when he'd asked her to save every dance for him? With a twinkle in his eye, Mark stood next to Charlie and jigged along with him. They looked adorable together. She joined them and her earlier disappointment began to lift. Spending time with Charlie, and Mark, gave her a sense of lightness that was becoming increasingly familiar. The Rascals, the Rolling Stones and the Supremes came and went on the jukebox as Charlie insisted they keep dancing. When 'Yellow Submarine' started to play, he yelped with excitement. 'My favourite.'

As the song ended Catherine begged off any more dancing. 'I need a drink.' She smoothed her hair into a semblance of respectability, and headed in the direction of her creaming soda, probably warm and flat by now.

She didn't notice Tim until she almost bumped into him.

'Hello,' he said. 'Come here often?'

'Tim.' She was aware of sweat under her arms, and a flush on her cheeks. He in comparison was cool and serene, with his blond hair and those blue eyes. She touched his arm, the suede of his sheepskin jacket soft under her fingers. 'You're here.'

'And you seem to have some fans.' He nodded behind her.

She turned and saw Charlie and Mark had followed her. 'Oh, this is Charlie.' She put out a hand for him to take but he hid behind his dad's legs.

'And this,' Tim looked Mark in the eye, 'is Mark Davis.' He turned to Catherine. 'You didn't tell me you were hanging out with pop stars.'

Something in Tim's voice pulled her off balance. It was a tone she hadn't heard before. 'I've been hanging out with Charlie, mainly.' Why did she suddenly feel so defensive? 'I told you about him.'

'Ah, yes. Little Charlie.' Tim shoved his hand towards Mark. 'I'm Tim Walsh. I'm sure Catherine's told you all about me.'

Mark shook Tim's hand. 'Sorry, mate, we usually talk about Charlie,' he glanced around the packing shed, 'or apples.'

'Right.' Tim nodded tightly. 'So, *mate*, why aren't you in the UK with the rest of The Scene? I hear they're doing really well.'

'Family obligations,' Mark said, his face impassive.

'Yeah, I read that in *Go-Set*.'

Catherine's sense of unease grew. She'd never seen either of them like this. Tim must have meant what he said about her saving all the dances for him. And she knew Mark was sensitive about being a so-called pop star.

'You're a married man, aren't you?' Tim nodded sharply at Charlie. 'With a kid even.'

'Yep.'

'Right then.' Tim turned to Catherine. 'Come on, let's get a drink.' He took her arm in his and started moving away, then stopped and looked over his shoulder towards Mark. 'Nice to meet you, mate.'

'What was that about?' Catherine asked, once they were out of earshot.

'You know what everyone here is talking about?' Tim didn't look at her.

'No.'

'You really can't guess?'

His grip was tight on her arm. Some of the women were staring, but not in the way she'd hoped. She shook her head in confusion.

'You and Mark.' His voice was a low growl. 'So, you ask me what *that* was about?' He looked at her now, his eyes dark with anger. 'You know that reputation you're always so worried about? Well, that was me, saving it.'

16

February 1968

Catherine

A year after Black Tuesday, Tasmania still bore the scars – swathes of scorched trees and scrub, the crumbling bones of burnt-out homes, and a sense of despair that was rarely voiced. The death toll had risen to sixty-two with the passing away of a few poor souls who'd succumbed to their burns. Nearly 1,300 houses had been destroyed leaving over 7,000 people homeless. More than 1,700 other buildings had been burnt, including churches, schools, shops and factories. All of this in the course of one day, with the worst of the firestorm lasting only five hours. Recovery was slow, but ironically the rebuilding had created a kind of economic boom.

Catherine's father's pigheadedness had come in handy when it came to their new house. He'd pushed through the bureaucracy and paperwork, then badgered a local construction team into doing the build. The result was worth it. A model home higher up the hill, and a different outlook without a glimpse of their old place, as her mother had wanted. After a year of living in the poky old cottage, it was a luxury to unpack their possessions into the clean expanse of the three-bedroom brick house. The new home was pristine; creamy white walls, carpet in a stippled green, a screened verandah to keep the flies out, and generous-sized bedrooms with built-in wardrobes. But the pride of the house, and her mother's favourite room, was the kitchen. When it was finally finished, Catherine's mother had opened and closed the olive-green laminated cupboards and touched every new appliance, from the refrigerator with its separate freezer compartment to the shiny chrome pop-up toaster. 'It's all so easy to keep clean,' she'd murmured. 'So much more efficient.'

The recent anniversary of Peter's death had seen her regress to shutting herself away in the darkened bedroom again. Catherine had enticed her out by begging her to cook something delicious in her new kitchen. 'You're such a wonderful cook, Mum, much better than me. I think Dad's pretty sick of my efforts. And I know how much you love the new oven.' It was such a pleasure to use after the portable gas stove and toaster oven they'd made do with in the old cottage. Even through the winter, when Catherine was long over her reluctance to use the wood stove, her mother had refused to have any form of fire in the house. Instead, they'd spent the long evenings huddled around a two-bar radiator.

Eventually Catherine's mother had emerged and her father had patted Catherine's hand in silent gratitude at seeing his wife busy in the kitchen instead of crying in the bedroom. And it had worked, to a degree. As long as she was absorbed in making something, her mother seemed almost content, if only fleetingly. This morning she'd baked a batch of Anzac biscuits. 'Why don't you pop over to

Annie's,' she suggested to Catherine. 'I'm sure her boys would love some of these biscuits.'

It was Saturday afternoon and Catherine's chores were done for the day. She'd been looking forward to reading one of the many books waiting in a pile by her bed but she knew it would make her mum happy if she took the biscuits over to Annie's. 'That's a lovely idea.' Catherine filled the biscuit tin and kissed her lightly on the cheek. She'd do anything to see her mother smile.

On the way, Catherine made a slight detour. Last year she'd planted a walnut tree at the site of the family home where she and Peter had grown up together, a tree that would grow slowly and spread its strong branches over the place where her brother had died. She knelt beside the sapling and opened the biscuit tin, placing an Anzac beside its slender trunk. 'There you go, little brother,' she whispered, brushing away her tears. 'I know how much you loved Mum's Anzacs.' The biscuit would most likely be eaten by birds or a possum, but she liked to think Peter's spirit appreciated the sentiment.

Along the familiar road to Annie's, the small scrubby bushes were beginning to grow back, along with the ever-tenacious bracken. Some of the eucalypts on the hill line sprouted fluffy new growth, but others would stay as they were, stark reminders of a day no one would forget. Before she reached Annie's house, Catherine could hear the familiar ruckus of the boys. She didn't bother to knock, calling out a 'yoo-hoo' as she made her way down the hall. The scene greeting her was the usual chaos of the Pearsons' kitchen. Four muddy boys, a screaming toddler and little Angela, looking like a doll in her pink romper suit. She kept herself upright by clutching on to the leg of the kitchen table and watching her brothers with her amazing eyes. They'd been blue when she was first born but had quickly begun to change.

'The boys have been fishing.' Annie put her hands on her hips. 'Or so they say. I don't see any fish. All I see is mud.' She stared at each of her four oldest in turn. 'This one,' she nodded at Scott, 'is going through the terrible twos, and terrible it is.' To prove her point Scott started his wailing again, falling to the lino floor and pounding it with his fists. 'But my little girl ...' Annie's face opened up in a joyful smile. 'She's a treasure, aren't you, my darling.' She wiped her hands on her apron and smoothed down Angela's dark hair.

'A treasure with the most extraordinary eyes,' Catherine said. 'They really are beautiful.'

Annie tensed. 'It's a family thing.'

Annie rarely spoke about her family. Who could blame her after the way they'd treated her? Cutting her off completely like that. Even after the devastating fires there'd been no contact.

'Aunt Marjorie,' Annie added. 'She had eyes just like Angela's.'

Something in her tone told Catherine not to pursue it. She cleared a space on the table crowded with baby bottles and sippy cups, glasses coated with the dregs of Milo, and plates with discarded crusts from Vegemite sandwiches. 'Mum made Anzacs and thought you might like some.'

'Great,' Michael said. 'All we ever get are apples.'

'Can we have one now, Mum?' Eric begged.

'Okay. But only one each.' Annie waggled a finger at them.

The two older boys immediately grabbed the tin and started to battle over it.

'Boys! One biscuit each. And take them outside.' Annie shook her head as her brood grabbed their biscuits and ran out the back door. She handed one to Scott who immediately stopped his wailing. 'Please thank your mum for me. Her biscuits are better than a dummy. How's the new house?'

'Very new, very shiny. Mum loves it. You'll have to come over and have a look.'

Annie snorted. 'As long as I don't bring my lot. They'd destroy it within moments.' She sighed. 'Lord, how I'd love a new house. Mind you, I'd settle for just a new kitchen. Rip this one out and start again.'

'And replace it with what?' Catherine had always loved the warm familiarity of this room combined with the nurturing Annie brought to it and the thriving, tumbling, endless energy of her brood. The kitchen in her parents' new home was certainly impressive but the clean lines and shiny surfaces stirred no emotion. There was no history there. Catherine knew that was exactly the point for her mother. Still, the room seemed soulless, even when filled with the sweet scent of oats and golden syrup.

Annie surveyed the mess around her. 'I'd rip it out and build everything out of concrete. Hose it down three times a day, along with the boys. Just like at a fish market.'

Catherine laughed. 'Is there anything I can do to help?'

'Only if you've got a concrete mixer out the front.'

Annie started collecting dirty dishes and Catherine gave her a hand. 'It'd be nice to see you at the new house,' Catherine said. 'Why don't you ask Mark to look after the kids so you and Dave can come over for lunch one day?'

She huffed. 'I wouldn't trust him with Angela, not one bit.'

Catherine didn't think Annie would trust anyone with Angela. Every time she'd offered to babysit, Annie had come up with an excuse.

Annie filled the sink with hot water and detergent. 'How's the new job?'

'I'm getting used to it. Teaching Kindergarten is a lot different from Grade One. Instead of exercise books and pencils, I'm dealing with smocks and finger-painting. I'm brushing up on my piano playing for the morning sing-a-longs. And I always have a pile of clean underpants in my desk drawer for the inevitable accidents.' It had been tough to find teaching work, especially as she'd refused to leave the valley. Before landing the position in Cygnet, Catherine had picked up some relief teaching from time to time, but mostly she'd spent the months since last year's harvest alongside her father; grafting, hoeing, spraying and thinning. She'd learnt about the irrigation system, gravity fed from the dam at the top of the property, and had grown stronger lugging the heavy pipes around. Her face and arms were sunburnt, her hands callused, and her body leaner and more capable than it had ever been. Her father never thanked her as they worked the long days together, but she knew he was glad of the help. Even though it was heartbreaking in some respects, it felt right to be working in the orchard again. It was how she'd grown up, working and playing in the open spaces of the countryside and river. When she'd started her new job a few weeks ago her parents were pleased, but the more time Catherine spent in the orchard the more she was convinced it was where she was supposed to be. There was still so much that needed doing. The grafts and young trees she and her father had planted to replace the rows of burnt trees would take years to bear fruit. Catherine missed the long days in the orchard, but at least she came home to it every day.

'And how's it going with Tim?' Annie asked as she began washing up. 'Aren't you supposed to be seeing him tonight?'

Catherine chewed her bottom lip. Annie had been her Agony Aunt over the past few months as Tim's behaviour had become increasingly erratic. The gallant, kind-hearted and patient Tim was frequently replaced by someone whose glazed eyes and strange behaviour was often worrying. 'Yeah, we were supposed to go up to

Hobart. The Kravats are playing at the Beachcomber.' She tried to keep the disappointment out of her voice.

'Were?'

Catherine instinctively reached for a tea towel and started drying up. 'He was surfing down at Cloudy Bay. Missed the last ferry.'

'Really.' The disdain in Annie's voice was obvious and Catherine knew why. Tim 'missing the ferry' from Bruny Island meant the surf must be pumping.

'Why don't you go out anyway?' Annie asked. 'I know how much you love the Kravats. You could catch up with some of your old friends from Hobart. You haven't seen them for ages and you can't spend every Saturday night at home with your parents.'

'Why would I want to go up to Hobart when I'm having the time of my life with my best friend, doing the dishes?' Catherine's laugh fell flat. The truth was her old friendships had fallen away. Time, distance and, more crucially, the way her life had been changed by the fires and Peter's death meant she had little in common with those friends now. In contrast, the tragedy and loss had only strengthened her bond with Annie. Annie was always the one she turned to, as she had from the age of thirteen. 'Besides, Tim said he'll come over tomorrow afternoon.'

'Well, that's all right then.' The sarcastic arch of Annie's eyebrow spoke volumes.

Scott began crying again, indignant his biscuit was gone. Relieved by the distraction, Catherine put down the plate she was drying and scooped up Scott instead. 'What's all that noise about, my little godson?' She jiggled him on her hip. 'My, you are becoming a big boy.' Scott let out another wail. 'With a very big voice.'

'I think he's overtired.' Annie dried her hands. 'Nap time for you, young man. And Angela too.'

'Do you need a hand?'

'Nah. But thanks.'

Catherine said her goodbyes and began the short walk home, while the summer light slowly began to fade and the afternoon shadows lengthened. Annie was right. She couldn't spend every Saturday night at home with her parents. Instead of heading back to the house she turned in the other direction, further up the gentle slope towards the pickers' hut Mark called home.

17

February 1968

Mark

He watched her walking through the orchard towards him. Strange how his heart lurched at the sight; half joyful, half full of dread. It had been over a year since Lara had left and still no word. It was as if she were a figment of an imagined other life, so different from the one he lived now that it was hard to reconcile. But he was a married man, no matter how estranged his wife might be, and the ache remained every time he saw Catherine. Charlie ran towards her, his love clear for all to see, while Mark sat stoically on the porch of the pickers' hut, his arms wrapped around his guitar. Benno lumbered to his feet, his tail the only spritely thing about him. He clambered off the porch to greet Catherine.

'Daddy, it's Cat,' Charlie whooped in delight. He tugged on her hand, pulling her towards the hut.

'Hi, Mark.' Catherine waved, a little awkwardly, with her free hand. 'I was in the neighbourhood. Thought I'd drop in and say hello to Charlie.'

He nodded. Their friendship started and ended with Charlie. There could be nothing else. Not in this close-knit valley. 'Welcome to our humble abode,' he said. 'Always good to see you. And Charlie's stoked. He hides his feelings well, but I can tell.'

Catherine laughed. 'Old poker-face Charlie.' She swung Charlie's hand in hers.

He looked up at her quizzically. 'Poker face? Like what you poke the fire with?'

'No.' Catherine bobbed down. 'It's a card game like Go Fish.'

'Can we play Go Fish? Can we?'

Catherine turned towards Mark. 'Looks like your dad is playing the guitar.'

'But you can play with me while Daddy plays music.'

'Sounds good to me.' She looked up at Mark. 'Is that okay?'

Mark shrugged. He was grateful Catherine had kept in contact with Charlie after the picking season was over, even though it caused Mark some anguish. 'Sure. Go get the cards, Charlie.'

Charlie raced up the steps onto the porch, 'One, two, three,' he counted.

Catherine bent to pat Benno, her fair hair swinging to cover her cheeks. She looked up at Mark with a questioning frown. 'I wasn't expecting to see Benno here.'

'Didn't Annie tell you?'

'Tell me what?'

A familiar tension gripped his stomach. Bloody Annie. 'Well ...' He hesitated but the truth was best. 'She was worried about having a dog around Angela, now she's walking. Annie thought it would be better for everyone if Benno came and lived with us.'

'Oh, I see.' Her hand reached up to touch the base of her throat. 'I was just over there and wondered why Benno didn't come and say hello. Annie probably meant to tell me, but she's always so busy.'

'Yeah.' Mark didn't trust himself to say anything else. 'Are you okay with Benno being here? Charlie adores him.'

'Of course, if you are. I can take him to the hydatid station to have him checked. And bring food for him too.'

'It's okay. I'll be careful.' Mark and Dave were still at school when Dave's father had first been diagnosed with hydatid cysts in his liver. His friend had explained how people became infected from dogs that had eaten offal. The dog would be okay, you might never know it was infected, but hydatid cysts in humans could be fatal. The last time Mark saw Dave's father he was almost unrecognisable – a frail jangle of bones and jaundice. Who'd have thought a tiny tapeworm could do so much damage?

Her shoulders relaxed. 'As long as you're sure.'

'Charlie's never had a pet and takes his responsibility seriously. And they have a lot of fun playing together. I think it's good for them both.' Plus it would give her another excuse to come and visit. Charlie, now Benno. Two out of three wasn't bad.

Mark strummed a C chord. He hadn't played for anybody except his son in a long time. 'Charlie's not a big fan of my songs,' he said apologetically. 'But he likes nursery rhymes.' He only played the songs he'd written for the band when Charlie was asleep. In the evenings, with no one else around, he'd let his fingers settle on the frets in the old familiar patterns and softly sing the words he knew so well, though it had always been someone else who'd sung them. He'd wanted to sing his own tunes, but the rest of the band had voted him down. 'What am I going to do if you're singing?' their lead singer had said. 'Play the fucking tambourine?' Mark had resigned himself to the situation, but Lara was furious.

'You're the brains of the band. You should be the star as well.' She'd wanted to be the wife of a front man and made his life miserable for weeks.

Catherine sat on one of the old rickety chairs while Benno flopped down beside her. 'If you had a piano we could perform a duet. All I ever play are nursery rhymes too. I'll know all the words.'

'How's it going, being back in the teaching gig?'

'It's not quite what I had planned, but it'll be a while before the orchard is fully productive again. And the children are wonderful.' Charlie came rushing out, waving a pack of faded cards. 'None as wonderful as this one though.'

Charlie had flourished in the year they'd been here. He was much more confident with Annie's boisterous clan and he'd grown more adventurous. He was turning into a country kid, catching tadpoles, running around until he was exhausted and falling asleep as soon as Mark started reading him a bedtime story. Charlie was proud of the scabs on his knees and the dirt on his clothes. Annie's kids had taught him how to be a boy, but Mark knew it was Catherine who'd led him there. He'd always be grateful to her.

Charlie gave the cards to Catherine so she could deal. 'When do I get to go to school, Daddy? I want Cat to be my teacher.'

'You're not quite old enough yet.'

'But I'm almost four.'

Mark laughed. 'Of course you are.' Charlie's birthday was over six months away.

Catherine leant towards Charlie. 'You can go to school when you're five, but I mightn't be a teacher by then. I'm just waiting for the trees to grow so I can work in my orchard all the time.'

Charlie's face crumpled. 'But I want you to be my teacher.'

'If I was your teacher you'd have to call me Miss Turner and never Cat. Where's the fun in that?'

'That's no fun at all.'

'We'll still be friends. And I'll teach you things outside of school.'

'Like what?'

'How many cards do you have?'

Charlie picked up his cards. 'One, two, three ...' As he counted he laid them on the table, face up.

'Charlie,' Mark said. 'You've got to keep your cards hidden or Catherine will know what you've got in your hand.'

'That's right,' Catherine said. 'Be like your dad, keep your cards close to your chest. Oh, I didn't mean—' She was flustered. 'Why don't we start again and this time keep your cards hidden.'

Mark watched as she shuffled the cards. She was right. He knew he was guarded. He'd had to be. When the band became big, everyone wanted something from him. Here in the valley he was more relaxed and open with Catherine than with anyone else besides Dave. Even so, he had to keep his feelings for her a secret. Another thing he needed to keep hidden.

Catherine began to deal the cards. 'Can you count along with me, Charlie? Five cards each.'

'I can count to ten,' Charlie said proudly. 'Sometimes twenty.'

'You're very clever for your age. Most children can't play Go Fish when they're almost four.'

'I can catch fish. Real fish. In the river.'

Mark smiled. 'Yeah, but mainly tadpoles in the creek.'

'They turn into frogs. I like frogs.' Charlie watched Catherine as she dealt the cards. 'One, two, three, four, five.' He beamed at her.

'Very good.'

The game continued with Charlie winning more than his fair share of hands. Mark suspected Catherine was complicit in the results. He strummed a few nursery rhymes and Catherine sang along, her voice a smooth alto. He was delighted when she sang a harmony; it seemed instinctive to her.

'You've got a great voice,' he said.

She looked up. 'Really? *You* think I've got a good voice? Wow.'

'Have you done much singing?'

'Oh, you know. Church choir, school choir and now nursery rhymes. Nothing like you.'

He humphed. 'All I sang were backing vocals.'

'But still—'

Charlie stood up, clearly impatient with the adults talking. 'I'm hungry.'

Mark looked at Catherine. 'We eat early around here. You're welcome to join us. It's just mashed potatoes, sausages, carrots and peas though.'

Catherine hesitated. 'That would be lovely. I like bangers and mash.'

'Me too,' Charlie beamed. 'And fish fingers and baked beans and egg on toast.'

'That's about my entire repertoire,' Mark admitted.

'Can I help?'

'That's okay. The kitchen's tiny and not really a kitchen. Only room for one, if that.' It was true. The pickers' hut had three small rooms. The middle one with the fireplace served as their lounge room, dining room and kitchen. The two smaller rooms on either side were bedrooms. The bathroom, if it could be called that, was a drop toilet out the back and a wood-chip heater and rusty old bath in the lean-to. Mark propped his guitar carefully against the wall and went inside. God, he hoped he didn't burn anything.

Later, when Charlie was asleep, Mark and Catherine sat on the porch, Benno happily snoring between them.

'I can't believe it's still so light,' Mark said, topping up her wine. 'It's after eight.'

'The delights of daylight saving.' Catherine raised her glass.

'Why does Tasmania have daylight saving? None of the other states do.'

'Because of the drought. Our electricity runs on hydro power. Less water means less power. Daylight saving gives us an extra hour of light at the end of the day. No one needs to turn the lights on until late in the evening.'

'I'm lucky Charlie runs around all day. If we were still in Melbourne and they brought in daylight saving, I'd never get him to sleep while it was this bright.' He downed the last of his wine and watched the patterns of twilight flicker in the apple trees. The first of the earlies would be ready to pick any day. At least he knew what to expect this time.

'Why aren't you back in Melbourne, where it would be an hour earlier right now?' she asked, almost dreamily. 'Why have you stayed here?'

Mark stood, swaying slightly. 'More wine? I can't believe the bottle's empty.'

'Not for me.' He watched her as she swirled what was left of her wine in the Vegemite jar that served as a glass. 'I haven't drunk wine for ages.'

'Me neither. Dave was given a couple of bottles by a mate, but Dave's more of a beer man.'

'And he pegged you for a wine buff?'

'To tell you the truth, the bottles have been gathering dust. I've had no one to drink with. Charlie prefers orange cordial.'

'I'm glad to hear it.'

'That I've had no one to drink with or that Charlie prefers orange cordial?'

The colour flushed in her cheeks. 'Charlie never struck me as either a beer man or a wine man.'

'I'll get the other bottle.' He knew his question had been a bit forward. The wine had loosened his tongue. It had been a while since he'd drunk this much but it was a beautiful night and he was with a beautiful girl. He returned with the wine and settled in happily beside her. 'Won't your parents be wondering where you are?' he teased. 'It's getting late.'

'They'll think I'm at Annie's. That's where I went first and then ...' Her voice trailed off.

Mark studied her profile. Fair hair, bleached lighter by the summer sun, strong tanned limbs in shorts and cotton shirt, and a sprinkling of freckles over her nose. She looked like a kid on summer holidays. Catherine turned to him and caught him staring. He looked away, too late.

'When I tell them what I had for dinner they will think I was at Annie's.' She laughed lightly.

'I hope it wasn't too horrible.'

'Nope, it was delicious. Especially with lots of tomato sauce.'

'Damning with faint praise.' He grinned at her.

'No, really. It was great. Annie couldn't have done better.'

'You won't tell your folks you were here?'

Her gaze shifted again, away from him. 'I don't think so.'

'Why not?' His glass was empty again. How had that happened? She shrugged. 'It's just easier.'

Mark knew what she was getting at. No matter how innocent their friendship was, he was a married man.

'And what about your parents?' Catherine asked. 'Are they in Melbourne? Or here in Tassie?'

'Nah. They're overseas somewhere.' He thought his parents were in Hong Kong, but wasn't sure – they were always moving.

His father worked all over the world while his mother enjoyed the indulgent expat lifestyle. Mark, an only child, had been raised by nannies and then shunted off to boarding school at a young age. He quickly changed the subject. 'It's Saturday night. Why aren't you out on the town with Tim?'

A frown crossed her face, then turned into a smile of resignation. 'The surf's pumping.'

'Oh.' He always suspected Tim was an idiot. What bloke would stand up a girl like this for a slab of seawater?

'He sees himself as a pioneer, of sorts.'

'Tim?'

'Yeah. There aren't many like him. Not in Tasmania. He and his mates drive all over the place searching for waves. Places where nobody's been before. They're mapping new territory. He sees it as a bit of a mission.'

'Right. And you don't want to be a pioneer alongside him?'

She chewed her bottom lip. 'Not really my style. Besides I have too much to do. A full-time job plus the orchard.' She turned to him again. 'I've answered your questions, but you haven't answered mine. I understand you needed to get away from Melbourne. I'm sorry about your wife and I know you were hoping she'd come back. But now? I don't know why a guy like you is still here, living in a pickers' hut so far away from everything.'

Mark filled his glass. 'I like it here.'

'Really?'

'Yeah, I like using my hands for something else other than playing guitar. I like learning about the seasons and apples—'

'And fat cattle.'

'Hmm, not so much.' He waggled his hand from side to side with fingers splayed. 'And there's Charlie. He's a different boy here. A happy one.'

'I'm going to be really nosy, but how do you afford it? I mean, I've had to go back to teaching. Dave and Annie's orchard is doing a whole lot better than ours but still, the fire and this drought has made things tough.'

'I don't pay much rent. Actually I don't pay any rent.' He grinned. 'Dave and Annie pay me a bit for the work I do around the place. Plus I have money coming in from my songs.'

'How does that work?' She shifted forward, her elbows on her knees, as the old chair creaked in complaint.

'Royalties. Every time my songs get played, I get paid. Not a lot. But enough.'

'Wow. I never knew that.'

'Most people don't. Most musos don't either. They get themselves stitched up in bad contracts and never see a shilling.'

'A shilling?' She wagged a finger at him. 'Get with the times, mister.'

'Yeah, all right. They never see a dollar.' Two years after the change to decimal currency he was still getting used to it.

'Well, strictly speaking a shilling is ten cents, but okay.'

'I stand corrected.' Mark poured himself another glass of wine. 'Here's to a Saturday night in the country. If I was back in Melbourne I'd have done at least one gig by now and have three more left to go.'

'Your band played four times a night?'

'Yeah. Saturdays were the busiest. We'd start in the afternoon and just keep going. But every week was pretty full on. Touring was rough. Weeks on the road in a smelly van packed with all the gear along with the band, our roadie usually off his face on something. We were lucky to get back alive.' He raised his glass in a mock toast. 'Good times.'

'Don't you miss it?'

'What part?' Mark scoffed. 'The groupies tearing my clothes and ripping out my hair? Trying not to get stuck in a clash between the sharpies and the mods?' He rubbed the small scar on his chin. 'All the men wanting to fight me and all the women wanting to—'

'I'm sorry,' Catherine stammered. 'I shouldn't have asked.'

'Nah, it's cool.' He leant towards her, his vision slightly blurred. 'Wasn't just me who got jack of it. Lara loved the fame but hated everything else about it.' He felt a sudden surge of anger towards Lara for the mess she'd left behind. 'She got so jealous. Made my life hell. For no reason. I was always a one-woman man.' He took another slug of wine. 'The only good thing about going on tour was leaving all that shit with Lara behind.'

Catherine stood quickly. 'I've got to go.'

Too late, Mark realised he'd offended her. It was the last thing he wanted to do. He stood. 'Sorry, I—'

'No, it's my fault. I'm too curious for my own good.' She began to walk away.

'It killed the cat, you know.'

She startled and turned towards him.

'Oh, God. I don't mean you.' He was horrified at his faux pas. 'Only Charlie is allowed to call you Cat, so I couldn't have meant you.'

She stared at him as if he was an idiot. He was an idiot. He'd had way too much wine.

'He loves you, you know.' Mark needed to make things right.

'Pardon?' She touched the base of her neck.

'Charlie. He loves you.'

A strange expression crossed her face. He couldn't read the mix of emotions. 'I love him too.' It was almost a whisper. She walked away into the fading light.

18

February 1968

Catherine

Tim's car was parked beside the house when Catherine and her parents returned home from church. Catherine's first thought was the surf must have dropped off, blown out or whatever happened to waves that rendered them useless to him. He jumped out of his car, tousled and salty, and beamed at them as they pulled up.

'Howdy, Mr and Mrs T. Hi, Catherine.' He opened the car door for her, gave her a brief kiss on the cheek then rushed around to open her mother's door.

'You'll do me out of a job,' her father joked.

'Never,' Tim said. 'There's only one man for your wife. Isn't that right, Mrs T?' He winked.

Catherine usually loved how attentive and respectful Tim was to her mother, but today it felt jarring. There was something off about his demeanour.

'Oh, Timothy.' Did her mother actually blush? 'Would you like to stay for lunch? Or do you and Catherine have plans?'

'Love to. Sure it's okay?'

'It would be our pleasure.' Her mother led them into the house, basking in Tim's compliments about the decor and the furnishings. Catherine knew her mother hoped for news of an engagement soon. She and Tim had known each other for a respectable amount of time and Catherine had recently turned twenty-four. There was nothing her mother would like more than to see her married and with a baby on the way as soon as possible.

'Can I help?' Tim asked.

'A man's place isn't in the kitchen.' Catherine's mother had already slipped on her apron. 'Catherine and I look after Sunday lunch. I do hope roast lamb suits.'

'Cool. But can I have a word with your daughter first, before she disappears into your beautiful kitchen?'

Catherine wondered if she had a say in any of this.

'Of course. Why don't you go out on the verandah? You'll have some privacy there and it's screened, so no flies.'

'Great idea.' Tim took Catherine's arm in a hard grip. 'Come on, Catherine.' His tone was brisk, not like the sweetness he'd used with her mother.

She was unimpressed. After he'd cancelled their plans yesterday, flowers would have been a nice apology, even if he'd stolen them from someone's garden like he usually did.

As the door shut behind them, Tim threw a grubby white envelope onto the table.

'What's that?' Catherine asked.

'It's got your name on it.' His eyes were wild. 'That man delivered it while I was waiting for you.'

'A man?'

'That pop star.' He snorted. 'Ex-pop star since he chucked it in and his mates got famous without him. That *married* man.'

Catherine watched Tim with a steady gaze. The more he ranted, the less attractive he became. He'd been a hero to her once, a man of salty mystery. She'd been amazed anyone as cool as him would be interested in her. Because of that, she'd put up with more than she should have, she realised that now. Catherine picked up the envelope. A jagged rip exposed a slip of paper inside. 'It's been opened.'

'Had to check what my chick was up to, didn't I?'

Tim had always been jealous of Mark, while Mark had never shown the slightest interest in Tim. Even last night when she'd let slip that Tim had stood her up, Mark didn't criticise him. Who was the better man in that equation?

'You've read it,' she said, trying to keep her voice steady. 'What does it say?'

Tim shifted his stance. 'Something about being sorry and Charlie.'

Catherine closed her eyes for a moment in relief. Mark was sorry. Last night had confused her. Even though his ugly words had given her a much better idea of why he'd left Melbourne, she wished he'd never said them. Then there was that strange interaction before she'd left. She thought she'd heard him say he loved her. The idea had thrilled her, much more than Tim's proclamations of devotion ever had. Neither she nor Tim had ever mentioned the word love, but even so, last night she'd felt guilty about her response to Mark saying it. But no, he was talking about Charlie. Catherine put the envelope back on the table. She was an idiot to think Mark could love her. It was Charlie who adored her and she loved him back with a fierce intensity. Catherine had grown wiser and sadder since her brother's death. Only Charlie brought the sun back into her heart.

Catherine took a slow breath to ease the aching in her chest. 'I went to see Charlie, not Mark.'

'So why the sorry note? Did he try something on? Pop stars are all the same. Think they can screw anyone they like.'

'Tim, stop it.' It was like dealing with a child. 'Like I said. I was there to see Charlie.'

'At his place?' Tim's voice was a whine.

'Honestly, Tim, you've got nothing to worry about. He's not interested in me and I'm only interested in Charlie.'

'Is that true? For real?'

'Yes.' Tim was right about one thing. Mark was a married man. They could never be anything but friends.

Tim reached out and held her, his strong arms pressing their bodies together. 'I get scared, Catherine.' His voice was a fraught whisper in her ear. 'We almost died in the fire. You were my angel. You saved me. We have to be together. If we're not, we'll die, don't you see? This morning, I got dumped by a massive wave. The ocean was pushing me down, pinning me under her weight. My chest was bursting, my head was exploding. I've been dumped before but never like this. Everything was black, freezing, and so heavy. Then I heard a voice. It was the ocean herself, giving me a warning, telling me what I had to do. She said she'd release me if I came straight here to you. Told me I'd die if I didn't. That you were the only one who could save me, again, always. I made a promise in that darkness, to her and to you. Then the light broke through. I headed towards it. And here I am. Don't you see, I can't live without you.'

Catherine felt that same pressure, as if she was being crushed under a wave. Tim's arms were too tight. She couldn't breathe, couldn't think. He was suffocating her. 'Tim, please.'

His grasp tightened further. 'Then I saw that man, here, with that letter, for you. He's the devil, Catherine, he wants to keep us apart. He wants me to die.'

139

She heard her father's polite cough. 'What are you two lovebirds up to, eh?'

Tim released her. 'Sorry, Mr T. Got carried away. Your daughter is so beautiful.'

'Yes, well, Catherine's mother needs her in the kitchen. Something about the potatoes not peeling themselves.'

'Yes, of course.' Catherine tried to smooth down the creases in her dress caused by Tim's intense embrace. Her thoughts were in turmoil. Was Tim mad? The fire had been horrendous and many people hadn't recovered emotionally or mentally. Could Tim be one of them? Had the experience altered him in some way? That could explain his erratic behaviour. The mood swings. Or was it something else? Annie had asked her if Tim was into drugs. He'd offered her some marijuana once, but her staunch refusal ensured it had never happened again. But she wasn't naive. She was sure he smoked it when she wasn't around.

She left Tim and her father talking about cricket and fishing, things Tim wasn't the slightest bit interested in but would never admit to her dad. She knew her father would take Tim on a tour of the orchard, showing him the new trees and the growth on the block they'd managed to save. The equipment and spray sheds had been rebuilt and the packing shed was next on the list. Tim would say the right things and nod in the right places, but now Catherine knew it was all an act. Underneath that extremely thin veneer lay an unstable mind.

Catherine sat quietly during lunch. Warily she watched Tim, waiting for another outburst, but he maintained an air of civility, flattering her mother and listening politely to her father. A few questions were sent her way, about her new teaching position and whether she'd help Annie and Dave again this season. There'd be very little to harvest in their own orchard this year, so Catherine would spend her after-school hours and Saturdays in Annie's packing shed. The extra money would help, but more than that, Catherine was yearning to see Charlie every day, with no questions asked.

Her father patted his stomach after two bowls of dessert. 'Fabulous lunch, girls.' He turned to Tim. 'We know what Catherine will be doing in the coming months. You'll hardly get a chance to see her. So, what'll you be doing with yourself?'

'Glad you asked, Mr T. Some interesting things coming up. The Summer of Love is over and it's time to protest.'

Catherine's father leant back in his chair. 'And what, exactly, will you be protesting?'

'A bunch of us are marching against the Vietnam War. I was hoping Catherine would join us.'

'Catherine?' Her father frowned at her.

Catherine raised her eyebrows. 'This is the first I've heard of it.' There was only one direction this conversation was going to go. She was tempted to leave the room, but part of her was fascinated by what was about to unfold. Like a spectator at a car crash.

'You don't believe we should be involved in the war?' her father asked Tim.

'No, siree. Not us. Not the Yanks. Not anybody.'

'You don't believe in freedom then.'

'But I do. Absolutely. That's why we oppose the war.'

Her father leant forward and placed both hands on the table. 'Son, are you a Communist?'

'No.' Tim's voice wavered.

Catherine watched him closely. Surely he must realise he was in dangerous territory. Should she save him? She could suggest they retreat to the kitchen to do the washing up, but there was a part of her that really didn't want to protect him, and that part was winning.

'I fought against the Japanese in World War II,' her father said. 'I didn't have to, but once they bombed Darwin nothing was going to stop me. I fought on the Kokoda Track, you heard of it?'

Tim nodded. 'Papua.'

'The terrain was much like our brave young men are in now, fighting for freedom against the Commies.'

'But it's not our fight. It's not like anyone is bombing us this time round.'

'The Reds are everywhere, all through Asia and heading this way. Why on earth would we wait until they're dropping bombs on us again?'

'We're only there because Harold Holt was putty in LBJ's hands.'

Catherine's father slapped his hand on the table. 'If you're going to go up against something, at least get your history straight. It was Menzies who committed Australia to supplying infantry.'

'That's my point. Conscription. If I had a draft card, I'd burn it.'

'And you'd be sent to jail.'

'Better jail than the stinking jungle, killing innocent people.' Tim turned to Catherine. 'How old was Peter?'

Catherine tensed. Why was he asking?

'Eighteen.' Her mother's voice was shaky. 'He would have been nineteen last June.' She clutched at the serviette beside her plate.

Catherine reached for her mother's hand but it remained a hard fist and didn't yield. The anniversary of Peter's birthday last year had been hard for them all but especially tough on their mother. She'd insisted on recognising the date and even wanted to go as far as cooking his favourite meal for dinner, roast chicken. But the primitive nature of the makeshift kitchen at the cottage and her ongoing grief had caused the plan to unravel. She'd returned once again to the darkened bedroom and her sobs had continued late into the night.

'So he'd have turned twenty this year, right?' Tim was oblivious to the pain that clung as heavy as mud to the others around the table.

Her father's face grew livid. 'Don't you dare.'

'He would've had to register for the draft this year.' Tim blundered on. 'Sent to fight an unfair war we shouldn't be in. He'd've had to murder people. Could've come home crippled or died in some swamp, shot by a sniper. The way I see it, he was lucky.'

The silence had an edge to it so sharp that Catherine was afraid to move. Tim looked around the table. 'All I'm saying is he had a pure death. Better than dying far away with blood on his hands.'

The crack of her father's chair falling over was like gunfire. He stood, moving faster than Catherine thought possible.

When he left the house, Tim was bleeding. Possibly a broken nose. Catherine searched herself for any sliver of sorrow or heartbreak, but all she felt was relief. The decision had been made for her. Tim would never be welcome in this house again.

19

May 1969

Annie

Where was Dave? He was the only one who could adjust the grader.
It was a mystical art, passed down from father to son through
the generations. It appeared to be such a simple thing to rejig the
graduated roller. When an apple fitted under the roller, it went
into a particular bin depending on its size. But if you didn't get it
right there'd be trouble. Trying to pack three-and-a-halfs when you
thought you were packing three-and-three-eighths was a disaster.
The last of the Red Delicious had been packed and the team needed
to start on the Democrats – big, round, easy to grow and easy to pick.
Annie found them tasteless, but the Germans loved them. Because
the apples were different shapes, the grader needed to be adjusted.
Annie paced impatiently while Angela played close by in an apple
bin, unaware of the tension. The shed team waited around uselessly.
Some had gone outside for a smoke and others sat on apple boxes,
resting their legs. It was hard work standing on concrete all day.

A commotion by the front doors caught her attention. Dave came rushing in followed by most of the pickers.

'What's going on?' She worried constantly about accidents in the orchard. The three-legged wooden ladders were handy on the sloping blocks, with the third leg used for balance, but even so there were falls. Whatever was going on now looked serious. Had the tractor rolled?

'Stan just got back from taking the last load to the dock,' Dave explained, his face bright with excitement. 'The ship was topping off and was 10,000 cases short.'

Stan pushed forward. 'They told me if I could get back by 4 pm we could have a free load.'

Dave slapped him on the back. 'So the good man came racing back.'

'Took out a few guideposts along the way.'

The men laughed. During the season the trucks wiped out every guidepost along Huon Road. The road was so narrow, trucks couldn't pass each other if they didn't.

'Free space?' Getting room on the ships was tough. The valley grew more apples than the ships could take, so the exporters gave out coupons to allocate a certain number of cases per grower per ship. If the growers couldn't get enough space, the apples went to the factories, or worse, had to be tipped. It meant a dramatic drop in income. Annie did a visual check of the pallets of Red Delicious packed and ready to go. They didn't have enough. She glanced at her watch. It was 45 miles to Hobart, along steep and winding roads. 'I don't think we can do it.'

'I think we can,' Dave said. 'This is why we have our own truck, Annie, so we can take advantage of fortune when she smiles on us. Let's face it, she hasn't been smiling much lately.'

Annie knew it. It had been more than two years since the fires, but making a profit from apples was becoming even tougher. There was a lot more competition from other countries for the export market. Thank goodness Australia had preferred nation status with Britain. Without it they'd be sunk. She lifted her chin. 'What are we waiting for? You'll have to adjust the grader. We've got bins of Democrats ready to go.'

Dave winked at her and called all the pickers over. 'Beer's on me if we get this done. We'll have to pack flat out, but I reckon we can do it. But be careful. We don't want inspectors sending the whole lot back.'

The inspectors at the wharf knew and respected Dave, but it wouldn't stop them from unloading the truck and checking the boxes. Some growers tried all sorts of tricks to pass off bad fruit as fancy grade – if their fruit wasn't coloured enough they'd hide all the green ones down the bottom, or they'd put a case with spider mite or bitter pit in the middle of the load. If they were caught, the inspectors put their name in a little black book and sent the whole lot back to the orchard. Annie and Dave would never try to cheat the system, but mistakes could be made. All it took was three bad apples and the whole lot would be rejected. Dave worked his magic with the grader while Annie organised the men into teams of graders, packers and luggers. An air of excitement filled the shed. All of them wanted to beat the clock, and not just for the free beer. The grader leapt back to life with a noisy roar. Annie took her place at one of the rotary bins, ready for the apples to start rolling towards her.

Exhausted but happy, Dave and Annie sat together in the kitchen drinking their last cup of tea for the day. The kids were asleep, the packing over for now. The night gang had finished getting the boxes and cartons ready for tomorrow. Finally they could relax.

'That'll make a nice addition to the balance sheet,' Dave said. 'My dad always said having a truck would pay for itself.'

146

Annie smiled despite the exhaustion seeping through her body. What a day. She'd never seen her team pack so fast. They'd all done well. Mark had worked at the grader and seemed to have an eye for it. And maybe for more than that. Catherine was spending more time at his place. It was a bad combination – a married man, a single woman, and the speed at which gossip spread through the valley. Why couldn't Catherine settle down with a nice man? It'd been over a year since Tim had been on the scene. Annie couldn't say she was unhappy to see the back of him. It had never been a good match. Catherine was straight as a pin and Tim loose as a wonky bicycle wheel. Annie understood circumstances could bring people together, but couldn't keep them that way. Unless there was love. Like the love she had with Dave.

Annie leant over and kissed him gently. 'You're a good man, Dave Pearson.'

He kissed her back. 'What's that about, darl?'

'There are some men out there who aren't so good, that's all. I'm glad you're not one of them.'

'Like those bloody wharfies.'

Annie stood up. 'Time for bed.' If Dave got wound up about the wharfies they'd never get to sleep before midnight.

'They're ruining us. Waterside workers in New Zealand can load a ship three times faster than our blokes.'

'Yes, dear,' she said, collecting the tea things and taking them to the sink.

'And the waterfront strike at the start of the season. Could have sent us all under.'

'I know, darling.'

'They hold everyone to ransom.'

Annie filled the sink with soapy water. She didn't mind washing up in the colder months when the water was warm and her hands chilled. 'Look on the bright side. We got free space on a ship. A whole load. And it *was* loaded by the wharfies. We're going to make money we weren't expecting. It's been a good day.'

Dave joined her at the sink and nuzzled her neck. 'You're right. It has been a good day. Shall we make it even better?'

'Why, David Pearson, are you propositioning me?' She turned to face him.

He answered with a kiss which deepened as she pushed herself against him despite her soapy hands. Even after all these years, he always awoke the desire in her. Her wet hands in his hair reminded Annie of the day they'd met back in 1957 in all that rain. When her bus had arrived he'd asked for her phone number but she'd said no, her mother would never allow it. Instead he gave her his number and asked her to call him. When Annie finally got up the courage, she told her mother she was ringing a friend to ask about a homework question. Dave's mother answered. She already knew about Annie and was delighted. Annie could only think of how her own mother would've responded. A country boy would be okay as long as he was from an old sheep and wheat family in the Midlands, but an orchardist? It would not be tolerated. But Annie liked Dave in a way that surprised her. Dave told her he'd been in town the day they'd met to take his father to the hospital for tests. His health was failing and the doctors had confirmed another hydatid cyst. Dave would be in Hobart again soon to take his dad to the hospital for an operation. When he asked her whether she'd meet him, she said yes.

They met at the Green Gate Milk Bar one afternoon after she'd finished school. As soon as they began to talk she found herself relaxing, letting down the defences she kept in place with boys – always on guard, hoping to impress, but not trying too hard, not wanting to be seen as easy or as a prude. It was a constant guessing game and exhausting. With Dave there were no games. His plain way of speaking was reassuring to her – he had no pretences, nor strange angles she couldn't see around. When he touched her hand it was the most natural thing in the world to entwine her fingers with his. From then on he'd come up to town whenever he could, even though it was at least a three-hour round trip along the treacherous roads.

If she'd had any doubts about Dave, they'd melted away like spring snow when he kissed her. Everything about it felt right. The kiss was gentle but firm, respectful but passionate. She knew she was in control if she ever wanted to stop. But she never wanted to stop. The first time they had sex it was a surprise to both of them. A kiss deepened into more and they both became oblivious to anything other than each other. She was tall, strong and headstrong. He was tall, strong and willing. They were equals. Always. Neither of them tricking or conniving the other into anything they didn't want.

The first time she missed her period it didn't even register. She was too excited about her blossoming relationship, too nervous about her parents finding out, and too in love to think anything bad could happen. But when two months went by she knew she was pregnant. She and Dave were sitting in his ute at Long Beach, looking out over the water, when she told him. To her surprise and deep relief he was thrilled and immediately asked her to marry him. Annie didn't hesitate in answering. She didn't want any of those snobby Sandy Bay boys with their pedigrees and their expectations. She didn't want to be a society lady and play mahjong and arrange charity balls. She wanted to marry Dave Pearson and have his baby.

That was eleven years and six children ago, and she'd never regretted it.

20

21 July 1969
Catherine

It seemed as if half of Cygnet was crammed into the school's assembly hall. Catherine's Kindergarten class sat cross-legged at the front, the older students on chairs behind them, arranged by class, with the parents jostling for space along the walls. Not many families in the area owned television sets and only those children had been allowed to stay home. The Pearson clan would be in their lounge room right now, with a roaring fire and warm cups of Milo. Catherine shifted her weight. There was nowhere for her to sit and she'd already had a tiring day. The children were overexcited and her efforts to get them to paint astronauts had floundered. All they wanted was to see a man on the moon.

At least it was warm in here. The extra bodies added to the meagre heat of the wall radiators. Winter in the valley meant bitter, dark mornings, the sun barely peeking over the hills until noon and then rapidly disappearing without providing a hint of warmth. As children, bundled up in jackets, scarves and mittens, she and Peter had loved to crack the ice on the puddles. Sometimes Peter found ice so thick he'd kick it down the road, laughing with delight as it skidded along. Even on the coldest of days he always found joy – in the frost creating a white wonderland on the paddocks, the steam blowing from his mouth like dragon fire, and the freshly toasted crumpets and honey their mother would have waiting when they returned home.

A commotion by the door attracted Catherine's attention. A couple of late arrivals. Mark squeezed into the room with Charlie close beside him. She was surprised they weren't watching the moon landing with Dave and Annie. Catherine raised an eyebrow at Mark. He shrugged and mouthed 'sorry'. Charlie was quickly lost in a forest of adults' legs and the chairs of the senior students. He'd never see anything back there. 'Charlie can come and sit up the front near me,' she called over the hubbub.

As the small boy pushed his way to the front, an uncomfortable silence crept through the room. The hush was only disturbed by the whispers of some mothers and a few nervous coughs from their husbands. A prickle of unease spread across Catherine's skin. Tim's warnings had been easy to discount as mere jealousy but when Annie had told her, more than once, that there'd been gossip about her and Mark perhaps she shouldn't have been so quick to dismiss it as nonsense. She and Mark were just friends, nothing more, and only because of Charlie. Now she wondered if she should have been more concerned.

Charlie happily squeezed in with the Kindergarten class, saying hello to some of the children he knew from the packing shed. He'd been longing to start Kindy this year but his fifth birthday wasn't until next month. Perhaps, after the moon walk was over and the children were given an early mark, she and Charlie could find some puddles and crack the ice on them together.

The headmaster stood beside the television, which sat on a high trolley to afford everyone the best view. 'It's wonderful to see so many of you here.' His eyes swept the crush of adults at the back of the room. 'In years to come, I think we'll all remember exactly where we were on this day. And we'll also remember, with pride, the part that Australia played in this historical broadcast, thanks to NASA's space tracking satellite near Canberra and the mighty Parkes radio telescope.' With a flourish he turned on the television. The air was electric with anticipation as they waited for the set to warm up and the black screen to become a vision of a new future, where all things were possible.

Catherine had wondered about the wisdom of showing the moon landing live to young children. What if something terrible happened? No one could be certain the landing module would make it safely. It could crash. There might be a fault like the one in the launch pad test two years ago where three astronauts had died in a flash fire. What if the surface of the moon was covered in a mile-deep drift of dust and the module was swallowed up whole? There were no guarantees in this world and even less on the moon. It wasn't until she heard the words 'The Eagle has landed' that her shoulders relaxed.

The younger children wriggled restlessly. There wasn't much to see as yet and she could sense their disappointment after the enormous build-up. The first images from the moon were just slabs of fuzzy black and white, but when the camera angle changed they could see a foot coming down the ladder. A collective gasp reverberated through the room. The foot hovered tentatively as Neil Armstrong talked about the distance from the ladder to the moon's surface. It didn't matter that his words were mundane, he was talking to them from the moon. The camera angle changed again and, though very shadowy, they could see the astronaut still hanging on to the ladder. Finally he took the plunge and stepped onto the moon.

'That's one small step for man—' Static broke up the sound. His words were indecipherable.

'What did he say?' one of the fathers asked.

'That's one small step for man,' the headmaster replied.

'Yeah, I got that, but what about the rest?'

'I think it was something about one giant leap,' one of the mothers said.

'Right.' The father frowned, still baffled.

The television announcer must have realised that all of Australia was wondering the same thing. 'And those were the first words spoken when man walked on the moon, "That's one small step for man, one giant leap for mankind",' he reiterated.

'Oh.' A murmur rumbled through the room as heads nodded in understanding.

Neil Armstrong continued talking about the surface of the moon and the nature of the dust, giving a commentary on everything he could see. Catherine was riveted, despite the indistinct images and the static. How many times had she gazed at the bright light of the full moon, mysterious and glorious? And now a man walked on the surface, so many thousands of miles away.

The children laughed as Armstrong zipped in and out of view collecting samples, his bulky space suit causing no hindrance in the low gravity. When Buzz Aldrin finally descended the ladder and bounced around like a kangaroo, the children laughed even louder. As the broadcast went on though, Catherine's class began to fidget. She knew if she didn't take them out of the assembly hall soon, they'd disrupt the rest of the broadcast for everybody else. She bent down and, with her fingers to her lips to indicate quiet, beckoned them to follow her. It was too cold to take them out to the playground, but Catherine hoped they might be ready for a nap.

Charlie tagged along. His eyes widened as he walked into the classroom, taking in the potato-cut paintings pinned on the back wall, a frieze of the alphabet, the piano in the corner, low tables and chairs, and the pile of mats for nap time. 'This is your classroom?' he asked.

Catherine nodded as she began to put out the mats.

'This is where I'll be when I turn five,' he announced proudly.

'Not until next year, mate.' Mark stood by the door watching with a smile. He must have followed them out of the assembly hall. 'We've talked about this.'

'Now, children,' Catherine addressed her class. 'It's been a big day. Tomorrow we'll talk about everything we saw on the television. But right now, even spacemen need to have a nap, so let's settle down for a little while.'

To her surprise the children took off their shoes and lay down without any complaint. There was some whispering and giggling, but that was normal.

Charlie tugged on her sleeve. 'I think I need a spaceman nap too.'

Catherine laughed gently. 'Do you now?' What harm could it do? Today was a special day. If things weren't done exactly by the book she didn't think anyone would mind. She looked at Mark. He shrugged with an 'it's okay with me if it's okay with you' expression.

'All right.' Catherine laid out another mat. 'Take off your shoes, lie down and close your eyes. Dream about the moon and the men on it.'

'What about the Man *in* the Moon?'

'Maybe they'll get to meet him.' She didn't mind her young charges believing in the myths and fantasies. Cold reality would come soon enough. Santa Claus, the Easter Bunny and the Tooth Fairy were all welcome in her classroom, along with the Man in the Moon.

As Charlie settled down, a broad grin on his face, Catherine moved to the doorway to stand beside Mark. They both watched his son, contentedly lying down with the rest of the class.

Mark reached for her hand and squeezed it. 'Thank you. I think being in this classroom is just as thrilling for him as watching a man land on the moon.'

His touch sent sensations fluttering through her body and she turned towards him to find his eyes gazing into hers. She'd never dared to believe, until now, that Mark felt something for her. The breath she'd been holding left her body in a sigh as he smiled, his hand still enfolding hers. 'Catherine,' he whispered.

The sound of voices in the corridor was like a slap. Catherine pulled her hand away and cleared her throat. 'Yes, we're excited about the new CA store at Cradoc,' she said, her voice tight and louder than necessary. 'Dave's glad he didn't rebuild the cool store. CA is going to change the way apples are marketed. We can store the fruit for much longer.'

Mark frowned in confusion, but she nodded in the direction of the two men walking towards them. A look of understanding spread across his face. 'CA? What does it stand for again? You've got to forgive this city slicker, I'm still catching up with all the jargon.' He chuckled. It sounded forced to Catherine's ears, but hopefully not to someone who didn't know him.

'Ah, Mr Davis.' The men were upon them now. Catherine knew them. Mr McKinley was raw-boned and red-faced, his fair skin roughened by decades of sun, wind and sleet. The McKinley boys were known to be bullies. Mr Stacey was small and dark; his children were wary and sneaky.

'City slicker, you say.' It was McKinley who addressed them. 'But you've been in the district for what – over two years? Surely you're up to speed by now. Or do you still need lessons from our pretty young school teacher?' He gave them a lewd wink and his friend snickered.

Catherine stepped forward. 'Did you enjoy the broadcast, gentlemen? An exciting day, isn't it?'

'Lot of money wasted, in my opinion.' McKinley scowled. 'Going to the moon? It's just rock and dust. What good does it do anyone? The Yanks only wanted to beat the Commies, plant their Star-Spangled Banner and claim it for themselves. Bah!'

'But what an achievement. It's captivated the world.'

'They shoulda spent the money helping the farmers who are doing it tough. We're the ones who put food on the tables of all those eggheads and flyboys. All them millions? Should have thrown some our way.'

'Coulda got me a new tractor at least,' added Stacey.

Catherine's forced smile was in danger of fading. 'The government helps out with subsidies and concessions. And there was all the help we got after the fire and through the drought.'

'Yeah, like your nice new house. The fire did you a favour there.'

Catherine stepped back. How could anyone say that? Mark put a steadying hand under her elbow.

'Come on, mate,' Mark said. 'You know Catherine's family did it tough. They had the worst of all possible losses.'

A flicker of shame clouded McKinley's eyes. 'Yeah, well. There was that.' He rallied. 'But I had fruit locked up in the Suez Canal that year. Hell, it's still there. Ain't seen no insurance for it yet either.'

Catherine couldn't believe it. The Six-Day War and the blockading of the Suez Canal had put some orchardists out of pocket, but they were all insured and would see the money one day. How could it possibly compare to her family's loss? She still missed her brother constantly and her mother was slipping back, not getting better. The crying at night had begun again, and the listlessness.

'I need to check on the children.' Catherine's voice trembled and she hated herself for it. The last thing she wanted to do was show weakness in front of these men. No wonder the McKinley boys were bullies. Their father had taught them well.

'I'll come with you,' Mark said.

Mr Stacey sniggered and nudged McKinley. 'I bet he will, too.'

'Pardon?' Mark squared up to the men.

'Don't get your knickers in a twist, pretty boy.' McKinley stepped closer. 'Everyone knows about you and the lovely young teacher here. The women don't approve, but I reckon they're jealous. And me,' he looked at Catherine with another suggestive leer, 'I gotta admit I wouldn't mind a bit myself.'

Mark's face reddened, his hands clenched at his sides. 'What?' The word exploded out of him.

'You're a married man. I'm a married man. Clearly she likes them married.'

A sour taste rose in Catherine's throat. He was talking about her as if she were a harlot. She turned to Mark. If he did anything it would only make this worse. 'Leave it,' she croaked. 'Please.'

'Yeah, you'd better listen to your girlfriend, otherwise you might not look so pretty any more.' McKinley postured like a rooster and Stacey strutted like a bantam, backing him up.

'Daddy?'

All heads turned to the classroom. Charlie was propped up on his mat, frowning at them, his hair mussed from sleep. One look at his innocent face gave Catherine the strength she needed. A searing heat raced through her as she turned back to the men. 'Mark and I have done nothing wrong.' She kept her voice low. 'All we have done is love and care for a young boy who desperately needed it at a difficult time. It's people like you who've made it ugly with your small minds and vicious tongues. Tell that to your wives. Tell that to the whole valley.'

McKinley and Stacey leant away from her onslaught. Expecting a fight with Mark, they'd been caught off guard by her words. McKinley huffed awkwardly and Stacey's eyes darted back and forth from his accomplice to Catherine and Mark.

'I think you'd better leave,' Mark said.

His words snapped McKinley out of his trance. He shook himself like a dog. 'That'd be right, pretty boy. Getting a woman to fight your battles for you.' He swaggered past Mark, bumping hard up against him on his way.

Mark shot a quick look at Catherine who shook her head. He let the men past.

McKinley turned back towards them and called out down the corridor, 'Oh and pretty boy, CA stands for Controlled Atmosphere. That's something you and your pretty teacher should learn more about – controlling your atmosphere.' He let out a cold bray of laughter as Stacey sniggered beside him.

Mark tensed. Catherine touched his hand. He shot her an agonised look and then watched the men walk away.

Charlie ran up to him and threw his arms around his legs. 'I don't like those men, Daddy.'

'That's okay, we don't like them either.' Mark hoisted Charlie up and hugged him.

Charlie wriggled free.

'I'm a big boy now. I'm at school.' He grinned, his small white teeth in a perfect row.

'Yes, you are,' Catherine said. Her heart rate was beginning to slow, but the anger remained.

Mark touched her arm tentatively. 'Are you okay?'

'Truthfully, I don't know. Those men are vile but they just said what everyone must be thinking.'

'Not everyone.'

A child's voice called out from the classroom. 'Miss Turner. I need to go to the toilet.' It was Sally Meadows. She had the smallest bladder of any child she'd ever taught.

'I have to go.' Catherine lowered her head, not wanting to meet his eyes.

'We can stay if you need us to.'

'No.' If he stayed, everyone who left the assembly hall would see them together. She'd had more than she could stand of poisonous thoughts and tongues.

'We'll see you later, then.'

'Sure.' But she knew she was lying. She bent down to give Charlie a hug goodbye, pressing all the love in her heart into his small body. It wasn't his fault. Nothing was, but he wouldn't understand. Finally she stood, forcing back the tears. She was going to miss him.

21

24 August 1969

Mark

Charlie's murmured words made no sense, garbled nonsense from a fretful mind. Mark rested the back of his hand on his son's forehead. So hot. Outside, sleet battered the hut, searching out the cracks in the wooden boards, under the door and between the window frames. During their first winter at the orchard, Dave had helped Mark line the hut with layers of newspaper and straw, keeping it in place with thin sheets of plywood. This rough insulation helped a little, but when the southerlies hit, the frigid air penetrated the smallest of openings. But today, even the icy draught was no help in lowering Charlie's temperature. Fever raged through his small body. Mark pressed a cold washcloth to Charlie's face, dabbing his cheeks, his neck, his chest, anything to cool him down. Less than a week ago, when news of the Woodstock Festival had filtered through to the valley, Mark had wished he was there, either as one of the muddy thousands gathered to hear the music or, even better, up on that stage. Now all he wanted was his son to be well.

A glass of water sat on an apple box beside Charlie's bunk, the dissolved aspirin turning the water cloudy. With a rising sense of helplessness, Mark dribbled some of the liquid into Charlie's mouth, hoping his son would swallow more than last time. He'd learnt to cope with scrapes, bruises and bee stings, along with colds and coughs, but nothing like this. It had been days now of fever and coughing, telling his daddy that 'everything hurt'. Charlie's bright eyes had dulled over the previous few days, clouding over with pain and confusion. And disappointment. He'd been looking forward to his birthday. Turning five meant so much to him. He'd be able to go to school next year and see Catherine every day.

'I miss her, Daddy,' he'd said. 'Why doesn't she come and play any more?'

Mark had tried. Over the past month, he'd hand-delivered letters to the Turners' house but they went unanswered. Once Catherine's father had intercepted him at their gate. 'Best leave it alone, son,' he'd said. 'No good can come of it.'

A week ago he'd asked Annie to invite Catherine to the party for Charlie's birthday, but she'd been dubious.

'Catherine has the right idea,' she'd said. 'You can claim your innocence until the cows come home, but the only thing that'll stop this gossip is if you two never see each other again. Honestly, Mark, it would be best if you left the valley altogether.'

'Better for who?' He'd felt the familiar anger rising in his throat.

Annie had glared at him. 'You can ruin your own life any way you choose, but I'll be damned if I let you ruin the lives of those I love.'

Her meaning was clear but the words rankled. 'I'll see you on Saturday at the party,' he said, through tight lips. 'Please ask Catherine to come. For Charlie.'

Then Charlie had fallen ill. The party was cancelled and now Mark hovered by his side, frantic with worry and a sense of inadequacy. Annie had said that kids got sick, and if she went into a tizzy every time one of her boys had a cold or an earache she'd have worried herself into an early grave. Hadn't she seen them all through the measles, not to mention chicken pox? She'd maintained Charlie would get well soon enough, but Charlie was far from well, and getting worse.

A gentle knock cut through the relentless wind. Mark hurried to open the door.

Catherine stood on the porch, clutching her rain jacket to her neck as the southerly threatened to whip it from her grasp. Her hair was wild and her cheeks flushed with the cold. Had she grown more beautiful since he'd seen her? It had been over a month but felt like an age. Mark ushered her inside, out of the bitter weather.

She shed her rain jacket, water dripping onto the floorboards. 'I've come straight from Annie's. I didn't know Charlie was sick until just now. I would have come sooner—'

'It's okay.' Her mere presence was enough to make him feel as though everything was going to be all right.

'I'm sorry.' She ran her hands through her tangled hair. 'About everything.'

'It doesn't matter. I'm glad you're here. Charlie's getting worse and I don't know what to do.'

'Right.' She pointed to the room on the left. 'Is he in here?'

Mark followed her to the bedroom where Benno lay on the floor next to the bunks. He hadn't left Charlie's side since he'd become ill.

162

'Hello, Benno,' Catherine said. 'Have you done a good job looking after Charlie?' The old dog's tail whumped against the floorboards. 'Good boy. Now, how's my little mouse?'

Mark heard her catch her breath as she pressed her hand against his son's forehead.

'He's so hot. Annie said it was just a winter bug.'

Charlie opened his eyes at her touch, murmured some gibberish and closed them again.

'How long has he been like this?' Her voice had an edge that made Mark's stomach contract.

'The fever? A couple of days. Much worse since last night. He had a cough first, about a week ago, and was a bit wheezy in the chest. It got worse from there. He's been sick before, but nothing like this.'

'When was the last time you took his temperature?'

'What? With a thermometer?'

'Yes.'

'I don't have one.'

Catherine lifted Charlie's pyjama top, revealing his pale chest. She checked his arms, his back, and gently touched his neck under his jaw.

'Has he been able to drink anything? Flat lemonade is best. Or some sugar water with a pinch of salt.'

Flat lemonade? Sugar water? His mind was spinning. How could he not know any of this? 'Just water with an aspirin dissolved in it and not much of that.'

Catherine kept her attention on Charlie. 'It's not measles or mumps. But I'm worried—'

'You think it might be the Hong Kong flu?' Thousands of Americans had died from the flu brought into the USA by soldiers returning from the Vietnam War. Then it had reached Australia, first in the West and then spreading rapidly to the other states.

'I don't think we should take any chances. It would be best to take him to the health centre. They can put him on a drip if necessary, to keep his fluids up. I've got my car here. I drove because of this weather.'

'What do I need to bring?'

'Some clean pyjamas. And a change of clothes. When he's well I doubt he'll want to leave the health centre in his pyjamas.' He knew she was trying to ease his fears, but there was no way he'd relax until Charlie was running around, getting muddy and catching tadpoles again.

The smell of antiseptic greeted them as they pushed through the doors of the Cygnet Community Health Centre. Charlie lay limp in Mark's arms, his hair plastered to his forehead with a combination of sweat and sleet. The nurse sat behind the counter in her starched uniform and cap.

'Please,' he said, his voice cracking. 'Can someone help us?'

'Yes, of course. Oh, my,' she said taking in the pale and shivering child in Mark's arms.

Mark realised how young she was, probably fresh from nursing training and sent to a country posting. 'My son. We think he has influenza. It's bad.'

'Right. I'll pop down your details.'

'My name is Mark Davis, and this is my son Charlie.'

The nurse scribbled a few lines on a form. 'And how old is he?'

'He's five. It's his birthday today.'

'Oh, the poor darling. What a horrible way to spend his birthday.'

'Yes.' Mark was impatient. It should be obvious, even to an inexperienced nurse, that his son was extremely ill. 'If you could look at him urgently we'd be grateful.'

Catherine touched his back, a soft reassurance against the emotions raging inside him. 'I think he's dehydrated,' she said. 'And we're worried this could be the Hong Kong flu.'

'Yes, of course, Mrs Davis. I'll get Sister Mason. Take a seat. She's just with one of the other patients.' She left through a pair of swinging doors.

Mark sat in one of the uncomfortable plastic chairs, Charlie murmuring feverishly in his lap.

'It's okay, little mouse.' Catherine wiped the damp hair from Charlie's forehead. 'Cat is here. You'll feel better soon, I promise.'

Mark relaxed, just a little. Catherine was by his side. Charlie would recover. Everything would be okay. A smile formed slowly on his lips. 'Mrs Davis, eh?'

Catherine tensed beside him. 'She's new. She doesn't know who we are. Sister Mason will set her straight.'

'I didn't mean ...' He'd put his foot in it. She was skittish after the gossip she'd endured. 'I kind of thought it was funny.'

Catherine kept her attention firmly on Charlie. 'There's already a Mrs Davis and it's not me.'

'You're right. But she's not here. Her son is seriously ill and where is she?' His mind churned with anguish, regret and anger. 'It's his birthday, for God's sake. She's missed the last two. Not even a card.' He knew because he'd rung their old place in Melbourne. He checked in with his friends there regularly to ask whether Lara had turned up or written or sent her son a present for Christmas or even remembered his birthday. Nothing.

'Mr and Mrs Davis?' Sister Mason stood in front of the still swinging doors, clipboard in hand, glaring at Catherine.

Catherine scrambled to her feet. 'An innocent mistake, Sister. It's Charlie's birthday today and he was supposed to be having a party at the Pearsons' place but as you can see—' she gestured towards

Mark and Charlie. 'I drove them here. I think Charlie might benefit from a saline drip. He's very ill and dehydrated.'

'*I'll* be the judge of that, *Miss* Turner.' Sister Mason turned towards the young nurse behind her. 'Bring the gurney.' She addressed Mark. 'If it is Hong Kong influenza we'll need to keep the boy isolated. Influenza has been rife this winter but everyone under my care has recovered. I'm sure this young boy will too.'

Mark laid Charlie gently on the gurney.

'Family only, *Miss* Turner.' Sister Mason stared hard at Catherine before indicating that Mark should follow her. Mark turned to apologise to Catherine, and to thank her, but saw only a glimpse of her faint smile as the doors swung shut behind him.

The afternoon disappeared in long anxious hours by Charlie's bedside. 'Nasty chest infection,' the Sister said. 'The antibiotics will help.' She hadn't gone as far as to mention the word 'pneumonia' but Mark was certain that's what she'd inferred. At least it wasn't the Hong Kong flu. When Charlie was finally resting comfortably, Sister Mason insisted Mark take a break. 'There's nothing you can do here. Your son will recover.'

Wearily, Mark pushed through the swinging doors into the waiting room. He was surprised to see Catherine, huddled on a plastic chair. 'You're still here.'

'I couldn't leave.' She looked as exhausted as he felt. 'How is he?'

'Sister Mason has decreed he will survive.' He tried to smile but his face hurt from hours and days of worry. 'He'll take some time to recover but he's going to be okay.'

'I'm so sorry.'

'Why? Whatever for?'

'I should have been there. For Charlie. But those men, at the school.' She took a shuddering breath. 'It was so … horrible.'

Mark longed to put his arms around her and hush her anguish away. Instead he just nodded. 'Yes, it was.'

'I couldn't—' She faltered.

'It's okay. I understand.'

Her eyes flashed, shimmering with her tears. 'No. It wasn't okay. Those men stole something from me that I loved. They made it dirty and small and—' She shook her head. 'I didn't know people could be so disgusting. And so mean.'

A bitter taste rose in Mark's throat. He should have punched those men.

'I thought if I stayed away, if I never saw you again ...' Catherine's freckles were stark against her pale winter skin. 'But all I did was cause more pain. I couldn't answer your letters, or visit. I didn't dare. I missed Charlie so much. When Annie gave me the invitation to his birthday party I thought, well, it'd be safe. At Annie and Dave's place with all the kids there. No one could turn it into something smutty, could they?' Her tears spilled, slowly etching a path down her cheek. 'We did nothing wrong. Nothing. But their filthy minds turned something innocent into something so ... so ...'

Mark couldn't bear it. Gently he took one of Catherine's hands in his own. 'I understand. I do.'

'But did Charlie? How could he when I deserted him? And now he's so sick.'

Charlie hadn't understood. He'd waited for Catherine every afternoon after school. On weekends, he wouldn't leave the pickers' hut in case she turned up. His mother had abandoned him and now Catherine. It had broken Mark's heart to see his happy, outgoing son become withdrawn and sullen again.

A different young nurse approached, carrying two cups of tea. 'I thought you might like these,' she said. 'I've put sugar in them both. It'll help.' Visiting hours had come and gone. Mark and Catherine were the only ones in the waiting room. 'He's going to be all right, your son.' She put down the cups on a small table beside them. 'He's going to be fine.'

'Thank you.' Mark was genuinely touched by the young woman's thoughtfulness.

The nurse nodded at Catherine, who was wiping her eyes with her handkerchief. 'It's always tougher for the mums.'

'Oh, I'm not – never mind.' Catherine paused and smiled up at the nurse. 'Thank you.'

'Please let me know if you need anything.' The nurse returned to her station.

Catherine hadn't corrected the nurse. Mark wondered if she was too tired to bother, exhausted from the unfolding of an emotional day. Catherine snuffled beside him. He thought she was crying until he realised her shoulders were shaking with suppressed laughter.

'What is it?' he asked.

Catherine looked up. 'How wonderful it would be. How simple.'

'I don't follow.'

'If it didn't matter what anybody else thought? If all that mattered was what *we* thought? What then?'

Mark knew what he'd do, but didn't dare say.

'You know what I'd do?' Catherine's eyes brightened.

'What?'

'I'd take Charlie to the Saturday matinee at the Town Hall every week. The three of us would have chocolate milkshakes at CB Thorp's shop and cream buns from the bakery. We'd walk down Mary Street together and swing Charlie between us. I'd move back into my grandmother's cottage and live there, on my own and independent. That's what Peter was planning to do if ...' Her face paled again. 'I miss him. And then to miss Charlie as well – it was too much. I've lost so much. I can't lose Charlie as well.'

'It's okay, Catherine. He's going to pull through.'

'It's not that. I refuse to let bullies and gossips ruin my life and take away the little happiness I have.' She nodded her head once in a determined fashion. 'I've decided.'

'Decided what?' He waited, not daring to hope.

'I'm going to do all those things. Move into my grandmother's cottage. And talk to my father about working full-time in the orchard.' She turned to him, clasping his hands in her own, her soggy handkerchief pressing into his skin. 'And I'm going to keep seeing Charlie. Go to the movies and on picnics, all of us. We're going to play cards and read. Oh, guess what I bought him for his birthday?'

'A frog? He does like frogs.'

She smiled. 'He finds his own frogs. No. I bought him a set of Little Golden Books, about fire engines and trucks, space ships and puppies.'

'He'll love them.' Charlie's books were all hand-me-downs from Annie – scribbled on, dog-eared and ripped.

'I've missed him so much.' Catherine sighed.

'And I've missed you,' he blurted. And he had, so sharply it made his chest ache.

Catherine looked at him shyly. 'I've missed you as well.'

Mark met her gaze, not trusting himself to say anything more. How could he tell her how much he longed to be with her? How the days without her had been agony and how, much as it pained him to realise it, he was grateful to Charlie for getting sick. It had brought her back into his life. Outside, the sun had long since set. The darkness held nothing but biting cold and black ice. But inside, with Catherine beside him, Mark was encircled in warmth and light. And hope.

22

Spring 1969

Catherine

The snows on the range across the river had finally thawed and the sun gradually shed its winter reluctance. Fine weather and bright skies brought the tourists back to the valley for a springtime pilgrimage. They came in their thousands, indulging in the stunning display of pink and white, and the sweet, heady scent of apple blossom. Catherine and Charlie counted the tour buses as they lumbered by, while Mark navigated the narrow road in Dave's old farm ute. The three of them sat along the bench seat with Charlie wedged in the middle. After a slow and careful month, Charlie was finally well again. To celebrate, the three of them were going to the pictures. *Chitty Chitty Bang Bang* was showing at the Town Hall. Afterwards they'd promised Charlie a milkshake and a cream bun.

In front of them, one of the buses pulled over to the side of the road. An excited group of tourists spilt out to take photos of the sea of blossom.

'It's such a shame the Apple Festival doesn't happen any more,' Catherine said. 'You'd have loved it, Charlie. There was a parade, and lots of games and competitions. One year they made the world's largest apple pie. It was on a huge trailer and they needed a knife as tall as your dad to cut it.'

'Wow,' Charlie said. 'Did you get a piece?'

Catherine laughed. 'Everybody got a piece and there was still plenty left over.'

'Where was it held?' Mark asked.

'Just up the road in Cygnet. Thousands of people came. The traffic backed up for miles.' She remembered the days when their parents helped out with the stalls and chatted with friends while she and Peter ran free. 'The parade was always the highlight and the Apple Queen had a special float of her own. When I was younger I always dreamt of being the Apple Queen.' She laughed to cover her embarrassment.

'The Apple Queen?' Mark turned to her with a small smile.

'Yeah, silly, I know, but there was a time I thought I was in with a chance.'

'You'll always be our Apple Queen, won't she, Charlie?' Mark's eyes were gentle and she knew he wasn't making fun of her.

'Thanks,' she said softly.

'What happened?' Charlie asked. 'Why did the festival stop?'

'I don't know. I was studying in Hobart by then. It's a shame though. It was always such fun.'

'Well, there's always the Huon Show in November,' Mark said.

'Can we go to the show, Daddy? Please, Cat?' Charlie looked at them both with imploring eyes.

'What do you reckon?' Mark shot her a hesitant smile. 'Are you game?'

Catherine paused. Once the three of them were seen together in Cygnet this afternoon there'd be no stopping the gossip. She knew, as a woman, she'd suffer more from the slurs than Mark, but she'd promised herself she would never again let the meanness of small-minded people stop her from doing what she loved. 'In for a penny, in for a pound.'

'What does that mean?' Charlie asked.

Mark chuckled. 'It means some things will never change to decimal currency.'

'What?' Charlie looked confused.

Catherine kissed the top of Charlie's head. 'It means yes.'

In the last week of the school year, the headmaster called her into his office. Catherine's heart beat faster at his summons. Annie had warned her once again about the gossip. It had been bad before, Annie said, but it was much worse now. Catherine had held fast. She and Mark had done nothing wrong. She wouldn't stop seeing him or Charlie. Even so, when she walked into the Four Square supermarket or Varian's Chemist and conversations stopped, she could imagine what was being said. *A good Christian girl and a married man. Disgraceful. A teacher should set an example.* Maybe someone had spoken to the headmaster. Was he calling her to his office to dismiss her?

'Ah, Miss Turner.' Mr Agnew rose from behind his desk, indicating she should take a seat. He was an old-fashioned man, his suit always neatly pressed and moustache perfectly trimmed. He preferred not to fraternise with his staff and was almost a stranger to her.

Catherine sat, sweaty hands folded on her lap, awaiting her fate.

'Miss Turner, you've been with us two years now.' His tone was grave.

'Yes, Mr Agnew. I've enjoyed the work and the children have been wonderful.' She clamped her lips together. She mustn't grovel.

If he was going to sack her then best he do it quickly. Her father would be furious, but she'd deal with that later.

'Good. Good.' Mr Agnew shifted in his seat. 'It's been rare to have one of our old students working with us as a teacher.'

Catherine nodded once, not trusting herself to speak, and waited. She was dreading having to pack the small mementos she kept in her desk drawer – the photo of her and Peter in the orchard, the kewpie doll Mark had won for her at the Huon Show and a pink plastic monkey Charlie had given her from a cereal packet. The walk from the classroom to her car would be worse. She could already imagine the whispers.

'As always there's an intake of young teachers coming through next year and there's one I think will make an excellent Kindergarten teacher.'

'I see.' There it was. The end of her teaching career. She inhaled a shuddering breath. The laughter of children in the playground outside drifted through the window, a sharp reminder of what she was about to lose.

Mr Agnew picked up a sheaf of papers from his desk. 'Mrs Sadler is leaving us at the end of the year.'

Catherine was confused. Mrs Sadler was the Grade Two teacher. 'Leaving?'

'Yes.' He cleared his throat. 'In the family way, so she informs me.'

'Oh. I'm—' Catherine stopped herself.

'That's the thing with women. You're good teachers, but always going off to get married or have children.' He frowned at Catherine. 'You're not planning on getting married, are you?'

Heat rose in Catherine's cheeks. 'No, Mr Agnew.' She wasn't sure where the conversation was heading.

'I'm glad to hear it. The Arbitration Commission's decision to grant women equal pay is all well and good, but it doesn't take into account the turnover of female staff.' Mr Agnew sat back in his chair. 'You can depend on men. They'll stay in a position for life. Mr Graves has been here for nearly twenty years.'

Catherine stayed silent. Mr Graves was the Grade Six teacher, set in his ways and lazy with it. He bossed the younger female teachers around terribly, insisting they make him cups of tea in the staffroom and bullying them into doing his playground duty. Most of the female teachers worked twice as hard as Mr Graves but still weren't paid the same. The recent arbitration ruled that women's wages would increase in stages. It would take another three years until their pay was equitable.

'Mrs Sadler's imminent departure means I'm in need of a Grade Two teacher,' the headmaster continued. 'I've looked over your performance both here and at the previous schools where you've taught. I see you've taught Grade One before and a composite class up to Grade Three.'

'Yes, that's right.' A lightness filled Catherine's chest. She dared to look Mr Agnew in the eyes for the first time since she'd entered his office.

'Given the circumstances, as of next year you'll be our Grade Two teacher.' He rose and stuck out his hand. 'Congratulations.'

It was one of those perfect late summer days, the sun like honey and the air as soft as silk. Catherine and Mark were free of work and responsibilities for a few hours. She'd packed a picnic of Vegemite sandwiches, jam drops and homemade ginger beer and they'd decided to spend the afternoon at Petcheys Bay, a small and usually deserted cove of sand on the banks of the Huon River not far from the orchard. Charlie had embraced the water during the summer, learning to dog paddle with the help of Mark and Catherine.

After a swim, Charlie and Benno went hunting for crabs among the rocks, while Mark and Catherine took advantage of the break to laze on the sand.

Mark leant back on his elbows. 'Are you looking forward to being the Grade Two teacher, Miss Turner?'

Catherine picked up a handful of sand and let it trickle through her fingers. 'I know Charlie's disappointed I won't be his teacher, but it's for the best. I'd be under too much scrutiny with him in my class. Hopefully, by the time he's in Grade Two, the orchard will be in full production. Then I'll quit and work full-time there.'

'You're always thinking ahead, aren't you?'

'If you fail to plan, you are planning to fail.'

'Who said that?'

'I'm not sure who said it first, but my grandfather drummed it into our heads when we were kids.'

'Luckily, I have a plan.' He sat up and dusted the sand from his palms.

'You do? What is it?'

'Lunch.' He grinned, then looked over to where his son was splashing around a shallow rock pool. 'Charlie,' he called. 'Time to eat.'

Catherine dished out sandwiches wrapped in rainbow waxed paper. Charlie ate in quick bites, ripping off the crusts and throwing them to Benno. The dog caught every one, then turned in circles, snuffling around for any he might have missed.

'I'm thirsty,' Charlie said.

'The ginger beer's keeping cool in the water.' Mark pointed to the spot.

Charlie bounced up to get it and came running back, proudly waving the bottle above his head.

Catherine laughed. 'Oh dear. This'll be a disaster.'

Sure enough, when Mark opened the bottle the ginger beer fizzed everywhere, covering them all in sticky liquid. Catherine and Charlie raced each other into the river to wash themselves clean, with Mark and Benno following closely behind.

While Charlie and Benno played in the shallows, Mark swam up to Catherine in the deeper water.

'I love days like this,' he said. 'I wish it could last forever.'

'Me too.'

Their faces were level, eye to eye, nose to nose, and lips to lips. He moved closer, the surface rippling gently around them. 'If only the water wasn't so cold, even in summer. I think it's time to go in. Would you like a lift?'

She smiled into his eyes. 'Sure.'

He wrapped his arms around her, their bodies tight against each other, his bare chest pressed to the flimsy material of her floral Speedos. She saw his eyes change and felt the stirring of something hard against her leg. Catherine laughed and gently pushed him away, making her own way back to the shore, but the sensations the embrace stirred in her refused to be quietened.

Back at the pickers' hut, Catherine taught Charlie and Mark the rudiments of gin rummy, surprised Mark had never played before. Tea was basic fare of eggs on toast, and afterwards she and Mark took it in turns to read bedtime stories to Charlie.

When Charlie was finally asleep, they sat on the porch, with Mark absentmindedly strumming his guitar.

'What song is that?' Catherine asked.

'This? Nothing. I'm just making it up.' He strummed a few more chords.

Catherine began humming a melody.

'Hey, that's pretty cool,' Mark said. 'Keep going.'

'Really?'

'Yeah. I dig it.'

'Wow, okay.' Catherine fought nervousness as she sang along to his chord changes. She'd never made up a tune before but with Mark beside her it felt natural. The notes flowed easily as her hum turned to oohs and aahs. She didn't need words; the melody was enough.

Mark's last chord rang out in a slow sustain. 'You've got a great ear.'

'All that singing in the church choir.'

'Well, praise the Lord.' Mark grinned.

'How about another song? Our favourite?'

'Yeah.'

Mark played the intro to 'Going Up The Country', the Canned Heat hit, while Catherine sang the flute part. Mark had told her it had been the unofficial anthem of the Woodstock music festival. It had become their anthem as well. They sang it together on the porch, in the car and on walks by the river. Everywhere they went, it came with them.

When they got to the lyrics about jumping in the water, Mark's eyes changed, the way they had when he was holding her close in the river. He stopped playing, put his guitar to one side, and reached for her. She didn't resist. His lips were soft but insistent and his kiss resonated deep in the core of her. More than just in her heart, it was in every cell, and in her soul. It was as if a brilliant light opened up within her, racing outwards, engulfing both her and Mark, and changing the very air around them. She pressed against him, feeling his pulse against her skin, the heat rising in waves, their breath changing and quickening.

Then, like a switch being flicked, her thoughts took over. This was a sin. He was a married man. What would her parents say? Hadn't they had enough pain? All those cruel gossips, she was proving them right with her wantonness.

'I can't.' She pushed Mark away. Their connection broke with a crack.

'I'm sorry.' His eyes mirrored her own pain.

'No, don't be. I want to, but—'

'I know.' Mark stood up, looking out over the orchard, the trees dark against the night sky. 'I think I should go to Melbourne.'

'What?' Panic rose in her throat. Was it because she wouldn't do what they both wanted? Had he given up on her that easily? Even Tim had been more patient, although he had started to complain towards the end.

'I'm going to find my wife.'

'But—'

'I'm going to find Lara and get a divorce.'

'Oh.'

'I'm sick of waiting for her to come back and put me out of my misery.' Mark turned to her. 'I need to be free. So I can live my life with you.'

She struggled with the tumble of her emotions. Could they be together, Mark, Charlie and her, like a real family? Would it actually be possible? 'But you've tried to find her before.'

'I'm determined this time.'

She believed him. He was a man with something to fight for.

Mark left shortly afterwards, leaving Charlie with Annie. Catherine was off balance the whole time he was away, as if part of her was missing and she could no longer find her centre of gravity. She longed to tell Annie about the anguish, the excitement, the fear and the joy she was going through, but she knew she couldn't.

How would Annie respond if she knew that Catherine was falling in love with Mark? Annie had warned her, more than once, not to get involved – Mark was married, Mark would leave the valley eventually, in short, Mark was not to be trusted. And always the warnings about the gossip. Catherine couldn't bear to hear those words again from Annie, but, without her friend's counsel and with Mark gone, she was left rootless. The days stretched out and her nights passed with little sleep.

It was ten days later when he returned. Catherine had counted every one. She was at Annie's, playing in the backyard with Charlie and her godson, Scott. The boys had become good friends over the past year, bonding over their love of frogs and Matchbox cars. The crunch of tyres in the gravel of the driveway announced the return of Dave from running an errand up in Cygnet.

'That'll be your daddy,' Catherine said to Scott.

'Not only *his* daddy,' Dave said, rounding the corner of the house.

Catherine looked up to see Mark following behind Dave. Her breath stopped. A fierce hope blossomed in her chest.

'Daddy.' Charlie ran towards his father and wrapped himself around his legs.

Mark lifted his son into his arms and held him close. 'I missed you.'

Catherine stood, dusting the dirt from her clothes. 'I didn't know you were coming back today.' Something was wrong. He was avoiding her eyes.

'Didn't Annie tell you?' Dave asked. 'That's why I was in Cygnet. To pick up Mark from the bus.'

'No.' Catherine kept her eyes on Mark, aching for any clue, but Mark hid his face in Charlie's hair.

'Well, here he is.' Dave cleared his throat. 'I'd better get back to it. I guess you two have some things to talk about.'

Catherine met Dave's eyes and saw only kindness and concern. He knew. Of course he did. He and Mark were close. Mark would have told him everything – how he felt about her, why he went to Melbourne and what had happened there.

'Let's go home, Charlie.' Mark put his son down and turned away. 'Thanks, Dave, for everything.'

Dave clapped him on the back. 'No worries, mate. But I think you're forgetting something.' He nodded towards Catherine.

Mark took Charlie's hand. 'I don't know ...'

The hope in Catherine's chest turned to pain. She could barely breathe. She tried to speak but her mouth was dry.

'Tell you what,' Dave said. 'Let's grab your supplies from the ute and then why don't you three head up to the pickers' hut.'

Mark's shoulders slumped in defeat. 'Okay.'

Dumbly Catherine followed Mark and Charlie to the pickers' hut. This wasn't the homecoming she'd envisaged, full of love and kisses and plans for the future. This was a funeral march.

Charlie, thankfully, was unaware. He chatted happily about all the things he'd done while his daddy was away. How he and Scott had slept in the same bed and got in trouble for talking after they were supposed to be asleep. About the games they'd played, what the big boys had got up to, the biscuits Catherine had brought over. Mark remained mute as they trudged up the hill.

Once the supplies were packed away and Charlie had talked himself out and was happily drawing a picture of a frog, Catherine and Mark sat on the porch, the air heavy between them.

Mark looked at his hands. 'I'm sorry, Catherine. I really am. More than I can say.'

'Lara?' It almost hurt to speak. Had he found her? Had she refused to get a divorce? Or worse, did she want him back? Had he agreed? Was Annie right and he couldn't be trusted? Her head throbbed, her mind taunting her.

'I tried. I really did. I looked everywhere, asked everyone. And then I looked and asked all over again. It was pointless.'

'You didn't find her.' Finally she let out the breath she'd been holding.

It was only then Mark met her eyes. 'I failed. I failed you. I failed us.'

Catherine shook her head. She'd been an idiot to get her hopes up. There was no happy ending.

'There's no sign of her, anywhere. I have no idea what to do now.' The pain in his eyes was intense. It matched the pain in her heart. She could hardly bear it. He had done his best. He had done it for her, for them. 'Damn that woman,' he muttered. 'Damn her to hell.'

Catherine reached for his hand. He took hold of hers and there was a desperation in his grip. Lara might have disappeared, but she wasn't gone. She'd become a ghost who haunted him. And Catherine.

23

March 1970

Catherine

Catherine enjoyed the challenges of being a Grade Two teacher, though she'd forgotten how much more work was involved. Today she'd stayed after class to catch up, which meant she was running late for the packing shed. On her way home to get changed, she popped in to apologise to Annie. Her friend was at the grader, tossing rejected apples into one of the bins bound for the factories.

'Sorry,' Catherine said. 'I'll be back in twenty minutes.'

'Don't worry. It's nearly teatime anyway. Why don't you come over to the house and have it with us?'

Catherine smiled knowingly. 'You're hoping I'll make a pudding, aren't you?'

'Oh, what a lovely idea.' Annie grinned. 'The thought never crossed my mind.' She took Angela by the hand, and together they walked towards the house.

In the kitchen, Catherine noticed the unusual quiet. 'Where are the boys?'

'Making the most of the twilight. Either down at the river crabbing, or up in the bush building forts. Lately though, it's billy carts. Michael and Eric are trying to outdo each other, seeing who can build the best one. And the younger ones watch on, dying to be like their big brothers. The old pram got taken apart for the wheels. Just as well I'm not having any more children. They'll be back when they get hungry.' Annie began preparing dinner, pricking sausages for the pan and choosing potatoes and carrots for the pot.

Catherine looked around for Angela, who just a moment ago had been at her mother's side. 'And Angela?'

'She'll be in the lounge room having tea with her dolls. She does it every evening. It's the sweetest thing.'

'How adorable.'

Annie sighed in contentment. 'She certainly is.' Her expression changed as she looked Catherine up and down. 'Is that what you wore to school today? I know you love that dress, but really.'

'What?' Catherine ran her hands down the skirt of her favourite dress. She'd bought it with her first pay cheque. How proud she'd been that day, with her own money to spend. As soon as she'd seen the frock on the rack in FitzGerald's, she knew she had to have it. The light blue of a springtime sky and sprays of tiny pink flowers had reminded her of apple blossom. 'Oh.'

Annie gave a quick nod. 'You understand, don't you?'

The dress belonged to a simpler time. Before the fire, when her brother was still alive. The sixties were over, both the good and the bad. Times had changed and so had fashion. 'I guess so.'

'You can't meet the Queen wearing a dress like that. Even she's more up to date than you.'

'I'm not meeting the Queen.' Catherine laughed. 'Most likely I'll be squashed behind rows of children all waving Union Jacks and lucky to catch a glimpse of her.'

In less than a fortnight, the Queen was coming to the valley as part of her Australian tour. Her Majesty wanted to experience first-hand the crop that had seen Tasmania dubbed the Apple Isle. The royal entourage, including Prince Philip, Prince Charles and Princess Anne, were going to visit the Coombes' orchard at Longley to wander through the trees and talk with the pickers. Then they were to travel to the Francombs' at Ranelagh, to watch apples being graded, packed and loaded. Mr Francomb had installed a brand-new toilet in case one of the royals was caught short.

The whole of the Huon Valley was dizzy with excitement. Every schoolchild in the district, and most of their parents, would be descending upon Ranelagh for the royal walkabout, to cheer and wave flags.

Annie turned back to the stove. The smell of cooking sausages made Catherine's mouth water. She'd had a long day at school, only managing a couple of bites of her sandwich while on playground duty at lunchtime.

'How about you pop up to Hobart after school on Friday for late-night shopping,' Annie said. 'Buy yourself a few nice things, including at least one new dress.'

'Can you spare me in the packing shed?'

'I'll manage. Don't worry about me and the packing shed, or your own orchard, or the school. Go up to town, do some shopping, see some friends. Think about yourself for a change instead of being a slave to everybody else.'

A tightness in Catherine's throat prevented her from saying anything. Is that how Annie saw her, as some kind of martyr? It was true she'd worked almost non-stop since returning to the valley.

The orchard needed so much attention and was reliant on her wage from teaching. It took everything she had and still demanded more. The new trees were all growth and the fruit wouldn't set. The disappointment had hit both her and her father hard. The Ag Department was helping them with solutions – different trees for cross-pollination, bringing more bees in and grafting other varietals, but the results wouldn't be known until next year. Another year of teaching at the Cygnet school, another season packing for Annie and Dave, and another cold winter reworking and pruning in the family orchard for no return. What had she expected when she'd raced back to find the orchard in ruins three years ago? The endless work and worry had left her exhausted. It was as if she'd forgotten herself and buried her true nature deep along with Peter. Only Charlie had brought her back into the light. The Sunday afternoons she spent with him and Mark were her source of sustenance and joy. Mark and she had moved on from the disappointment of Lara being untraceable, but there would be no more kissing, no more thoughts of a future together. Their friendship was purely platonic, even though their love of Charlie made their bond stronger than most. Even so, Catherine's father outright refused to let her move into the old cottage, implying she couldn't be trusted because of her association with Mark. His disapproval was so fierce she'd resorted to stretching the truth. She told her parents she was spending her Sunday afternoons at Annie's. Her father didn't need to know that 'Annie's' could mean any part of the Pearsons' place, including one particular pickers' hut.

'You need to find a different way of having some fun.'

Annie's words pulled Catherine up sharply. It was if Annie had been reading her mind.

'Remember fun?' Annie continued. 'I do, somewhere in my distant past. But I'm a married woman now with six kids and an orchard to help run, not to mention the cattle. But you? You're still relatively young and unattached.' She gave Catherine a penetrating look. 'You are unattached, aren't you?'

'Relatively young?' Catherine huffed, but made sure Annie saw her smiling. 'I'll take that as some kind of backhanded compliment.' It wasn't really though, was it? Catherine would be twenty-six soon. She'd used everything from her career, to the fire, to the orchard as an excuse not to be married, not even engaged. The truth was, the only fun she wanted to have was right here in the valley on those golden Sunday afternoons.

'And unattached?' Annie persisted.

It was clear Annie wanted one of Catherine's regular assurances that nothing was going on between her and Mark. Not that it would dispel Annie's concerns in any way. She'd always had a set against Mark. It went beyond her concern for Catherine being associated with a married man. Catherine wasn't sure what it was, but the atmosphere between the two of them was charged with something antagonistic which bore no relation to what Catherine and Mark did or didn't do. 'Yes, unattached.'

'Good, because Prince Charles is available. He's probably coming to Australia looking for a bride. He'll take one look at you and think, "Perfect. We need new blood in the family and this fine colonial gel is just the ticket."' Annie's impersonation of the royal accent was spot on.

'You're trying to matchmake me and Prince Charles?' Catherine laughed. 'He's too young for me. Besides, a Tasmanian marrying royalty? That'll never happen.'

'You might be in with a chance – with the right dress.'

'Annie Pearson, you're a wicked woman.'

'Well, that's always been true. But prince or no, promise me you'll go up to Hobart and buy yourself something at least halfway fashionable.'

Catherine knew her friend was right. It was time for a change.

Annie's voice softened. 'I'm not criticising, Catherine. You look beautiful no matter what you wear. But the orchard takes all your wages and you never think of yourself. All I'm saying is, go and spend some of your hard-earned pay. You deserve it.'

Catherine nodded. A new dress would be lovely and a trip up to Hobart a real treat. If the fire hadn't ruined the orchard, if Peter hadn't died, she'd still be living in Sandy Bay and buying new dresses on a whim. She closed her eyes for a moment. It wasn't often she thought of how things might have been. It was an indulgence she couldn't afford. Her life had changed forever on that day, as had many others'. The orchard was her focus now, her brother a memory she cherished even though it brought her pain.

'Good,' Annie said, as if putting a full stop to the discussion. 'Now, I believe you offered to make a pudding. Those Gravensteins need using up.' She nodded to the bowl of apples on the kitchen bench. 'And the rhubarb has gone berserk in the garden.'

'I can make a crumble if you like. Or whip up a sponge topping instead.'

'That'd be wonderful. But first, go and take a peek at what Angela's up to. It's sure to make you smile.'

'Okay.' Catherine stepped quietly down the hall. There was something delightful about watching a young child at play in a world of their own. She paused just outside the lounge room door and peeped in. Angela was, as usual, dressed in pink, her dark hair swept back with a hairband. Her dolls were neatly arranged around her on the floor and each with a toy plastic cup, saucer and plate in front of them. Angela pretended to dish something out from a small plastic bowl. 'No, Lucy,' she said sternly to the smallest doll. 'You're too little to have peas. You'll just spill them on the floor.'

Angela must have sensed her presence and looked up.

'Hello, Angela. You're doing a very good job.'

'Thank you.' Angela's manners were lovely; her mother had made sure of that.

'I'm helping your mummy in the kitchen. I'm making an apple and rhubarb sponge.'

'We're having cake, but only after they've eaten all their vegetables.'

Catherine tried not to laugh and returned to the kitchen where Annie was cutting up potatoes. 'She really is the most beautiful child,' Catherine said. 'With such wonderful manners.'

'It's hard with her brothers setting such a bad example, but I do my best.'

'And those gorgeous eyes,' Catherine added.

Annie paused, then continued with the potatoes. 'Yes.'

Catherine pulled on an apron, worn and faded, but clean and smelling of lemon Fab, and began the all-too-familiar task of peeling apples.

'Thanks,' Annie said. 'You always were much better at puddings than me.'

'I was taught by the best.' Catherine had grown up cooking beside her mother, learning all the tips and tricks. Annie, with her wealthy parents, had been destined for a life buffered by a housekeeper and a nanny.

'I've heard Prince Charles is partial to a good jam roly-poly.' Annie winked at her. 'If you know what I mean.' She snorted with laughter and Catherine couldn't help but do the same.

'Excuse me.' Angela stood in the kitchen doorway. 'How are my dollies supposed to sleep with all this racket?'

The women looked at each other with glee. Angela's words were the exact imitation of her mother's when she was trying to get her younger children to sleep. Their laughter bubbled out uncontrollably.

Angela shook her head in a disapproving fashion, tsk-tsked, and walked back down the hallway.

Annie slumped into the chair next to Catherine, holding her sides with her hands. 'Oh, stop. It hurts. My laughter muscles are out of practice.'

Catherine dabbed at her eyes with her apron. She couldn't remember the last time she'd laughed so much. Tears, yes, there had been plenty of those, but laughter? She put her arm around her dearest and oldest friend. On the hardest days Catherine had doubted her decision to return to the valley, but here, in Annie's kitchen with all they'd shared, she felt she was exactly where she was supposed to be.

24

April 1970
Annie

Annie put the last candle on Dave's hurriedly iced birthday cake. Why did his birthday have to fall at the height of picking season? She hardly had time to go to the toilet, let alone make a cake. Here it was almost six in the evening, and she had to be back in the packing shed by seven. Today had been stressful. She hated it when the inspectors turned up, poking their noses into everything. When they'd started pulling apart a pallet that was packed and ready to go, she'd wanted to scream. Most inspectors were ex-orchardists who couldn't make a go of it and now made other orchardists jump through hoops. It felt like being back at school with the teachers checking her work and itching to write a big red F.

'Hi there.' Catherine bustled in, rosy-cheeked from the brisk autumnal air, her arms laden with Tupperware. 'My mother sends birthday greetings to Dave with some of the latest treats from her

190

kitchen.' Carefully she unloaded her cargo onto the kitchen table. 'Enough to feed an army.'

'Luckily I have an army.' Annie gave her friend a quick hug.

'Where are they all?'

'Outside. They kept sticking their fingers in the icing, the bowl and the cake.'

'Surely not Angela?'

Annie inclined her head to indicate that Angela was under the table.

'Oh, I see. There's a fairy in the kitchen.' Catherine bent down to take a peek. Annie knew what she'd see. Angela had lined up her teddy with the pink bow and one of her dolls under the table and was whispering to them sternly about not putting their fingers in icing. It melted Annie's heart. Not that she didn't love her boys but she and Angela had a bond that was special.

'How is your mum?'

A cloud passed over Catherine's face. 'Not so good at the moment.'

Annie knew Judith Turner hadn't been doing well. Catherine had mentioned her mother was spending more time in her room again. There were some who might say that Judith Turner should be over her grief by now, but Annie understood that losing a child was the sharpest loss of all.

Catherine opened another container of party food. 'Fortunately cooking still seems to help, so I don't think anyone will go hungry this evening.'

'Oh, I don't know. Bottomless pits, every one of them.' Annie sighed. If it wasn't for the veggie garden and the chooks she didn't know how she'd manage. Dave ate like a horse and his sons all took after him. The housekeeping money always ran out before the end of the week. She'd sworn to never ask her parents for money, but as the years went by, her resolve was weakening. Impatiently she brushed the thought aside. The food might not be fancy, but there was love at her table.

'There.' Catherine stood back. 'Looks like a pretty good birthday feast to me.'

'I'm just going to mix up some Tang and we're done. Could you see if Dave's on his way? He should be close by now.'

'Sure.' Catherine went out the back door.

Annie could hear her boys mobbing her, asking what food she'd brought and when they could eat it.

'Mummy?' Angela emerged from under the table, and Annie felt the familiar flutter in her stomach. When her daughter was little, the feeling had been more of a violent lurch, almost painful at times. The fear of losing her was always so strong. 'Mummy. I'm hungry.'

Annie bent down and swung Angela up for a cuddle. 'Anything your heart desires, my darling, you can have.'

Angela smiled at the sight of the pink-iced patty cakes with red glacé cherries on top. Judith must have had Angela in mind when she'd made them. 'Please?' she asked. Annie picked one up and put it into her daughter's waiting hands.

Dave came bursting through the back door surrounded by a tumble of children, with Catherine, Mark and Charlie bringing up the rear. 'Wow, what a spread,' Dave said. 'Anybody hungry?'

The boys roared with approval and in a few minutes the sausage rolls, party pies and patty cakes were demolished.

When it was time for the birthday cake, Annie lit the candles. 'Make a wish, darling.'

Dave blew them out with a puff and she knew what he was wishing for. Good prices for apples and cattle, fair weather for grafting, decent rains for growth, and no hail. Then he winked at her and she knew his last wish was one she would happily grant later tonight, no matter how tired she was.

When every last crumb was gone, Mark stood up. 'Catherine and I have a little birthday surprise for you, Dave.'

His use of 'Catherine and I' grated on Annie. She'd watched them warily over the past couple of years, especially after Charlie's illness. As the gossip mounted she had to wonder. Catherine had always confided in Annie, ever since she was a young teenager, but she'd become tight-lipped about her friendship with Mark, despite Annie's constant questioning. Annie consoled herself with the thought that if there was something going on, they'd be more discreet. Maybe what Catherine said was true. They had nothing to hide. She hoped so.

When faces and hands had been washed, teeth brushed and pyjamas put on, the children and Annie joined the others in the lounge room where the open fire popped and crackled. Dave sat in his armchair wearing the gold paper crown the kids had made him. Catherine was at the old piano and Mark had his guitar strapped over one shoulder. He didn't look much different to the photos she'd seen of him and his band in the clippings he'd sent Dave ages ago. Dave had been proud to be best mates with someone famous. Annie hadn't been impressed. What did a man like that know about hard work and family values? She had to admit he'd surprised her over the past three years. He'd turned out to be a diligent worker and a good father to Charlie. It didn't stop her wishing he'd pack his things, go back to Melbourne and never return.

'We've been practising. I know Mark will get it right but as for me—' Catherine put her hands in the air as if surrendering. 'All I can say is, "Don't shoot the piano player, she's doing her best."'

Annie wondered where they'd been practising. At the school? Surely not.

Mark put his hand on Catherine's shoulder. 'You're better than you think.'

Catherine inclined her head towards his hand, making Annie frown. It was the move of a woman in love, whether Catherine admitted it or not.

'Happy birthday, Dave.' Mark nodded to Catherine and softly counted them in, 'One, two, three, Hey Jude ...'

Catherine began to play the chords as Mark strummed and sang in a voice so lovely Annie shook her head in disbelief. She couldn't help but join in and wasn't the only one. The whole family clapped, swayed and sang while Mark did a perfect rendition of Paul McCartney's scream-singing over the top. The old piano wasn't exactly in tune but it didn't matter. Catherine thumped out the chords with growing confidence and Mark threw his head back and put everything into the song. Angela slid from her lap, toddled up to the piano and swayed to the rhythm. When the song finally ended, the family burst into applause and laughter.

'Wow,' Dave said, a wide grin creasing his eyes. 'Bloody bonza.'

Mark gave a little bow and then turned to Catherine, applauding. 'Catherine deserves all the praise. That's a piano song and there's no way it would work without her.'

'But your voice, mate,' Dave said. 'Why didn't you ever sing in your band?'

Mark shrugged. 'Just one of those things, I guess.'

'I know they're doing really well overseas,' Dave continued. 'But I reckon they'd be doing even better if you were still with them.'

Annie tried to catch Dave's eye. They both knew Mark had his reasons for quitting the band, but with The Scene so famous now, he must regret it.

'More, more,' Michael shouted, and the rest of the boys joined in.

194

'Encore,' Dave cheered.

Catherine shushed them all, like the school teacher she was. 'We do have another song. Dave, I hear you can't decide whether you're a Beatles or a Stones man.' She looked up at Mark with a shy grin. 'Maybe we can help you choose.' She settled herself at the keyboard and nodded to Mark.

As soon as Annie heard the first notes she knew what they were going to play. It might have been a hit around the world a few years ago, but she didn't think it was appropriate. A song about not getting any satisfaction – could the implications be any more obvious? Her older boys ran into the kitchen and returned with saucepans and wooden spoons, banging along with gusto. The cacophony threatened to drown out Mark and Catherine, which might've been a blessing, under the circumstances.

When the song finished to enthusiastic applause, Mark turned to Dave. 'Well, Dave, does that help you make up your mind? Beatles or Stones?'

Dave shook his head. 'I don't know, mate. What I do know is you're bloody good.'

'Language, Dave,' Annie said.

'What, darl? You didn't mind when I said the Beatles song was bloody bonza.'

The boys tittered among themselves like sparrows.

Annie raised an eyebrow at him. 'I guess it's obvious who gets my vote.'

'I think you're right. I'd love to hear "Hey Jude" again. It's a cracker of a song.'

A single note from the piano rang out in a slightly out-of-tune way. Then another. Angela had edged closer to the piano and was steadying herself with one hand while reaching up with the other to hit the notes.

Catherine laughed. 'You might have a little musician in the family.'

Mark shot a glance at Annie, but she avoided his eyes.

Catherine bent down to Angela. 'Would you like to play along with me?'

Angela nodded. 'Yes, please.'

'Well, you put your fingers up here.' She guided her small fingers to the top of the keyboard. 'And when I start playing, you hit this note as many times as you like.'

Mark and Catherine began to play 'Hey Jude' again, and the energy in the room lifted. Angela's one note was completely out of place but it didn't matter. Even Michael and Eric's percussion was bearable. Before the song reached its crescendo there was a banging on the front door. Dave turned to Annie. She shrugged and got up.

The cold air slipped around her as she opened the door. The night was still and clear, with the moon fat and low in the sky. Everything looked silver, including the two policemen on her front verandah. She'd sometimes wondered whether they'd show up. The thought always turned her stomach to water. These two weren't local. An unwelcome thought popped into her head – *out of towners to do the dirty work.*

'Mrs Pearson?' the taller one asked.

'Yes?' It came out as a question. Their presence made her unsure of everything. She shifted her gaze out towards the valley where the moonlight shimmered.

'We're looking for Mark Davis. We believe we might find him here. Is he in?'

'What's this about?'

'We need to speak to him regarding a matter of importance.'

'Ah.' She paused. 'I'll get him.'

Annie walked inside, but stood by the lounge room door for a moment watching Mark and Catherine play, with Angela hitting her one note, and her boys singing along with enthusiasm. Only Dave, with his gold paper crown slightly askew on his head, turned to her, a question in his eyes. She took in the scene with a chilling knowledge. It was all about to change.

25

Hobart, April 1970

Mark

The buzzing of fluorescent ceiling lights set Mark's teeth on edge. One of them flickered in an arrhythmic tic that stretched his strained nerves further. He placed his hands on the table in front of him. Tanned by the sun and roughened through his work in the orchard, they didn't seem to belong to him. There was a time when his hands were precious things, to be cared for, and the only calluses were on the fingertips of his left hand from years of pressing metal strings to a wooden fretboard. Now his hands were covered in scars and multiple calluses from pruning, digging, fencing and the endless hoeing around the trees. Three years he'd been living and working at the orchard. Years of wondering and waiting. And now this.

The policeman sitting opposite him wrote a few notes then turned his attention back to Mark.

'And that was definitely the last time you saw her?'

'Yes.' Mark rubbed a hand over his eyes. How many times did he need to answer the same questions?

'February fifth, 1967. Two days before the fires?'

'That's what I don't understand. Why was she still in the valley?'

'You never reported her as missing.' He looked at Mark with a questioning expression.

'My wife had a habit of running off. She was what you might call highly strung. She'd usually come back after a few days, once it was weeks.' Mark cleared his throat. His mouth was bone dry. Lara. Found in the burnt-out wreck of his car.

'But why not report her missing?'

Mark's voice rose. 'The fire came through on the seventh of February. All phone lines were down and no power. People were dying. A young man was burnt alive on the neighbouring property and—'

The policeman interrupted. 'Just answer the question, Mr Davis.'

'Am I under arrest? Do I need a lawyer?'

'You're not under arrest. In any reportable death we are required to collect statements and evidence for the coroner's report. You are Mrs Davis's next of kin and the last person, that we know of, to see her alive. And I fully understand the circumstances of the seventh of February 1967. I was on duty here, in Hobart.'

Mark noticed the hitch in the policeman's voice. What kinds of things had he seen that day? Much worse than anything Mark had encountered, for sure. The best thing was to cooperate fully and use the kind of language they understood. 'Because my wife had gone missing before the fire, I didn't think there was any connection or concern. I waited for her to return.'

'To the Pearson farm at Wattle Grove.'

'Yes. The clean-up after the fire was exhausting, and I didn't think to follow up at first.'

'And after that?'

'I tried. Contacted all my wife's friends and family then returned to Melbourne to try to find her. We have a young son. I left him with the Pearsons to see if I could find her in any of her usual haunts. I wondered whether she'd asked her friends not to tell me where she was.'

'Why was that, Mr Davis? Did your wife fear you for any reason?'

'No. In fact quite the opposite. Lara was the one who used to lash out. As I mentioned, she was highly strung.'

The policeman made a note. 'She "lashed out".' He looked Mark straight in the eye. 'And you were never tempted to retaliate?'

'No. Never. I'd leave her alone. Get Charlie out of her line of fire and leave.'

'Your son?'

'Yes.'

'Were you concerned for his safety?'

Mark hesitated. He was away so frequently, and even when he was based in Melbourne the band had so many gigs he often wouldn't see them all weekend.

'Lara could be … unpredictable.'

'Did she ever hurt your son, Mr Davis?'

He shook his head. 'No.' He wasn't sure, but he couldn't give the cops a reason. Could they possibly think he'd murdered Lara?

'How did you get that scar?'

'Pardon?' Mark frowned.

'The one on your chin?'

His hand reached up to touch it. The skin was raised in a small, jagged line from below his bottom lip to the left-hand side of his chin. 'I got caught up in a fight, not of my making or of my choosing.'

'Where was this fight?'

'In Melbourne, at a gig. The sharpies decided they wanted to kill the mods. Nothing to do with me.'

'At a gig?'

'I used to play in a band.'

'So you weren't always a farm labourer?'

'No.'

'An interesting change of career.'

There was a knock on the door of the interview room. The door opened and another policeman entered, handed over a plastic bag and left. The policeman's face assumed a different expression, gentler, more concerned.

'May I be honest with you, Mr Davis?'

Mark swallowed but nodded.

'Your car, as you know, was found down an embankment, deep in a gully. The vehicle had exited the road with some force.' The policeman looked down at the contents of a slim folder in front of him. 'From what we can deduce, the car must have been engulfed in flames during the fires of the seventh of February 1967. But as the body remained in situ for over three years there were disturbances—' He pressed his lips into a thin line. 'Wild dogs, most likely.'

'Oh.' The room swayed. Mark closed his eyes. Breathe in. Breathe out. The room steadied.

'Mr Davis? Would you like a glass of water?'

'No. Thank you.' He wanted to get this over and done with.

The policeman continued, his words slow and measured. 'The forensic pathologist will be able to ascertain the sex and the age of the victim, but any further identification will be difficult under the circumstances. However, we did find this.' He pushed the evidence bag across the table to Mark.

Tentatively, Mark smoothed out the plastic for a closer look at the contents. The silver chain was blackened and melted, but the stone was recognisable. His heart thudded painfully against his ribs. He'd found the pendant in a tiny shop hidden away in Flinders Lane. It'd caught his attention in among the other necklaces and bracelets, moonstones, crystals and incense. He knew it was meant for Lara. 'His Lara' as she was back then – wild and free and beautiful. Their passion was limitless. His friends warned him she wasn't the kind of woman you married and it would only lead to trouble. But her eyes had haunted him day and night. He'd wanted her, always and forever. Charlie made his presence known soon after the wedding, although Lara had baulked at the idea of a child. When the baby arrived, squirming and screaming, she'd handed him to Mark. That was the first time she disappeared. Only for a few days. But history repeated itself, again and again, until finally—

'Mr Davis? Do you recognise this pendant?'

'Traditionally, it was carried as a way of fending off curses.'

'I beg your pardon?'

'Tiger's eye. It's also supposed to help alleviate fear and anxiety.' It hadn't worked. Her moods had grown worse. Mark called in favour after favour as he learnt how to look after his young son. Lara's parents were a godsend. Her mother was eager to spend time with her grandson, especially under the circumstances. That first year had been hell for all of them. When Lara was home she spent most of her time crying, or pacing and fretting. The weight fell off her already slim frame and her hair became dull and brittle. She couldn't bear to be in the same room as Charlie and would sleep on the couch, if she slept at all. Mark turned to his old friend Dave, the only person he knew who had kids. He rang him regularly for advice, even though Dave had little, Annie having never behaved in such a way. But Mark could always rely on him for words of comfort and encouragement. During the worst of it, it was Dave who prevented him from being crushed under the weight of it. Then when Charlie was just over a year old, something changed. Lara seemed to accept the situation, and although the boy was still a toddler, he would go where she went, and do what she did. As Mark's band became more popular he spent less time at home. Lara had sometimes forgotten Charlie, leaving him at a cafe once, and a wine bar late at night. Charlie had, by necessity, grown so quiet and compliant as to be almost invisible. In the months preceding their trip to Tasmania, she'd grown restive again, disappearing all day and sometimes overnight. Mark saw the old pattern repeating itself – the anxiety, mood swings, and insomnia – and had hoped a complete change of scene would help. He'd been wrong.

'Mr Davis. Again, for the record, do you recognise this pendant?'

Mark pressed the plastic tight against the stone, trying to feel the tiger's eye beneath his fingers, to somehow conjure the soul of Lara and touch her one more time. 'Yes,' he said.

'And did it belong to your wife, Lara Virginia Davis?'

'Yes, yes it did.'

'And was she wearing it the last time you saw her, on the fifth of February 1967?'

'Yes.'

'Thank you for your cooperation. We will need to speak to Mr and Mrs Pearson to corroborate your statement. Unless there are any complications we should expect a report from the coroner within the next few days. You will be informed of the findings. Do you have any questions?'

Mark's eyes remained fixed on the tiger's eye. Did he have questions? None the policeman could answer. His wife was dead. But was she finally at peace? And would she ever forgive him?

26

Late April 1970

Catherine

'Hello?' Catherine called. 'Where are you?'

Sometimes Charlie would hide when she arrived on Sunday afternoons, prompting a game of hide and seek, but today there was an odd stillness to the pickers' hut. Mark wasn't on the porch waiting for her, and Charlie hadn't given away his hiding spot by giggling as he usually did.

Her sense of unease grew as she walked inside. The small rooms were silent and bare. In the bedrooms, the beds were made, with sheets and blankets tucked in tight and the pillows in straight lines. It was as if Mark and Charlie had never lived there.

It had been almost a fortnight since the discovery of Lara's body. During that time Mark had become withdrawn and distracted. She'd wanted to offer comfort, but he'd kept her at a distance. He'd been impatient for the coroner's report and anxious to put Lara's remains to rest. Catherine had known he'd have to go to Melbourne to sort

204

things out, but she'd thought she would've seen them before they left. Why hadn't Mark said goodbye?

She moved heavily to the porch, disappointment creating its own sense of gravity. Her eyes scanned the ground where Charlie had played with his hand-me-down Matchbox cars, making roads in the dirt, but there was no trace of the young boy she loved. She walked down the steps, counting in her head the way Charlie used to – one, two, three – and headed to the back of the hut. There, in the small clearing before the rows of apple trees began, a small wooden cross still stood. One thing had not been erased.

'Good boy, Benno,' she whispered. 'Good boy.'

Ever faithful, Peter's best friend and then Charlie's beloved companion, Benno, had succumbed to old age with patience and acceptance. He'd made it clear when he was ready to go, and the vet had come to them. Benno went to sleep peacefully among the apple trees where he'd spent his life. Catherine had cried so much, even the vet was moved to tears. Another part of Peter gone.

And now Mark and Charlie were gone as well.

They'd had their own loss, of course, and it had been unexpected and shocking. Catherine would never admit it to anyone, but her first thought when she'd heard Mark's wife was dead was that finally they could be a happy family. That she could become, legally, the mother Charlie had always needed. She knew she should feel guilty for having such thoughts, but the relief of Mark finally being free had been overwhelming. Perhaps their sudden disappearance was her punishment.

She stumbled back to the porch. They'd sat there so often. Catherine remembered Mark's eyes, his hands, his touch. The memory of their only kiss, his lips firm and warm against hers, still lingered like a flower pressed between the pages of a book. The colour had faded, but the imprint remained, fragile and thinner than paper, but still real, and more precious because of its frailty. She'd put a stop to the kiss because he was married. And all that time, Lara was dead, down a gully along the treacherous Huon Road. All the slander she and Mark had endured. For what? Now, when they were finally free to take up from where that kiss had been leading, he'd shut her out then left without a word. Had she been a fool all this time? A diversion to entertain him while he was playing at being an orchard hand? Had Annie been right? He couldn't be trusted. A hard lump formed in her throat. No. She refused to believe it.

Catherine didn't know how she found the strength to get up. She walked through the trees towards Annie's house. The pickers had done the first pass through this part of the orchard and the remaining apples were colouring up. They'd need to be harvested within a few days to be right for export. These thoughts kept her mind busy; a distraction she knew wouldn't last.

Annie's kitchen was in its familiar disarray with piles of washing heaped on the table.

'Have you come to help with the ironing?' Annie looked exhausted. Two months into the picking season, her workload was relentless. 'I could use a hand.'

The sound of the boys playing footy in the backyard filtered through closed windows, along with the crack and clatter of Dave splitting wood. Angela was playing with her dolls under the table. Catherine couldn't believe everything was so normal here. 'Mark's gone. And Charlie.'

Annie kept her head down, busying herself with the washing. 'Other pickers are moving into the hut tomorrow. Mark doesn't know when he'll be back. Couldn't have come at a worse time. As if I didn't have enough to organise with the harvest.'

'He didn't tell me.'

'You knew he had things to take care of. The funeral.'

'I know, but I thought he'd say goodbye before—'

'I don't understand why he lied about going to the police.' Annie sounded angry, suddenly.

'What do you mean?'

'A couple of weeks after the fires, Dave and Mark went to Huonville. Mark said he was going to the police station to report Lara missing. Thing is, he never did. He told us he did, but he didn't.'

'Why would he do that?' Catherine was already bewildered by Mark's disappearance. Annie's words added to the doubts she was desperately trying to push aside.

'We didn't know he'd lied until the police interviewed us after her body was found.'

'What did he say?'

'Put us through our paces. Those coppers ask a lot of questions.'

'No. Mark.'

'Not a lot.' Annie looked Catherine in the eye for the first time since she'd arrived. 'I never did like him or his wife. Something off about the pair of them. He's done you a favour by leaving without letting you know. Shown his true colours. You should forget about him.'

Catherine was shocked by Annie's words. 'How could you say—'

'He doesn't belong here, he never did. Mark turned your head and it was a disaster. I never told you the worst of the gossip. I'm glad he's gone back where he belongs. You should be too.'

'But Charlie—'

'Honestly, Catherine. I have a ton of work to do. If you're just going to mope I'd rather you left.'

Annie had never spoken to her like this. She'd come here hoping for answers, but instead found hostility. This day had brought nothing but confusion and sorrow. Mark and Charlie gone, and now Annie angry with her for a reason she couldn't fathom.

Despite her mounting turmoil and despair, Catherine held it together. 'You know what? I've got work to do at home, the kind I can do while moping.'

She walked down the hallway, expecting Annie to call her back with an apology. By the time she reached the front door, Catherine knew it wasn't going to happen. At the end of the driveway she turned towards the ever-flowing river, beyond to the purple peaks of the Hartz Mountains and the arcing vault of cold blue sky. So much space. So much emptiness. And her, so small in the midst of it. So small and so utterly alone.

27

7 February 1971

Catherine

The year unfurled through the seasons; a bleak winter, a bright spring and then the long clear blue days of summer. Not a word from Mark. The grief that had roared through her in the weeks and months since he'd left had now steadied to a constant familiar pain. It had become part of her, like the stone she carried in her heart for Peter.

It was four years to the day since she'd lost her brother.

The rector was at the door as she left the church. Usually he would shake hands with his parishioners after the Sunday service but Catherine was supporting her mother.

'Bless you, Catherine,' the rector said. He laid a gentle hand on her mother's shoulder. 'And may God give you strength, Judith.'

Catherine's mother dabbed her eyes with an already sodden handkerchief.

Catherine's father was behind them. 'Wonderful sermon, Rector.'

209

'Thank you, Jack. Are you joining us in the church hall for morning tea?' He always asked. Catherine thought he should know by now what the answer would be.

'Not today.' He inclined his head towards his wife. 'A quick visit to say hello to Peter and then home. I think that's best.'

The rector nodded. 'If I can do anything, please let me know.'

'Right you are.'

A few women approached Catherine and her mother with the concerned expressions Catherine had come to know so well – pity tinged with the relief it wasn't their son who'd died in the inferno of Black Tuesday. Soon they would be talking in low serious voices about how, yes, they'd spoken with Judith Turner and no, she wasn't doing well, even after all these years. Catherine fended off their platitudes with a few of her own and helped her mother towards the cemetery, with her father beside them, his steps almost as slow. The anniversary of the fire was always hard, and it falling on a Sunday this year made it worse. Her mother had been fragile even before the sermon began. The rector's words were too much – he spoke of loss and tragedy, the heroism of those who fought the fires, and the ultimate sacrifice some had made. He'd gone on to talk about resilience and the new growth that occurs after fire, but those words had been lost on Catherine's mother as she sobbed in the pew beside her husband and daughter.

At the cemetery, Catherine's father stopped by the gate. 'Perhaps it's best to leave it for today. We could come back tomorrow.'

'He would've been twenty-three this year.' Her voice was surprisingly clear. 'A man. Married, even children. I need to see him. He needs to know I haven't forgotten.'

Catherine had tried, but her mother had refused to see a social worker, saying no amount of talking could ever bring Peter back. Not even the rector had been able to help, she'd said, and he had a direct line to God. Catherine watched her mother diminish a little more with every anniversary, lost in her grief. She took no interest in the orchard even though the new trees were finally bearing. Every tree was productive again and Catherine was determined to work full-time beside her father. It was time.

As soon as they arrived back at the house, he disappeared into the bedroom and emerged wearing work clothes. 'Just off to check the irrigation system,' he said, picking his battered old hat off the hook by the back door.

The new drip irrigation saved time, water and electricity, but it had its drawbacks. Sometimes the drippers got blocked, and frogs and tadpoles needed to be cleaned out of the lines daily.

'I'll come with you,' Catherine said.

'No.' His voice was firm. 'Look after your mother. It's a tough day for her, you know that.'

'If I was working in the orchard full-time I could be here more for her. She might start feeling better knowing her daughter was close by at all times.'

'We've talked about this.'

'But all the trees are in fruit. We'll have a good crop this year, enough to make up for my teaching wage.'

Her father's jaw was set in a grim line. 'The new trees are still coming good. The fruit might be small this year and you know the prices for apples fell last year. New Zealand and South Africa beat us on every level and shipping rates have gone up again. Best you stay a teacher if you want to keep this orchard going. That's where you're the most help.'

'But, Dad—'

'Catherine, you're the first person, *ever*, in this family to receive a tertiary education, and you want to throw that away? To do what?

Work like a slave, day in and day out, year after year, for just enough money to live on if you're lucky?'

Catherine took a shaky step backwards. 'If that's how you feel then how could you have expected Peter to do it?'

'It's what he wanted.' He glared at her, daring her to deny it.

Catherine held her tongue. This wasn't a wound she wanted to reopen. Instead she took another tack. 'You've been asking around for someone to work in our orchard. Annie told me.' Catherine's father had been overheard in the hardware store, asking about experienced orchard workers. Catherine had been furious. She still was. 'Why not let me do it, instead of using my wages to pay someone else?'

'What I do here is my business.' Her father's face was rigid with anger. 'Do you know how much he'll be paid? If you did, you wouldn't be mewling about wanting to do the work. You'd be grateful for the job you've got.'

'But the orchard is why I quit my job in Hobart. It's why I came back to Wattle Grove. It's what Peter really wanted.' Despite her previous intention, the words were out before she could stop them.

'Peter?' Her father stepped towards her, his voice harsh and his eyes fierce. 'You think your mother would feel better if you were here all the time? You're wrong. She doesn't want her daughter close by. All she wants is her son back. You can never, ever, replace Peter. Not for her. Not for me.' He opened the door, letting in a gust of hot air and closed it hard behind him.

Catherine slumped against the wall, breathless. It was as though her father had slit her open and gutted her like a rabbit. Tears of frustration and rage ran down her cheeks. She should pack her car and drive away. Leave this valley and not look back, just like Mark. But she couldn't. With Mark and Charlie gone, the only sense of belonging she had was in the orchard. She measured her weeks and months by the turn of the seasons, the cycle of the trees, the steady repetition of the work. Peter's spirit lived on in this orchard and she wouldn't desert him. Neither could she leave her mother, racked by a grief that didn't abate.

Catherine took a deep breath and dashed away her tears. Annie had been right. Catherine had become a martyr. But no more. It was time she began to shape her own destiny. She'd help her mother with the Sunday dinner. But she wouldn't sit down and eat at the same table as her father, not today. Maybe not ever again. She would leave this house. Her father had forbidden her from moving to her grandmother's cottage because he feared the gossips more than he trusted her. But after today, she no longer felt the need to obey his commands. She'd read *The Female Eunuch*, secretly in her room at night, devouring every word. It had questioned everything she'd thought was true. There was one truth remaining that couldn't be denied. She was a grown woman with her own life to lead.

28

March 1971

Catherine

The sound of wheels on gravel confused Catherine for a moment. No one ever drove up this way. She stood on the verandah and shielded her eyes from the late-afternoon sun. A familiar car came into view. Could it really be Erica Jane? How long had it been since she'd watched the car hightailing it off their property with a bleeding Tim at the wheel? Catherine ran her fingers through her hair and regretted her work clothes of shorts and a faded blouse. Then she caught her thoughts. It didn't matter what she looked like, not any more.

A figure emerged from the old Holden, leaner and more tanned than she remembered. His hair was still bleached by the sun, but longer. Miss Downie would never approve. And was he wearing an earring? He looked up at her and waved. 'Hi ya, babe, long time no see.'

She shook her head at the incongruity of his words, but was surprised to feel a frisson of excitement.

214

'Didn't want to go near the new place,' he drawled. 'Not after last time. But I saw the Hillman parked up here. So here I am.'

'Here you are.' She smiled despite herself. Could she actually be pleased to see him? 'Come on up.'

'You sure? The old man's not around, is he? Don't want to cause any hassles.'

'No. Just me, the chickens and a cat.' Catherine had felt lonely when she'd first moved back into the old cottage. The solitude had wrapped around her day and night. She'd needed more than the breeze blowing through the trees and the screech of cockatoos as they helped themselves to another feed of apples for company. She'd come to love the chickens, each with unique personalities and strange little quirks, but with them came rats which in turn attracted snakes. A cat was the logical answer. Mickey was not only good company, he was also a stone-cold killer, depositing proof of his prowess on her doormat every morning.

Tim hoisted himself up the steps. 'Cool.'

They stood face to face, a little shy.

'This is kinda weird,' Tim said. 'What do you say to a chick when the last time you saw her everyone was a bit unglued?'

'You start by telling her what on earth you're doing back in the valley. Come and sit down.' Catherine indicated the two wicker chairs. In her grandmother's day they had been pristine and white, now the paint was all but gone and the wicker missing in places.

He sat beside her and casually touched her hand. 'No rings. Thought you'd've got hitched by now. That ex-pop star seemed a bit keen. What happened to him?'

Catherine shrugged. The last thing she wanted to talk about was Mark.

'That's right, he was married. Wife disappeared or something.'

She was suddenly restless. 'Do you want a drink?'

'Nah. Just wanna drink you in.' He gave her the lazy grin she remembered so well.

Catherine laughed. It sounded strange, in a place where there'd been so much silence. 'What *are* you doing here, Tim?'

'Gotta job at the wharf.' He nodded towards the river. On the opposite bank to Wattle Grove lay Port Huon, where ships from all over the world waited three deep to load their holds with Tasmanian apples.

'Really?'

'Yep. Got my stevedoring ticket through a mate whose old man's a wharfie. We're both doing a season to save up some dough. I'll be here for months.'

'A girl in every port.'

'Nah, just this one.' He smiled at her, his tanned skin crinkling around his sea-blue eyes.

'Who's the lucky girl?' Catherine relaxed into the harmless flirtation.

'You might know her. Pretty. Obsessed with apples. Makes me wish I was an apple.' He chuckled.

Catherine hadn't missed Tim, hadn't even thought about him over the past few years. But now he was here, sitting next to her, she found herself remembering the good times they'd had together, before he became jealous and obsessive.

'There's something different about you,' she said.

His face became serious. 'I'm real sorry about when we were together. I stuffed it up. Kinda went a bit crazy, you know? All those magic mushies.'

Catherine nodded silently. That explained Tim's strange behaviour. She'd heard about magic mushrooms, a kind of hallucinogenic available for free in the fields. The information had come with a warning. They were dangerous and best avoided.

216

'After what I said that day ...' Tim touched his nose. 'Don't blame your old man for having a go at me. But I was right about Vietnam.'

Catherine chewed her lip. She could barely bring herself to follow the news with its endless depictions of the suffering in the war.

'I was there at the marches.' His eyes burnt with a zeal that both scared and excited her. 'They were unreal, massive. People waking up, coming together. And it made a difference. Our troops are coming home. We should be out of this shithouse war by next year. Shoulda never been involved in the first place.'

'It's horrible, for both sides.' Catherine had thought about going to Hobart for the moratorium march last year. Over 200,000 people had marched, Australia wide. After what had happened to those women in My Lai, and countless others, she'd wanted her voice to be heard. But the thought of what her parents would think, especially her father, had stopped her.

'I'm stoked to hear you say that. Got this idea in my head you'd be more tuned in these days.' He leant in, his eyes searching hers. 'You should come to Bali with me.'

'Where's that? In Vietnam?' She'd heard of Saigon, Hue, Khe Sanh and Long Tan, but Bali?

'Nah, Indonesia. An island off the east coast of Java. Went there over summer with some dudes I met on the march. Blew my mind. That's why I'm here, working on the wharf. Saving up my bread to go back. You can live like a king there for next to nothing. The surf's radical, rolling barrels all the time. And it's paradise. Just narrow dirt roads and shacks on the beach. Living on fish, rice, and the most amazing fruit you've ever eaten. Pineapples, bananas, mangoes and things called dragon fruit – bright pink and purple. You scoop out the flesh and eat it, tiny black seeds and all.'

'Dragon fruit?' She'd never heard of such a thing.

'Yeah, and coconuts so fresh you just knock the top off them and drink the juice. Unreal. But you probably wouldn't like the place. No apples.'

She laughed. 'You're probably right. What do you do there?'

'Surf, babe. What else is there?'

Catherine raised an eyebrow; there was a lot more to life than surfing. 'And you're going back?'

'Yep. Reckon I can save enough to live over there for the rest of the year. The waves are unreal and the water, it's so warm, not like here. You can surf all year round without freezing your bits off. Hardly anyone else out there surfing. A few Yanks, some Aussies and that's about it.' His eyes grew distant. 'There's something about the place, you know. The people are real cool. They leave these little offerings outside their homes every day – fruit and flowers – as gifts for the spirits. They're happy all the time and it rubs off on you. So different from being here where everyone's so aggro. Working on the wharf? Well, enough said.'

Catherine was hypnotised by his words. This place called Bali did indeed sound magical.

'Once the cold season hits, I'll be gone. It's perfect there in winter.' Tim grasped her work-roughened hands. 'Come with me, if only for a holiday. You'll be warm, and far away from the frost and ice and sleet.'

'But I don't surf.' Much as she was enjoying his attention, the idea was ludicrous. 'What would I do there?'

'Do? Nothing. That's the point. Relax, eat, swim. You gotta be respectful of the locals, they're a modest bunch, but there are spots where the only creatures watching you are the monkeys. You can strip off and swim, sunbake on the white sand without a stitch on, just as nature intended. We'd be like Adam and Eve in the Garden of Eden.' His thumb gently rubbed the back of her hand.

His blue eyes were so clear. She'd forgotten. 'Adam and Eve didn't come to a happy end.'

'Ah, but remember what I said about Bali? No apples.' He winked.

The picture he painted of a tropical paradise, his hands on hers and the closeness of his body stirred something she'd suppressed since Mark had left.

'I've never forgotten you,' he said. 'Or the day of the fire. How could I?' She pulled away, remembering his fixation on her as his saviour.

'Hey, don't worry.' He lifted her hand to his mouth. His lips brushed her skin, setting off tiny sparks of electricity through her body. 'For sure, I was a bit crazy back then. Guess I freaked you out. That's history. The Balinese have taught me about respect for others, for nature and for myself.' He was still holding onto her hand. 'That's not to say I don't want to kiss you right now. What do you say? Come to Bali. You'd fall in love with the place. And me.'

She leant back in her chair. 'You certainly are a charmer. How many girls have you spun this line to?'

His face fell. 'None. Only you.'

'Really?'

'Yeah.'

It was getting late. She should be locking up the chickens and feeding the cat. But it was nice here, with him. It had been so long since she'd been flattered or admired. 'Well, in that case, I'll think about it.'

He sighed. 'I know you, Catherine Turner, and that means no.'

Did he know her? They'd been together, if you could call it that, for little over a year, one of the hardest years of her life. So much had changed since then.

'And I know that look,' he said. 'Can't blame you. Here's me lobbing up out of the blue and saying come away with me.' He shifted closer. 'Tell you what, I'm going to change your mind. Being on call at the port, the hours are crazy, but every chance I get, I'm gonna be here with you. I want you to be my lady. Sure, I've met a lot of fine women, but none I dig as much as you. You're a fox and you're strong. You gotta be a bit tough in Bali. It's blissful but basic. What do you say?'

Most women would jump at the chance to live in paradise with a handsome man. And here was Tim – with his brilliant eyes, winning smile and golden tousled hair – throwing himself at her. Still, she hesitated. He said he'd changed, but had he? He'd once thought of her as an angel keeping him alive. His fixation had scared her and pushed them apart. Now he'd waltzed back into her life assuming she'd want to be Jane to his Tarzan, in some place called Bali. He hadn't seen her for years and yet had already mapped out her future. Wasn't this the very thing she was trying to escape? Men deciding what she could and couldn't do?

Catherine and her father had come to an awkward truce. There was no avoiding each other, even with her living up the hill in the cottage. Without ever mentioning that day and the harsh words spoken, they'd managed to come to a working agreement. Catherine knew she was stubborn. She and her father were the same in that regard. Peter had been more like their mother, gentle and dreamy, with a tendency to waver between joy and melancholy, but always seeing the beauty in everything. Catherine was tougher – not physically stronger, but definitely stronger in mind and spirit.

Tim reached over and caressed her cheek. 'What are you thinking? Am I in with a chance?'

'Maybe.' Catherine knew she was taking a risk. Tim had made it clear that everything was on his terms. He'd only be able to see her when he had a break from the wharf and, she reminded herself, if the surf wasn't pumping.

'Let's see if I can make that a yes.' He pulled her closer and kissed her neck.

She took a steadying breath, fighting the sensations that swamped her body. But why? Tim was offering an escape from the drudgery her life had become. Since Mark and Charlie had left, her life had seemed little more than a husk – dried out and brittle. She needed something more. In a blink she made up her mind. He wanted a strong woman? She'd show him one.

Catherine kissed him back, hard.

29

April 1971

Catherine

In summer, when the sun rose early, Catherine never needed to set an alarm, but now the valley was deep in autumn, with its crisp mornings and a sharp bite to the air. Even the sun seemed reluctant to get out of bed. She leant over and switched off the alarm, stretching out to touch the warmth of Tim's body but only finding the cold space where he'd lain. He must've had another early start at the port and not wanted to wake her. She hugged herself tight, remembering the things they'd done last night. In the month they'd been together, she'd broken every edict imposed by teachers, doctors, the church, her parents and society. The world hadn't ended, and God hadn't struck her down. In the mirror, she could see no change at all, except a secret smile at the corners of her mouth. Sometimes, when thinking about Tim, a warm glow would spread from deep between her legs. She'd have to pull away from the sensuous echo of the night before, back into the present of her workaday life.

They did what they could to prevent their affair being discovered. Tim had swapped cars with his friend from the wharf so if her father saw a car at Catherine's place, he wouldn't recognise it. Usually Tim left the car in Huonville, a natural halfway point between Port Huon and Wattle Grove, where Catherine would pick him up. Last night had been unexpected – a last-minute change to the roster at the wharf. Tim had turned up late, promising he and the car would be gone before dawn. A promise he'd kept. Catherine touched her swollen lips, delighting in the memory of his ardent kisses.

In the kitchen, she thanked him silently for stoking up the wood stove before he'd left. The kettle sat on the edge of the hot plate, warming gently for her morning cup of tea. When she'd moved into the cottage she'd cleaned her grandmother's old stove, sweeping out the flue and the firebox, and scrubbing the oven and hot plates. It had taken a while to work out how much wood was needed to keep the fire going overnight, to keep the draughty old cottage warm as summer had stealthily slipped away. Getting the temperature right for cooking was another skill she was slowly mastering. Even so, the old camp stove and toaster oven were used more often than she'd hoped as she battled the vagaries of the wood burner.

Catherine gazed out over the apple trees and the mist nestling in the valley, as the day slowly lightened. The kettle came to the boil, its whistle a happy promise of a hot cup of tea. Mickey yowled outside, demanding to be let in after a night's hunting. She opened the door just wide enough, closing it quickly as a blast of chilly air rushed in. The cat wrapped himself around her ankles, then settled into his favourite spot in front of the stove. Tim had taken a shine to Mickey, and the feeling was mutual. What was it about Tim? He was thoughtful, funny and a sensational lover, not that she had a basis for comparison, yet she hadn't fallen in love with him. When he went to Bali she'd miss him, but not badly. Sometimes she wondered why love hadn't come, but in her heart she knew the answer. Catherine closed her eyes, remembering the cold winter evenings playing cards and singing songs by the fire in the pickers' hut, and warm summer twilights eating peaches and wading in the river. Tim was fun, and a guilty pleasure, but she could never love him. There was only room in her heart for one man, and he had left without a word.

April turned to May and the season drew to a close. Night came early as the pickers finished up, rubbing icy fingers and bustling into the packing shed to pick up wives and children before heading home to a hot meal. The wives would return after tea, to continue with the packing, having put children to bed or settled them with their homework.

Dave came over to Catherine as she was getting ready to leave. 'Haven't seen you at our place for a while,' he said. 'Not avoiding us, are you?'

Catherine went to object, given she saw Annie and the kids in the packing shed every day. Then she noticed the twinkle in his eye. 'Just waiting for an invitation,' she teased.

'Since when do you need one? But if that's the way it is.' He spotted Annie by the grader. 'Hey, Mrs Pearson, is it okay if I extend an official invitation to Miss Turner to come for tea tonight?'

Annie looked puzzled. 'Since when does Catherine need an invitation?'

'My thoughts exactly.' Dave looked pleased with himself. 'Consider yourself invited, if you can stand the thought of a rowdy meal with our tribe.'

'It sounds delightful.' Catherine wasn't expecting Tim tonight, and the prospect of her humble tea of eggs on toast didn't compare.

On the short walk to the house Dave turned to her. 'So, what does your dad think about the Board of Inquiry's decision?'

Catherine masked her annoyance. Why did Dave assume her father was the only one in the family with an opinion? 'Our lack of long-term planning is a disaster. Have you read the report?'

Dave shook his head. 'Nah, just going on what I've heard from other growers.'

A major restructuring of marketing was vital to the survival of the apple industry. Catherine had read everything she could get her hands on. 'It's damning. Unless things change soon, our livelihoods could be gone within a few years.'

'That bad, huh?'

'We need to be organised and speak with one voice.'

Annie laughed. 'You sound like one of those leftie pinkos.'

'If that's true, the Board of Inquiry must consist purely of Communists,' Catherine replied. Annie's flippancy irked her. The work of generations was at stake.

'I'm glad we diversified,' Dave said. 'But I gotta say, the prices for cattle aren't good. Our mainstay will always be apples.'

'And the mainstay of our puddings and cakes will always be apples,' Annie said, as they arrived at the house. 'I was thinking of an apple charlotte tonight, to use up some apples and stale bread. What do you think, Catherine?'

'I think she's volunteering you to make it,' Dave warned.

'Well?' Annie smiled at Catherine. 'It'll fit right in with your philosophy of all for one and one for all, comrade.'

'How could I refuse?'

Dinner was indeed a rowdy affair. Michael, now thirteen and starting to test his boundaries, was sent from the table without pudding. Eric, not to be outdone by his older brother, attempted to be banished as well. Scott argued with Paul about who was going to win the TFL grand final, which was months away, and Greg, who was in Catherine's Grade Two class, attempted to impress her with his knowledge of rocks. Only Angela was quiet, as she sat in her chair, bolstered by cushions, and ate her dinner of shepherd's pie without any fuss.

Dave pushed his chair back from the table. 'Delicious dinner, girls. Eric and Paul, you're on washing-up duty. Decide between the two of you who's washing up and who's drying.'

'But, Dad,' Eric whined.

'You know the roster. That's why your mother had so many children – to help with the chores around the house. You want to eat, you've gotta work. A hard lesson in life, son, best learnt early.'

Annie whispered to Catherine, 'I'll have to wash them again afterwards but they are getting better.'

'I'm going to warm up the TV.' Dave stood, stretching his back. 'Gotta watch *GTK* tonight.'

'No, Dave.' Annie's voice held a warning.

'What's on the show?' Catherine didn't have a TV at the cottage. She had books and a transistor radio to keep her company, and Tim.

Dave hovered awkwardly. 'Oh, nothing really.'

Catherine didn't believe him. 'I think I'll watch it too. Consider it payment for making the apple charlotte.'

Annie seemed perturbed. 'Boys, time to do your homework.'

'So we don't have to wash up?' Paul asked.

'You can do it later,' Annie said, her mouth pinched. 'Out. Now.'

As the children filed out of the kitchen, Annie was quiet.

'What's going on?' Catherine was baffled.

It was Dave who answered, keeping a careful eye on Annie. 'Mark's new band is on *GTK* tonight to launch their latest single. Mark tells me it's the best song he's ever written.'

Catherine swallowed. Part of her wanted to make excuses and leave, but her overwhelming desire to know more won out. 'So, he's been in touch with you?'

'Yeah.'

Catherine realised how naive she'd been in assuming Mark had cut off everyone when he'd left the valley. Of course Mark had kept in contact with his best mate. And he hadn't missed a beat from the sound of it. He'd happily carried on with his glamorous, famous life while she pined for him back in Wattle Grove, wondering what she'd done wrong and agonising over why he'd never got in touch with her. 'I want to watch it.'

'What?' Annie looked startled.

'Let's hear this fantastic new single.' Anger stirred inside her.

'I don't think that's such a good idea.' Annie looked to Dave for support.

He moved towards the door. 'I promised Mark I'd watch it. If either of you want to join me, that's fine.'

Catherine followed him out of the kitchen, leaving Annie at the table staring at her hands.

Mark has a beard, Catherine noticed. And longer hair. Apart from that he looked exactly the same. He began to sing. That's his voice, she thought, the one I've sung harmonies with. The camera cut to his fingers playing guitar. Those hands have held mine and pressed against my skin. The song was melodic, with an easy loping beat. It was about having a simple life in the country and being free. Mark had a harmonica in a cradle around his neck and replicated the riff he was playing on his guitar. It was effective. She could see this being a hit. It caught the fantasy of a generation, fitting right into Tim's ethos and those like him. But it was far from her reality. Country life was about work and toil; battling the elements and bureaucracy to eke out a living.

The song ended and the host appeared, asking Mark what had inspired the band's new single. 'Some of the best days of my life were spent living on an orchard in Tasmania,' Mark said. 'I still long for the happiness I found there.'

'Why did you leave?' the host asked.

A shadow crossed Mark's face. 'They say the greatest writing comes from pain.' Then he laughed, a self-deprecating chuckle. 'Not that I'm saying this song is the greatest. But it's about something I long for every day.'

The *GTK* theme song began as the credits rolled. Catherine realised she was crying.

Dave touched her hand. 'Guess that's why Annie didn't want you to watch. She knew you'd be upset.'

Catherine rummaged in the pocket of her cardigan for a hanky. She nodded as she wiped her eyes.

'If you missed him so much why didn't you write back to him?' he asked, his eyes gentle and concerned.

'What?'

'His letters. He told me you never answered them.'

'What letters?'

'He sent them to your house. And rang your folks' place all the time. Charlie really wanted to say hello too, but you'd never come to the phone.'

Catherine blinked. None of this made any sense. She hadn't received any letters from Mark, or calls. Then slowly, memories hit her like cold metallic blows. Her father always insisted on answering the phone at the house. He'd jump up to get it, leaving the room to stand in the hallway and talk, though rarely for long. Sometimes he'd just hang up, saying it was a wrong number. Catherine had never considered her father might be lying to her.

'Mark asked me to talk to you,' Dave continued. 'But Annie thought it wasn't a good idea. Best not to get involved, she said.'

Catherine shivered despite the warmth of the fire. *Bellbird* was on the television now, but she wasn't interested in what Lori was up to with Charlie Cousens or what Adeline Phillips had to say about it. Her own soap opera was unfolding right here in the Pearsons' lounge room.

'He was worried when you didn't answer that first letter. But when you didn't reply to any of the others either, he was really hurt.'

'I never received that letter. Or any others.' Catherine couldn't think clearly. There was a buzzing in her head.

'He gave it to me to give to you. I left it in the kitchen. When it was gone I assumed Annie—'

They both turned to see Annie standing in the doorway, her arms crossed protectively over her chest.

'You gave it to Catherine, didn't you, darl? We talked about it.'

'I thought I had. We'd all had a big shock with Lara being dead and all. It was a tricky time. And hectic, with the harvest and the kids to look after. Maybe one of the kids got hold of it. I don't know.'

Catherine listened to her excuses knowing none of them rang true. Annie hadn't given her the letter. She'd admitted to never liking Mark. She was always warning Catherine about him. And as for the other letters? If her father was capable of blocking Mark's calls, what was he capable of doing with his letters? Catherine was never home when the post arrived. She was at school, making money to keep the orchard afloat. A cold blackness threatened to engulf her, but she refused to let it. Other priorities were more urgent.

'I have two questions,' she said to Dave, deliberately turning away from Annie. 'Do you have a phone number for him?'

'Yes. What's the other question?'

'Can I use your phone?'

30

May 1971
Mark

Mark had never meant to lie. And he hadn't meant to stay away so long. But after Lara's funeral some old friends had persuaded him to come over for a jam session. One session turned into many more. Their drummer, Tigger, booked them some gigs at the Thumpin' Tum, then word spread and the crowds increased. When the record companies started sniffing around, the band found a manager and from there the whole thing had escalated. Mark went along for the ride. After years of heartache, confusion and hard physical labour, he was happy to be swept up in the flow. Gigging and touring with this band was different from the start – they were older, wiser and battle-scarred. Mark was thirty-two now, and the rest of the band were a similar age, happily no longer the target for screaming teenagers. Television made it easier to reach a wider audience without having to drag themselves around the country. Even so, on the back of this new single, and the album, Mark had committed to an Australia-wide tour. Why not? He had nothing to lose.

He knew he'd pushed Catherine away before he'd left Wattle Grove, but at the time he was capable of little else. Lara's death had been such a visceral shock. Guilt tormented him. The fact her body had been down a gully for so long, ravaged by fire and animals, disturbed him still. Any emotional reserves he had left went to comforting his son. Charlie barely remembered his mother, being only two when she'd left, but he knew he was supposed to feel sad. But it was Catherine Charlie had yearned for after they returned to Melbourne. When Mark's letters went unanswered he'd been hurt but unsurprised. Lies escalated, even the small ones. He should never have kept anything from her. He'd said that, in his letters. But instead of bringing them closer his words had blown them apart. It had been nearly a year now and Mark could only blame himself.

The closing credits rolled on *GTK*. The rest of the band were watching it at Tigger's place, where a party was sure to be raging, but Mark had wanted to watch it with Charlie. 'What did you reckon? Did your dad do all right?'

'You look funny in black and white,' Charlie said.

Mark chuckled. He could always trust Charlie to keep his feet on the ground.

The phone rang in the hallway. It'd be the band bragging about their performance. 'Hey, guys,' he said into the mouthpiece, ignoring the pips. 'Yeah, it was real cool.'

There was a pause on the other end of the line and an intake of breath. Mark hesitated. He should have known the pips meant a long-distance call. It wasn't the band.

'Who is this?'

Still nothing, except an odd snuffling noise.

'You're wasting your money calling long distance. I'm going to hang up.'

'Mark?' The woman's voice was trembling. 'Is that you?'

The voice sounded familiar but he wasn't sure. 'Yeah, this is Mark.'

'I never received your letters.'

The blood hammered in his head. He slumped onto the stool next to the phone table. 'Catherine.' Why was she calling? 'Are you all right?'

'I'm sorry.'

'What for? It's all my fault.' He talked quickly, frightened she'd hang up like her father had so many times. 'I felt so guilty about Lara. If I hadn't dragged her to Tasmania she'd still be alive. I couldn't bear it. I couldn't think about anything else for a while there. I tried to apologise in my letters.'

'My dad, he must have thrown them all away. And Dave told me you tried to call.' He could hear her crying down the line.

'Shh, it's okay. We're talking now.' After all the months of hurt and bewilderment, he felt nothing but relief to hear her voice again. To know he wasn't responsible for her long silence.

'It's not okay. I'm angry with my father. And with ...' She paused. 'I'm devastated to think I hurt you in any way. I never meant to. If I'd known—'

He hushed her gently, making soothing sounds down the line. 'Darling Catherine, I thought I'd scared you off with my stupid lies. I was hurt I never heard from you, but I could understand why.'

'What do you mean?'

'About reporting Lara missing. I never got to do it.'

'Oh, that. Annie ...' Her voice almost strangled the name. 'She mentioned it. I wasn't worried. Just confused.'

Mark tightened his grip on the receiver. 'It was a stupid mistake. I was embarrassed and didn't tell Dave the truth. When I went to the Huonville police station, I was recognised by a couple of teenagers. They started hassling me. Jesus, the whole place was still in bedlam after the fires and all they wanted to do was give me the third degree about The Scene. I tried to shake them off but they followed me. I couldn't report Lara missing with them hanging around. Those kids would've run to the papers with any whiff of a scandal. It was stupid to lie to Dave, but I felt like an idiot, you know. Worried about teenagers when there was so much more at stake.'

'I get it.' Her voice was calmer, steadier.

'Yeah, well. After Lara's body was found, the police weren't so understanding. The whole thing blew up in my face. I never want to lie again. Especially not to you. I—' Mark stopped himself. He'd made a promise to Dave.

'Come back, please. I've missed you so much.' The yearning in her voice matched his own.

'Who you talking to, Daddy?' Charlie emerged from the lounge room.

Mark heard Catherine gasp. 'Is that Charlie?'

'You want to speak to him?'

'Yes, please.'

Mark held the receiver out to Charlie. 'You'll never guess who. It's Catherine.'

'Cat? Really?'

Mark watched warily. Over the past year, Charlie had drawn her pictures, signing each one very carefully with his name, which Mark had posted with his letters. He'd told his son that Catherine thought they were great and sent him all her love. Another lie.

Charlie pressed the receiver to his ear. When he heard her voice, his face brightened. 'I lost my front tooth ...'

'Yes, the Tooth Fairy came ...'

'Ten cents ...'

'I spent it on mixed lollies. A big bag of milk bottles and freckles and clinkers.'

As Mark listened, he began to relax. What he'd longed for this past lonely year had happened. Catherine was back in his life. And Charlie's. Mark had a tour to get through but after that, just like his latest song, they were going home.

31

May 1971

Annie

The flames started slowly, licking their way through the dry grass and kindling. There was a moment of hesitation when the fire could either fizzle in a whisper of grey smoke or forge on to catch the larger sticks and branches. The orange glow increased, the flames licked at the carefully placed wood, snaking its way up until at last it reached the top, and exploded in a shower of sparks. For a moment Annie's thoughts darted to another time, another fire. The smell of burning eucalyptus always conjured the fear and panic of that day. Tonight's bonfire was different – a celebration deep in the heart of winter with a welcome warmth for all those gathered around in jackets, scarves, hats and mittens.

Michael whooped with glee. 'See, I told you it'd work,' he said to Eric. 'You just gotta angle the wood right.'

'But that was my idea, stacking the old palings like that. That's why it went up.'

236

Annie sighed. Her oldest boys were always trying to outdo each other. Tonight the result was worth it. The kids shouted and squealed as they ran around the burning heap, some waving sparklers in the air. Cracker night was always exciting for the children, almost as much as Christmas. They could hardly wait for Dave to put a match to the fireworks. Her husband, always cautious around fire, had cleared a patch in the paddock for the Roman candles and set up bottles for the rockets.

There were always some who complained about cracker night – it wasn't safe, it scared the dogs and spooked the horses – so Annie had invited all the neighbours. Many families had turned up with thermoses of tea, marshmallows for the kids to toast, and more fireworks. Annie searched the faces in the glow of the fire, hoping to see Catherine's among them. She was disappointed, again.

Dave hugged her from behind. 'The boys did really well,' he said, a note of fatherly pride in his voice.

'You sure it's okay to let Michael light the rockets?'

'He's thirteen now, and'll do a good job, I'm sure.'

Still, Annie worried. The government had banned the sale of double bungers this year. The stories of children losing a finger or of being badly burnt always concerned her. 'Angela, darling,' she called to her daughter. 'Come closer to Mummy, that's the way.'

'The apple wood is burning well.' Dave smelt of smoke.

'At least it's good for something.'

They'd grubbed out more apple trees from the Fletchers' old place. The trees were past their prime anyway, but it was a sign of how troubled the industry was when not even the Cleopatras could get a decent price. Another shipping strike hadn't helped. Over a hundred ships were tied up in Australian ports all because some stewards had been fired.

'We'll be okay,' Dave said. 'This new stabilisation scheme will help.'

'How, exactly? If we ever get decent prices again, we'll have to pay it back to the government. I don't see the point.'

'Well, at least it'll help us get through this year.' He straightened up. 'Now, I think it's time we put on a show. Come on, kids. Who wants to see some fireworks?'

The children came running, faces flushed from the bonfire and eyes wide with excitement. Annie kept a protective hand on her daughter as Michael lit the first rocket, his tongue sticking out between his teeth as he concentrated on the task. The rocket flew into the sky, exploding into a shower of gold and red. Dave let Eric light one of the Roman candles, and Michael, not to be outdone, launched another rocket into the clear night sky. When the light show was over the kids were given rows of tom thumbs to throw into the fire. Annie was keen to get Angela away from the pops and bangs of the crackers. The bonfire had settled into itself, the glowing coals sending out a steady heat, but only feet away the winter night was bitter.

As they picked their way across the paddock by torchlight, Annie's thoughts turned to Catherine. She wasn't surprised Jack and Judith Turner hadn't turned up tonight. They'd be tucked up in bed by now with hot water bottles warming their feet. But Catherine was a different matter. She'd always loved cracker night and since her return to the valley had never missed one. Even last year, without the company of Mark and Charlie, she'd been here helping the smaller children with their sparklers and admiring the fiery display in the sky. Now she wouldn't even talk to Annie. She'd turned up at the packing shed each afternoon after school to help with the harvest but kept contact to a bare minimum. It hurt, but Annie knew she'd brought it on herself. Destroying Mark's letter had been a risk, but there was no alternative. As soon as she'd read his words to Catherine about no more lies, Annie had panicked and thrown it in the fire. For the first few months she'd been on edge, but as time went by she'd begun to relax, believing the danger was over. She was wrong. Why did Mark have to become famous again? Didn't he come to their orchard to get away from all of that? Why did he have to be on that stupid TV show, looking like a hippie with his long hair and beard, singing a sappy song about making his way home? Catherine need never have known. But instead here they were, enemies instead of friends.

Back in the house, Annie helped Angela wash the last of the toasted marshmallows from her sticky fingers and brush her teeth. She popped her into a clean pair of pink pyjamas, nicely warm from the clothes airer, and tucked her into the small bed in the corner of their bedroom. They'd been hoping to build an extension on the house, but the prices for apples were dismal. Annie had thought about asking her parents for help but couldn't bring herself to beg. Instead, Dave, with some help from Michael and Eric, was painting the sunroom pink. It would be a pretty room when they were done, but even so Annie would miss having Angela in the same room where some nights she'd stay awake just to watch her daughter sleeping.

The house was silent, but Annie's thoughts were in turmoil. She wasn't the only one who'd lied to Catherine. The rift between Catherine and her father was worse than ever. Annie didn't care if they never made amends, but she urgently needed to be reunited with Catherine before Mark came back. Clearly he hadn't told her yet; he must be waiting until he returned to the valley. Then she was sure he'd reveal everything. She had to make Catherine listen to her side first. Annie checked her daughter. Angela's breath was calm and even, indicative of a deep sleep. Annie so rarely had a moment to herself, let alone the ability to do something without her family knowing. This might be her only chance. She agonised about leaving Angela, but at four years old she was too heavy to carry all that way. Better she stay here, safe and asleep. Annie grabbed the torch and quietly left the house.

The gravel of the driveway crunched under her feet as she avoided the ruts and potholes leading to Catherine's door. The faithful old Hillman sat beside the house as usual, but behind it was a car Annie didn't recognise. Curious, Annie crept up the steps to the verandah. She could hear Catherine speaking, along with the low murmur of a male voice. Annie peeked in the window. The lamp in the lounge room cast a dim glow. Catherine sat at one end of the small couch and next to her was a blond, long-haired man. Was that Tim? Annie was baffled. Catherine had treated Annie like a pariah over that letter, never believing Annie's claims that it was a simple mistake, yet here she was getting cosy with another man, with Mark all but forgotten. Annie felt something shift inside her.

She knocked. 'Catherine, it's Annie. Just wanted to check you got our invitation to cracker night.'

Catherine opened the door. Her face was tight. 'What are you doing here?'

'We missed you tonight.' She peered inside. 'Tim? Of all people. I didn't expect to see you here.'

Catherine took a step backwards. 'He was just leaving.'

Tim didn't take his eyes off Catherine. 'But I love you.'

'We've been over this. You don't love me. You're in love with your idea of me.'

'Please, Catherine. We had such plans. You and me in Bali. The beaches and the dragon fruit.'

Annie was transfixed by the scene playing out in front of her. Tim might be good looking, but he'd always been slightly unhinged.

'They were your plans. Not mine.'

240

'But—'

'Please, Tim.' Catherine's voice was cold. 'Just leave.'

Tim had the look of a man who knew he was beaten. 'All right, I'll go.' He picked up his jacket from the arm of the couch, then paused by the doorway, addressing Annie for the first time. 'Try to change her mind, please. I know she digs me. No woman can do the things we've done without being in love.'

Annie shut the door behind him, thinking hard about what to say. Catherine stood, arms crossed, glaring at her.

Annie had some ammunition. But would she use it? She'd come here to try to patch things up, not make them worse. 'That was unexpected.'

'Why are you here?'

'I was hoping you'd come to cracker night. It's not the same without you. Nothing is.'

'You should have thought of that before.'

'It was one small mistake. I honestly thought I'd given you the letter.'

'How dare you talk to me about honesty? Why didn't you tell me about Mark's calls to Dave? He rang constantly, desperate to get a message to me.'

'I thought it was for the best. Least said, soonest mended.'

'What does that even mean?' Catherine's face was white with anger. 'He loves me, Annie. Mark loves me. And I might never have known. I spent a year in agony, despising myself because he'd rejected me. I thought I'd be alone for the rest of my life. I only did this—' she flung out an arm, words escaping her for a moment, '— this *thing* with Tim because of that. I just wanted to be with a man. To know what it was like. And it felt good. *I* felt good. Powerful, you know?'

Annie knew too well. It had led to a shotgun marriage.

'But it never would have happened if you'd been a true friend. If you hadn't lied.' Catherine almost spat the words at her.

'You don't understand,' Annie pleaded. This wasn't the scenario she'd painted in her head. She'd imagined the two of them talking out their differences and becoming friends again. Only then could she trust Catherine with the truth. 'There are things you need to know but—'

'Now you want to tell me things? You deliberately kept information from me knowing how heartbroken I was. How could you?'

'It's Mark. Not me.' Annie's voice rang high and shrill in her head. 'He could ruin everything. I'm just trying to protect my family.'

Catherine frowned, as if calculating Annie's words and coming up with an odd equation.

Panic rose in Annie's chest. 'Forget what I said.' How could everything have gone so wrong so quickly? Frantically she tried to think of a way to turn it around. Her frenzied mind found another tactic. 'He could make trouble for you.'

Catherine paused. 'Who, Mark?'

'Tim. What would your dad say? What would people think?'

'My father thinks what he likes, most of it lies.' Catherine glowered. 'And as for the rest? I really don't care.'

'But what if Mark knew?' The threat lingered in the room like the cloying stench of rotting apples.

Catherine stared at Annie, fierce and unflinching. 'I'll tell him myself. I have nothing to be ashamed of. It's not as if we were married. He and I will have no secrets between us. No lies.'

Annie swayed. The light changed as if darkness was pressing around her. She found the solid door behind her and reached for the knob. Catherine stood, strong and proud. Annie remembered the first time they'd met. Catherine had been barely a teenager, awkward and shy, hiding behind her long straight hair. Annie had sensed a need in her, a yearning to connect, despite her parents' initial disapproval of any friendship between them. Annie, knowing friends would be hard to find in the small and close-knit community, was keen to nurture that connection. Catherine could be the younger sister Annie had always wanted but never had. The idea especially appealed since her own family had so recently rejected her. Catherine had eagerly fallen into the role and Annie had relished taking her under her wing.

But who was Catherine now, this woman of the world, so certain of herself? Catherine was a stranger to her, and dangerous. When Mark returned that threat would grow. Together, there was nothing Catherine and Mark couldn't destroy. Her thoughts fled to Angela tucked up in bed, alone in the house. What had she been thinking? Without another word, she rushed back out into the frigid night.

32

July 1971

Catherine

The fallen leaves crackled under Catherine's feet as she walked through the orchard. Her breath hung in a heavy cloud just beyond her lips and frost remained in the shadows, even past ten in the morning. The trees were all but naked – only a few tenacious leaves, brown and withered, still clung to branches here and there, a reminder of the season past. She and her father had begun the pruning last month to remove the unwanted growth and to help control the crop for next season. More pruning remained to be done in the short, cold afternoons after school but the coming season held promise. Yesterday, while her father ploughed the dirt, Catherine had bent her back to the thankless task of hoeing around the trees. They maintained a cold civility, for the sake of the orchard, but little more.

Today was Sunday, her one day off. Sometimes she drove to the church in Cygnet, but this morning she wouldn't be part of

244

the congregation. Mark had called last night. He and Charlie had crossed Bass Strait safely and were on the way to Launceston. By now they'd be heading towards the valley, to her.

They'd be hungry after the long drive, and Charlie had always loved scones, so she'd baked some fresh this morning. They nestled under a clean tea towel in her basket along with a pot of clotted cream, a box of tea, a bottle of milk and a jar of her mother's homemade blackberry jam. Her mother would never visit her at the cottage. It reminded her of those hard months after the fire, when the grief was too raw to bear. But sometimes she'd go with Catherine to pick blackberries growing wild along the fence lines. The thorny bushes were considered a pest, prolific and hard to destroy, but no one could deny the deliciousness of the berries. Her mother was still subdued, barely the woman Catherine remembered from before the fire, and hardly left the house. Catherine was grateful that, once in a while, she'd join her and they'd walk in the fresh air together.

Catherine's pace quickened as she crossed the dirt road and made her way through the Pearsons' orchard towards the pickers' hut. It felt good to stretch her legs and use some of the pent-up energy humming through her body. She'd admitted to Mark that she was nervous. 'It'll be just like old times,' he'd said. But it wouldn't. So much had changed. Mark and she were finally free to be together. Tim was long gone. She didn't miss him, but she was grateful. He'd been a caring and generous lover, teaching her about her body and the pleasure it gave. One day she would share that pleasure with Mark.

The hut came into view through the trees, the wood greyed with age and the corrugated iron roof faded to a patchy red. Her heart soared, imagining Mark stepping through the door with Charlie pushing past to fly down the wooden steps towards her. But the door remained closed, the curtains drawn. It would be dusty in there and in need of a good airing.

After making the hut as hospitable as possible and laying out the scones and jam, Catherine turned her attention to the fireplace. With some encouragement and the addition of more kindling, finally the fire burnt brightly in the hearth, dispelling the winter chill from the hut. It was too cold to sit outside on the porch but even so Catherine placed the old rickety chairs out there, just as they were before Mark had left. She wanted everything to feel as familiar as possible. Catherine heard the sound of an engine, a low throaty burble. Mark's new car. Charlie said it looked like a bee, bright yellow with black stripes, but roared like a lion. Catherine peered down the rutted track, hoping the car wasn't too low slung or it would never get up the driveway. The car eased along the track, coming to a stop in front of the hut.

Mark jumped out and beamed at her. 'Hi, honey, I'm home.'

The hammering in her chest threatened to burst it wide open. Mark was here and he was hers. She drank in his eyes, his face, his body. The beard made him look older, but he was still the handsome man she'd fallen for.

'Cat!' Charlie pushed open the heavy car door and clambered out. He was taller and his face a little longer, losing the chubby cheeks she remembered so well.

Catherine ran down to meet them, longing to feel Mark's arms around her, but it was Charlie who was at her side first. 'Charlie. How's my little mouse?'

He hesitated.

Had she said the wrong thing? Was he too old for childish games? She tried a different tack, struggling to keep her voice steady. 'I've missed you so much. We've got a lot to catch up on. I bet you could thrash me at gin rummy these days.'

Charlie's face changed and he burrowed into her arms. 'I missed you too,' he said, his voice muffled.

246

Catherine hugged him tight, overjoyed. She felt Mark's hand touch her shoulder. 'Can I join in?'

Catherine had planned to look stunning and composed, dressed in her new tight v-neck jumper and flares. She'd wanted to show him she was as good as any of those city girls. Instead her face was probably a mess, with mascara running and her nose red from the cold. It didn't matter. The look in Mark's eyes was enough to dispel any lingering doubts of how he felt about her. Charlie nestled into her side as Mark's strong arms encircled them both. She breathed them in with a shuddering sigh. This is what she'd yearned for and now, after so long, it was happening.

Charlie was the first to break away. 'I'm hungry. Is there anything to eat?'

'I made scones, just for you.'

'Yay.' Charlie raced up the steps and disappeared into the hut.

Mark took her hand. It was smoother than she remembered, except for the calluses on his fingertips. She stroked them gently. 'Someone's been playing a lot of guitar.'

'From east to west, and north to south. But that's done with now. I think you might be interested in how smooth my lips are though. Unlike my fingers, they haven't had a lot of use at all.'

Catherine lowered her eyes to take in those lips. 'I've never kissed a man with a beard.' The energy fizzed through her body, little sparks igniting every nerve.

'I'm glad to hear it.' His voice was husky as he pulled her towards him, and his body warm as she pressed against him. Mark lifted her head to meet his lips.

'Stop all that yucky kissing stuff.' Charlie was on the porch, waving a scone at them. 'Come and have scones.'

Catherine laughed. 'The way to a man's heart.'

'You already have my heart. It's never wavered.'

She touched his lips with her fingers. 'So smooth,' she said. 'And all mine.'

Catherine took in the bright yellow car with fancy black stripes. It was certainly going to turn heads in Cygnet. 'Charlie's right, it does look like a bee.'

Mark pretended to frown. 'I think it looks more like a tiger.'

'Of course, I see that now.' She snuggled close to the warmth of his body. She never wanted to stop touching him, if only to be sure he was actually here. 'What kind of car is it?'

'HG Monaro. A GTS 350 V8. Came out last year.' Mark spoke with a pride she found fondly amusing. 'Driving down from Launceston today was the first time I could really let her rip. What a blast.'

'How nice for you and HG. I hope you'll be very happy together for many years.'

'I think we're all going to be very happy together.' He bent to kiss her.

'Scones.' Charlie's voice was insistent. 'Please.'

Reluctantly they broke away but their hands remained enfolded in each other's as they walked inside.

Charlie proved just how hungry he was by scoffing down three scones, topped with jam and cream. Catherine only nibbled at hers – her appetite for food had been replaced with a hunger for Mark's touch. 'Is the band really okay with you coming back to the valley?' she asked. 'With all your success I would've thought they'd want you to stay in Melbourne.'

Mark finished his scone and licked a smudge of jam from the side of his mouth. 'They're more than okay, stoked actually. Our manager said it was a masterful stroke of publicity.' He put his plate down on the apple box serving as a side table.

'In what way?'

'"Long Road Home" is a massive hit, and now here's the man who wrote it living what the song is about. I've come home to the simple life and the woman I love. *Go-Set* did a whole feature on it and our album went skyrocketing back to number one.'

'But don't they want another album? Another tour?' Catherine couldn't suppress the worry in her voice. Now he was back she never wanted him to leave again.

Mark leant forward, his knees touching hers. 'Here's the thing. The hardest part about being in a band is being in a band. You spend all your time together; gigging, recording, touring. It can start to bum you out. With these guys, all of us are old enough to know how quickly a good thing can go bad. We're going to take it easy, do the odd gig, maybe some festivals, but after this tour we all knew we needed a long break.' He stroked her fingers, sending sparks through her body. 'A really long break.'

'Yeah,' said Charlie, wiping jam and crumbs from his mouth. 'Like me and Granny and Grandpa. We like hanging out together but sometimes it gets boring.'

'I'm sure they love you very much.' Catherine knew Lara's parents doted on Charlie. Mark had been grateful to have such enthusiastic babysitters, especially when he was on tour. Before Lara's death they'd been confused and saddened by their daughter's behaviour. Mark had told her that Lara had shut them out of her life in the months before they came to the valley. Her death had left them shattered, but having Charlie around had eased their pain somewhat.

'They're pretty cool, but not about my frogs.'

'You still like frogs?' Catherine glimpsed the young boy she used to know.

'Hard to find in Melbourne. Can I go down to the creek and look for tadpoles?'

'We might have to wait until spring,' Catherine said. 'It's a bit cold for tadpoles at the moment. But we can still go and try.'

'Now?' Charlie jumped off his stool, sending crumbs flying, and raced for the door.

Mark smiled apologetically. 'Sorry. He's been cooped up in the car for so long. I think he needs to let some of that energy out.' He stood, offering his hand to Catherine.

'I know how he feels,' Catherine said softly, blushing at the inference of her words. She took Mark's hand to stand, leaning close against him. In his eyes she saw a desire that matched her own.

'There will be a time,' he whispered, his voice low and throaty. He traced her jawline with his fingers. 'Soon.'

'Come on,' Charlie said, struggling into his parka.

Catherine kissed Mark lightly on the lips. 'I'm going to hold you to that.'

Charlie returned to school in Cygnet and, almost as if he'd never been away, quickly became a country kid again, with scabbed knees and muddy gumboots. Mark began work in the orchard with Dave, living the country life he'd sung about. It had only been a few days, but Catherine could hardly bear to be apart from him. At night her sleep was restless, dreaming of his touch. Her days were distracted. When Mark turned up at the cottage without Charlie the following Sunday afternoon, she was overcome with relief and a delicious sense of anticipation.

'Dave offered to take Charlie fishing with his boys.' Mark chuckled. 'I think he might've guessed we wanted some time alone.'

Catherine pulled him inside, hungry for the taste of his lips. 'The whole afternoon and you're all mine.' They fell onto the couch laughing and kissing, finally free to explore each other's mouths and bodies. Catherine tugged at Mark's jacket as the desire hummed through her. She wanted his skin against hers, his hands on her body, and the hunger she had for him quenched.

'Whoa,' Mark said, through her kisses. 'Let's slow this down, just a little.'

Catherine stopped, confused. 'Why? I'm not ... well, you know.' Before he'd returned to the valley, she'd told Mark about Tim. Even though it would have broken her heart if he'd changed his mind about coming back, she wanted him to know the truth while there was still time. His reassurance had been a balm. But he did admit to hoping he'd be the only man she wanted from now on. It was a promise she was happy to give.

'Don't get me wrong.' He cradled her face in his hands. 'I want this as much as you. But there's something I need to do first.'

Catherine watched him as he rummaged in the pocket of his jacket. 'Ah, here it is.'

He went down on one knee in front of her, holding a small velvet box.

Catherine pressed her hands against her chest. She hadn't imagined this might happen so soon. They'd talked about love and being together, but never marriage.

Mark smiled into her eyes. 'Catherine Turner. Would you do me the honour of being my wife?' He opened the box and inside was a delicate ring studded with tiny sapphires encircling a diamond that threw out prisms of light.

She couldn't answer. Words had deserted her. Instead she lowered her head and extended the fingers of her left hand.

Mark slipped the ring on her finger.

She stared at her hand, silent and awestruck.

'Are you okay?' he asked, gently touching her arm.

'I never expected ... I didn't think ...' She looked at his face, the laugh lines round his eyes, the dark beard surrounding his lips. This was the man she loved, and he wanted her to be his wife. She sighed with a deep happiness. 'We're going to get married.'

'Yes, we are.' Mark joined her on the couch. 'So, shall we take up from where we stopped? I believe you were tearing my clothes off.'

'Yes, but not here.' She led him to the bedroom, kicking off her boots and socks as she went. He followed suit and they stood, barefoot, pressed against each other, their kiss deep and urgent. She felt a familiar hardness press against her leg. Playfully, she pushed him onto the bed, following him down. They lay beside each other gazing into each other's eyes for a moment. She drank in the reality of Mark here, in her bed, then his lips were on hers, his tongue hot in her mouth and the passion flared again.

Wrapping her legs around him, she rolled him over on to his back, grateful for the lessons she'd learnt from Tim. She straddled his body and leant over to kiss him, her hair falling loose around her cheeks. Mark reached up, pulled her jumper off over her head, and began unbuttoning her blouse. Slowly his fingers worked their way down, brushing against her skin and sending delicious shivers through her body. She closed her eyes, relishing the sensation, and delighting in the knowledge of what was to come. They had waited so long.

Catherine let her blouse fall from her shoulders and reached back to unclasp her bra, watching Mark's expression when he saw her naked breasts. His eyes darkened with desire.

'My beautiful Catherine,' he whispered and raised himself up to kiss her lips, her throat, her breasts.

She rolled away and stood beside the bed. Shimmying out of her jeans and panties she stood completely naked in front of him. Catherine enjoyed the sense of power she had in her nakedness, quite the opposite of what she'd been taught by the Church and society. She might well be a temptress here in the orchard surrounded by

252

apples, the fruit of knowledge, but there was nothing evil here, nothing to be ashamed of, just her and Mark and their love.

Mark groaned and reached for her.

'Let me undress you,' she said. She leant over and pulled his jumper off along with his T-shirt, then slowly, with a knowing smile on her face, she unzipped his jeans and tugged them down over his hips.

'I want to kiss you, now,' he said, his voice low and thick.

Catherine removed his last piece of clothing and let her eyes wander over his body, strong and lithe, with a smattering of dark hair leading down to the place she longed to touch. 'Where would you like to kiss me?' she asked.

'Everywhere.' He pulled her to him and pressed his body against her. His fingers and lips explored her body, then his tongue traced a line over her stomach and down between her legs. Her body pulsed with a need so deep it made her moan. She reached for him. As he moved inside her she dissolved into a state both familiar and strange. The world she knew slipped away and there was no going back. She was light, she was energy, she was everything. And then she was nothing. Drifting like a feather on the breeze. Later Catherine lay her head against his chest and swayed with the rise and fall of his breath. She was home.

33

August 1971

Catherine

'So, Mark's back, then.'

It was a clear, still morning. The mist had burnt off early, leaving the pale sky cloudless and bright. But the cold was always there, turning toes and fingers numb. Catherine and her father were pruning in the lower block and had paused for a warming cuppa from the thermos.

'That's right.' Catherine stopped herself from adding, *No thanks to you.*

'You know what everybody's talking about?'

Catherine said nothing. No doubt the gossips were indulging in their usual tittle-tattle.

'That car.' He slowly shook his head. 'Hardly suitable. What was he thinking?'

'Not that he'd be coming back to Wattle Grove.' Her words had a bite to them she couldn't hide. She was willing to work with her father,

254

but his betrayal still hurt. In time she'd forgive him, but sometimes the anger rose unbidden.

'I only did what any father would. You can't blame me for trying to protect you.'

Catherine buried her response by taking a sip of tea. Her father had admitted what he'd done, but had never apologised for it. In his mind his actions were justified. It was a fight she wasn't going to win. Her victory came in being with Mark.

'He's asked me to marry him.' She watched the expression on her father's face change from righteous to worried.

'What answer did you give?'

Catherine took off her work glove, displaying her left hand and the ring that sparkled there. 'I said yes.'

'Right.'

'That's it? I thought "congratulations" might be more appropriate.'

'In my day a young man asked the father's permission first. Everything's changing so fast, and not always for the better.'

'Gee, thanks, Dad.' Catherine threw the last of her tea on the ground and put her glove back on. 'I'm going to work on the trees in the second row.' She needed some distance.

'Are you certain, about him? The rumours—'

Catherine turned to face him. 'What rumours, Dad? There've been so many.'

'He lied about reporting his wife missing. There's some suspicion he might have—'

Catherine threw her hands up in frustration. 'The police investigated and found there was no foul play. Who do you believe? Them or some troublemakers at the pub?'

'If you're sure—'

'I love him, Dad. And Charlie. And they love me. It's as simple as that.'

Her father sighed. 'Well then, I guess you'd better bring him home to meet your mother.'

Later in the week, Mark and Charlie arrived at Catherine's cottage dressed in their best clothes. Charlie's hair was neatly brushed, and Mark looked more like the man she'd first met, now he'd shaved off his beard.

Catherine touched his smooth cheek. 'I kinda liked that beard. I'm going to miss it.'

'Well, I can always grow it again.' He held her fingers in his own. 'But for now it's best to look less like a hippy and more like a respectable suitor.'

'Are you nervous?'

'Of course. Your dad is formidable.'

'What does that mean, Dad?' Charlie asked.

'It means he's a tough old guy. So make sure you're on your best behaviour.' His smile softened his words.

Catherine was on edge as well. Not only was she marrying a man widowed in extraordinary and much talked-about circumstances, but one with a young son. She wasn't sure how her mother would be, as her moods were often bleak. It might have been better to ease her into the situation, Mark first, then the both of them. But Mark had joked that her father would be less inclined to punch him if there was a child present, having heard the story about Tim.

Charlie dawdled on the walk to the house, wrapping his woollen scarf high around his chin. The winter sun was already waning and the temperature dropping with it. Mark and Catherine held hands and said little. Mark had generously forgiven Catherine's father for his subterfuge but seeing him face to face would be a test of his resolve.

At the house, Catherine's father met them at the door but instead of ushering them inside he joined them in the cold, closing the door behind him. Catherine's heart dropped. What was he playing at? He'd wanted this meeting to happen. Had he changed his mind?

She held her voice steady. 'Dad, this is Mark Davis, and Charlie. This is my father, Jack Turner.'

Mark reached out a gloved hand. 'Good to see you, Mr Turner.'

Catherine held her breath as her father hesitated. Finally he took Mark's hand and shook it, but with little more than a grunt.

'Is there a problem, Dad? Why are we out here?'

He crossed his arms. 'Before we go in, I want to know if you've set a date. For the wedding.'

Catherine looked at Mark in surprise. They hadn't talked about it. 'The sooner the better I think. A spring wedding.'

Mark nodded. 'I agree.'

Catherine's father looked less than pleased. 'No. That's not a good idea. And I'm only thinking of your mother here.'

'Mum? What do you mean?'

'You know how fragile she is. All of this is going to be a shock for her. She hasn't heard any of the—' He cleared his throat. 'As far as she's concerned, you two hardly know each other. She doesn't get out much and hasn't heard any different. The proper thing would be to introduce Mark as a friend first, announce your engagement in six months' time and set the wedding for next spring.'

'A year away?' Catherine was aghast.

'I think it would be best, for your mother.'

Catherine seethed. She should have known he'd try to complicate things, but how dare he use her mother as leverage. This was just a ruse. He had so little faith in her, or Mark, that he expected they'd break up before a year had passed. Or hoped they would. 'No, Dad. I have a ring on my finger and I'm not going to hide it from Mum.

Have you stopped to think that a wedding might make her happy? Having something to celebrate would lift her spirits.'

Mark stepped in. 'With all due respect, sir. I love your daughter and she loves me. I know the circumstances haven't been ideal—'

'You're right about that,' her father growled.

'But we've waited long enough. I think it's important Mrs Turner know how much I treasure her daughter and will do until the day I die. I don't want to lie to your wife, do you?'

Catherine stiffened, catching the hint of aggression in Mark's tone. How would her father respond?

'There are some things she might be better off not knowing,' he said, staring Mark in the eye.

Charlie was restless. 'It's cold. When are we going to go inside?'

'Soon, Charlie,' Mark said. 'We've just got to sort something out first.'

'When people see the ring, they're going to know I'm engaged.' Catherine's voice had an edge. 'Do you want me to lie to everybody?'

'All right, all right. Keep your voice down. You can announce your engagement today, but for God's sake, postpone the wedding for a while.'

Catherine looked at Mark. He nodded. She turned back to her father. 'Under duress. But not until next August. How about January?'

'It's too close to the anniversary of the fire. Your mother won't cope.'

'I'll be back teaching in February.'

'And then there's the harvest. No time then.'

Catherine knew her father was playing her, but she was willing to let this slide, for everybody's sake. Her father had done his best to keep her and Mark apart. He'd failed. Mark and her were committed to each other, the formality of a wedding could wait. 'June. Right after the harvest. But no later.'

'Done.'

'My June bride.' Mark squeezed her hand.

Laughter drifted from inside the house along with the enticing smell of home baking. Catherine noticed the door was ajar. 'Charlie?'

They found him in the kitchen with Catherine's mother, eating a chocolate biscuit. 'I've got a new granny.'

'What's that, son?' Catherine's father looked horrified.

Her mother put her hand on Charlie's shoulder. 'This young man tells me he has a granny in Melbourne but doesn't have one here.'

'So, I asked her to be my granny here,' Charlie said.

Catherine's mother smiled wistfully. 'I always wanted to be a grandmother.' She looked at Mark and then to Catherine with a quizzical expression. 'Do you have something to tell me, dear?'

34

February 1972
Catherine

The season turned, the trees blossomed and budded, and now the fruit was ripening on the trees. Catherine's father slowly came around to accepting Mark, mainly thanks to his wife's devotion to Charlie. The two of them spent many afternoons cooking up treats in the kitchen or piecing together jigsaw puzzles. Catherine was grateful to see a contentment and happiness, missing for so long, returning to her mother's life. Her father never acknowledged it, but Catherine was sure he knew his wife's wellbeing improved with each of Charlie's visits.

During the long summer break from teaching, Catherine worked with her father in the orchard; ploughing, hoeing, spraying for codling moth, looper grub and red spider mite, and checking and thinning the budding fruit to ensure the best crop possible. And it was going to be a good one this year. They were expecting a record harvest now the Red Delicious had finally come good. Hong Kong had opened up a brand-new market for Tasmanian apples, and the exporters and agents were beating a path to her father's door. He was smiling more these days, and easier to get on with.

Spraying was done early in the morning before the breeze picked up, so later in the day her time was her own. When Mark wasn't needed on the Pearsons' orchard, they spent long, slow afternoons with Charlie down by the river, swimming and fishing. Tea would often be flathead cooked over an open fire on the small beach at Petcheys Bay, followed by juicy apricots and nectarines from the home orchard. The twilights ebbed away slowly, with Catherine wrapped in Mark's arms, gazing across the river to the mountain ranges beyond, while Charlie waded through the shallows in his endless hunt for crabs. On the afternoons he wasn't with them or his granny, Charlie often played with Annie's boys. They were building a top-secret fort up in the bush beyond the orchard, no adults allowed. Today Mark and Catherine were grateful to the secret fort and the few hours alone it gave them.

Catherine took Mark's hand in hers and led him towards the cottage. She paused to kiss him on the verandah, their lips warm against each other's. His hands brushed gently along her arms and enfolded her in an embrace. Catherine leant her head against his chest.

'Happy?' Mark asked.

'Very.'

'Only three more months until you're my wife.'

'Three months?' She smiled up at him. 'Just as well we don't have to wait until then.' She opened the front door and backed slowly towards the bedroom, keeping her eyes on his.

Mark kicked the door closed with his foot as he followed her, taking hold of her outstretched hands. They fell on the bed in a tangle of hands and lips and arms. Catherine was always astounded by the passion she felt for Mark and the freedom she experienced when naked in his arms.

It was the distant rumble that roused her from a late-afternoon drowsiness. Catherine raised her head to find Mark smiling at her.

'Hello, beautiful,' he said and tucked a strand of her hair behind her ear.

She stretched and pressed against him, indulging in the sensation of his body strong against her own. Then she noticed the dimness of the room. 'What time is it?'

'It's only three. We still have plenty of time.'

'Then why's it so dark?' She clambered out of bed, instantly awake. Outside the bedroom window the sky was ominous. Huge banks of dark cloud tinged with an eerie green shifted and billowed, coming in fast from the south-west. 'No, no, no.' Catherine grabbed her clothes and began to dress, the panic rising in her chest.

Mark raised himself on an elbow. 'What's wrong? It's just a thunderstorm.'

'I've seen this before. The green light in the clouds. This is bad.'

'Why?' Mark swung his legs off the bed and sat up.

'I have to talk to my dad. The hail rockets went up in the fire and we didn't replace them. But someone must have one somewhere.'

'Hail rockets? What, like fireworks?'

'Not quite but the same concept. Two pounds of TNT blasted into the clouds to stop hailstones forming.'

The wind picked up, rushing through the valley along the river and pushing the storm towards them. A flash of light filled the room and within seconds a crack of thunder shook the window panes in their frames. Catherine stamped her feet into her boots and headed towards the door. Hail had ripped through the valley, wiping out the apple crop every leap year from the 1940s through to 1964. She'd heard the stories and seen the damage; the year's work gone, useless ravaged fruit going to waste, the trees damaged and battered. There hadn't been hail for so long now, they'd become complacent.

The rattle of wind and rain on the tin roof grew stronger, drowning out Mark's voice as he called out to her. 'Don't go out there.' He was shouting to be heard over the roar of the storm.

'It's 1972.'

'What?'

'It's a leap year.'

Mark shook his head, clearly thinking he'd heard her wrong through the howling wind buffeting the cottage. Catherine tried to open the door but the storm snatched it from her and slammed it shut. She tried again but Mark laid a hand on her arm. 'You'll never get to your dad's place. Not in this.'

Another crack of thunder, so close the floorboards trembled under her feet. Mickey jumped from his comfortable spot on an armchair and ran to hide under the couch.

There was so much fear in Catherine, stirring from deep inside. She'd seen the hail rockets go up when she was a kid, always from a safe distance, but even so the boom they made shook the ground. She and Peter would watch as the trail of smoke headed into the inky darkness of the clouds. It was like magic. The blackest of clouds would turn white. The hail melted and fell as rain. She had to talk to her dad, now. As she reached for the phone, Mark blocked her way, shaking his head. She could see his mouth forming the word 'no', but couldn't hear him over the storm. Lightning flooded the cottage with a light so pure it made her wince and the force of the corresponding thunder almost threw her off her feet.

The sharp tapping on the roof sounded like hungry birds trying to peck their way in. The tapping grew stronger, fiercer, until it was as if nature was throwing rocks at them in her fury. Catherine closed her eyes and ached at the sound of destruction. All that work, and heartbreak. So many disappointments over the years and then the jubilation of a record harvest on the way, until this. She threw herself at the front door, forcing it open against the wind and cracking it back against its hinges. The storm rushed in around her, lashing her with its brutality. The sharp hard ice of the hailstones ripped her skin and bruised her body. Catherine fell to her knees and screamed into the howling wind in frustration.

Strong arms pulled her back into the living room. Mark cradled her as they crouched dripping on the floor, her body leaning into his. He whispered in her ear, words of comfort and love, words she could barely decipher over the sound of the storm. They stayed, huddled together, until the wind dropped and the roof no longer rattled under the weight of the hail.

'It's okay, Catherine. Everything will be all right.' Mark's voice was like a chant, soothing her as her heartbeat steadied and her breathing eased.

A calm settled over the cottage. Sunlight broke through the dispersing clouds. Catherine scrambled to her feet. She had to see the damage. Like pulling off a Band-aid, it was best done quickly. She knew what she would see. The orchard in ruins, the apples destroyed, all of the years of sweat and toil since the fires wasted. She took a breath and walked outside. Hailstones littered the ground like ice cubes glinting in the sun, out of place but oddly beautiful. The trees around the cottage were shredded, battered and stripped by the storm. She lifted her gaze to take in the rest of the orchard. Mark came and stood beside her, taking his hand in her own. She frowned through narrowed eyes, not making sense of what she was seeing.

'Far out,' Mark said. 'That's crazy.'

Catherine nodded. She'd heard hailstorms could happen this way – ravaging one block of orchard or one complete strip, leaving the trees on either side untouched – but she'd never seen it so clearly demonstrated before. The cottage sat in a line of ruined trees barely four rows deep. On either side the leaves glistened green in the sunlight, the small apples perfectly preserved, the trees healthy and whole. The shrill ring of the telephone interrupted her astonishment. She walked in a daze to pick up the receiver.

'Catherine, it's your father.' He always introduced himself to her on the phone as if she'd never recognise him otherwise. 'I can hardly believe it. The Red Delicious are good. They're undamaged.'

'Oh, Dad. When the hail started ...' She took a breath, the nightmare still so close.

'I know, I know.' His voice held a warmth she'd missed for so long. 'But the orchard has survived. We're going to harvest a record crop and by next year I reckon we'll be set.'

'What do you mean?'

'I think it's time.' He cleared his throat. 'Next year you can give away the teaching and come work in the orchard full-time.'

Catherine held her hand to her heart, feeling it race under her fingers. Mark stood beside her, a questioning look in his eyes. She grabbed his hand and held the receiver between them so they could both hear her father's words. 'Sorry, Dad, could you say that again? I couldn't quite hear you.'

'Next year,' he boomed down the line, 'I'd like you to work with me in the orchard full-time. What do you say?'

35

March 1972
Annie

The wooden bulk bins piled up around Annie, all of them full of ruined fruit. She took a cursory glance at the latest load, picked up a scarred apple and threw it back. She'd held a faint hope that some of the pitting caused by the hailstorm would grow out. No chance now. The entire crop was going to the factories this year, and mostly for juicing for a fraction of the price she and Dave would normally get. Another lean year. And would the government help them out? No. They'd done away with the hail insurance back in 1966 because it was costing them too much. She scowled at the bulk bins; nothing worth packing there. A lot of the crop had rotted on the trees after the hail left ragged holes that made the apples fester and spoil. The air in the packing shed was thick with the sickly reek of decay. Annie was worried though. With so many orchards damaged by hail, the factories had a glut of fruit at their disposal. This lot might have to

266

be tipped, all of it left to rot up in the bush, feed for possums and insects.

Dave and Mark were doing most of the picking this year. There were no wages to pay their usual gang. Usually at this time the shed would be full of women yelling over the sound of the grader, laughing and gossiping, their hands flying, dipping in and out of the rotary bins and filling the boxes for export. But instead it was as if something had died; the silence and the stench. It made her feel wretched, but where else did she have to go? Her home was empty and silent as well. Angela was in Kindergarten this year, and much as it broke Annie's heart to be parted from her every day, it had made sense at the time. Annie would be free to run the packing shed without the additional responsibility of children to look after, at least during school hours. But now? What an absolute debacle.

She turned at the sound of footsteps. Mark. A rush of anger filled her chest.

'Dave asked me to drop over and tell you we're finishing up for the day. The rest of the Goldies aren't worth picking and he wants to leave the Sturmers for a few days, possibly a week.'

Annie nodded. The Sturmers were headed to the evaporating factory in Franklin where they liked them as sweet as possible.

'He's gone to check the Granny Smiths. He said he'll meet you back at the house.'

'And you? What are you going to do? Run off over the road to the Turners'? He's employing a few of our pickers this year, I hear.' Annie had recovered from the initial blow of the hailstorm that had ripped through their orchard, only to be left with a dull throb of resentment and flashes of anger. Hail could be unpredictable and capricious, but to see her apples ruined and the Turners' virtually unscathed had left her breathless. With so many orchards suffering damage, the crop would earn premium prices. Jack Turner was crowing with delight and Catherine was telling anyone who'd listen that she'd be working full-time in the orchard next year. Her excitement was salt in Annie's wounds.

'Good luck to them, and Jack,' Mark said. 'I think the Turners deserve a break.'

'Jack, is it now?'

'What's wrong, Annie? He's had one bit of good luck and you act as though it's happened just to spite you.'

'You know what I don't get?' Her finger jabbed at the air between them. 'You know this year's crop is lousy and there'll be no money to pay you. Mind you, even in a decent season we've never paid you much. With all your success in Melbourne, why are you back living in a pickers' hut? Why not get a place in town? You can't expect Catherine to live with you in that hut?'

'I have plans. But you know why I stay in Wattle Grove. Don't pretend you don't.'

'Well, Dave likes having you around, I guess.' Annie picked up another apple. Rotten, like so much else.

'If that's the way you want to play it. At least he kept me up to date with what was happening here while I was away. I missed out on a lot, but not everything.'

Annie saw her moment to strike. 'Kept you up to date, did he? What about Catherine's little affair? Bet you didn't hear about that. She kept it a secret from everyone.' Her hands were shaking. She knew she was crossing a line but she wanted to lash out, to offload some of her desperation and hurt. She missed Catherine, especially now. But their friendship was as fetid as the rotting apples and Annie felt helpless to repair it. She had nothing left to lose. 'Tim came back while you were gone. They had a very torrid time together, by all accounts.'

'I know all about Tim.' Mark's face was impassive. 'What are you trying to do here, Annie?'

'Just making sure you have all the facts.'

'That'd make a nice change, but right now I gotta split. The insurance company is finally giving me the cheque for the Monaro.'

Annie smirked. That was the only good thing to come out of the hailstorm. Mark's ridiculous car had been severely damaged, with both windscreens shattered and every panel dented. The insurance company had deemed it a write-off. 'Interesting, isn't it? How one minute everything is perfectly wonderful then the next it's a wreck.'

Mark's jaw tightened. 'Could be worse. I'm getting a new car out of this.'

'A brand-new car and soon to be married. Yeah, life's good for you.'

'Don't forget, life's been pretty good to you too, Annie. You got what you wanted, at the expense of others.'

She went to answer, to object, but he turned and strode out of the packing shed.

Annie slumped onto an old apple box. The anger inside her chest slowed but didn't dissipate. It was exhausting carrying it around all the time. She couldn't help but feel some lingering resentment towards Catherine. Mark would never have come back to the valley if it wasn't for her. If only Mark would go away – take Catherine with him if he had to, but just leave. But Catherine would never leave the valley and because of that Mark was here for good. There was only one glimmer of hope. Clearly Mark hadn't told Catherine all his secrets.

36

April 1972
Catherine

It wasn't only the crisp autumn day that made Catherine shiver, but the strange stillness of the Pearsons' orchard. Over the road, the harvest was in full swing with pickers working steadily and the tractor chugging down the rows to collect the bulk bins. Her father had made the right decision in not rebuilding the packing shed. It made sense to send the apples to Cradoc for packing and cool storage, and it certainly made Catherine's life easier. She felt for Annie, despite everything that had happened between them. She knew what it was like to have no viable fruit to harvest. She picked up her pace and headed towards the house.

It was almost a year since she and Annie had fallen out. A year of wonder and miracles for Catherine. A year of hardship and heartbreak for Annie. Catherine had mellowed over the months as her happiness grew. And now with the devastating hail damage to Dave and Annie's orchard she was able to feel compassion for her oldest friend. Annie had always been there for her through all her trials, disasters and grief. It felt wrong now, to be separated because of something that was over and done. It was her mother's words that had strengthened Catherine's resolve to rebuild her friendship with Annie. 'You and Annie have been friends for so long,' she'd said. 'It would be a shame to lose that, after everything else that's been lost.' Catherine wasn't sure how much her mother knew about the situation. She'd certainly never burdened her with it. Maybe it was a mother's ability to sense when things were painful.

It had hurt like a thousand stabbing knives at the time, but it had become easier to overcome the hurts of the past with so much happiness in her life. Perhaps it was a simple mistake, as Annie had said, the misplacement of Mark's letter. And Annie was always worried about the gossip, with Mark being a married man. Could that concern have continued, even when it was no longer needed? If so, it might explain why she never told her about his calls. Catherine asked Dave about it when she'd enlisted his help in arranging today's reconciliation with Annie. Dave had looked away and rubbed his chin. 'She did worry about you,' he'd said. 'You know, she always thought of you as the little sister she never had. And she didn't know Mark the way I did. He was a stranger to her when he arrived here. She was always suspicious, I guess.'

His explanation was unsatisfying, but Catherine hadn't pressed the point. Dave had quickly changed the subject to how grateful he was that Catherine wanted to patch up their differences. 'She's missed you,' he'd said. 'And with this dreadful season and Angela starting Kindergarten, she's been bereft.'

It felt strange to knock on the Pearsons' front door after a lifetime of just walking straight in with a 'yoo-hoo'. Annie answered the door, her expression unreadable. Dave had told Catherine she'd agreed to this meeting without reservations, but now Catherine was unsure. Her stomach twisted with nerves. Maybe this was a mistake. 'Hi, Annie.' Her voice sounded stiff, unnatural. 'Thanks for agreeing to see me.'

Annie's mouth crumpled and she took in a shuddering breath. 'Oh, Catherine. I'm so sorry.' She held out her arms towards her.

With a sigh of deep relief Catherine stepped forward into Annie's embrace, her senses filling with Annie's familiar scent of Sunlight soap, lemon Fab and home cooking. The memories of all the times Annie had held her, wiped her tears, and given her words of comfort, whether it be over the end of a silly schoolgirl crush or the death of her beloved little brother, came flooding back. 'I'm sorry too,' she murmured into Annie's hair and held her tight.

They didn't talk about what had happened between them, or the cruel words that were spoken – neither of them wanted to reopen old wounds. Instead they fell back into their friendship, both relieved to let bygones be bygones. It wasn't until a few weeks later, when Catherine's mother suggested she ask Annie to be her matron of honour that Catherine felt a sense of the old tension. Annie had always been opposed to her relationship with Mark and she was loath to jeopardise their fragile friendship with the request, but her mother insisted. Annie was her best friend and Catherine must have a matron of honour. After a few days of procrastinating, Catherine steeled herself and made her way to the Pearsons'. Inside Annie's kitchen, she found the usual chaos and clutter created by six hungry children.

'As soon as I tidy it up, the boys come through and mess it all up again,' Annie complained, mopping up a puddle of milk on the table with an old Wettex. 'Here.' She dusted off some crumbs from a kitchen chair. 'This is the least grubby spot. Have a seat and I'll make some tea.'

Catherine placed the Tupperware container on the table. 'A coconut jam slice from Mum. Still warm from the oven.'

'Your mother's feeling better then?'

'Yes. Knock on wood.' Catherine rapped the table sharply with her knuckles. 'Charlie's given her a new lease on life. He's over there now, helping her make a chocolate cake. I don't know how much help he is, but he's very good at licking the bowl.' Catherine paused. 'Plus she's really looking forward to the wedding.'

'Right.' Annie busied herself with the kettle and teapot.

Catherine watched Annie warily. 'You know how Dave's going to be Mark's best man ...'

'Uh huh.'

'I was just wondering ...' Catherine chewed her bottom lip. She felt as though she was on a tightrope, precariously balanced at a great height.

'Mmm?'

Catherine took a steadying breath. 'Would you be my matron of honour?' She almost winced as she said the words, not knowing how Annie would react.

Annie placed the teapot on the table and sat down. 'And I was wondering when on earth you'd get around to asking. Dave and I even had a small wager on how long you'd leave it.' She poured the tea with a cheeky smile. 'I'm glad to say, I won.'

Annie's response was a balm to Catherine's anxiety. Why had she been so worried? 'So you will?'

'Of course. How long have we known each other? Plus you're Scott's godmother – we're more or less family.'

'Thank you, thank you so much,' Catherine gushed. Her last concern about the wedding evaporated. Annie would be there, beside her. Her happiness was complete.

'Here's to the bride.' Annie raised her teacup in a toast.

'And to her wonderful matron of honour.' They clinked cups.

Catherine relaxed into her chair. Everything was going to be all right. An enticing idea popped into her head. Something she was sure Annie would love. 'Where's Angela?'

'In her room, playing.'

'I just had a thought. Mum's making my wedding dress.' It was a simple gown, with a fitted bodice, flared sleeves and a maxi-length skirt. Catherine had refused to wear white, saying she wanted to be able to wear the dress more than once, so she and her mother had settled on a sky-blue fabric that highlighted the colour of Catherine's eyes. She knew some guests would raise their eyebrows at her choice, but she was twenty-eight years old, for goodness sake, and this was the seventies. 'It's almost finished and it looks fabulous.'

'I'm sure it does.'

'She has some material left over. I reckon there'd be enough to make Angela a dress. How about if she was my flower girl?'

'I don't think so.'

Catherine noticed the edge in Annie's voice but pushed on. 'Imagine her walking down the aisle in a pretty dress, carrying a basket of roses and daisies. It would be the sweetest thing.'

'No, Catherine. I don't think it's a good idea.'

The mood in the kitchen shifted with a tension that made Catherine nervous. Why wouldn't Annie want her darling Angela to be the flower girl? She usually relished any opportunity to show off her daughter. 'I only thought—'

'I didn't have a flower girl.' Annie cut her off. 'Let alone a matron of honour. Hardly a wedding to speak of. Just me and Dave and his parents at the registry office in Hobart. My father wasn't there to give me away. My mother wasn't there to weep.' Annie snorted. 'She did plenty of lamenting though, before the event.'

'I'm sorry.' Catherine hadn't thought her wedding would bring back painful memories for Annie. She so rarely mentioned her family, the two estranged brothers and the parents who had cut her dead.

Annie straightened her shoulders as if shrugging off the past. 'Their loss. I gained great parents-in-law, may Keith rest in peace, and a whole new sprawling family. And now I'm going to be your matron of honour. Of course, to fulfil my duties, we'll have to have a hens' night.' The cheeky glint was back in Annie's eyes. 'Us, on the town in Cygnet, with a choice of three pubs. We could do a pub crawl!'

'Sounds like a blast.' Catherine relaxed again. 'But I think I'd be happier with an evening on the verandah, the two of us, and a bottle of Ben Ean.'

'Give me an endless supply of brandy alexanders and I'll be a happy woman.'

'The perfect hens' night. Let's do it. But not the night before the wedding. Oh, my head.'

'Done.' Annie chuckled. 'I tell you, being a matron of honour is a snap.'

'Thank you. I mean it. For saying yes. It means a lot to me.'

Annie fiddled with her teacup. 'Sorry about going on about my wedding day. I don't know what got into me. I just get a bit grumpy sometimes.'

'Happens to the best of us.' Catherine could understand. Six kids to feed and a failed crop – she was surprised Annie had a sense of humour left at all. She opened the Tupperware container. The smell of coconut, butter and jam wafted towards her. 'Would you like some? Before the boys descend and eat the lot.'

'Don't mind if I do. But only until the brandy alexanders come along.'

Catherine bit into a piece. The homemade strawberry jam oozed onto her fingers. The two of them ate in silence.

Annie finished hers with a satisfied sigh. 'That's better. You know, I blame the metric system for making me grumpy.' She gave a quick huff of laughter. 'I've barely got used to the new decimal currency and now there's centimetres and kilograms. And what is Celsius anyway?'

'Oh, that's easy.' The change over to the metric system had been gradual and Catherine had been preparing her students for it. From next year all primary schools would teach only the new system. 'You take the temperature in Fahrenheit and subtract thirty-two then multiply that number by five and then divide by nine and you have the temperature in Celsius.'

Annie rolled her eyes. 'Easy, she says. I give up. Pass me another piece of slice, but don't ask me what temperature it is, because I wouldn't have a clue.'

They were interrupted by the sound of Annie's boys whooping outside and the crunch of tyres in the driveway. Catherine looked questioningly at Annie.

'I'm not expecting anyone and certainly not anyone who'd get the boys that excited.'

They were almost at the front door when Michael came bursting through. 'I saw it first,' he shouted.

'Did not,' yelled Eric, hard on his heels.

Annie held up her hands. 'Stop. What's going on?'

'It's a Mercedes.'

''Tis not. It's a Bentley.'

Paul pushed his way into the hallway, puffing to catch his breath. 'I think it's a Rolls Royce.'

His older brother sneered. 'It's not a Rolls. What do you know about cars anyway?'

The boys wriggled like puppies, each clamouring for attention. 'We saw it from the upper block. Coming down our road.'

'Raced it all the way down the hill.'

'Real slow for a fancy car.'

'And then it turned into our driveway.'

'It's right outside.'

Annie untied her apron, hung it on a coat hook and smoothed down her hair. 'Well then, we'd better see who it is.' She pushed past the boys and opened the door.

A large black car sat on the driveway in front of the house. Catherine knew about the almost mythical wealth of Annie's parents. Could this be them? Why would they come now, unannounced, after all this time?

The boys rushed down the steps, gathering around the front of the car. Greg and Scott came straggling up the driveway, holding their sides and puffing. 'What kind of car is it?' Greg called out.

'Mercedes,' Annie said.

The driver's door opened and a man wearing a chauffeur's cap and uniform emerged. A quietness fell over the scene. Even the boys were silent. The chauffeur opened the rear passenger door and a foot appeared wearing the highest platform boots Catherine had ever seen. It would be like walking on stilts. The other foot appeared, and then two impossibly long legs. Finally a tall slender woman unfolded herself from the back seat of the car. She wore tiny red hotpants, a skin-tight top and a cropped white fur jacket. Her hair swung long and dark, and her eyes were covered by a pair of sunglasses so big Catherine could hardly see her face. Annie stiffened beside her.

The woman looked around slowly. 'The old place has hardly changed.' Her voice was melodious with a touch of a British accent.

'Boys,' Annie snapped. 'Go get your father. He's in the spray shed.'

'But, Mum,' Eric whined.

'Now.' Annie's voice was fierce. 'And make sure he brings Mark with him.'

They ducked their heads as if expecting a clip around the ears and ran off.

The woman laughed, a gentle tuneful sound. 'No, nothing's changed.' She walked forward in those impossible boots with grace and confidence, pausing at the bottom of the steps. 'Aren't you going to ask me in? I've come a very, very long way.'

Annie's fists were clenched. 'I don't understand – how are you here?'

The woman opened her arms, her hands upwards, as several heavy bangles jangled on her wrist. 'Surprise.'

Catherine was confused. Annie appeared to be terrified of this woman.

'Where's Emily?'

Annie's voice was little more than a croak. 'There's no Emily here.'

'I know this is a shock.' The woman touched her delicate fingers to her heart. 'Believe me, I was more shocked than anyone. But now there are certain things I need to take care of.'

'What are you doing here?'

'I won't stay long. But I would love to see Emily.'

The door creaked open behind Catherine. She turned to see Angela peeking out. 'Mummy?'

The woman advanced up the first step. 'Is that her?'

'You'll scare her.'

'Emily. You won't remember me.'

'Leave her alone, I said.' Annie's voice was harsh, pressed out between clenched teeth. 'Angela, go back inside.'

The woman crept up another step. 'Oh, Angela, is it? What a pretty name. And what a pretty girl. Let me look at you, my darling.' Her voice was like a purr, warm and enticing.

Angela looked at the arms stretched out towards her. 'Is that a snake?'

'Why, yes it is. Made of pure gold, with emeralds for eyes. Would you like to wear it?' She slipped the bracelet off her wrist and held it out.

'Angela, go back inside.'

But her small hands reached, hypnotised by the bangle.

The woman took a breath and her smile widened, revealing rows of perfect white teeth. 'It is you. I know it is.'

Catherine watched them both. There was something wrong here, but she didn't know what. Was it her place to intervene? Annie certainly knew this woman. Catherine was in the dark.

The woman took off her oversized sunglasses. Her face was intensely beautiful – chiselled cheekbones, a wide smooth brow, elegant arched eyebrows and a perfect full-lipped mouth. And her eyes, there was something familiar about them, a kind of bronze and highlighted with dramatic slashes of gold. 'Emily,' she whispered again.

Catherine followed the woman's gaze and her hands flew to her mouth. It was if she was seeing the very same eyes.

Dave came barrelling around the corner of the house. 'The boys said it was an emergency. Are you okay?' He stopped short to stare at the car.

The woman straightened and turned towards him. 'Hello, Dave.'

He looked at her, startled. 'Do I know you?'

She laughed gently. 'But of course.'

Mark appeared, wiping grease from his hands. 'What's going on?'

'Ah, there he is.' The woman's voice was like a sigh.

A cold sensation hit Catherine in the stomach. This woman knew Mark? How?

Mark stumbled and sank to his knees. 'No.'

'Yes,' the woman said. She appeared calm in the face of such an odd reception.

'It can't be.' He shook his head. 'It's impossible. You ... you're ...'

'Darling, it's a long story. I know it's a bit of a surprise, but you know how I love surprises.'

'I don't understand.'

'I'll explain everything. I would never have come back, but I had to see you.' She looked back towards Angela. 'And our little Emily.'

Mark's face collapsed in anguish. 'But, Lara—'

Catherine took a step back, and then another, until she felt the weatherboards behind her. She leant against them to steady herself, but it was no good, the earth was shifting beneath her feet. She had no bones, no breath. He called her Lara. How was that possible? She slid to the wooden deck of the verandah and clasped her hands around her knees, rocking in the storm that engulfed her. She tried to find a true horizon, something to steady her. Beside the big black car, the chauffeur stood unmoved by the drama unfolding around him, the only form of certainty in this dangerous sea.

37

January 1967

Annie

Annie remembered everything. She'd tried to forget, but that night remained deeply etched in her body and her heart. It had been hot, in the way only a January night could be – dry, fierce and unrelenting. But worse was the dread that something was wrong with her baby. There'd been no kicking, no movement at all for days. The pregnancy had been hard from the start with unrelenting nausea and a body that ached all over, the pain a constant drumbeat. Annie was incapable of doing all the things that needed to be done so Dave had picked up the slack around the house and with the boys. Part of her had wished the pregnancy was over, but now, with the baby so still in her womb, she feared the wish had cursed her unborn child. 'Stay with me, little one,' she whispered, touching her distended stomach gently. 'Please stay.'

She was in her third trimester. The danger should be over, but instead a sense of dread filled her waking hours and the nights stretched out endlessly. If she did manage to drift off, her dreams

281

were full of shifting, formless frustration and fear – nightmares of trying to escape but getting sucked down into blackness. In less than two months her baby would push into the world, healthy and strong like all her boys. Fierce little fighters, every one of them. But, oh, how she yearned for the softness of a girl, and for all the things they would do together as mother and daughter. She'd given this baby a name that evoked her longing. Angela.

She was in bed when it hit. Pain rocked through her body from deep in her pelvis, a burst of fire unlike anything she'd known. She was booked into the Cygnet Community Health Centre for her delivery, although sometimes things moved too fast. Both Eric and Paul had been born right here in the house. But she'd never felt like this. A gush of warm liquid rushed from between her legs, soaking the bedding.

'No, please no,' she whimpered.

Dave woke beside her. 'What's wrong?'

'The baby.' Annie sobbed. 'It's too soon. Not yet.'

Another wave of agony rocked her body. She clutched at her belly and squeezed her eyes shut. The flare of red that danced beneath her eyelids turned white hot as the pain intensified. 'No, little one. Please stay with me. Just a while longer.' Her voice was a hoarse pant through gritted teeth.

There was a deep stab of pain, and a sudden release. Dave cut the cord as he had done with the boys, but this time there was no little bundle in her arms, no mewling infant searching for her breast. 'Where is she?' Annie was certain this one was a girl. 'Where's my baby?'

Dave kissed her gently on the top of her sweat-soaked head. 'The boys might've woken up. I'll go check on them. When I come back we'll clean you up and change the bedding.'

Annie struggled to rise, but pain and exhaustion won out. 'I want to see her. I want my baby.'

Tears spilled from Dave's eyes. 'My darling Annie. She's gone.'

Annie screamed at Dave for taking her baby, and then fell into a blackness that had no time, only pain.

Mark

On that night Mark had been woken by a frenzied banging and the sound of the front door being thrown open with a crack that echoed through the still night. It had been hot, as always, a dense dry heat making every surface warm to touch and the cold water in the taps tepid. Mark and Lara slept naked but never touching, the bulk of her belly keeping them apart more than physically. Often she would spend the nights pacing restlessly until exhaustion overtook her, then slump onto their bed in the early hours, still tense but tired enough to doze. That night the violent sounds jolted them both into wakefulness. Lara's eyes were fearful as she grabbed the sheet and wrapped it around her body.

'Stay here,' Mark said. He pulled on a pair of shorts and headed up the hallway.

'Daddy?' Charlie called out sleepily from his room.

'It's okay. Go back to sleep.' Mark closed the door to his son's bedroom and kept walking.

The front door was wide open. Mark heard a strangled sound coming from outside. A thin edge of grey light silhouetted the surrounding hills. Mark's eyes adjusted to the semi-darkness. A man was slumped on the front steps. His shoulders shuddered with sobs and he was hunched over a small object.

'Are you okay, mate?' Mark asked. This man might have thrown the front door open, but he hadn't entered and he seemed too distraught to be dangerous. Still, Mark was wary, his body tense.

The man turned. His face was distorted by fierce emotion, but even so Mark recognised him in the dim light. 'Dave?'

'Oh, God.' Dave sucked in a gulp of air, trying to calm his breathing.

'What's happened?' Mark dropped to sit beside him.

'The baby came early. Too early.' Dave rocked back and forward, clutching the object in his arms. Mark could make out a small blanket-wrapped bundle. 'Annie's crazy with grief. Won't accept what's happened.' He stood suddenly, his eyes darting back and forth. 'I've got to get back before she comes to. The boys'll be scared shitless. All that screaming.' Tears etched furrows in his face.

'God, Dave, I'm so sorry.' His words were inadequate, Mark knew, but what else could be said? Annie had been looking forward to this baby, certain it was a girl. And now? Dave's face told the story – the raw grief and trauma of it.

'I hate to ask this of you.' Dave turned, a frenzied look in his eyes. 'Annie – I can't leave her alone for long. And I can't let her near—' He stared down at the blanket in his arms.

Mark flinched. It couldn't be? Surely not.

'Please,' Dave's voice was desperate, a small keening sound. 'Bury her somewhere Annie will never find her. High up in the bush where the ground is too steep to be cultivated. Deep though, so the animals—' He shuddered.

Mark pulled back sharply. Weren't there rules around this kind of thing? Procedures? A baby had been born. Not alive, but even so. Was this how it was done? He had no idea. 'What about a doctor?'

Dave shook his head. 'Not yet. Right now, I gotta look after my boys. And my wife. This has torn her apart. Annie refuses to believe the baby is gone. I don't know what else to do.'

Mark had never seen Dave in such torment. He got to his feet, searching for another solution but finding none. His best friend was begging him for help. The grief on Dave's face told a story neither of them had ever expected to experience.

Mark nodded. 'Okay.'

Dave's face collapsed in gratitude. He gently untangled the bundle from his arms. The growing light of dawn echoed the shade of the blanket, a delicate pink. He took a small step towards Mark.

Mark tightened his jaw, willing himself not to react. He took the baby from Dave's arms, expecting the warmth and softness that was Charlie when he was born, but this was just a tiny thing, so light as to be almost unnoticeable. With Lara's due date so close, only a matter of weeks now by her rough estimate, Mark couldn't help wondering how he'd cope if he were in Dave's position. He glanced down and was grateful the blanket was arranged like a shroud, hiding any sight of the baby.

Dave reached out to touch his daughter one last time before he turned and walked away.

Mark's progress up the hill was awkward and tentative, marred by the shovel he held in one hand while keeping his small charge tucked into his side with the other. He wanted to blank out the truth of what he was doing. It was too awful to be real. Any moment he'd wake to discover this was just a fitful nightmare brought on by heat and the closeness of the air. The path he needed to take through the scrub, native grasses and eucalypts became clearer as the sun began its relentless ascent. Already the day was heating up and sweat made the bundle clammy as he climbed the steep slope. Almost at the top, in a hidden place no one would ever find, he put his burden down and began to dig. The shovel bit into ground that was hard and dry, parched from drought. Sweat stung his eyes but Mark kept digging, the steady rhythm and exertion helping to dull his thoughts. He didn't stop until the hole was deep, much deeper than needed, but finally he had to lay the small pink bundle in her unmarked grave, far from her mother and father. So far from anyone who might have known her and loved her. He knew it wasn't right. He also knew he'd always feel guilty. But if he'd refused Dave, the guilt would be worse.

A rustle in the dry grass and the sharp snap of a twig caused him to falter, shame and fear roaring in his ears.

'Mark?'

Lara had followed him, leaving Charlie on his own, as was often her way.

Mark stared into the hole; the evidence was there, barely covered with earth. 'Born too soon.' His voice was thick. 'A girl. Dave said she never had a chance.'

Lara showed no surprise. She must have overheard him and Dave talking. She knelt beside the grave and sprinkled some dirt into the hole. 'Darling girl, may the angels take you home. Peace and love be yours forever.'

Mark berated himself silently. He hadn't thought of saying a few words over the grave. Part of him was grateful Lara was here to make his grisly task more bearable.

'Poor Annie.' Lara struggled to her feet and brushed the earth from her hands. 'She wanted this baby so badly. She told me our babies would almost be twins.' She smiled wistfully. 'Can you imagine? Both of us with girls so close in age – we couldn't help but feel a bond.'

'Two girls?'

'Oh, yes. I'm certain this is a girl.' She rubbed her stomach. 'Even more so now.' Her smile had a strange quality to it.

Mark felt off balance and for a moment wondered why. Then he realised – this was the first time he'd heard Lara refer to their unborn baby in any way approaching fondness.

From then on Lara softened towards the child in her womb. Up until the death of Annie's baby, Lara had either railed against her condition or been in complete denial. When she'd first fallen pregnant again she'd raged at Mark, blaming him for ruining her life. She'd refused to tell anyone about the baby, even her parents, and her behaviour had become erratic again. Lara sometimes disappeared all day and into the night. On the days she didn't sneak away, she stayed in bed, hardly eating and screaming at Mark if he suggested calling a doctor or even worse, her mother. He'd feared for the wellbeing of their unborn child, but neither begging, cajoling nor threats had led to a different outcome. When she could no longer disguise her growing belly she'd refused to see her parents or any of their friends. She hated the way she looked, she told him, she couldn't bear anyone seeing her. Between keeping an eye on Lara and looking after Charlie it became harder for Mark to keep his commitments to the band. When they'd decided to make a go of it in Britain, he knew they'd be leaving without him.

At his wit's end, Mark had rung the only person he could trust. Dave had suggested they come and stay at the orchard for a while, which had seemed like a godsend. They'd have a house of their own, away from the prying eyes of the press and the clamouring of fans. Hopefully Lara would relax once she was away from the city and in a place where no one knew her. The pressure of the constant lies to their friends and Lara's parents about her pregnancy had worn on Mark. It would be best for everyone if his family got out of Melbourne for a while.

They'd arrived at the orchard in the first week of January and within less than a week his hopes were dashed. Lara didn't want to see the valley or the orchard, rejecting suggestions of country drives or walks by the river. She'd refused to go to the health centre in Cygnet. She'd even stopped Mark from making an appointment for her, saying once people realised who Mark was they'd have no privacy. It would be Melbourne all over again. Dave had told him about Annie's two homebirths and that she could help if Lara wouldn't go to the centre when the time came. Mark was not greatly reassured.

And in all that time Lara had never referred to the child in her womb with love or affection. When Annie had come to visit them in the old house, chatting about preparations for a new baby, Lara had refused to engage. The only time she'd showed any interest was when Annie had joked that their babies would almost be twins. Lara had become animated, asking Annie how she'd cope with twins. Mark had found it curious, but there was so much about Lara that never made sense to him.

Now, although he'd never admit it to anyone, he was grateful that the loss of Annie's baby had impacted Lara so profoundly. It was as if the tragedy had shocked her into realising how fortunate they were. When the baby kicked she pressed her hands against her belly and laughed, reaching for Mark's hand so he could feel a tiny foot stretching against its confines. She asked Mark to sing lullabies for their daughter, convinced the baby would be a girl.

'What shall she be called?' Lara asked one day. They were sitting in the shade of the verandah where a slight breeze eased the searing heat a little.

Mark was caught by surprise. The past months had been so difficult, he was yet to become used to Lara's change in attitude. 'I'm not sure.'

288

'I had a great-aunt called Emily. Sensationally creative and completely mad. I've always liked the name.' Lara's smile was so open and appealing he felt himself relax in its warmth.

'Emily it is then.'

Lara nodded and rubbed her belly. 'Little Emily. You will be the most adored little girl in all the world.'

A lump formed in Mark's throat. He'd wished for things to be different for so long and now his wish had come true. His small family was happy and content. Life was good.

Another hot day. Even the birds were struck dumb with the heat. The orchard shimmered in waves and Charlie was fretful and grumpy. Mark took him to the main house to give Lara some peace. Charlie was shy around Annie's brood, unused to other children. But it was good for him to experience the rough-and-tumble of play, instead of the adult-centred life in Melbourne. The boys were in the backyard, playing under the sprinkler. Mark encouraged Charlie to join in but he clung to his father's leg. 'What about the sandpit?' Mark suggested. 'There's a Tonka truck just waiting to make some roads.' Charlie silently walked over to the sandpit and began to push the truck through the sand.

Mark found Dave in the kitchen, looking as dishevelled as the house, with dirty dishes and piles of laundry on every surface. It had been over two weeks since Annie's baby had been stillborn. Mark hadn't seen her since. 'How's Annie?'

Dave shook his head, his face grey with fatigue. 'She stays in the bedroom, crying. Doesn't come out, not even for the boys. I don't know if I did the right thing, asking you to – you know.' Dave frowned and looked away. 'Now we're stuck. We've lost a child, but nobody knows except us. I can't go into town, don't think I could face people. Eventually they'll find out. I mean, everyone knew we had another one on the way. It's such a mess.'

Mark had no words of reassurance. 'I'm sorry, mate.'

'And I'm sorry I dragged you into this. Come to Tassie and get away from it all. Relax and enjoy the country life.' His smile was a grimace. 'You'd've been better off staying away.'

'No, mate. I'm glad I'm here. No matter what.' He couldn't tell a grieving father that Lara was finally happy about having another baby. 'Thanks for looking after Charlie. I'd better head back.'

'I'll keep an eye on him. Least I can do.'

Mark felt awkward leaving Charlie there, but Lara was so close now he didn't like leaving her alone for long. Her refusal to go to the health centre still worried him. He thought she would've changed her mind by now, but she was adamant.

When he got home she was still in bed, the door firmly closed. He opened it gently. 'Can I get you anything?'

Despite the heat, she'd pulled the sheet over herself. 'Nothing.' Her voice was muffled and tense.

Mark backed away. He'd learnt to leave her alone when she was like this. He took his guitar out onto the verandah and began composing a new lullaby for little Emily.

It was some hours later when he heard a low moaning. Lara. He rushed into the bedroom to find her on all fours on the floor, her naked body dripping sweat and her face contorted in a silent scream. He dropped to the floor beside her. 'Lara, c'mon. Let's get you to the health centre, now.'

'No,' she growled.

His mind raced. Annie was in no state to help and he couldn't leave Lara, not like this. The only thing to do was get her into the car and drive her to Cygnet. 'Lara, please. We have to go to Cygnet.'

'I'm not going anywhere.' She grabbed his arm in a vice-like grip. 'You got me into this.' Her grip tightened as a contraction racked her body. 'Get her out of me,' she bellowed. 'Do it now.'

The stream of abuse that followed was shocking. Mark knew pain and fear were causing the vindictive tirade, but the depth of her anger was unnerving. As the labour progressed he floundered, knowing he was out of his depth. All he could do was follow her lead – walking with her when she wanted to pace, swaying with her as she rocked, and kneeling beside her when she dropped to the floor to push. He rubbed her back, gave her water, and brought hot water and towels although he wasn't sure why. Mark was astounded by her strength and determination. His wife was an Amazon, enduring an agony he was sure he could never survive. She abused him, bit him and bruised him, but he knew his pain was nothing compared to hers.

When at last their baby slid into the world, wet and red, he laughed with relief. The towels and water were put to good use as Mark nervously cut the cord and wiped their daughter clean. She filled her lungs with air and announced her presence in the world. To Mark she was beautiful, even with her wrinkled skin and elongated head. 'Look, darling, our little Emily.' He held her out to Lara in wonder. 'She's perfect.'

Lara crawled onto the bed. 'She's not my baby,' she muttered.

Mark joined her, carefully cradling their daughter. 'Would you like to hold her?'

Lara turned away.

Mark didn't know what time it was. The bedroom was dark and still. They must have fallen asleep; him, Lara and their daughter, all exhausted from the birth. He reached out but the bed was empty. He padded into the lounge room expecting to find Lara feeding their daughter there. Empty. As were the kitchen, the other bedrooms and the bathroom. Charlie would still be at the main house. With the events of the afternoon and evening, Mark hadn't found time to collect his son. Dave would understand. But what about Lara and Emily? Where were they? The car was missing. Had Lara taken the baby to the health centre to have her checked out? But why not wake him so he could drive them there? He pulled on his shoes and headed towards the main house. He'd pick up Charlie, borrow the ute and head into Cygnet.

At Dave's he let himself in the back door and walked up the hallway, checking the bedrooms for Charlie. He spotted him asleep, top and tailing with one of the boys. Best to leave him for now. He heard murmurs from Annie and Dave's room and noticed a crack of dim light under their door. He knocked.

'Come in.' It was Annie. Her voice sounded light, not full of sorrow as he'd expected.

He opened the door. Annie was sitting on the bed, with a beatific smile on her face and a baby nestling against her chest. Dave was the mirror opposite, hovering beside her, his face grey with worry.

'Mate, I'm sorry,' Dave said.

'I have a daughter.' Annie was beaming. 'She's beautiful.'

Mark reeled back. He'd buried Annie's daughter with his own hands.

Dave took a faltering step towards him. 'It was Lara. She didn't seem herself. I tried to stop her. But she insisted. I didn't know what to do. And Annie ...' He turned towards his wife.

'She's mine.' Annie clutched the baby closer. 'Lara said. She said she was always meant for me. My precious daughter.' She stroked the baby's cheek. 'So perfect.'

Mark stared in horror. Annie had his daughter. 'I don't understand. Where's Lara?'

Dave shrugged – a pathetic gesture that made Mark furious.

'Give me my daughter,' Mark said.

'She's not yours,' Annie said. 'She's mine. Lara said so.'

Mark growled in frustration. He couldn't bear to be in the room any longer. 'Dave.' He indicated towards the door.

On the verandah Mark couldn't keep still. 'Tell me what happened. And where's Lara? The car's gone.'

'Said she needed to get away. Didn't say where. Mate, I'm sorry. There was nothing I could do. By the time I realised, the deal was done.'

'The deal?'

'The women made some kind of pact. This is the first time I've seen Annie happy for so long. Honestly, I never thought I'd see her smile again.'

'For God's sake, Dave. The baby's not hers. She can't keep her. This'll only make things worse.'

Dave slumped like a beaten dog. 'I know. But just for a little while. Just until Lara comes back. Let her look after your daughter. Please?' His eyes held a sorrow Mark could never imagine. He realised his friend had lost a baby daughter and his wife too, in a way.

Mark shoved his hands in his pockets and stared out towards the river. The sun would be coming up soon. He'd have to begin his search for Lara. How could he do that with a young son to take care of and now a newborn daughter as well?

'We'll take good care of her, you know we will.' It was as if Dave had read his thoughts.

Mark closed his eyes for a moment. 'Only until I find Lara.'

Dave let out a sigh. 'Okay.'

But Mark didn't find Lara. And she didn't come back. He realised, too late, that she'd fooled him. She'd planned to give their daughter to Annie as soon as she heard about the stillbirth, maybe even before with all that talk of twins. She'd hidden the signs of her labour until there was no choice but for her to give birth in the house with only the two of them there, and he'd played right into her hands. Had she always planned to give their baby away? Is that why she'd never let anyone know she was pregnant? Just how much of a sucker had he been?

The change in Annie was dramatic. She doted on the baby and was back to her happy, capable self, whipping the house and the boys into shape. Mark knew she could look after his daughter a lot better than he could, given his circumstances – homeless, jobless, and with a young son to take care of. But only until Lara was back. He wasn't to know the lengths Annie would go to to keep his daughter.

38

May 1972

Mark

For the first time the pickers' hut felt poor and shabby. Mark had never noticed, until Lara sat down, how decrepit the old chairs were. She was like an exotic creature out of place and time; at odds with her scruffy environment. He sat down too and tried to comprehend what was happening. Lara was dead yet here she was, with a Mercedes, a chauffeur and a slight British accent.

He watched her warily as she swung one long leg over the other and reached into her handbag, pulling out a packet of menthol cigarettes. 'Do you have a light?' She stretched a bejewelled hand in his direction.

'I don't smoke any more, but I've got matches.' He began to rise, but she motioned him to sit and produced a gold lighter from her handbag with a sly smile. She was testing him. Making sure he was still malleable and compliant. He grabbed a saucer to act as an ashtray, knowing she'd ash on the floor otherwise.

Lara lit the long cigarette and sucked the smoke into her lungs before releasing it in a steady flow. 'I don't remember it being this cold.'

Mark could offer to light the fire, but didn't want her getting too cosy. 'It was summer. I'm surprised you remember it at all.'

'Darling man, don't be like that. It was a hard time for me. You know how devastatingly ragged I used to get.' She waved her hand as if batting away a fly. 'All in the past. Do you have anything to drink?'

'Tea, water. Or perhaps you'd like an orange cordial. It's Charlie's favourite.'

Mark watched her mouth as it encircled the cigarette and took a drag, that luscious, ripe, ridiculous, lying mouth. She pouted as she blew the smoke out slowly. 'Really, lover. Nothing else? A nice bottle of wine or a finger or two of whiskey?'

Mark rubbed his hand across his eyes. As always with Lara she never divulged anything easily. Once he was over the initial shock, he'd asked her the obvious questions. She'd been declared dead, for God's sake! But she'd dodged his queries by asking Annie and Dave about their health and the children, though it was obvious she didn't really give a damn. Dave had answered in monosyllables while Annie was stiff with anger and fear. Mark had finally suggested that Lara come to the pickers' hut with him where they could be alone and he'd have more chance of finding out what he desperately needed to know.

'Who was it down in the gully, in the car?' He'd insist she answer. 'Clearly it wasn't you, but the woman was wearing the pendant I gave you. You were listed as legally dead. How can you be sitting here, smoking a cigarette?'

'Quite easily, darling.' She took another drag. 'See? You suck on this end and then blow out.' She exhaled and tapped the end of the cigarette, spilling ash into the saucer.

'Lara.' He tried to mute the frustration in his voice. He'd have to keep his anger in check if he wanted answers. And he did, badly.

'You really are no fun any more. But then you hadn't been for a while.' She twirled a strand of her long dark hair around the fingers of her free hand. 'How can I be here? I flew in from London. Swung by Mummy and Daddy's on the way through. They were surprised to see me, I have to say.' She laughed low in her throat.

Mummy and Daddy? Lara had never called her parents anything but Mum and Dad before. 'Why didn't you call? Or write?'

'You don't have a telephone, silly. Mummy and Daddy told me that. They wrote you a letter. Clearly I arrived before it did.'

'I mean, ever. Not even a note.'

She shrugged languidly.

Mark knew he'd get nowhere so changed tack. 'Who was it in the car?'

Lara pouted. 'I assume it was the woman I sold it to. I threw in the pendant as well since she seemed to like it.'

'What woman?'

'Oh, I don't know. Canadian from memory. On a trip around Australia in a Kombi with her boyfriend, but she didn't look like a hippy. Old money I'd say, indulging in a bit of rough before having to settle down. She and her boyfriend had a huge fight and she'd been desperate to get away. We were driving to Hobart, but when we hit Fern Tree she changed her mind. The stupid girl wanted to go back to her boyfriend. I told her where you were and that you'd pay her back for the car, but I was keeping her dough. She took off, leaving me stranded.'

'But where did you go?'

Lara stretched like a cat, slow and lazy. 'I don't know, darling, it's all a bit of a blur. There was some hitchhiking, I think.' Her golden eyes widened. 'Oh, now I remember. A very nice man picked me up.

Turns out he was travelling to Melbourne on the boat so I tagged along. The crossing was hideous and I wasn't all that well so the darling gave me his cabin and slept in his car.' She studied her nails. 'He was extraordinarily kind, but ended up being way too clingy.'

That explained why Mark hadn't been able to find any record of her using their return ticket. 'But none of our friends in Melbourne saw any sign of you. I went over and looked for you. There wasn't a trace.'

'Melbourne held no appeal.' Lara waved her hand dismissively. 'I ended up in Sydney. Now that was a lot of fun.' Her laugh was low and throaty.

'Why didn't you tell us where you were?' He couldn't help but ask again, the hurt was still so close to the surface.

Lara dragged hard on her cigarette. 'Might have been the people I was with or the substances we were indulging in. Both, probably. Honestly, darling, what does it matter? I'm here now.'

'But what about Charlie and our life together? And Angela?'

'I'll always think of her as Emily.'

'That's when she was our daughter. You gave her away. I had no say in it.'

Lara's eyes went cold. 'You'd rather put me through the hell I endured after Charlie was born?'

Mark was amazed at her selfishness. 'The birth certificate was signed before I could think about what to do – how to cope with two on my own.'

'Talking about certificates. I have a tiny little favour to ask.'

Of course, that's why she'd finally turned up, back from the dead. Because she wanted something. She'd never cared about Charlie and had never wanted Angela. Had she ever loved him? Mark said nothing. He'd make her work for a response.

She leant forward, her bracelets chinking gently against each other. 'I hardly think you'll mind, given the circumstances.'

'So, you were in Sydney all that time? Doing drugs?'

'Oh, no, darling. I skipped over to the UK. A British band was touring Australia and we hooked up. One of them couldn't live without me, naturally.' She ground her cigarette into the saucer.

'England?'

'Lucky I had a passport. Remember when we both got them?' There was a glimpse of the old Lara in her eyes, the fierce, combative nature that had made their marriage such a fury. 'It finally came in handy.'

She'd never let him forget what a disappointment he'd turned out to be. Mark was supposed to go to the UK with the band and take her with him. He was supposed to be famous and keep her in the lap of luxury. 'You were pregnant and we had a child. It was never going to work.'

'Children!' She spat the word. 'I wasn't going to get sucked down into a pathetic little life saddled with two brats.' The cool, elegant woman was gone. Even her accent was less British.

'So you gave our baby away, abandoned your son, and me, and never let us know where you were.'

'I could hardly escape if you knew where I was. And admit it, Emily has had a better life here than I could have given her. It's obvious Annie dotes on her.'

'Annie was out of her mind with grief. You took advantage of her.'

'Interesting.' Lara looked at him shrewdly. 'You're defending Annie? Did she ever offer to give Emily back?'

Mark said nothing, his jaw clenched tight with anger. He remembered how furious and how utterly powerless he'd felt when he found out what Annie had done, and there'd been nothing he could do about it, nothing at all. It had been not long after the fires and the world was still in disarray when Dave came to him with a stricken expression on his face.

'I'm sorry, mate,' Dave said. 'I didn't know anything about it. She told me she was going into town to pick up some supplies from the Red Cross. That's all.'

'What are you talking about?'

Dave shook his head slowly. 'Annie.' He paused and took a deep breath. 'She's registered your baby as ours. She's showed me the birth certificate. Angela Pearson, born to Anne and David Pearson on the fifth of February 1967. It's all signed, stamped and legal.'

Anger and disbelief exploded in Mark's chest. 'What the hell? How? How could she do that? How could you let her?'

Dave was close to tears. 'I didn't know. Honestly. You've got to believe me. She even went to the Four Square in Cygnet on the way home, she told me, to show Angela off.'

Mark began to panic. By now the whole valley would think Emily Davis was Angela Pearson. Everybody had known Annie was expecting and now there was the baby to prove it. No one in the valley had ever caught a glimpse of Lara, let alone known she was pregnant, she'd made sure of it. Mark would look crazy if he declared the baby didn't belong to Annie, but to him. The realisation slammed into him – first Lara and then Annie had taken advantage of him. The trap had been set and he'd walked right into it.

'She also said—' Dave's voice faltered.

'What?' Mark was almost shouting, his voice high and strained in his head. 'What else did she say?'

'She said it was Lara's idea. To register your baby as Annie's. That Angela had always belonged to Annie, not her.'

'Emily,' Mark hissed between clenched teeth. 'Her name is Emily. And I'm going to get her back. She belongs to me. I'll tell everyone what Annie's done.'

'Please, mate, please.' Dave was crying now. 'It'll break Annie if the truth gets out, but not only that, it'll break everything – me, the boys, it'll ruin us all.'

Mark felt as though *his* world was breaking apart – Lara gone, his daughter stolen. He clenched his fists and walked away.

Eventually though, he promised Dave he'd keep the secret. He would never do it for anyone else and certainly not for Annie, but for his best friend, who'd always been there for him. But part of him had never given up. Annie couldn't stop Mark from staying in the valley, or from keeping an eye on his daughter. It broke his heart to see the similarities between Charlie and Angela as they grew, brother and sister, but to never be able to tell them, or to be the father to Angela that he wanted to be. He couldn't deny that Dave was a good dad and Annie, despite his antipathy, was a much better mother than Lara. But the antagonism between Mark and Annie was ever present, a fire that kept burning long after the bushfires were over.

Lara was still waiting for an answer. Mark remained mute, the frustration grating on his nerves.

'No.' Lara laughed softly. 'I didn't think so.'

'What do you want, Lara?'

Her composure was back; her face a beautiful mask. 'What do I want? I want a divorce.'

A bitter sound erupted from his mouth.

'You won't have to do much,' Lara said. 'Just appear in court. My lawyer, well, Bobby's lawyer actually, will take care of everything.'

'Bobby?'

'Oh, you've probably heard of him.' She lit another cigarette and inhaled deeply. 'Fabulous guitar player. Wonderful songwriter too. Hugely famous. Stonkingly rich. The car and the chauffeur were his idea. Didn't want me running off the road and ending up in a gully.' Her smile was little more than a smirk.

She had the nerve to joke about her supposed death, and worse, the death of a woman whose name she hadn't even bothered to remember. He'd felt wretched with guilt when the police had told him Lara was dead. It was his fault. He'd brought his family to the valley and Lara had ended up in that gully. He'd blamed himself for everything and pushed Catherine away in his anguish. Bile bit the back of his throat.

'Anyhow, darling, he wants to marry me. It's all very sweet. I hadn't been using my real name, oh, for some time, but when it came to the wedding things came a bit unstuck. So here I am.'

'To stick them together again.'

'Well, quite the opposite actually.' She brought the cigarette to her lips then paused. 'At least as far as you and I are concerned.'

Mark rested his elbows on his knees and ran his hands through his hair. He couldn't get his head around the idea of it. Divorcing a dead woman.

'So.' She stretched the word out into a question. 'Will you? Then I'll be out of your life forever.'

'I thought you were. We all thought you were dead.'

'All you need to do is appear in court in Sydney. That's where I'll be staying until this little mess is tidied up, away from prying eyes.'

'Sydney?' Mark could only assume she wanted as little contact with her parents and their old friends as possible.

'Bobby's flying out incognito for a secret holiday. It's all so delicious. The lawyer's taking care of everything. He assures me that because we've been separated for over five years we'll get a no-fault divorce. No need for one of those horrid private detectives.'

Mark slowly shook his head. It was as if he was in a bad dream – no, a farce. Except nothing about this was funny.

'Being declared dead will actually help. We couldn't have been together if I was dead, now could we?' Her smile was sly. 'He'll also obtain affidavits from mutual friends saying we never co-habitated after I left Wattle Grove. Dave and Annie won't mind giving a statement, will they? Considering everything.'

Her words whirled through Mark's head. Lara had clearly been clued up by her lawyer on how to present her case. But his mind was a jumble of thoughts and emotions.

'If you just sign a couple of teensy documents we can have a court appearance in a month. My lawyer is confident we'll be granted a decree nisi without any problems, and you'll get sole custody of Charlie. There's no record of Emily being ours. Then three months after that, the decree absolute will be declared and we're both free.' Lara took a last deep drag on her cigarette and exhaled the smoke in a satisfied sigh.

'You don't want joint custody of Charlie?' Mark's throat was dry, his tongue thick.

'Don't be silly, darling.' She waved her hand again. The sunlight filtering through the window caught the gemstones in her rings, including the large diamond on the third finger of her left hand. 'What would I do with Charlie? No. He's much better off here with you. Where is he, by the way?'

'With his grandmother.' Judith was as good as Charlie's grandmother and loved it when he called her Granny.

'His grandmother? Have your parents finally stopped living abroad? I never imagined them settling in Tasmania after such an exotic life.'

'Forget it.' He wasn't sure where his parents were. They never wrote to him, or called. He realised now he'd married a woman just like his mother, one who wanted nothing to do with her own child.

'Well, he's certainly not with my mother. Although Mummy and Daddy said how much they loved spending time with him. Positively gushed.'

'Do you want to see him? Charlie?'

'I don't think so, darling. He thinks I'm dead. Wouldn't want to confuse the little mite.'

'But you're not dead. He has a right to know.'

'Maybe I'll write him a letter.'

'Right. Because you're so good at writing to let people know where you are and what you're doing.'

'There's no need to get snarky. Snarky Marky.' She laughed. 'It rhymes. Perhaps I should write songs too instead of being everyone else's muse.'

This was such a mess. He was marrying Catherine in a month. Oh God, Catherine. She'd been at Annie's place when Lara had turned up. He had to see her. 'A month till the court case, then another three and the divorce is final?'

'Yes, darling. A minimum of fuss. Nothing for the papers to sniff out for their tawdry rags. Bobby's lawyer will keep it all very hush-hush. He knows the right people.'

No June wedding then. It'd be four months until he could legally marry Catherine. A spring wedding after all. A celebration under the apple blossom. It could work. 'Fine,' he said. 'I'll sign the papers and come to Sydney for court. But on one proviso.'

'Hmm?' She raised one perfectly plucked brow.

'That we never see you again.'

Her laugh was honey sweet, but laced with bitter almond. 'But, darling, that's exactly what I want too. Now everybody's happy.'

As soon as Lara left, Mark sought out Catherine, anxious to set things right. When he opened the door of her cottage her face was swollen with tears and white with rage. Before he could say a word, she launched into him.

'You've got a lot of nerve turning up here. You've been lying to me since the day we met. How could you not have told me about Angela? You've strung me along for years. You told me you loved me, but it was all lies. Everything that's come out of your mouth. Lies. Angela is the reason you stayed here. It was nothing to do with me.'

Mark deserved her anger, he knew it.

'And what about Charlie?' she continued, jabbing him in the chest with her finger. 'Does he know he has a sister or have you lied to him too? You can't keep your stories straight, your life's such a mess. Are you going to tell him his mother is alive? What if he finds out one day and knows you lied to him for so long?' There were tears of anger and pain in her eyes. 'I know how awful that feels.'

'Lara doesn't want—'

'Lara!' Catherine almost screamed the name. 'It's always been about Lara. Even when you thought she was dead, it was still all about her and your grief and your guilt. When have you ever put me first? When have you ever treated me like the woman you loved? You told me lies and gave me scraps.'

She pushed at him blindly, tears streaming down her face, trying to force him off the verandah.

'You told me there'd be no secrets between us. You're a liar and a fraud. I don't even know who you are. Certainly not the man I fell in love with. That man doesn't exist.' Catherine wrenched the engagement ring off her finger and held it out towards him. 'I'm not going to marry you. How could I? You're still married. But worse than that – you're a stranger to me.'

He stepped back. 'The ring is yours. Keep it. I hope one day you'll think me worthy of being your husband. I'm not going anywhere, Catherine. I love you.'

'Love? How dare you?' She gave him one final angry shove, spun on her heel and slammed the door so hard the cottage shook.

Mark stayed still for a moment, staring at the door. He had to fix this. But he had no idea how.

39

June 1972

Annie

Another wet, dreary day of trying to get endless loads of washing dry and school uniforms ironed. The pile of mending would have to wait until later, after Angela was asleep, the boys finally in bed and the household quiet. That was the time of day she relished – just her and Dave sitting quietly in front of the open fire, him reading the newspaper he hadn't had a chance to glance at all day, and her with the mending.

The tension between them was slowly abating. After the shock of Lara's return, Annie had clung to Angela with a fierce desperation that had scared the child. She'd kept her home from school, refusing to let her out of her sight. The fear of losing her was overwhelming. At first, she and Dave had hardly known how to speak to each other, and when they did it was in hushed tones away from the keen ears of the children. Their muttered discussions about what to do had

307

finally been resolved. Only then did Annie begin to release her grip on Angela and allow her to return to school.

Mark had been in no state to argue. His whole world had been tipped on its head. He'd left in a daze for Sydney and the divorce case, leaving Charlie in their care. And the wedding? It wasn't even talked about, a detail abandoned in the chaos Lara had left in her wake.

A sharp knock on the door jolted Annie out of the rhythmic swoosh of a hot iron on cotton school shirts. She wasn't expecting anyone and her tribe weren't due home from school quite yet.

'Hi, Annie.'

A shot of guilt hit her in the stomach. It was Catherine. They hadn't had a chance to talk since the day Lara's return had shattered their world. Annie had been secretly relieved. How could she explain? Catherine's face was drawn and set in a determined frown.

'I left school early. I wanted to see you, on your own.'

Annie recovered her senses and forced a smile. 'Come in. Since when do you knock?'

'Since I have no idea where I stand any more, or who to trust. Since I don't know what's true and what's a lie.'

Annie took a deep breath but said nothing as Catherine followed her through to the kitchen. She turned off the iron. Housework would have to wait. 'Cup of tea?'

'We don't have much time. The school bus will be here soon. I need to know what happened, Annie. I've been going crazy. I guess you know I sent Mark packing.'

'Sit down, at least. I'm going to. Been on my feet all day.' Annie shoved a pile of washing to one side and sat at the kitchen table. Slowly Catherine followed suit, sitting opposite her. Her eyes were fierce and Annie steadied herself for the onslaught.

'Tell me what happened. I've been left in the dark. I doubt Mark has said a true word to me since we met. You've been no better. Lie after lie. Now I need to know the truth. From the beginning.'

'From the beginning?' A lump formed in Annie's throat. She had longed for a girl, swearing she'd never treat her daughter the way her parents had treated her. She'd love her no matter what. 'My baby died. My little girl. She came early.' At the time Annie had felt as though she was being punished all over again and that her mother was right. Annie was unworthy. She didn't deserve a daughter of her own.

'I'm sorry, Annie. I never knew. You never told me. I could have—'

'No, you couldn't. No one could help. I was in a dark place.' She closed her eyes briefly, remembering. The hole inside had deepened endlessly, plunging her into a place so bleak she thought she'd never find her way out. Part of her had never wanted to. 'Then Lara came with Angela. She said, "Take her, she's yours." She hadn't known what to do when Charlie was born and never wanted to go through it again.' Annie's voice faltered. 'Lara said her baby girl was meant for me, not her. I swore that nothing would take Angela from me.'

'But what about Dave? What did he say?'

'He protested at first, but Lara left that same night and I—' She faltered. 'My arms were aching to hold a newborn baby. I'd made all the preparations ...' Annie took a breath. 'Dave knew the arrangement made sense. But the thing you have to understand is that I was broken by my baby's death. Finally a girl, but gone before she'd even lived. I couldn't do anything. Couldn't get out of bed. I was useless as a mother and a wife. Dave was suffering as well. But he couldn't afford to grieve because he had to look after me as well as the boys.'

'I tried to see you before I left for Hobart. Dave turned me away. He said you were struggling with the pregnancy. He never told me.'

'We didn't tell anyone except Mark. He must've told Lara.'

'And Mark? Was he happy to give his daughter away too?'

Annie slumped. The weight of Mark's anger and resentment was still a burden Annie carried every day. 'No. But Lara was gone and he had Charlie to take care of. How was he going to look after a baby as well? Even if Lara came back, he knew what an unreliable mother she was. She could never cope with two.' Annie had used that to justify her actions. Some women didn't deserve to have children. 'Then the fires came and everything changed.'

'Yes.' Catherine chewed her bottom lip. Annie looked at her properly for the first time since she'd arrived, remembering the tragedy her friend had suffered because of the bushfires.

Annie's happiness had come at a price. She'd been wary at first; worried someone would find out, and terrified Lara would waltz back into her life and take Angela back as easily as she'd given her away. Then her fear was that Mark would try to reclaim his daughter, even though he was working in the orchard as well as caring for Charlie, and a baby would have been too much for him to handle. He'd hung around though, always keeping an eye on the baby, which made Annie anxious. It didn't feel safe having him so close. She'd felt completely self-righteous about registering Angela's birth in her own name. When Lara had thrust Angela into Annie's empty arms she'd said, 'Your baby was never reported. Nobody knows she's gone. This is your baby now. Make it legal. Register her in your name. Yours and Dave's.'

Annie was certain she'd done the right thing. Dave wasn't convinced. His anger took her by surprise. But it was too late. He knew when he was beaten. It had been left to him to tell Mark and she knew it hadn't gone well. Another reason to fear Mark's presence. He mightn't have a legal leg to stand on, but he could make trouble if he put his mind to it.

'Didn't you ever feel guilty? So many lies.' Catherine sounded as though she genuinely wanted to know.

'You don't understand. Angela was mine. She was always meant to be mine. Lara said so herself. I never felt as though I was lying to anyone, especially not to you.' And not to her mother. Annie had written to her mother to tell her about Angela, as she had with all her children, but this time it was different. She wanted her mother to know this daughter was loved, cherished and protected. She sent photos and regular updates, each one of them reminding her mother that Annie was better at raising a daughter than she was, that Annie was everything she wasn't. Her mother never replied.

'But your baby—'

'I couldn't bear to think about what happened, let alone talk about it.' Somewhere on the property her baby lay. She'd never asked where. The thought only came to her occasionally now, fainter every year.

'Surely you worried that the truth would come out one day?'

'I was terrified. But after Lara was declared dead it made sense. Angela was better off with me and Dave, always had been.'

'But Mark didn't feel that way.'

When Mark finally went back to Melbourne, it had felt like the perfect outcome. Annie began to feel truly safe for the first time. But then he'd returned to the valley and proposed to Catherine, making the old fear raise its ugly head. Annie had become distracted and angry, always on edge and waiting for the axe to fall. Mark would tell Catherine the truth, claim Angela as his child and raise her with his new wife. But she could never admit this to Catherine. 'No.'

'And now Lara ...'

Annie had fretted over every scenario, but she'd never expected this. Lara, back from the dead, and bringing the lies crashing down around all of them. 'Yes, Lara. Like Lazarus, but in this case it was a miracle we could have done without. Especially you. I'm sorry, Catherine, about the wedding.'

Catherine blinked rapidly and looked away. 'I'm too angry to even think about it.' She faced Annie again. 'So, what are you going to do now?'

The clatter of boys on the front steps, the front door opening, the thump as school bags were dumped in the hall and the calls of 'Hi, Mum, anything to eat?' stopped the conversation cold.

'I'm going to get back to what I do best, being a mother.' Annie rose and started fussing with the piles of washing.

'Annie?' Catherine's voice was insistent.

Catherine would never understand. Her world was black and white – truth or lies with no room for anything in between. Annie saw things differently. When Lara had reappeared she'd made it clear that she wanted nothing to do with Angela other than a moment of curiosity, or Charlie for that matter. Her antipathy filled Annie both with rage and relief. How could a mother be so indifferent to her own children, abandoning them, just as Annie had been discarded by her mother? But her failure was Annie's gain. Angela was hers and would always be. She raised her head. 'I'm going to do the right thing.'

40

January 1973

Catherine

When the dreadful news rocked the valley, part of Catherine wasn't surprised. England joining the Common Market meant the collapse of their main export market and their primary source of income. It spelt ruin for the valley. To Catherine it was yet another catastrophe in a long line of disasters. The past months had been hell. Lies had created more lies. After everything he'd said and done to keep them apart, Catherine couldn't bear to admit to her father that he'd been right about Mark all along. When he'd asked why she wasn't wearing her engagement ring, Catherine had told him she didn't want to lose it in the orchard. The lack of a wedding was explained away with another lie – Mark had a contractual obligation to do an extended tour of the mainland with his band. In reality, after the divorce proceedings in Sydney, he'd spent time with Lara's parents in Melbourne trying to figure everything out, including what to do with the ashes buried under the plaque with Lara's name on it. Once

313

again Lara's lawyer had stepped in and taken care of it all, with everything hushed up by whatever means necessary. It had added to the layers of deceit and disrespect that Catherine hated.

Poor Charlie had been kept in the dark about everything. He'd stayed with Annie and Dave while Mark was away but shielded from what was actually going on. Catherine was forced to lie to Charlie too, because of decisions she didn't agree with. It created a tension whenever she saw him. Would Charlie ever know he had a sister? And would Angela ever be told? Annie still refused to consider it. The birth certificate named her and Dave as the parents. Angela should never know any differently. To anyone who asked, Lara was explained away as an eccentric aunt of Annie's. Everybody knew how rich her family was, and there'd been no hiding the expensive car with a chauffeur cruising through Cygnet that day.

Mark's lies were the worst. She'd been uncertain of him from the beginning, thinking he was waiting for Lara to come back. Then, after Lara's 'death' and Mark's return to the valley, she'd foolishly believed it was for her. But it was because of his other child. A daughter he'd given away. A secret he'd kept from her all this time. If he was capable of lying to her about something so important, what else was he capable of?

Catherine knew some of this mess wasn't Mark's fault. He'd honestly thought Lara was dead. But he'd gone along with so much deceit; the lies Lara wanted, Annie wanted and the lawyer wanted. There was no room left for what Catherine wanted. Charlie was the one who suffered most. He was looking forward to being the ring bearer at the wedding, and part of a whole new family. Instead, Mark and Catherine were like strangers. Since Mark had returned to Wattle Grove they had spent Sunday afternoons together, either at the river or the pickers' hut, but only for Charlie's sake and she never stayed long. She missed the afternoons and evenings she and Mark had spent in her bed, hungry for each other's touch, and afterwards lying tangled together, unwilling to let each other go. But she couldn't give herself, body or soul, to a man who'd lied about so much for so long. When people asked about when the wedding would be now Mark was back, Catherine gave vague unconvincing answers that never assuaged the doubt in their eyes.

And now, more bad news. Catherine trudged through the orchard towards her parents' house, pausing to touch a few of the growing apples. But what was the point of tending to them now? The heaviness in her heart filled her days with despair. She could see no glimmer of hope. The fire in 1967 had been devastating, and Peter's death heartbreaking, but she'd had something to fight for – getting the orchard back up and running. Then Charlie had given her joy and Mark's love had transformed her life. That had ended in deceit and pain. And now England had perpetrated the greatest betrayal of all.

Her father sat at the kitchen table, the orchard ledger in front of him along with assorted files and papers. His mouth was a grim line. 'We've got the Hong Kong market for the Red Delicious, but that's not enough. We could try to increase our sales to the mainland, but everyone's going to be doing that, and even when times were good those sales hardly paid enough to cover costs. The Jonathans, the Golden Delicious and Sturmers are dead in the water, I reckon. I was counting on the Brits to take all of them.'

There'd been rumblings about what might happen if England joined the Common Market, but no one had planned for this. With the stroke of a pen Tasmania, along with the rest of Australia, had lost its favoured nation status. The orchardists used to joke that England would buy every variety Tasmania chose to grow. Now England would be taking very little. Instead, a committee in Brussels would dictate which markets Britain would buy her apples from. Tasmania was a long way down the list. No longer would the apple ships wait three deep at Port Huon. No more would the trucks packed with boxes of apples line up through the streets of Hobart on their way to Constitution Dock. It was over.

Catherine's mother placed a teacake and two plates on the table next to the teapot and cups.

'Not having any cake, Mum?' Catherine asked.

'No appetite, darling. It's all a bit of a worry.' Her face brightened. 'Is Charlie going to come over today?'

'Not today.' Catherine was glad, in a way, that her mother didn't know about Lara. At least Charlie had one adult in his life who wasn't lying to him. But even so, with everything that had happened, Catherine kept his visits to a minimum.

'Oh.' Her mother sighed, her face contracting again. 'I might go and have a little lie down.'

Catherine's father waited until his wife was out of earshot. 'She's taking this pretty badly. As we all are. I can't believe Britain would do this, after all we've done for her.'

'What do you mean?'

'Helping in her darkest hour. Sending our young men over to fight in their thousands. Many never returned. Our best helped her win not one, but two wars, and now she's turned her back on us. It's a disgrace.'

Catherine's father had been born here, as had his father and grandfather, but there was still an enormous attachment to the 'Mother Country'. So many of the older generation referred to England as home, even though they'd never been there. And now their mother had abandoned her children.

'Doug Anthony is furious,' her father said.

'I'll bet.' Doug Anthony was the leader of the Country Party. Her parents were dyed-in-the-wool Country Party supporters, as were most farmers and orchardists.

'Been a monarchist all his life, but now he reckons he's going to join the Republican Movement. Don't blame him. Not the Queen's fault though. It's the bloody British Government.'

'Our government knew this was going to happen. I can't believe they didn't put anything in place.'

Her father shook his head. 'I reckon the Libs were too busy worrying about winning the election. Lot of good that did them.'

'The new government might do better.' The Labor Prime Minister, Gough Whitlam, had only been in power a little over a month, but already Catherine was impressed by how he was shaking things up.

'Bunch of radicals. Where's the money going to come from to fund all their promises? Anyway, the horse has bolted. I can hear the Argentinians cheering from here. They'll be shipping their cheap fruit into Europe holus-bolus. It was hard enough to compete before, but now?' He turned up his hands in a gesture of defeat.

One good year, Catherine thought. That's all they'd managed despite the endless work, season after season, with early mornings, late nights and no holidays. It had seemed worth it with a goal in sight. But now the goal posts had been moved. They had no hope of scoring, let alone winning.

Her father patted her hand. 'You're lucky you have a profession to fall back on. Me and your mum? What have we got? Worked all our lives for nothing.'

Tears sprung to her eyes, unbidden and unexpected. Her father had always been a figure of resilience and certainty. Yes, she'd battled against him, both of them being so stubborn in their own way, but he'd been her rock, no matter the circumstances. To see him crumble now, beaten by a political decision in a distant country, was too much. 'We've been through worse than this. We've got to keep trying. What about the stabilisation scheme? That can keep us going until we figure it out.'

Her father dropped his eyes to the ledger. 'The scheme won't last. Not now. It'll cost the government too much. There was a point to it when there was a market but it's gone.'

'But the Red Delicious – the Asian market. We still have that.'

'And it'll be a good selling point.'

'For what?'

'We have to get out now, before the rush. We're too small to survive. One of the bigger mobs might find our Red Delicious an attractive option.'

'What are you saying?'

'I've decided. Your mother's never been the same since Peter's death and being here is a constant reminder. The fire. Costs going sky-high. The competition from other countries. And now this.' His shoulders slumped. 'It's time to let it go.'

A hard cold band clamped her chest, restricting her lungs and stilling her heart. 'Dad?'

'I'm selling up.' He nodded his head slowly. 'I'm selling the orchard.'

41

January 1973

Mark

She came striding through the orchard towards him. The sight of her made the breath catch in his throat. She was angry, that much was clear – her hands were clenched and her jaw tight – but he was grateful to see her. Even though she had closed her heart to him, he was still at his happiest when they were together. He longed for her touch and the secret places he used to kiss her, but that was lost to him now. The joy he'd felt at their upcoming wedding was a torn shred of a memory blown away in a relentless wind of hurt and lies. He slipped the pruning scissors into the pouch on his belt and wiped his brow. The day was hot and still, the only sound was the drone of the ever-present flies. There were so many of them since Dave had started running more cattle – another reason to prefer apples as far as Mark was concerned.

'Annie told me I'd find you here. Don't know why you're bothering with the thinning. Might as well let them all grow wild.' She threw out a hand indicating the entire orchard.

'The Common Market.' He'd heard all about it from Dave.

'I've just been to see Annie, but she's too busy to talk. Worried about her own problems. And besides, she agrees with my father.'

Mark had no idea what she was talking about but didn't interrupt – he was thankful she was talking to him at all. She'd been so cold since his return from the mainland.

Catherine paced restlessly in front of him between the rows of trees, her hands shoved into the pockets of her shorts, kicking at stones and creating little puffs of dust with her work boots. 'Sell the orchard! How can he sell the orchard? It's my orchard too. Did he ask me? Did he ever talk it over with me, see if there was another solution, or something we could do together to fix this? Nope. He decided, just like that.' She clicked her fingers. 'If I was a man, I would have been consulted. If I were his son, he'd pass the orchard on to me. He wouldn't sell. If I was a man. If I was Peter.' Her eyes were wild with grief and anger, shards of blue swimming in unspilled tears. 'But you know what the really crazy thing is? Peter never wanted it. *I* was the one who always wanted to run the orchard. Peter's dream was to be a vet. He was always saving the possums from the traps, and rabbits. Drove Dad wild. He'd spend more time with our house cow and the chickens than any other of his chores. And then when Benno came along—' Catherine pressed her lips together and looked up into the flat blue sky. 'I told him I'd take over the orchard and he could be a vet if he wanted to be. I told him I'd help him. But Dad was right; it was a pipe dream. Peter's dead and Dad's going to sell the orchard. I don't know what to do. I really don't.' She sunk to the ground, burying her face in her hands.

Her despair was awful to watch. Mark knelt beside her, avoiding physical comfort since any touch from him had made her recoil in recent months. 'What does your heart tell you?'

'My heart?' She spat the words at him. 'My heart! I can't trust my heart. It trusted you. And my father. My heart trusted the orchard, and this land. My heart is an idiot. It's the last thing I should be listening to right now.'

'Okay, well, what do you want?'

'I want Peter to be alive. I want the orchard to be successful, with me running it. I want – to be loved.' Her face crumpled. 'To love you. But it hurts too much.' She shook her head. 'My heart is an idiot and so am I; believing in happy endings, in love, in England, believing in anything. It's all ruined. And I tried so hard.'

He reached out to help her up from the dirt, but she pulled away.

'I'm so sick of being angry all the time. With you, my father and Annie,' she took a shuddering breath, 'and I'm angry with Peter. Why did he have to die?'

'I'm sorry, Catherine, I truly am. For everything.' Mark's words were inadequate, he knew, but he felt helpless in the face of such distress. He'd never seen her like this.

'Sorry? Hah!' The rage was back in her eyes. 'You're to blame for so much of it. You lied to me. You, who stayed here for Lara and for Angela, not for me. It was never for me.'

He was grateful for her anger. For months their conversations had been polite and perfunctory, with Catherine putting up a wall of ice he couldn't penetrate. Now, at least, they were getting to the truth of things. 'You're right, to a point. I stayed, at first, because I was waiting for Lara to return and because of my daughter. By the time it became obvious that Lara wasn't coming back, it was too late. I'd fallen in love with you.'

Catherine looked down, her fair hair falling around her face. She stared at her hands and rubbed a callus on her index finger.

He spoke gently, not wanting to be shut out again. 'I was grateful for how you helped Charlie. He was so lost, and you brought him back. I will never be able to repay you for that.'

Catherine's voice was softer. 'He reminded me of Peter, when he was little. It felt as though I'd been given a second chance.'

Mark nodded. He'd always suspected as much. 'I fell in love with you, Catherine, and it tore me apart that Lara had disappeared and left such a mess. I couldn't be with you because I was married. I couldn't tell you about Angela because I'd promised Dave. He was hurting too. His daughter had just died. And all Annie did was shut herself away and cry until the day Lara gave our baby to her.'

Catherine nodded. 'She wouldn't see me, or even come to the door. I didn't know what was going on. Certainly not that her baby had died.' Despite the summer heat Catherine wrapped her arms around herself, as if cold. 'But you didn't tell me. You didn't trust me. You kept the lie alive.'

'I tried not to, truly. In the letter I wrote to you when I went away for Lara's funeral, I said I didn't want any secrets between us and when I came back I was going to tell you everything.' He sighed. 'But I never heard back from you, and you wouldn't take my calls—' Catherine went to object but he held out a hand. 'I know it wasn't your fault, but think about it. There I was in Melbourne, not knowing what you were feeling. I'd written you a letter saying there was something I needed to tell you, and you never responded. The moment you called me – you remember?' His fingers gently touched hers and she nodded slowly. 'I immediately set the wheels in motion to return, to you. I didn't come back for Angela. After Lara was declared dead I knew there was no chance. I came back for you.'

'But you stayed away so long.'

'Yeah, I did and I'm sorry. If I'd known ...' He risked taking her hand and to his relief she let him nestle her work-roughened one in his. 'The band's success was unexpected, but it happened and then I had obligations to them. And to Charlie. His mother was dead but his grandparents adored him. But all my thoughts were of you.' He stroked the back of her hand with his thumb. 'You are the seed, grown where you were planted, strong and true, reaching deep down into the soil and finding the essence of life. Me? I'm just the graft.'

She frowned and withdrew her hand. 'Have you learnt nothing? The graft is the bearer of the fruit. Without the graft there'd be no crop, no livelihood. Seed can never produce an apple that's true to type. The fruit is unpredictable, inconsistent. Is that how you see me?'

He laughed softly in exasperation. 'Here I am trying to be poetic and you bring me back down to earth. That's exactly what I'm talking about. You are my solid ground. I need you.'

'And yet you hurt me. So badly.'

'Yes, I did.' Mark shook his head. 'It was stupid of me to give that letter to Dave. I should've known Annie would read it. That's why she never told you about the letter or my calls. She was desperate to keep the truth about Angela hidden.'

'And you played along.'

'Not for her, for Dave. He'd seen his wife break apart, helpless to do anything about it. He was terrified of what would happen to Annie if I tried to take Angela away. I made a promise to him. Not to Annie, but to him.' He rubbed his eyes. He'd been conflicted, wanting to tell Catherine the truth but also wanting to keep his promise to Dave. Had his intentions been honourable or had he just been a coward?

Catherine sat quietly, and Mark held his breath, waiting for her next words.

'What's it been like? Watching Angela grow up, knowing she's yours but never being able to tell her the truth or spend real time with her?'

A wave of grief he was powerless to resist crashed through him, a pain he'd carried since the day Lara had given their baby away. How could words describe how it felt to lose his daughter and yet see her every day? To watch with love and sadness as she grew and changed. And Annie there, every minute, keeping Angela from him and never letting his daughter out of her sight. To never be able to tell Charlie he had a sister and to see them grow up together and yet so far apart. Embarrassed, he dashed a tear away.

Catherine's hand touched his shoulder. 'What a pair we are,' she said gently. 'Crying in the orchard.'

'I'm sorry, Catherine.' Mark took a deep breath. 'For everything.'

'Me too.' She leant her head against his shoulder as they clung to each other in the finely tilled dirt under the apple trees.

42

February 1973

Catherine

The anniversary of the fire passed with the usual tears and regrets. After six long years from that awful day, so much remained unhealed. The countryside still bore the scars: chimneys standing in the ruins of burnt-out houses, dead gums like skeletons in the bush, and abandoned orchards overgrown and gnarled into a fester of codling moth and black spot. A despair had settled on the valley since the news of England's defection to the Common Market. Catherine had been too hasty in resigning from her teaching job last year. She met with the headmaster of the school at Cygnet, hoping some work might be available, but he shook his head regretfully. 'We're expecting more families will leave the area and may be looking at composite classes. I'll have to let teachers go, not employ them. I am sorry.'

Catherine left his office with little hope, despite his assurance she'd be the first to know if any relief teaching came up.

She dropped in at her parents' place on her way home to see how the meeting with the property appraiser had gone that morning. She found her father in the kitchen, frowning at some paperwork. Catherine poured herself a cup of tea from the pot on the table and sat opposite him.

'What did the appraiser say?'

'Nothing good, I'm afraid.' He ran his hand through his thinning hair. 'With the bulk of the export market gone there aren't many who want to take on an orchard, even one with a fine crop of Red Delicious and Asian markets to sell to.'

Catherine was relieved. Maybe the sale wouldn't happen after all. 'Really?'

'They see the Asian market as fickle,' her father said. 'It's "untested". That was the word he used. I told him it's a strong market and only going to get bigger, but he wouldn't budge.'

Catherine turned her cup of tea in its saucer and wondered what her tea leaves might predict. She wanted to tell her father, yet again, the Asian market was why they should hold on to the orchard, but she knew what the result would be. Another argument and no ground conceded.

'Why don't you apply for a teaching job up in Hobart, Catherine? It'll be easier to find a permanent position there.'

'I have some money saved. We need to keep the orchard productive to show buyers what they're getting.' She was resolved to hang on until the last possible moment.

Her father sighed. 'You're throwing good money after bad. Your mother and I just want to get out. We have our eye on a nice little house in Hobart, but it'll probably be gone by the time we sell this place.'

'And if Peter was still alive?' Catherine kept her head down, not wanting to meet his eyes. 'Would you sell up? Or would you hand over the orchard to him in the hope he'd make a go of it?'

'Peter's gone and that's that.'

'But this is my home too.' She persisted, despite the warning in his tone. If she was going to lose her dream of running the orchard, she wanted to know why. 'It's my inheritance. You can't sell it out from underneath me.'

'Your mother and I need to move on. It's the best thing for you too. Go work as a teacher. It's a cushy job with long holidays and good pay – more than you'll ever get from this orchard. There's precious little to show for all the work we've done. I'll have to find a job in the city. I'm hoping for something with the council, standing around leaning on a shovel all day. That'd suit me fine.'

Catherine pressed her hand to her forehead. She and her father had been going around in circles for weeks now. She'd hoped he'd let her buy him out. She'd pay him half and the other half would be her inheritance. But he wouldn't agree. It was impossible anyway. She couldn't afford it and the bank wouldn't give a woman a loan without a husband's or father's consent. She didn't have a husband and her father would never agree. She pushed her chair away from the kitchen table. 'I've got to go, Dad.'

'I'll be spraying the upper block at dawn.'

'Right. I'll meet you in the spray shed.' She poked her head around the door to the living room. 'See you, Mum.'

Her mother looked up from knitting another jumper for Charlie. 'Leaving so soon? I was hoping you'd stay for tea.'

'Can't, Mum. Gotta go.'

'Will Charlie be popping over this weekend? I thought we'd make lamingtons. You and Peter used to love rolling them in coconut when you were little.'

'He'll be here.'

'Bye, darling.' Her mother's smile was enough to take the edge off the conversation with her father. Februaries were getting a little easier for her, mainly thanks to Charlie.

Catherine walked up the hill to the cottage. If her father did sell, she'd miss her pretty little weatherboard home. Over the past two years she'd made it her own with bright geometric curtains and abstract floral throw cushions. She'd even bought herself a beanbag, not that she found it at all comfortable, but she'd felt up with the times and Mickey liked it.

Mark sat waiting on her small verandah. They were slowly making their way back to each other. He was gentle and patient, but sometimes she felt like a skittish colt, spooked by an imagined wrong or remembered hurt. Thank goodness he'd never mentioned marriage again, although a few days ago he'd said he had a proposal for her. She'd immediately baulked, but he'd said it wasn't *that* kind of proposal and he'd come over to go through the details. And here he was, sitting in the late February sunshine with a wide grin on his face as she walked up the steps towards him.

He stood and kissed her softly. Her body responded, yearning for more, but she pushed the sensations away, not wanting to be drawn down that enticing but dangerous slope. Slowly, slowly, she reminded herself as she pulled away. He had to earn her trust again, and she needed to find the faith that he would. It was getting easier.

'Hope you don't mind,' he said. 'I let myself in. I needed to set something up.' There was something of Charlie in his expression, the boy hoping for praise for his latest drawing or admiration of his tadpole collection.

'I'm intrigued.'

'Come in and I'll show you.' He opened the door and stood aside so she could enter first.

Catherine looked around the room, wondering if something was out of place. Mickey was curled up on the beanbag as usual – it was as if he thought she'd bought it just for him. Then she saw it, sitting on a small table next to the standard lamp. 'A record player.'

'Yeah. I thought you might like it.'

Her parents used to have a radiogram but it had burnt in 1967 along with all the 78s, LPs, and Peter's collection of singles. They'd never bought a new one and it wasn't until this moment Catherine realised how much she'd missed it. She stepped towards the stereo and touched the perspex lid covering the turntable. Two speakers stood on either side. 'But I don't have any albums.'

'We can go record shopping up in Hobart one day if you like.'

'That'd be great.'

'I did bring one record with me. It's just a single but I want to play it for you.'

'Okay.' Catherine wondered whether it was one of the singles he'd released with his band. Was that the reason for his hopeful smile?

'Take a seat and I'll put it on.'

Catherine perched on the couch, sitting forward with her hands pressed between her knees. The needle hit the record with a slight hiss of static and the song began. 'I know this song,' she said. 'I've heard it on the radio. Even the ABC.'

'I'm not surprised. It's been a hit just about everywhere.' Mark's face showed his pride.

Catherine listened carefully. 'It's Glen Carter, isn't it?' Glen was an American singer who'd been massively successful in the 1960s. This was his comeback song.

'Yep.'

'I don't get it. Why are you playing me this?'

'It's called "Cathy's Song".'

'Yeah, I know. So?'

'Hang on a sec.' Mark stood by the record player waiting for the song to finish. He carefully removed the single from the turntable, holding the edges of the record with the flats of his hands and offered it to her as if it were a precious gift. 'Have a look at what's printed on the label, under the song title.'

Catherine peered at the record label. She saw three names in brackets: G Carter, M Davis and C Turner. 'I don't understand.'

Mark put the single back in its sleeve and sat beside her on the couch. 'It was called "Catherine's Song", but Glen's producer didn't think it scanned well, so they changed it to "Cathy's Song". Glen gets a writing credit because, well, he's Glen Carter, and he added a few flourishes here and there. But most of the song belongs to you and me.' He took her hands in his own. 'Us.'

'I still don't get it.'

'Do you remember at the pickers' hut, when I was doodling around on my guitar and you sang a melody to it?'

The memory was vague. They'd spent so many afternoons and evenings with Mark playing guitar and her singing along.

'When I was in Melbourne, missing you, I remembered that tune. I wrote a song about how I felt to your melody. It didn't fit the band, so my publisher shopped it around. Getting a song placed in the States is a bit like winning the lottery. Doesn't happen very often. It helped that Glen was desperate.'

'I see,' Catherine said, not seeing at all.

'This was going to be my wedding surprise for you.'

Catherine pulled away at the mention of the word wedding. 'A record player?'

'It's okay, I know a wedding is off the cards, but you need to know about this. They're half yours.'

'What are?' Catherine frowned in confusion.

'The royalties.'

'Oh.' Catherine faintly remembered Mark telling her about music royalties years ago and how they'd helped him survive despite the pittance Dave and Annie paid him.

'At the time I thought when the money came through, we might buy a small farm with a house of our own, chickens and a small orchard. We'd stay in the valley, or go anywhere you chose. I didn't care as long as we were together. But now, seeing how distraught you are about your father selling up, I have a different proposal in mind.'

Catherine's mind reeled. He was going to buy her a farm? Or he wasn't? None of this was making any sense.

'I know I've caused you pain in the past, but that's over. And now the cheque's finally here, you can have what you've wanted for so long.'

'What? How?'

'We have the money, Catherine. We have enough money to buy the orchard.'

43

July 1974
Annie

Dave looked at the ground or at the lowering sky, anywhere but the orchard.

Annie touched his arm. 'We're doing the right thing.'

'Thank God my dad's not here to see it.'

'He'd do the same.'

'I'm going into town for a bit.' Dave waved a hand in the direction of the bulldozer. 'Jim knows what to do. He's done a lot of this in the last year. He doesn't need me around, or you. Go inside. Keep warm.'

Annie pulled her cardigan tighter. She should have grabbed a scarf. The air was cold and close with a dampness that insinuated itself into boots and clothing. It was one of those winter days when the sun barely rose above the hills, and the landscape was cloaked in a thin wispy mist. A southerly wind came in gusts, bringing the freezing air straight from the Antarctic. The apple trees looked like

332

ghostly Christmas trees with hardly a leaf left, but still abundant with apples that weren't worth picking. 'Perhaps we can use the money to buy a bulldozer. Plenty of work around for one of those.' Annie's joke fell flat, as she knew it would.

'Tomorrow, I was thinking, we could go up to Hobart.' Dave turned his back on the bulldozer. 'Have lunch at the Coles Cafeteria. Watch the Cat and Fiddle clock in the arcade just for fun. We'd be back before the kids get home from school. It'd be a nice break.'

'Sounds lovely.' Annie knew Dave was grieving, but he'd never admit it. He kept asserting that this was a sound financial decision. The orchard would drag them under. Being paid by the government to grub out the trees was an opportunity too good to miss. Yet here they were, on the first day of the bulldozing, and he couldn't wait to leave.

Dave turned and waved at Jim standing beside the dozer. 'Rightio. All set?'

'Yep.'

Jim was bundled up in a heavy jacket, scarf, hat and work gloves. It would be a long cold day's work for him today and into the following weeks. How did he feel, destroying the toil of so many generations? She supposed he was grateful for the work; anyone around here would be. A pall of depression had settled in the valley like a clammy fog. Orchards were disappearing under the relentless grunting pressure of bulldozers – the earth was raw where the roots had been torn away and long rotting windrows of ugly knotted stumps marred the hills where tourists once came to marvel at their beauty.

Dave hugged her briefly, and she sensed his apology in it. He felt he'd let her down. She grabbed his hand, clasping it tightly. 'I love you, David Pearson. Don't you ever forget that. I've never regretted one day of our lives together, and I won't regret this one.' She kissed him with the same passion she'd felt the day they'd met in the rain all those years ago. He clung to her like a drowning man.

It was only for a moment. Dave cleared his throat and straightened up, pushing his shoulders back with a sense of determination. 'Right. I'll be back before tea.' He waved once more at Jim, who was shuffling in embarrassment by his bulldozer. 'Thanks, Jim. I'm heading out. Any problems, we'll sort them out later.'

His expression caused Annie's breath to falter. Her husband had worked so hard to protect his family, provide for them and give them a good future. She'd seen the same look on the faces of the men in Cygnet and Huonville – shame and despair. Their livelihoods were gone, their sense of purpose and a place in this world snatched away. The apple industry had been faltering for years, but when England had joined the Common Market it was the death blow. The government had come up with the Tree Pull Scheme, but orchardists were still scrambling to find something to replace apples and support their families.

Jim climbed onto the dozer and the engine rumbled into life.

Dave recoiled from the sound; she could see it. Shoulders hunched, he walked to the car.

Annie waved goodbye as the roar of the dozer filled her ears. She'd have to get used to it; it would be the soundtrack of her life for the next few weeks.

It was always the same. Annie heard her horde of boys arriving home from school before she ever caught a glimpse of them. Today their whoops of excitement cut through the rumble of the dozer. Greg and Scott, her two youngest sons, threw down their schoolbags as soon as they tumbled through the door. 'Can we go out in the orchard and play, Mum? Please?'

'Change out of your uniforms and put your gumboots on first. And you might want to have a look in the kitchen before you go running off.' She marvelled at their ability to see everything as an adventure. They'd be clambering over the grubbed-out stumps, turning them into imaginary forts and mysterious hiding spots, never realising the agonising nights of discussion that she and Dave had gone through to reach their decision.

Paul and Eric ambled up the steps, both young teenagers now, their shirts untucked and their schoolbags heavy with textbooks and homework.

'We'll have a grouse bonfire at cracker night this year,' Paul was saying. 'Pile all those trees up, and bang!'

'I'm gonna check out the dozer,' Eric said.

'Bet he won't let you drive it.'

'Why not? Can't be much different to the tractor or the crawler.' Eric had proudly conquered the idiosyncrasies of their old tractor and had helped with the spraying in the early mornings before school over the past year. They'd keep the tractor – it would still be useful – but not the crawler, though no one would want to buy it now. It would lie useless and quiet, like the grader in the packing shed, gathering dust and mice.

'Hi, Mum.' They slouched into their room and emerged wearing old and patched farm clothes. She knew their school uniforms would be in a tangled mess on the floor. It didn't matter how many times she told them.

'I like cows better anyway,' Eric said.

'Cause you smell like them,' Paul retorted.

'There's a chocolate cake in the kitchen.' Annie cut into the brotherly taunts.

'Wow. Really?'

She usually offered them bread and jam after school, and a glass of Milo if there was any left, since the boys ate it by the spoonful. But today she'd needed cheering up and thought the boys would too. She was wrong. It reminded her of the bushfires. At the time they were too young to understand the extent of the destruction and the pain of the consequences, instead seeing the fire as exciting and dramatic. That was in 1967, when it all began to unravel. The fire, and then their fruit trapped in the Suez Canal incident, left to rot as the war raged on. The canal was still closed, but at least the insurance company had finally paid out. The money had helped them get through the aftermath of the hailstorm last year. Freight and oil prices had begun escalating after the canal closure, wages kept increasing, as well as the cost of sprays and fertilisers. Then the erosion of their export markets by other countries saw smaller returns for their fruit. It had been one thing after another. The only good thing to happen in 1967 was Angela, but even that joy had come at a cost. Would she ever tell Angela the truth? How could she explain it? They'd only heard from Lara once since she'd appeared back from 'the dead'. A parcel had arrived addressed to Emily. The postman had looked at Annie quizzically when he'd given it to her. Annie saw the British stamps and fear had gripped her. What did Lara want now? 'Oh, it's from my aunt,' she'd explained. 'She's always getting the children's names mixed up.' Inside was the gold snake bracelet with emerald eyes. No card. No letter. Annie had kept the bracelet hidden at the top of her wardrobe behind the boxes and bits and bobs that accumulated over the years. And here was Angela now, clambering up the steps, her extraordinary golden eyes a constant reminder of Lara. God, how Annie wished they'd been any other colour, but this was the truth she lived with.

'Hello, darling. Did you have a nice day at school?' When Angela had started going to school Annie had reluctantly begun to let go.

She'd had to, especially when Angela formed friendships with her classmates. It was natural that her daughter would want to spend time with girls her own age, surrounded as she was by brothers who never wanted to play with dolls or teddies. It had been a wrench at first, but Annie was pleased to see Angela blossom into a popular young girl.

'Yes, Mummy. I wrote a composition about birds.'

'How wonderful. Now run into the kitchen and get some chocolate cake before the boys eat it all.'

'Yummy.' Off she scampered, her long dark plaits bouncing on her slender shoulders.

Michael, her oldest, was last in. He always kept an eye on his brothers and especially his little sister, making sure they arrived home safely. Michael was growing into a fine young man, aware of his responsibilities and never shirking from them.

'Mum. The orchard.' His face was dark with concern. 'Is this really the only way?'

'I know it's hard, but it's for the best.'

'That's my future being torn to shreds out there.' There was no belligerence in his voice, only pained confusion.

'There's no future there. Not for any of us.'

'Catherine's not bulldozing her orchard.'

Annie swallowed her sigh. Catherine and Mark were idiots for paying Jack Turner as much as they had for the orchard. They'd have got it for half the price if they'd waited. Land prices were falling fast. Still, the money had come from nowhere, so it was fitting it was going nowhere. Royalties from songs? Who'd ever heard of such a thing? Not that it had done Mark any good. Catherine still wouldn't marry him. She'd insisted on his half of the money being a loan. She wanted to own the orchard outright and run it her way. How she would pay Mark back, God only knew. He and Charlie were living in the Turners' old cottage now, while Catherine rattled around in her parents' place. They all seemed happy with the arrangement. Catherine and Mark asked if Charlie could hang out with her boys from time to time. Annie was in no doubt as to what they got up to when Charlie wasn't around to interrupt them.

'They were lucky with their Red Delicious, Michael. Right apple at the right time. It's impossible to judge these things. You just don't know when you decide on a variety whether it's going to be popular down the track. The market changes so quickly. And some of our trees were planted by your grandfather. They're old and expensive to work.'

Michael jammed his hands in his pockets. 'Can I talk to you for a second?'

'Your brothers are in the kitchen eating all the cake. Are you sure you don't want to join them?'

'Nah, that's a good thing. It means we won't be interrupted.'

Annie cocked her head in curiosity, followed Michael into the lounge room and sat beside him on the couch.

'I've been thinking, Mum. I'm nearly sixteen and old enough to leave school now.'

'Yes, but you've still got five months to get your Leaving Certificate.'

'What good's a Leaving Certificate if I'm not doing matric? And what good's matric if I'm not going to uni?'

Annie had always hoped her children could go on to better things, but until this year wasn't sure if it would ever be possible. 'You could go to university, if you wanted to, now there are no fees.' The Labor Government had made all tertiary education free. Her parents had always been Liberal Party supporters and Dave naturally voted for the Country Party, but Annie had been one of many to back Gough Whitlam with his promises of free education and health care.

'Oh, Mum. I'm not cut out for uni. I've always been better with my hands than with books. I always thought I'd take over the orchard but now ...' He spread his hands in a gesture of defeat. 'There are jobs going at the new trout farm in Huonville. I could bring in some money for the family. I mean, things are going to be tougher than ever, right?'

Annie and Dave had always tried to keep their financial worries away from the kids and clearly had failed. But this? Michael going out to work to put food on the table? She couldn't bear it. 'No, darling. The government is giving us money to grub out the trees. Once we've paid Jim, there'll still be plenty left over. We have plans. Other crops, maybe hops or tomatoes, even berries.' They'd also thought about more cattle but the prices were so low right now. 'We'll get through this. What we need from you at the moment is to stay at school, get your Leaving Certificate and then think about what you want. Okay?'

Michael looked uncertain. 'Well, what I really want is to be a mechanic. Me and my friends have been talking about getting apprenticeships and studying at the Tech in Hobart. It's free to go there too.'

'Oh?' Another thing to blame Mark for. Michael had always been good with engines but after Mark had turned up in that ridiculous yellow thing, he'd become besotted with cars. Mark had encouraged him to poke around under the hood with him until the hailstorm had destroyed it and Mark bought a much more practical ute, but the damage was already done. Michael talked of nothing but cars for months. 'It would mean moving to Hobart.'

'I could look after myself. One less mouth to feed.'

'And you eat a lot.' Annie laughed when all she wanted to do was cry.

'There's nothing for us in the valley now. My friends and me, I mean. We're talking about getting a house together in Hobart, somewhere cheap.'

So this was it. Her first-born spreading his wings and leaving home. Memories of Michael as a baby, a toddler and a cheeky six-year-old made her heart ache. They'd all thought he'd take over the orchard one day, but soon there'd be no orchard. What remained for him here except hard work with no certainty of reward? A relentless grinding slog that ended in heartbreak.

'Mum?'

Annie contemplated her son. He would leave the valley. So many would, the young first. Maybe, one day, she and Dave would drive away and never look back. Families were already packing up and moving to Hobart or the mainland hoping for greener pastures. 'We'll talk about it when your father gets home.' She smiled. 'Now go get some cake.'

He left her sitting alone in the gathering gloom. In a moment she'd ask one of the boys to make the fire. The sun would be setting soon, as it did so early on these winter afternoons. The kitchen would be warmer, with the remnant heat of the oven and all her children bustling around the table, but she didn't want to join them, not yet. She finally allowed a tear to escape. Dave would see the sense in it. He'd want Michael to follow his dream. All Annie had to offer was love and chocolate cake. Once it had been enough. She sat listening to the grind and clash of the bulldozer while the darkness drew in around her.

44

July 1974
Catherine

Judith Turner had soundly rejected the idea of having a fireplace when their new house was built, unable to bear the smell of burning wood. Catherine huddled by the oil heater her father had so proudly installed instead.

'Efficient and economic,' he'd said at the time.

That was before oil prices had surged and heating oil became hard to come by. On these bitterly cold mornings Catherine sorely missed her grandmother's old wood stove. She wondered if Mark had mastered the art of keeping it burning all night so that he and Charlie awoke to a toasty warm cottage. She reached down to scratch Mickey behind the ears – he'd settled in a warm spot after a long night of ratting. He'd adjusted to the move, but Catherine wasn't so sure she had. This house was less draughty than the cottage and the hot water system certainly more effective, but it was still her parents' house. Most of the furniture had remained behind, with her

341

mother keen for a fresh start in Hobart. Catherine had left the main bedroom exactly as it was, preferring to sleep in her old room. There was one thing she'd changed. Her mother had raised an eyebrow on a recent visit when she'd seen the double bed in Catherine's room.

She wrapped her hands around the mug of tea, remembering a few days ago when she and Mark had ended up in that bed. They were supposed to be going through the yearly budget, but their hands had brushed up against each other, which led to lips and mouths and fingers touching and exploring. It had been a pleasurable distraction from the reality of the numbers, most of them written in red. He was coming over again this morning and they had to concentrate this time, even though the task was disheartening. The shipping line had recently announced a 25 per cent increase in freight rates for the Tasmanian run and as a result everything was more expensive. The Red Delicious were keeping the orchard afloat, barely. They needed to find new markets for the other varieties. Even with thousands of trees being grubbed out in the valley, the competition was still fierce and the apple industry in disarray. It was heartbreaking to see the ruin of Dave and Annie's orchard, the mangled heaps of broken trees amid the churned-up mud left by the bulldozer. But it was a solution she might have to confront herself when it was costing money to keep her unprofitable varieties in the ground.

The small amount of relief teaching available at the school helped with expenses, but she was loath to go back to full-time teaching even if there was a position. This was her orchard and she was determined to keep it that way. She was grateful for Mark's help and for his tireless work in the orchard. 'Just keeping an eye on my investment,' he'd say with a mischievous smile, and sometimes she wasn't sure if he meant the orchard or her. The cottage was certainly a more pleasant home for him and Charlie than the pickers' hut, and for now he seemed satisfied. There'd been no more mention of marriage. She did love him but was still finding her way in this ever-changing world, and marriage, she felt, would be one thing too many. She kept his ring though, safe in its box, tucked in the top drawer of her dressing table. To give it back would feel too final, and the one thing she was sure of was that she wanted Mark and Charlie in her life. The thought of living without them was unbearable.

A knock on the back door roused her from her thoughts. 'Paper delivery, ma'am.' Mark smiled as she opened the door and offered her the morning copy of *The Mercury*. 'While I was in Cygnet I dropped into the bakery. Couldn't help myself.' In his other hand he held a white paper bag. 'Neenish tarts.'

'My favourite.' The rich iced tarts were her guilty pleasure. Her mother used to make them, but Catherine had never mastered the art of getting the pastry, buttercream filling and two-tone icing just right. 'Come in and I'll make a fresh pot of tea. I've got us set up in the lounge room next to the heater.'

'Didn't think it could get any colder and yet here we are.' Mark took off his boots, leaving them at the back door, and padded after Catherine. 'The frost shows no sign of melting this morning.'

Catherine glanced through the newspaper while the kettle boiled. 'Politicians are giving themselves another pay rise, I see.'

'It's hardly news, it happens so often.'

Catherine huffed in frustration. 'Half their luck.'

'Yeah, but would you want to be a pollie?' Mark opened a cupboard and took out two plates. He knew his way around the kitchen. He'd even cooked dinner for Catherine a couple of times, and more than bangers and mash.

'No. But there are plenty of crackers in it.'

'I think you'd have to *be* crackers. I'd much rather be a neenish tart.' Mark grinned as he placed two tarts on each of the plates.

'Two each?' Catherine was delighted.

'I thought we'd need some sustenance to get through the paperwork. Besides, I want to sweeten you up.'

Catherine poured the boiling water over the tea leaves in the pot. 'Hmmm. Is this to do with your possible solution?' Mark had hinted at something that might ease the financial strain.

'Let's go sit by the heater. It's freezing in here.' Mark gathered the plates and slung a couple of empty mugs from his fingers. 'After you.'

When they'd settled close to the heater, Mark flicked through the orchard ledger. 'Not looking too promising, is it?'

'Do you regret it?'

'What?' He looked genuinely startled.

'Lending me your half of the money. There are so many other things you could've done with it.'

Mark reached for her hand. '"Cathy's Song" would never have existed without you. I can't think of anything more fitting for the royalties than buying the land you love. You know how I feel about you, and Charlie's the happiest he's ever been. I have no regrets at all.' He smiled, his weatherworn face showing laugh lines around his eyes and mouth. 'I'm here for the long haul. Which brings me to the idea.'

'Your solution?'

'Not so much a solution as a possible way of helping out.'

Catherine put her mug down on the coffee table beside the damning accounts. 'I'm listening.'

Mark pressed his lips together, appearing to be thinking carefully about his next words. 'The upper block is the hardest to work because of the degree of the slope.'

Her heart sank. If he was going to suggest applying to the Tree Pull Scheme and grubbing out the trees, did he actually think she hadn't considered it? The soil was the poorest up there behind the cottage. It cost more to fertilise, more in sprays because the trees weren't as resilient, and it was trickier to pick the apples.

'Well, I have some friends who'd like to lease it.'

'Lease the upper block?' Catherine was astounded. 'Whatever for?' The block was only a couple of acres, way too small to make a living.

'They're in Melbourne and want to make a change, like I did. They have a dream of living on the land, growing their own food, being close to nature. They were thinking of Nimbin, but decided they'd rather move here after I'd raved about how beautiful it is. Izzy sold her house in Fitzroy and land here is so cheap at the moment.'

Catherine winced. They'd paid too much for the orchard but Mark had never complained.

'I suggested they rent first to get a feel for it, you know, to find out whether it's really for them. Leaving the city for the country is a big change, and a massive challenge.' He chuckled. 'I know that from experience.'

'Izzy. Your old roadie, right?' Catherine had been fascinated when Mark had told her about Izzy, a woman doing what was usually a man's job. She'd felt a camaraderie with her even though they'd never met. Now, it seemed they might.

'Yeah. Great chick. You'll love her. She's capable and a real hard worker, but this whole move to the country thing was Stardust's idea. She's lived on a couple of communes. Got some interesting ideas about growing food and wants to try them here. And Izzy would do anything for her.'

'Stardust?'

Mark shrugged. 'It's a name she felt drawn to. Probably from the Joni Mitchell song.'

'You said they were a couple. They're both women?'

'Yeah,' Mark said slowly, concern in his eyes. 'Is it a problem?'

Catherine had never met any homosexuals. Most of them lived in cities, which she could understand. You'd want a lot of support if you were fighting a battle like theirs. Would it be a problem having lesbians living on the property? Her father would have a fit, but it wasn't his land any more. 'No, not at all,' she said. 'But it might be for Izzy and Stardust. Cygnet is a small town. I can't imagine they'll be readily accepted.'

'Small-minded people will always have small minds. Their kind will die out eventually. The world's changing all the time. Faster and faster.'

'Hmm.' Catherine wasn't so sure. This wasn't Sydney or Melbourne; this was a small town on an island at the bottom of the world. Attitudes were passed down through the generations.

'Haven't you noticed the changes? Even here?' Mark asked.

'Yes, but not for the better.' Cygnet was like a ghost town. So many people had left the area. Properties up for sale that'd never sell, houses for rent that no one wanted to live in, and clearing sales every weekend with owners desperate to get some money any way they could. The orchards that weren't being ripped out were simply abandoned and left to grow wild. 'Why on earth would anyone want to move here?'

Mark leant closer. 'Because it's beautiful. The air is pure, the water is clear. It's unspoilt. The fact that land and houses are cheap is also real attractive to certain people.'

'The hippies.' She'd seen them in town during the summer with their Indian gear and their bare feet. Deb at the Four Square supermarket had told her they'd bought some land along Nicholls Rivulet way. They were living there in their cars and vans, building some kind of shack. 'They're a rum lot,' Deb had said. 'But they seem quite nice. They only ever buy rice and beans, but at least they're spending money.'

Not everyone was so kind. 'They look untidy,' Mrs Smith had said at the hardware store. 'And no shoes. How can you work without shoes?'

'You can't,' her husband had answered. 'That mob's useless. They don't do anything. Not like us; we're used to work and plenty of it. Those layabouts wouldn't know what work was if it hit them on the head.'

Catherine thought if the hippies were making a go of it up in the back blocks they'd certainly know about work. It wouldn't be an easy life.

'Yeah, the hippies. And Stardust is proud to call herself one. Izzy?' Mark shrugged. 'Not so much. But they say opposites attract and it sure is the case with those two.'

'Okay, so they want to lease the upper block. But what about the trees? And where are they going to live?'

'One thing at a time. So, theoretically, you're okay with them leasing it?'

'They'll pay money to live here and take care of the trees?'

'That's the idea. They want to stay a year to begin with to see if it's what they really want.'

Catherine had no idea what would happen with two city women trying to work the trees, but she'd been considering bulldozing them into the ground anyway. 'Okay.'

'Are you sure?'

Catherine took a breath. Was she? No, not at all, but it would mean a small amount of income and a lot less work. Plus, she was desperate enough to try just about anything. 'Yes.'

Mark's face broke into a broad grin. 'Great, because they'll be here in two weeks.'

45

August 1974
Catherine

A blue Bedford van pulled up next to the house. Catherine wasn't sure what she'd expected, but something like a Kombi with flowers painted on the sides. This van was solid and practical. A lithe yet compact woman stepped down from the driver's seat, her hair a wild halo of frizz. From Mark's description, it had to be Izzy.

Mark waved from the verandah. 'Come on in out of the cold.'

Catherine hoped her smile didn't look forced. She was nervous about two strangers living on her orchard, looking after her trees. Mark hadn't told her much about their methods, preferring they tell her themselves. 'It's a bit different from what you're used to,' was all he'd say.

'Good to see you, mate,' Izzy said. Her voice was low and raspy, as if she lived on whiskey and cigarettes.

'Bit different to our usual gigs.'

'Exactly why we're here.' Izzy laughed, a deep throaty chuckle. She leapt up the steps. 'Getting back to nature. Living off the land. Who'd have thought?' She gave Mark a hug, slapping him on the back at the same time.

Catherine was baffled when she heard hippies talk about nature and the land, as if it was something they'd invented. It was all she'd known growing up. Living by the seasons, growing vegetables, with eggs from the chickens and milk from a house cow. She still missed Petunia. Their house cow had survived the bushfire only to die a few years later from a suspected snakebite. Probably just as well. Milking was not something Catherine was adept at, not like Peter or her mum.

'You must be the famous Catherine.' Izzy turned her smile on Catherine and thrust out her hand. 'I can see what all the fuss was about. No wonder Mark came running back here.'

Catherine blushed as she shook Izzy's hand. 'I've heard a lot about you too.'

'Yeah, I'll bet.' Izzy winked at Mark. 'The times we've had. The miles we've travelled in the old van.' She indicated the Bedford. 'You wouldn't recognise her inside now.'

'No?' Mark asked.

'I'll let Stardust tell you. She supplied the inspiration and I did the grunt work. It's how we roll. And talking of my beloved, here she is.'

Stardust floated up the steps, her hair drifting in Pre-Raphaelite waves of gold and accompanied by a waft of scent – woody and sweet. She was swathed in layers of tiered skirts, muslin scarves and a large white ribbed jumper with sleeves so long they covered her hands entirely. Completely impractical for orchard work. Then Catherine noticed her boots. They were serviceable and worn, like her own Blundstones. Perhaps there was more to this woman than her white jumper and skirts. Stardust joined them, making a small bow of greeting with her hands pressed together as if praying. 'Thank you,' she said in a voice soft as a gentle breeze. 'We're honoured you've chosen to share your beautiful piece of this planet with us.'

'Good to see you again, Stardust,' Mark said. 'Let's get inside though. There's a bite to this weather.'

They settled themselves in the lounge room by the heater with mugs of tea, or in Stardust's case a mug of hot water because she only drank herbal tea. Catherine had never heard of it.

'Apple cake?' Catherine had just taken it out of the oven. 'It's still warm.'

'Is it wholemeal?' Stardust asked.

'What?'

'The flour?'

Catherine shook her head. Why would anyone make a cake with wholemeal flour? It'd be too heavy and only good for feeding to the chickens. Mark was perfectly at ease with Stardust's odd ways, but Catherine was baffled by almost everything about her. Only her boots made sense.

'I'll have a piece,' Izzy said. 'I'm starving. It's a bit of a drive. Mind you, we won't be going far after today. We're looking forward to staying in one place and putting Stardust's plan into action.'

Catherine glanced at Mark as she passed him a slice of cake. He nodded, knowing she was bursting to ask the questions that had been buzzing around in her head for the past fortnight. 'What are your plans?' She tried to keep the nervousness out of her voice and wasn't sure she'd succeeded.

Stardust sat straight and serene in her chair. 'To start with I'll be getting in touch with the vibrations of the trees.'

Catherine blinked and looked at Mark for support.

'I see,' Mark said steadily. 'And how do you go about doing that?'

'Everything in nature has a vibration. I'll tune in to theirs so we may work together in harmony.'

Izzy stopped consuming cake for a moment. 'This is stuff Stardust picked up living on communes. It's fascinating and backed up with years of study.'

'Really?' Catherine wondered who'd conducted the studies. She was sure this method of agriculture wasn't taught in any of the colleges. Those poor trees. It looked as though she'd have to grub them out after all, once Stardust had finished vibrating with them.

'Can I have another piece?' Izzy inclined her head towards the cake. 'It's delicious.'

'Of course.' Catherine cut another large slice and placed it on Izzy's plate.

'There was this guy called Steiner,' Izzy said. 'He worked out all these theories about how to grow stuff naturally, in tune with nature. Biodynamics, that's what it's called, isn't it, Stardust?'

Stardust nodded. 'It's well established in Europe where they've been using the practices for decades.'

'And there's a biodynamic research institute near Melbourne.' Izzy wiped some crumbs from her mouth. 'Stardust has spent time there too.'

'I learnt so much from the institute. Which reminds me, I'll need cow horns and cow manure. Is there somewhere nearby that can supply me with some?'

'The Pearsons' place just over the road has plenty of both; can't get any closer than that,' Mark said. 'But why do you need them?'

'I'll put the manure into the cow horns and bury them. Winter is the time to do it. Later, in the spring, we'll dig them up and mix the humus with water.'

'There's a lot of stirring involved,' Izzy added.

'Then at night when the moon is new I'll use it to fertilise the orchard. We won't need any chemicals.'

Catherine sat, stunned. She'd never heard such poppycock.

351

Izzy smiled at Stardust proudly. 'And you've also developed some theories of your own, haven't you, my love?'

'Yes. I'm looking forward to putting them into practice in your beautiful orchard.'

Catherine wasn't sure what to make of all of this, but she knew about orchards. 'The trees are pruned, but you'll need to keep on top of the tilling and hoeing. You can borrow the crawler.'

'What do you mean?' Stardust tilted her head to one side, like a curious bird.

'The crawler? It's like a tractor but with tracks instead of wheels. Much easier to use on the slope.'

'No, about tilling and hoeing.'

'We've had a bit of rain and the weeds and grass are growing pretty quickly, even in this cold. Best to keep on top of them.'

'Oh, we'll let them grow.'

'But you can't.'

'Why ever not?'

Catherine paused. All orchardists tilled and hoed every bit of dirt around their trees. It was the way things were done. 'Because when we fertilise we'd just be feeding the weeds, which compete with the trees for nutrients.'

Stardust sipped her hot water. 'Grassing down orchards is popular in Europe and increasingly so here in Australia. Sod culture helps keep the moisture in the ground, and some so-called weeds, like clover, release nitrogen into the soil.'

Catherine glanced at Mark to see what he thought and immediately looked away. She knew more about apples than he ever would. He'd learnt a lot in his years working with Dave, but it was in her blood. 'If that's what you want to do, I wish you luck.'

'Thank you.' Stardust's smile was genuine and Catherine felt a stab of guilt that her own remark had been less than generous.

'I guess you'll be mowing then, once the grass grows, rather than ploughing? The crawler will come in handy then.'

'Oh, I think the chickens will help keep the grass down, as well as eating the bugs we don't want. And the sheep will certainly be happy to do the mowing for us.'

Catherine nearly choked on her tea. 'Sheep? In the orchard?' She'd seen the damage sheep could do. They chewed the bark, grazed on the lower branches and ate the apples. In some of the abandoned orchards, where the weeds grew out of control, farmers had opportunistically run sheep and the trees were ruined. 'But they'll eat the trees.'

Stardust's laugh was a gentle tinkle. 'I'll ask them very nicely not to. I might give them a couple of trees to keep them happy. The advantages of sheep are many. Their urine is high in nitrogen, and sheep manure is a superb fertiliser. They'll eat the windfalls, meaning less pests and diseases. Then there's their wool, so beautiful and useful.'

Catherine didn't trust herself to say anything. She knew Mark was willing her to keep an open mind, but sheep in the orchard? They'd have to build a fence between the upper block and the main orchard, which was something she hadn't factored in. She took a deep breath. These women were helping her keep her beloved orchard. If they had some ideas she didn't agree with, well, she'd have to learn to live with them.

'So, Izzy.' Mark's tone indicated a change of subject. 'Tell me about the van. Sounds as if she's changed since the days when we'd load and unload her ten times a week.'

As Izzy leant forward, Catherine was aware of the woman's strength even in that small movement. 'It's so cool. I built the interior. Compartments for everything, plenty of storage under the bed and I've attached an annexe that pulls out for a living room. But the decor is all Stardust's doing.' Izzy reached out and took Stardust's hand. 'She's magical.'

Stardust smiled at Izzy in a way that made the heat rise in Catherine's cheeks. The love between the women was palpable. Catherine had to admit to herself, if not to anybody else, that she'd need time to get used to seeing two women together like this.

'I do love stars, it's true,' Stardust said. 'Izzy and I have our own universe inside our tiny home.'

'Like Dr Who's Tardis,' Mark quipped.

Even Catherine laughed, grateful to Mark for dispelling her awkwardness.

After more tea, and more cake for Izzy, they walked up to the upper block. Stardust stretched her arms out wide. 'I embrace this land. I embrace these trees. I embrace all creatures and the part they play in our ecology.'

Catherine wondered if Stardust would want to embrace the possums and rabbits once she saw the damage they did, let alone the codling moths and looper grubs. As Stardust moved through the orchard, caressing the trees and whispering into their branches, Catherine shuffled and stamped her feet, pretending it was the cold making her fidgety. She loved the orchard, but the trees were to be worked to ensure they cropped reliably, free of black spot and blight and whatever else nature threw at them, not cosied up to like a lover.

'Right then.' Izzy clapped her hands together. 'I'll get the van and we'll start our grand adventure. Thanks again, Catherine. You won't regret this.'

Catherine gave a small, tight smile. She was regretting it already.

Winter rolled on in clouds of sleet and ice, the temperature barely registering in double figures during the day, and plunging at night. Snow draped in folds over the mountains behind the banks of the Huon River. Catherine went about her work rugged up in layers of jumper, jacket, rain jacket and scarves. Even so the relentless mist and drizzle managed to slip through, chilling her to the bone. She worried about Izzy and Stardust perched at the top of the orchard with only the dam for water and no electricity. She dropped in to see them from time to time with cakes and biscuits, gratefully received by Izzy who wolfed them down but not Stardust who, Catherine was learning, only ate whole foods, whatever they were.

'We're fine,' Izzy said when Catherine expressed her concern. 'Plenty of work to keep us warm during the day and our love to keep us warm at night.'

Catherine was glad her awkward expression was hidden, thanks to the scarf covering most of her face. She had to admit she was impressed by their campsite. Izzy had built a fire pit for cooking and warmth, and the annexe was covered on two sides by plastic sheeting to keep the rain and wind at bay. Izzy had also fashioned a washstand out of timber to clean their dishes and, she assumed, themselves. Judging from the ripeness of Izzy's odour, Catherine wasn't sure how often that happened. Not that she could blame them in this weather. She wouldn't want to disrobe and wash with the southerly blowing off the Antarctic and the sleet stinging like razor blades.

'I don't know why they decided to come here in winter,' Catherine said to Mark that night. She'd invited him and Charlie over for tea and Charlie, exhausted after a day of helping Izzy and Stardust, was fast asleep in the spare room. Izzy had put him to work nailing bits of wood together, for what purpose Catherine wasn't sure, but Charlie had boasted about it endlessly over their meal of lamb chops and three veg followed by golden syrup dumplings.

'Once they'd made up their minds to move, they couldn't bear Melbourne for a moment longer. And Stardust needed to bury those cow horns in winter, remember.' He winked at her, knowing how Catherine felt about it. 'But I think they hoped spring would arrive a bit sooner.'

'The weather is still freezing in spring. It takes months to warm up.'

Mark hugged his mug of tea to his chest. 'Don't I know it.'

They sat on the couch together, gazing into the sterile glow of the oil heater. Catherine seriously contemplated ripping it out and replacing it with an open fire. She should be grateful. Izzy and Stardust had no heating at all in their van. Even if they huddled up next to the fire pit, one side of them might be warm but the other would still freeze. 'I think they should move into the cottage.'

Mark frowned. 'Those two love their privacy. It's a big part of why they're living in a van on top of the hill away from everybody and everything.'

'I feel bad about charging them money to freeze to death up there. The cottage is close to the upper block. Maybe just until the weather improves.'

'Which, like you said, might not be for months. But yeah, I understand. Charlie and I can bunk in together in the same room. It's still a lot more comfortable than the pickers' hut, and we lived there for years. But I don't know if Izzy and Stardust are going to be stoked about being cooped up with us.'

A thought had fluttered through her mind a few times lately, but she hadn't wanted to pin it down and examine it. She loved the idea of having Mark and Charlie close, but would living in the same house be too close? 'You could move in here,' she said, tentatively.

Mark sat up so abruptly he spilt some tea on his jumper.

'I'll get something to clean it up.' Catherine went to get up, but Mark laid a hand on her arm.

'Nobody will notice a stain on this old jumper. Stay right here and tell me I heard you right. Did you just ask me to move in with you?'

Catherine blanched. The way he said it made it seem so salacious. 'Hold your horses.' She tried to keep her voice steady. 'There are three bedrooms. You can sleep in my parents' room and Charlie can have the spare room. I feel guilty having this big place all to myself while Izzy and Stardust are roughing it up there.' She nodded her head slowly, trying to reassure herself that it could work. 'I think this makes sense.'

'Okay. And if things get awkward we can always reconsider.' He held her hand gently in his own. 'I have one condition.'

'Oh?' Catherine thought Mark would jump at the chance of moving in with her, not that that's what they were doing. It was the logical thing to do, that's all. But if that was true why was her heart beating so fast? Why was the touch of his hand making her tremble inside? 'What's the condition?'

'There's no way I'm sleeping in your folks' bed.' He grinned, his eyes bright. 'Your dad would kill me.'

46

December 1974

Catherine

Catherine was surprised to see the verandah railing festooned not only with daisies, nasturtiums and geraniums, but also dandelions and thistles. Mark and Charlie followed her up the steps and she heard Charlie murmer a low 'Huh?' They'd all been invited to the cottage for a banquet to celebrate the summer solstice. Stardust didn't acknowledge Christmas, preferring to give her veneration to the sun and nature. She and Izzy had been hesitant about moving into the cottage at first, wondering whether they were 'selling out', but when Stardust saw the wood stove the matter was settled. 'Oh, you are a wonder,' she'd murmured while lightly stroking its surface. Catherine had given her some tips, and in time Stardust had mastered its idiosyncrasies.

'Welcome to our palace.' Izzy threw her arms wide. 'We're eating outside today. Much as we loved the stove in winter, it gets a bit hot inside now the weather's warming up. We'll be more comfortable eating outside.'

'What a wonderful idea.' When Catherine had lived at the cottage she'd always resorted to the toaster oven and camping stove in summer. She should have known Stardust would stay true to her love of the wood stove. 'And everything looks so beautiful.' The old wicker chairs were nowhere to be seen but in their place, crowded onto the small verandah, were the kitchen table and chairs. The table was covered with unbleached muslin and every place setting had a garland of daisies around it. In the centre sat an old jar crammed with more flowers and weeds.

'All Stardust's work,' Izzy said with pride.

'I brought beer.' Mark handed over a couple of longnecks of Cascade, cold from the fridge at the house.

'You beauty.' Izzy took the bottles from him. 'We'll drink them later. Stardust has other plans for lunch.'

'Do you need any help in the kitchen?' Catherine asked.

Izzy snorted. 'She won't let me anywhere near the stove when she's creating. She says they have a special bond and even the slightest variance in the energy throws it off balance. But thanks.' She raised the bottles. 'I'll just put these in the fridge. That's as far as she'll let me go. Back in a sec.'

Charlie fiddled with the decorations, taking a dandelion from the railing. 'I thought these were weeds.'

'Not to everybody,' Mark said. 'Stardust sees all plants as beautiful in their own way. Useful too.'

Catherine would never think to use dandelions decoratively but had to admit their yellow petals added joy to the table. But useful? She couldn't imagine how.

Stardust emerged from the cottage, her cheeks flushed, wearing an off-the-shoulder cheesecloth dress, dandelions and daisies in her braided hair, and her ever-present work boots. In each hand was a jug with condensation beading on the glass. 'Isn't it a glorious day?'

She smiled up to the summer sky. 'Welcome to our summer solstice celebration.'

'Thanks for inviting us.' Catherine smiled at her. Stardust always looked like a fey spirit from another realm, even when she was working.

'Our home is your home, in so many respects.' Stardust put the jugs on the table. 'Elderflower cordial and iced dandelion tea.'

'Dandelion tea? Sounds great.' Mark shot a look at Charlie.

Catherine was glad there was another option. 'I'll have an elderberry cordial, thanks.'

'Please, have a seat.' Stardust began to pour their drinks. 'Hestia has told me our feast is ready.'

'Hestia?' Catherine asked as they squeezed into their chairs.

'The stove. Goddess of the hearth and its fires.'

'Oh, of course.' Catherine had never thought to give the wood stove a name. Perhaps it would have been easier to tame if she had.

'And she and Stardust have done us proud.' Izzy carried a large tureen to the table. 'To begin with, lentil soup.'

'But first, we give thanks,' Stardust said. 'Let's hold hands.'

Catherine was used to saying grace, she'd said it with her parents before every meal, but never while holding hands. She should've known Stardust would do things differently. She took hold of Mark's hand on one side and Charlie's on the other, giving Charlie's a supportive squeeze.

'Thank you to the spirits of the land, of the water and the air, who made this food available,' Stardust chanted. 'And our heartfelt thanks to the sun, for giving us life. We are grateful.'

Catherine bit her lip to stop her automatic response of 'Amen'.

They released hands and Mark raised his glass of dandelion tea in a toast. 'And thanks to you for your hospitality and this wonderful food.'

'No worries, mate.' Izzy was dishing out steaming bowls of thick, brown soup. 'Dig in.'

Catherine took a tentative sip. It didn't look appealing but was unexpectedly tasty. She recognised the flavours of onion, garlic and bay but the other ingredients escaped her. Mark ate the way he ate everything, with enthusiasm, while Charlie prodded it doubtfully with his spoon.

Izzy polished off her soup and gave a sigh of satisfaction. 'And there's plenty more to come.'

'More soup?' Charlie's face fell. He'd hardly made a dent in his.

'If you'd like. But you'll want to save room for what's coming up. Hunza pie. And rice pudding for dessert.'

'I like pudding,' Charlie said, hopefully. Since he and Mark had moved into the house, Catherine loved spoiling him with steamed puddings, self-saucing puddings, and apple pies and crumbles.

'Did you hear the news?' Izzy said. 'You're looking at the new darts champion of the middle pub.'

'For real?' Mark seemed pleased, if surprised.

'Yeah. And they've asked me to join the team. We're going to take on the other two pubs.'

'Congrats,' Mark said. 'Cygnet has a reputation for being a bit rough on outsiders, but you two don't seem to have had any trouble.'

Catherine knew about Cygnet's reputation. She'd barely ever set foot in any of the pubs, but she'd heard the stories of punch-ups. For people who'd grown up here, the sight of the new arrivals with their flowing hair and tie-dyed clothes was a shock. The hippies were into peace not war, so she couldn't imagine it was them who'd started the latest fight. It had been over a small amount of money one of the new arrivals had won on a beer ticket machine. That one little thing had ignited the simmering resentment, and punches were thrown.

'Everyone loves Stardust,' Izzy said proudly. 'Who wouldn't?'

'We share a common bond,' Stardust said. 'All of us connected.'

'What she means is we're all dirt poor,' Izzy explained. 'The locals, the hippies, all of us. Nobody has much of anything, that's our common bond. Some of the locals hate us. They say we're good-for-nothing dole bludgers. But others can see we're trying to make a go of it, just like them. There's no landed gentry here, just the landed poor.' She laughed her deep rasping chortle. 'Plus I'm a shit-hot darts player. Everybody respects that.'

Charlie giggled and turned to his dad. 'Izzy swore.'

'Oh, God. Sorry, mate.' Izzy looked horrified. 'Forgot. Young ears and all that.'

'Yeah, we're not on the road any more, thank goodness.' Mark assumed a serious expression and turned his attention to Charlie. 'Izzy made a mistake and she's sorry. There's no need to use words like that, ever.'

Charlie shrugged. 'Okay.'

Catherine suspected he'd heard worse from the older kids at school. Izzy's and Mark's reaction was appreciated though, considering they would've done a fair bit of swearing on tour.

The next course arrived – a pie filled with rice and spinach, and a salad of unidentifiable greens, strewn with dandelion and nasturtium petals. It required more chewing than Catherine was used to, and she only managed to eat half before declaring she was so full she couldn't eat another bite.

Charlie patiently awaited the pudding, having only picked at the pastry of his pie, but when the dish of brown rice, raw sugar and soy milk arrived, his face fell again. 'Could I have a Vegemite sandwich, please?' he asked.

'Let me see what I can find.' Stardust floated back into the cottage and returned with a piece of her home-baked wholemeal bread. 'I've spread it with a special Middle Eastern delicacy. A paste made from chickpeas and ground sesame seeds. It's delicious.'

Charlie looked dismayed, and as soon as the meal was over asked to be excused to meet Scott and Eric who were fishing down by the river. Catherine suspected he'd go to the house first to fill up on white bread and Vegemite, plus a few rock cakes, before he went anywhere else.

Catherine helped clear the dishes, and as always did a double-take when she went inside the cottage. When Izzy had asked if they could do some redecorating, Catherine thought they meant some new curtains or a rug. Instead the kitchen was now painted bright orange, and the lounge room walls were a vibrant azure. Macrame hangings decorated the walls, batik material covered the couch and the cushions sparkled with little mirrors embroidered onto the multicoloured covers. The curtains were a rainbow of tie-dyed cotton and in their bedroom they'd painted not only the walls but the ceiling in a deep indigo, with the moon and stars in a constellation over it all. The scent of incense was heavy, and large half-melted candles sat on many of the surfaces. At least they were prepared for any power outages.

Back at the table, she settled into her seat. 'Thanks for a lovely lunch. There were a few ingredients I hadn't tasted before. Where do you find them? I can't imagine they're in stock at the Four Square.'

'Stardust has found her tribe here.' Izzy cracked open one of the bottles of beer. 'They've formed a sort of co-op.'

'There are many people who've come to the valley as we have, looking for a haven,' Stardust said. 'Naturally we gravitate towards each other.'

'They take it in turns to drive up to Hobart for their supplies,' Izzy explained. 'Works out a lot cheaper to buy stuff in bulk. And you can get things there you can't here.'

'Great idea,' Mark said.

Catherine nodded. These new arrivals were certainly resourceful.

'There's more happening than the co-op.' Izzy leant forward, her eyes bright. 'The friends we've made here are helping each other build their houses. Milled boards are cheap since the sawmills have started closing down, and you can buy windows for a song from the clearance sales, along with anything else including the kitchen sink.' She smiled at her small joke. 'I'm pretty good with a hammer and nails; turns out I'm not bad at plumbing either. One day we hope to build a little place of our own. That's our dream. Don't get me wrong, it's not that we don't love the cottage, it's just that having our independence is important.'

'We are all interdependent, my love,' Stardust corrected Izzy gently. 'Everything is in a state of connectedness.'

'Talking of which,' Izzy continued. 'Some of our friends have stalls at the market, selling the things they make – woodwork, pottery and the like. We're thinking we might join them.'

'What would you sell?' Catherine asked.

'You tasted some of it today. Pies, relishes and jams for starters. Stardust is pretty handy with the knitting needles, knows how to spin a fleece too. And we just happen to have some sheep.'

Catherine had checked the trees to see what damage the sheep had done. To her surprise, Stardust's efforts in 'connecting' with them seemed to have had some effect. The sheep had kept their bark-chewing to only a few of the trees. When Izzy and Stardust left to build their own place with their tribe somewhere else, Catherine could always grub those trees out if they were too far gone, that is if she didn't bulldoze the lot. 'Are you talking about the Huonville market?' She'd heard it was doing well with the tourists.

'No, up in Hobart at Salamanca Place, on Saturday mornings.'

'Isn't it only on over summer?' Mark asked.

'So far, but the first Winter Market kicks off next year.' Izzy clicked her fingers. 'Hey, you should get a stall too.'

'Us?' Catherine was taken aback. 'What would we sell?'

Izzy grinned. 'Your cakes and biscuits are pretty special. People would snap them up.' She often dropped in at the house at morning or afternoon tea time and could easily demolish half a cake in one visit.

Stardust shook her head gently. 'Izzy, we shouldn't be encouraging people to eat white flour and sugar.'

'Just saying.' Izzy shrugged. 'It's worth thinking about. Our friends are making a bit of money out of it, and God knows we could all do with some of that.'

Mark turned to Catherine with a look of enthusiasm. 'What do you think?'

It wasn't something Catherine had ever considered. A market stall? It'd be like being a shopkeeper. And all that baking meant she'd be stuck in the kitchen, instead of working in the orchard. 'I really don't think it's feasible.'

'Apply for the Winter Market,' Stardust suggested. 'It starts in April. We'll be selling our beautiful apples. You could do the same.'

'That could work.' Mark was clearly keen. 'I'll take care of it – pack the apples, load up the ute.'

'They provide trestle tables,' Izzy said. 'All you need to bring are your goods, a couple of chairs and a beach umbrella. The sun can get pretty hot.'

'It'll be winter, darling,' Izzy said.

'It'll help keep the rain off then.'

'It all sounds doable,' Mark said. 'What do you think? Wanna give it a go?'

Catherine had to admit another source of income, no matter how small, would be useful. And it'd only be one morning out of their busy week. She felt as though she was being pushed though, into something she wasn't sure about. 'I'll think about it.'

'While you're doing that, let's go for a swim in the dam.' Izzy stood up. 'It's really warmed up.'

'Wonderful idea,' Stardust said, rising to her feet. 'Hestia and I created a lot of heat together.'

'We didn't bring our bathers,' Catherine said. 'But I can scoot down to the house and get them.'

'Bathers?' Stardust seemed perplexed.

Izzy chuckled. 'No need for bathers. We swim as nature intended.'

'Skinny dipping?' Catherine knew people did it, including Tim and his friends, but for the life of her couldn't understand why.

'Haven't you ever done it before?' Mark asked.

A blush rose in Catherine's cheeks. Hopefully the flush already on her skin from the summer heat would provide some camouflage.

'Hey, remember that tour to Queensland?' Izzy said to Mark. 'When we stopped at a beach just before we hit the Gold Coast. All that white sand and blue water, and nobody else there.'

'How could I forget? Tigger almost got caught in a rip. We pissed ourselves laughing because if a boat picked him up they'd wonder why he was in the nuddy.' Mark ran his fingers up Catherine's bare arm. 'I think you'd like it. It's like being caressed all over by the gentlest touch.'

She shivered in pleasure.

'And don't worry,' Izzy chimed in. 'The dam's tucked away from prying eyes. Not that there are people around anyway. It'll just be us women, and a bloke whose bits I'm sure you've seen before.'

Now that summer was here, Stardust sometimes wore clothes so sheer little was left to the imagination, and Izzy often stripped down to only her shorts when she was working. Catherine found it confronting, but also intriguing. How could they be so comfortable with their own bodies? She'd been taught to hide hers away. But she'd had two lovers now and had enjoyed sharing herself with them completely. Perhaps it was time to let go of another taboo. She took Mark's hand. 'Okay.'

47

April 1975

Mark

The cool autumn breeze blew off the Derwent River, and over
Constitution Dock where the fishing boats bobbed at their moorings.
It raced through the plane trees flanking Salamanca Place straight to
where Mark stood, behind their market stall. He pulled the scarf
Stardust had knitted him higher around his neck. It wasn't the
prettiest of garments, but it was warm in all its natural and knobby
glory. The market sat between the docks and a row of old sandstone
warehouses. The buildings told the story of Hobart's history, from
the whaling days through to the apple boom and its demise. These
days many of the warehouses were abandoned and dilapidated, with
rusting gutters and boarded up windows, but on Saturday mornings
Salamanca Place was full of life – people bustled from stall to stall
shopping and eating, while buskers kept the crowds amused with
music and magic tricks.

'Are these fresh?' A woman with a basket in one hand and a young child clinging to the other pointed at the Golden Delicious.

'Picked them myself this week,' Mark replied with a smile. 'Would you like to try some?' He chose a sunny-hued apple from the pile in front of him and sliced off a piece with a knife, handing it to the woman, then cut another for her son. 'Want some too?'

The youngster nodded and wolfed it down.

'I'll take two pounds, please.'

'Would you like me to put in a few smaller ones? Easier for little hands and little mouths.' Mark nodded towards her son.

'Yes, please.'

Mark weighed two pounds of apples on the scales hanging next to the trestle table. Fortunately it measured both in pounds and kilos for anyone, Mark included, still having trouble with the metric system. He popped in a couple of small apples for free. 'There you go.'

The woman's smile was easily worth the price of a couple of small apples. 'That's very generous, thank you. I'll be sure to tell all my friends about your stall.'

Catherine had said he was a natural at selling. Maybe it had something to do with all those years on stage. But he genuinely enjoyed meeting and talking with people. It made him realise how isolated he'd been when he lived in the pickers' hut with only Charlie for company most of the time.

A small crowd gathered around the stall wanting to buy Cox's Orange Pippins, Cleopatras, Jonathans and the ever popular Golden Delicious. Some asked where his orchard was and how it was faring through the Tree Pull Scheme. The state of the Tasmanian apple industry often made the news, and none of it good.

Catherine and Charlie arrived back from checking out the other stalls just in time to help. Charlie was turning eleven this year, so weighing apples and counting change was great for his maths, plus he was paid pocket money for helping. Customers always loved hearing Catherine's story of growing up on an orchard that had been in her family for generations.

'What about the fires in '67? Was your place damaged at all?' one man asked as Catherine weighed some Jonathans.

'It was tough. We pretty much had to start again,' she said.

Mark noticed the corners of her mouth tighten. Seven years later and the fires were still a subject of conversation for locals and visitors alike. Catherine always bore the queries well, but he knew her heart still ached. Her daily visits to the walnut tree were proof.

When there was a lull Mark poured them a cup of tea from the thermos and gently kissed her cheek. She smiled up at him, her eyes still bearing a trace of sadness. He handed Charlie the smaller thermos full of hot Milo. 'Did you check out Izzy and Stardust's stall?'

'Yeah. They've just about sold out of pies already,' Charlie said. 'And they gave me a little apple tart.'

'Even those hunza pies sell well,' Catherine added. 'Brown rice in a pie. Very odd.'

'Tastes all right, though,' Mark said with a smile.

'Hmm.' Catherine sounded dubious. 'And their apples are a bit scabby and russeted, but their customers don't seem to mind.'

Mark always enjoyed strolling through the stalls when he had the chance. He'd say hi to Izzy and Stardust's friends behind tables laden with home-grown vegetables, leatherwork and pottery plus the homespun jumpers, scarves and beanies that always reminded him of lumpy porridge. There was a camaraderie among the stall holders. They'd swap goods, exchange tips, and take care of each other's stalls if the need arose. The market was like its own little village, built from scratch every Saturday morning and then packed away until the following week. Sometimes, when the rain and wind made the hours drag and Charlie was bored and irritable, the market was less appealing. Mark would find himself longing for his warm, dry armchair at home. Even so, he looked forward to Saturdays with a sense of anticipation.

'Do you have any Ladies in the Snow? They're so hard to find these days.' A woman peered at the piles of apples on the table and the boxes underneath.

'They're my favourite too,' Catherine said. 'My dad had to restructure the orchard and most of them went, but I made him keep a few in the home orchard. They sell out very quickly though. I might have to plant some more.'

'Oh, so you've sold out?'

'Afraid so. But give me your name.' Catherine pulled out a notepad from next to the cashbox. 'I'll have a few next week and can keep them aside for you if you'd like.'

'That would be wonderful.'

'In the meantime the Cox's Orange Pippins are very good at the moment.'

'Lovely. I'll take a kilo.'

Mark loved watching Catherine with the customers. She was always welcoming and warm. The three of them were a good team. Word was spreading about their stall and he wouldn't be surprised if they made $200 again this week.

At one o'clock, as the market was closing, the bargain hunters came around, hovering like crows hoping to score some cheap apples. Mark was happy to give them the smaller and marked apples for half price. The way he saw it, everybody was a winner as it meant less lugging for him. On the drive home they listened to the radio and sang along to their favourite songs. So many of them were about love. Mark snuck a glance at Catherine, her mouth wide and smiling, singing enthusiastically. She loved him. She hadn't told him, but he knew. When he and Charlie had arrived at the house with their meagre possessions in a couple of suitcases, she'd shown Charlie to the spare room and Mark to her old room. 'It was your one condition,' she'd reminded him with a grin. It made sense to have his room next to Charlie's, and during the nights when he found himself in Catherine's bed he was grateful to have his son's room a little further away. He treasured the nights he was with her, not only for their lovemaking, but also for the luxury of holding her as she fell asleep. It was then that he felt most at peace. When Catherine's mother came to visit, more to see Charlie than her own daughter, Mark suspected, he was grateful to have a room of his own. Judith would always do a little snooping, keeping tabs on what her daughter and almost son-in-law were doing. Catherine's father had pulled him aside on one of the rare occasions he visited.

'When are you going to make an honest woman of my daughter?' he'd asked, his eyes stern and his mouth a thin line.

'She is already, Jack. Living an honest life and making an honest living. If you're talking about marriage, I'd do it in a heartbeat, but the decision isn't mine to make.'

Jack had never asked again. Mark wondered if Catherine would ever marry him, but the longer they lived together in their strange but workable situation, the less important it felt. They were happy. Why push her into something and ruin it all?

As soon as they got home, Charlie rushed off to play with Greg and Scott over at Annie's place. They were building yet another fort in the bush and Charlie's carpentry skills were much in demand. Mark unpacked the ute and headed for the kitchen. The cashbox sat on the table and Catherine was counting the notes, mostly the browns and greens of one and two dollar notes but there were some purple fives and a few blue tens as well.

'Another good day's takings,' she said, tipping the cashbox up to empty the coins onto the table. 'Charlie will have fun counting all this later.'

'It's really making a difference, isn't it?'

'Yeah, it's helping.' She chewed her bottom lip. 'But it's still not enough.'

He pulled out a kitchen chair and sat beside her. 'There is something else that'll ease the burden a little.'

Catherine raised an eyebrow. 'Another of your famous solutions?'

'Yep.' Despite her doubts he'd been right about Izzy and Stardust and about the Salamanca Market. 'Izzy and Stardust would like to buy the upper block.' He paused, waiting for an objection from Catherine. It was her family's land and had been for generations. Leasing was one thing but selling was another altogether. Catherine remained silent so he pressed on. 'They're willing to pay above the going rate. They love it here. The trees, the view and the dam.' He smiled at the memory of the time they'd all gone skinny dipping. 'They want to build their dream home right here.'

Mark waited, but she remained silent. He let the silence stretch out, giving her time to think it through.

Catherine took a deep breath and exhaled slowly. 'If I pull those trees the government will pay us $350 an acre. I checked because I honestly thought Izzy and Stardust were going to ruin them. But they haven't. The trees aren't in as good a condition as I'd like, but their offbeat methods seem to be working, to a point. And if I pulled them what would I do with the land? Cattle, tomatoes and potatoes like Annie and Dave? That's not exactly working out for them. I grew up with trees. I like trees. They're rooted in the earth but they reach to the sky.' She snorted. 'Good Lord, I'm starting to sound like Stardust.'

'You like her and Izzy, don't you?'

'Much to my surprise, I really do. Stardust is completely wacky, but she's also very loveable, and both of them are such hard workers. I respect that. I couldn't sell my land—' Tears gathered at the corners of her eyes. 'I couldn't sell my land to just anybody. Not to people I didn't know.' She took a breath. 'But I could sell it to them. They'll have to pay more than the government would though. Even if I bulldozed the trees, the land would still be mine. If we can agree on a price then, yes, the land is theirs.'

Mark moved closer, engulfing her in his arms. 'I know this is hard but it'll all work out.'

'It's been hard for so long. I'd really like it to be just a little bit easier.'

He kissed the top of her head. 'I love you.'

'Thank you,' she said, nestling deeper into his arms. And for now, that was enough.

48

Catherine

Catherine read down her list of pros and cons. So far the first column was lengthy and compelling. It had been another disastrous year for Golden Delicious. A massive oversupply meant prices had plunged yet again. If it wasn't for the Salamanca Market they'd have had to tip most of the crop. The results for Sturmers were even more appalling, which was a shame because they were a sturdy variety and easy to grow. Freight rates to Europe were going through the roof so it had actually cost them more to send their Cleopatras to Norway and the Democrats to Germany than they'd made on the sale. The Red Delicious were still doing well in Asia, and the Granny Smiths were holding their own.

She eased the crick in her neck and looked out at the endless rain. If Mark didn't get home soon he mightn't be able to get through. Word was some of the roads in Huonville were going under. The weather made pruning miserable work, with cold water running down the back of her neck and up her sleeves, not to mention the mud up to the top of her gumboots. When she was working near Izzy and Stardust's block she'd keep check on the changes they'd made in the year since they'd arrived. Sometimes she envied the grass and clover growing like a luscious green carpet around the trees. The thick clinging mud wouldn't be a problem in their orchard. It was too early to tell how it was affecting the trees, but Catherine had looked into grassing down her own orchard and Stardust was right, it was becoming popular. Maybe it was time to invest in some grass seed rather than a new disc for the plough. The rain had been relentless for weeks. If it didn't ease up she was worried about an infestation of black spot; the fungus multiplied like crazy in damp conditions. There were other issues concerning her – electricity tariffs were way up meaning cold storage costs would rise, and interstate freight had jumped another 40 per cent. The apple industry wasn't the only one doing it tough. The newspapers were reporting unemployment rates as high as they'd been during the Depression.

Catherine picked up the letter from the Ag Department that had arrived the previous week. She'd read it at least ten times and could quote it verbatim without having to look at the words printed there in black and white. The government was extending the Tree Pull Scheme. Already more than two-thirds of Tasmanian apple and pear growers had applied for assistance. Others had tried to keep going and were struggling, as she was, but had finally been forced to give up. She glanced down at the balance sheet of the orchard ledger. Even with the extra income from the Salamanca Market, some varieties were definitely dragging them under. The obvious answer was to take advantage of the government's offer and grub out some trees. What would her father say? Catherine slammed the ledger shut. It didn't matter what he thought or said. The orchard was hers now, and always would be.

The sound of Mark's ute pulling into the driveway and the rumble of another larger vehicle drew Catherine away from her lists and budgets.

'Come round to the back door,' Mark called out to the driver of the truck. 'It's a flat entrance through there.'

Catherine peered out the kitchen window. Mark had been mysterious about his reason for a trip up to Hobart today. Two burly men jumped out of the truck's cabin, opened up the back, and locked a ramp into place.

Mark bustled in, water dripping off his hair, nose and clothes. 'What a day.' His kiss and the chill of his skin made her shiver. 'Sorry about letting the cold in but I've got to keep the back door propped open for a bit.'

'What on earth is in the truck?'

He gave her one of those smiles that made her bones weaken. 'You'll see.'

The men wrestled a large object down the ramp. It was covered in a blanket so Catherine couldn't be certain, but it looked suspiciously like a piano. With Mark's help the men manoeuvred it through the back door and, with some grunting and muttering, managed to edge it down the short hallway and into the lounge room.

'Where do you want it, mate?' One of the men, wet with rain and sweat, stood hands on hips surveying the room.

'What do you think, darling?' Mark's face was flushed from exertion and excitement. 'If we move this side table it would fit up against this wall.'

'A piano?' Catherine stared at the object. With all the trouble they were having trying to stay afloat, Mark had bought a piano?

'Second-hand and a real bargain. I couldn't resist.' He removed the blanket to reveal the lovely mahogany instrument. His eyes gleamed as he opened the lid to display the black and white keys just waiting for someone's touch.

The delivery man cleared his throat. 'So, along this wall then?'

'Catherine? What do you think?'

She wasn't sure what to think. Mark was usually as frugal as she was, but a piano was a pure extravagance. She wanted to say as much but instead pressed her lips together. They'd wait until the delivery men had gone to talk about it. 'Sure.'

After the truck had disappeared back into the rain, Mark sat at the piano and played a few bars of 'After the Gold Rush'.

'It needs tuning,' Catherine said, aware of the sharpness in her voice as well as the piano.

Mark stopped, his fingers hovering over the keys. 'I thought you'd be pleased.'

'I've been looking at our budget.'

'I thought it'd be a wonderful surprise. I know how much you love playing. We could have sing-a-longs, you on piano, me on guitar and I bet Charlie would be a natural on drums. I was thinking of buying him a set for his birthday. Just a small one.'

She thought Charlie would probably prefer a colour TV, but there was no way they could afford one. Catherine sat beside him on the piano stool.

'He has a great sense of rhythm. Maybe bass guitar.' Mark played a few more chords. 'You're right, it does need tuning.'

Catherine placed a hand on his. The notes fell away. 'Our budget. It doesn't look good.'

'It was really cheap. The delivery cost more than the piano. I paid for it with my latest royalty cheque, and I'll get it tuned as well.'

Catherine couldn't remember the last time she'd bought anything for herself. Any money she earned from relief teaching and the royalties that still dribbled in for 'Cathy's Song' went straight into supporting the orchard and their living costs. Mark had hoped another of his songs might have been picked up after his success with Glen Carter, but he'd been right, getting a song placed was like winning the lottery. Not that it would have made any difference to the orchard. Catherine would never accept his money as anything other than another loan and she was stretched to make repayments to him as it was. It was strange, though, how after each one of those payments something they desperately needed would turn up. The tractor would mysteriously have two new tyres, a local man would spend a day 'helping out with a few bits and pieces around the joint', or Mark would have found an 'amazing deal' on sprays or fertilisers. None of those costs ever came out of the orchard budget. Catherine had stopped questioning it because all she got from Mark was wide-eyed innocence and flippant explanations. He'd distract her with kisses and change the subject. The tension in her shoulders eased slightly and she laced her fingers through his. 'It's a beautiful piano.'

She turned her face up to his and they kissed with a passion that kindled sensations low down in her body. 'And we'll make beautiful music together,' he murmured.

Catherine pulled back slightly to look into his eyes. 'How about now?' She didn't want to think about freight charges or electricity bills. She craved his naked skin next to hers, ecstasy and oblivion. She stood and took his hand, leading him towards the bedroom. They fell onto the bed, pulling off clothes, each hungry for the taste and touch of the other. The sheets were cold with the clamminess of endless days of rain, but his body was wonderfully warm and his mouth hot. Mark's kisses traced lines of fire across her breasts and down her stomach. The glow between her legs grew in heat and intensity, sparking through her body. She moaned and pulled him up towards her, pushing hard against him as he thrust into her with the urgency she craved. He met her with an energy and intensity of his own, bearing down upon her with a combination of strength and lightness. He called her name and his body rippled beneath her fingers, then sighed and softened. Cradling her face with his hands, he kissed her lips, her nose and her eyelids, then held her tightly against the length of his body.

They lay together as little undulations of pleasure pulsed through her body. Mark pulled the blankets up to keep the cold away and she snuggled into his warmth. 'Beautiful Catherine. Beautiful music,' he whispered, his breath tickling her ear.

Slowly her body calmed and stilled. Her heartbeat steadied and the reality of the afternoon eked its way back into her consciousness. They needed to discuss her decision to apply for the Tree Pull Scheme and go through the budget together to see if there was anything she'd missed. There was dinner to cook and before she could do that she had to go out in the rain and pull some potatoes and carrots from the vegetable garden.

'Where have you gone?' Mark propped himself up on an elbow and looked into her eyes. 'You were here with me and now you've disappeared into a world of worry.'

'Just a few things on my mind.'

'I'll make a cup of tea and you can tell me all about it.' She watched as he dressed, the muscles in his back moving with ease under his skin as he pulled on a T-shirt and jumper. She'd never regretted asking him to move into the house. They might never marry. The idea was getting further and further away, like a small boat drifting away on the tide. She was reminded of the Joni Mitchell song about not needing a piece of paper to stay together. What would a wedding certificate give them that they didn't already have?

In the kitchen the window was fogged up with condensation from the recently boiled kettle. Mark had put out mugs, milk and sugar along with the chocolate coconut slice she'd baked yesterday.

He sat down opposite her to pour the tea. 'So, you really do like the piano?' he asked.

'It's beautiful. And I have missed playing.'

Mark put pieces of the slice onto plates, avoiding her gaze. 'Have you given any more thought to giving Angela piano lessons? She'd be old enough now.'

'Pardon?' Catherine hadn't been considering lessons at all. She and Annie had never discussed it. Was he referring to a comment made years ago, before Lara was mistakenly declared dead? It felt like a lifetime had passed since then.

'Eight years old is a good age, don't you think?'

Catherine rubbed her temple, easing the sudden headache that bloomed there. 'I see.'

'What?'

'The piano. It's not for me. You bought the piano as a ruse to get Angela over here, using me as the bait.' She couldn't even look at him.

'That's a bit harsh.'

'Is it? A piano arrives, and next you're asking me to give your daughter piano lessons. Not only that, but you distract me with sex, and when I'm all softened up and pliant you spring your real objective on me.' Catherine pushed the plate away. 'Honestly.'

'Hey, it wasn't my idea to have sex. You literally dragged me into the bedroom. And as for pliant? When have you ever done anything you didn't want to do? It's your way or no way. Every single time.'

'Well, if that's the case how come ...' she stopped.

'How come what?'

Catherine concentrated, thinking back over their time together. There had to be something. Some instance where he'd got his own way even though it went against what she wanted. He'd wanted to get married, she'd said no. He'd wanted to buy half the orchard and make them equal partners, and she'd refused. 'Izzy and Stardust.' She glared at him. 'That was your idea, not mine. You talked me into it.'

'You could have said no at any stage. It was always your decision.'

'Still.' She realised she was acting like a petulant child, but was unable to stop herself.

'And?' He lifted his hands in a questioning gesture. 'You love them. Was that so hard?'

'You never told me about Angela.'

'Not fair. We've been over that, more than once. It wasn't my secret to tell. Well, it was, but I couldn't. Anyway, I thought we'd got past it.'

He was right. She had understood, eventually, and forgiven him. She wasn't playing fair. 'Well, I think you're being underhand buying a piano and pretending it's for me.'

'It is for you. It's for us. You, me, and Charlie if he wants to learn. For Izzy and Stardust when they drop over. I bet Stardust can play the 'Moonlight Sonata', or 'Für Elise' at least.'

Catherine laughed despite herself. Every girl who learnt those pieces played them hoping to appear waif-like and ethereal. Stardust would pull it off better than anyone.

Mark took a breath. 'And I'm hoping it will be for Angela as well. I know Annie will object, but half an hour once a week, is that too much to ask? I miss her.'

Catherine's heart constricted. Of course he did. When Mark lived in the pickers' hut he'd see Angela almost every day – in the packing shed during the season, at the house whenever he'd go there, probably often just to catch a glimpse of his daughter. Angela was the secret he couldn't share, the lonely burden he carried. He'd had to watch her grow up from a distance, never being an integral part of her life. It was the kind of pain Catherine would never know, but one she could help ease. She studied his face and saw the anguish there, etched in the lines around his eyes. 'Yes,' she said.

He reached for her hand. 'You'll ask Annie then? She has a piano at home for practice. Just half an hour here a week, that's all.'

Catherine felt small and somewhat petty. Mark had missed Angela all this time but he'd never complained. She hadn't noticed, too wrapped up in her own troubles. He'd never said a word until he had a plan in place to change it. Her part here was simple. 'Yes,' she said. 'I will.'

49

March 1976

Annie

Annie turned the envelope over to read the address embossed on the back, just to be certain. Tentatively, as if it would come to life and bite her, she opened the envelope and unfolded the thick, textured paper inside. The words, in her mother's unmistakable handwriting, were sparse and blunt.

> *Dear Anne,*
> *Your father is dead. The funeral was last week.*
> *I'll expect you and Angela at the house this Thursday at 2 pm.*
> *Cynthia Nettlefold.*

Annie reread the letter. Her father was dead. Why hadn't her mother called? Or her brothers? And the funeral. Why hadn't they told her about it? Annie stared at her mother's signature on the letter. Her mother had signed off with her entire name as if her own daughter was a stranger. She might as well be. Annie and her mother had never been close; Cynthia wasn't the kind of woman who was close to anyone. Annie and her brothers had been kept at a distance by nannies and housekeepers. Dinner was always a formal occasion where neither she nor her brothers were allowed to speak unless spoken to. It was very different to Annie's rough-and-tumble table with laughter, songs and the natural exuberance of children. If her mother had been a stranger, then her father could only be compared to a complete foreigner. He'd been a solemn and impeccably dressed man who appeared at dinner and sat in the same pew as them at church, but his life and thoughts had remained a mystery to her. Annie clutched the expensive stationery to her chest, waiting to feel grief, or regret, but there was only a sense of irritation at her mother's words. Two pm on Thursday. No 'please' or 'if it's convenient'. It was a letter of demand. She wanted to screw it up and toss it in the basket with the kindling, but instead folded the paper and carefully inserted it back into the envelope. Part of her was tempted to write 'Return to Sender' on the envelope and take it straight back to the post office, but her curiosity was too strong. What on earth did her mother want? And why insist on Angela being present? Only one thing was reassuring – her mother must have read the Christmas cards and letters Annie had sent her over the years, even though she'd never once responded.

When Dave came in for lunch, Annie was waiting in the kitchen with slices of cold lamb, home-grown tomatoes and lettuce, pickled onions, mustard, thick slices of white bread and the letter.

'What's this, darl?' He washed the dirt off his hands at the sink.

'Lunch.'

'And it's a beaut spread.' He inclined his head to where the letter was propped up against the salt shaker. 'But what's that?'

'Read it.'

Dave dried his hands and sat down opposite her. His face closed in as he read the few words. His jaw tightened as he read it again and then placed the letter on the table. 'I'm sorry about your father.'

'Are you? I tried to be, but—' Annie lifted her shoulders in ambivalence. 'I didn't really know him.'

'But still, he was your dad. And not to be invited to the funeral? That's inexcusable.'

'I suppose they thought I'd be an embarrassment to the family. He was a pillar of society, after all, as my brothers are now, from all accounts. Can't have the black sheep sullying the ceremony.' It was only then she felt tears pricking at her eyes. Not because of her father's death, but from the way her parents had treated her. The hurt was still there. They'd cut her off completely, as if it was she who'd died.

'I'm sorry, darling.' Dave paused. 'Are you going to go and see her?'

Annie nodded. Curiosity had won.

'And will you take Angela? You'll need to take her out of school for the afternoon.'

'I want Angela to meet her grandmother. Worst comes to worst, we'll just leave. And who knows? Now my father is dead perhaps my mother has softened. She might even consider investing.'

'It doesn't sound like she's softened.' Dave sounded dubious. 'Do you really want to go?'

'This might be my only chance.' Annie had thought it through. They were in trouble. Her mother's wealth was their last chance. What did she have to lose that she hadn't already lost?

'Be careful.'

The concern in his eyes almost caused her to falter. Instead she clenched her hands under the table. 'There's nothing she can do to me she hasn't already done. Nothing at all.'

The house in Lower Sandy Bay was more impressive than she remembered. Most people would think of it as a mansion. A two-storey structure with huge bay windows looked out over the Derwent River, the tennis court and croquet lawn, and the immaculately trimmed hedges with a central rose garden. The size and grandeur of the residence caused Annie to pause for a moment. She was aware of her clammy palms, her racing heart and the fine sheen of sweat on her nose. Her mother had always made her nervous, but now a whole band of drummers were playing in her stomach, beating an erratic tattoo of anxiety. She stopped the car outside the converted stables that used to house her father's Bentley and her mother's Mercedes. She wondered if one of her brothers had claimed the Bentley, then realised her stupidity. The cars would've been upgraded many times over the years.

'Here we are, darling.' Annie pulled on the handbrake.

Angela swivelled in her seat, taking it all in. 'It's a very big house.'

'Yes, it is.' Annie checked her watch. She was five minutes early. Should they sit in the car for a moment? But her nerves were fast getting the better of her. Time to get this over with.

The doorbell rang its familiar chime deep within the house, and a woman she didn't recognise opened the door. 'Mrs Nettlefold is expecting you,' the woman said. They were ushered into the formal drawing room. 'Mrs Nettlefold will be with you shortly.' She gave a stiff nod and left the room.

Annie stood in the middle of the room, wondering how long her mother would keep them waiting. Just the right amount of time to make Annie more uneasy, she was sure. She glanced around at the couches and chairs, all upholstered in new material, and recently. The plush beige carpet was unfamiliar, as were the curtains. The view outside the bay window was almost unchanged though. The wide blue of the Derwent River and the hills beyond gave Annie a slight sense of nostalgia. The sight of the broken span of the Tasman Bridge brought her back to reality. Disaster could happen at any time and without warning. She had to stay on her guard.

Angela wandered over to one of the antique oak side tables, tentatively putting a finger on a small ivory carving of a woman. 'Don't touch that, darling,' Annie warned. 'In fact, don't touch anything.' Annie moved to one of the couches and sat on the edge of the seat. 'Come sit here beside me while we wait for your grandmother.'

It was another seven minutes before Cynthia Nettlefold swept into the room. Her mother's skin was as pale and fine as porcelain, showing minimal signs of ageing, and her nails perfectly manicured. Her hair was permed and coloured a faint shade of blue. The skirt suit was Chanel, as was the perfume, and her figure was as trim and her posture as perfectly correct as when Annie had last seen her, eighteen years ago. Annie stood, conscious of the extra pounds around her middle, the roughness of her hands, and the permanent tan of her face and arms.

'Just as I suspected,' her mother said in her cultured tone. 'Being a farmer's wife wreaks havoc.' She turned to peer at Angela. 'Good afternoon,' she said, her voice warm for the first time. 'I'm your grandmother and I'm very pleased to meet you.'

Angela curtsied shyly, making Cynthia smile in delight. 'What wonderful manners.'

Annie was gobsmacked. A curtsy? Did Angela think Cynthia was the Queen? Never mind, it had gone over well with her mother. Annie was glad she'd brought freshly ironed clothes and Angela's patent leather Mary Jane shoes when she'd picked her up from school. With her hair brushed and her favourite pink hairband keeping her long dark hair in place, Angela looked perfect. Her mother couldn't fault her there.

'Come here, child,' Cynthia commanded. 'Let me look at you.'

Angela stepped forward to stand in front of her grandmother.

'What extraordinary eyes,' Cynthia murmured. 'Must be on the father's side.'

Annie flinched but stayed silent.

Cynthia placed a finger under Angela's chin, lifting her face. 'Yes.' She nodded once and then walked around the young girl as if inspecting a piece of livestock. Angela stood stiff as a board, watching her grandmother with those wide golden eyes. 'Yes,' Cynthia said again. She picked up a small bell and rang it. The housekeeper arrived within a second. 'Mrs Parkes, accompany my granddaughter to the kitchen.' She turned back to Angela. 'There's a lovely afternoon tea waiting for you, and a rather large doll I think you'll like. She walks and talks and is wonderfully polite, just like you.'

'Thank you, Granny,' Angela said.

Cynthia came close to a frown. 'No, dear, that won't do at all. I am your grandmother and at all times you will call me Grandmother, and only Grandmother. Understood?'

Annie watched with concern. How could she have forgotten how terrifying her mother could be? Angela's bottom lip quavered for a moment and Annie stepped forward, ready to take her daughter and leave, but then Angela straightened and nodded her head. 'Yes, Grandmother.'

'Good. Now off you go.'

'I'll be right here,' Annie said, smiling in a way she hoped was encouraging.

Cynthia waved her hand at the couch, inviting Annie to sit. 'I don't think either of us are in need of afternoon tea, are we,' she said, eyeing Annie's waistline. 'Let's sit and I'll tell you what is going to happen.'

Annie was famished and thirsty after the long drive to Hobart but would never admit it.

Her mother sat on a chair to one side of the couch. 'As you know, with your father dead, I am now the head of the family.'

Annie wondered what her older brother thought of that, but in all honesty he'd probably agree. Their mother was indeed the matriarch.

'My granddaughter is in dire need of a proper education,' Cynthia continued. 'We should have removed her from that provincial country school years ago, but your father would never agree. How old is she now?'

'Nine.' Annie kept her voice steady. An ice-cold sensation clutched at her stomach.

'Best to have started sooner. No matter.' She smoothed down her skirt. 'We can soon correct any bad habits and traits. I've pulled a few strings and she's been offered a late enrolment at St Michael's Collegiate School. The school year has hardly begun and I'm sure, with some tutoring, she will catch up.'

Annie sat with a sense of growing horror blooming inside her. Her mother had planned this in advance, without so much as consulting Annie. The woman's sense of entitlement had not diminished but grown over the years. She struggled to keep her voice calm. 'Are you talking about boarding school?'

'No, not boarding school.' Her mother's tone had the edge that Annie remembered so well. 'She will live here, with me, during the week.'

The tension mounted in Annie's chest. So this is why her mother had summoned her and Angela. Cynthia planned to claim

Angela for her own. Despite her rising panic she played along. She wanted to know the extent of her mother's scheme. 'And weekends?'

'I'm a busy woman with my charity work, tennis and bridge. It's best if she goes home to you on weekends, but I don't want my granddaughter working in the fields like a navvy. You have enough boys for that. In time she will make new friends and be invited to their homes on the weekends from time to time.'

Her mother's arrogance was shocking. She had mapped out Angela's life without a thought for what Annie or Angela might want. 'What about school holidays?' Annie asked.

'Suitable friends may invite her to holiday with them, and when she's older I will take her travelling to expand her education. There are no decent art galleries or museums in Australia,' she sniffed. 'So little culture.'

Annie's anger began to build. She struggled to keep her voice steady. 'There are other considerations. Angela is learning piano. She's very good.'

Cynthia dismissed this with a wave of her elegant hand. 'She'll have the best of teachers in Hobart. Piano, ballet, and elocution to correct her speech.'

Her mother was waiting for her objections, not that she would take any of them into consideration. Cynthia's plans were always immutable. Annie held her nerve. 'She's my daughter. She's happy at Wattle Grove.'

Cynthia didn't blink. 'I find that hard to believe – a young girl with as much beauty and, as you've told me, talent as she. And as her mother, I would think that you'd desire her to achieve her full potential. A well-educated, accomplished daughter who can hold her own in society. I hardly think that's possible in Wattle Grove.' Her lips curled in distaste.

'I see.' Cynthia wanted to turn Angela into the daughter she'd always wanted. Annie's one mistake had deemed her ineligible and her mother expected Angela to fill that void while demanding Annie pay the price. The woman's egotism and selfishness were boundless. She was about to say as much, to stand and leave, taking her precious daughter with her, when the reality of what she and Dave were facing hit her. She'd watched with love and admiration as Dave had slogged away at the potatoes and tomatoes. He'd improved the herd but it was touch and go whether beef prices would rally. They'd even considered selling off some land to the hippies, or 'new settlers', as they liked to call themselves, but the money they offered was too low. Nothing was working. They were sinking further into debt. The broken remains of the apple trees mocked them from the windrows and heaps where they waited to be burnt. Their past was a twisted ruin. They had to look to the future and were certain what it was. They'd done their research and had endless discussions with the Ag Department. But the bank wasn't convinced and refused to lend them the money. They were already carrying too much debt and the word 'foreclosure' had been mentioned. Foolishly she'd hoped her mother might offer her some money today, as part of her father's legacy. But her mother had presented another option. Annie pushed down the nausea that rose at the thought – desperate times call for desperate measures. She swallowed. 'And what do I get in return?'

'I beg your pardon?' Cynthia straightened her shoulders in an effort to appear affronted, but Annie knew her mother too well. This is where the bargaining began. Annie said nothing, hating herself for what she was about to do.

The silence stretched between them. Birds twittered in the garden and the grandfather clock in the hallway ticked on steadily. Annie kept her hands clasped together, feeling the pulse in her fingertips keeping time. Her mind was in turmoil, as was her heart. Her mother could offer Angela the best of education and culture, but what about love? And how would Annie's days be without her daughter to brighten them? She was appalled at the bargain she was willing to strike, but her family was in danger. The threat of poverty and homelessness was real. Even those who had left the valley struggled to find work elsewhere. Businesses were laying people off, not employing them.

Eventually her mother shrugged in a bored and elegant way. 'Your father left a sizeable inheritance. If you hadn't been cut out of our wills, a third of the inheritance, including this house, would have gone to you.' She pierced Annie with a sharp look. 'Instead it will go to Angela.'

Annie's heart beat faster and her hands grew clammy. If there was ever a time to stand up to her mother, it was now, no matter how hard it was. 'No.'

'As I said, Anne, you were written out of both mine and your father's wills. I am being more than generous.'

'I have six children, not one.' Annie clasped her hands tighter to stop them from shaking.

'That's hardly my fault.'

'Dave and I have a business plan which will ensure the future for your grandsons as well as your granddaughter. We need financial backing.' Annie pushed on despite the look of disbelief on her mother's face. 'All I'm asking for is my share of the inheritance, or Angela's share if you prefer, in advance.' Annie swallowed the bile that was rising in her throat. She was doing the equivalent of selling her precious child, her beautiful Angela, to Cynthia. She was appalled at her own behaviour but couldn't deny there was a part of her that felt as though a sleek ocean liner had pulled up beside the stricken raft she and her family were desperately clinging to. Would the liner stop or would it sail past, leaving her tossed in its wake? And which of those two options did she actually want?

Cynthia raised a hand to her throat in mock horror. 'Why on earth would I consider backing you financially? In what way could I expect a better result than the apple orchard has brought you? Why would I squander Angela's inheritance?'

'Because it's my inheritance, it's also my sons' and your granddaughter's. If it makes you feel better, consider it a loan.'

'No, Anne. It will never happen.'

So, the ocean liner had sailed right on by. There was no lifeline. She closed her eyes against the confusing mix of dread and relief. Angela would stay with her, where she belonged. She and Dave would have to find their own way through their troubles, although she had no idea how. Annie stood. She hadn't forgotten where the kitchen was. Many was the night she and her brothers had been banished to eat their tea there when her parents had company. She'd collect her daughter, grab some afternoon tea for herself, and they would leave and never return. She got as far as the door.

'Stop.' Her mother's voice was low and firm, but there was a hint of a plea in that one word. A lifeline after all. Annie reached for the doorframe to steady herself. Was she really capable of relinquishing her daughter in order to save her family?

50

March 1976

Catherine

Angela usually made her own way to the house for her piano lessons, but today Annie was with her. Her face was drawn and puffy. Lack of sleep or tears, Catherine thought. Maybe both.

'I'm not staying,' Annie said, almost apologetically. 'But I wanted to walk over with Angela. It's so rare we get time together, just the two of us.' Annie was clasping Angela's hand and showed no signs of letting go.

'It's always good to see you. Sure you won't come in for a cuppa?'

'Not now. I'd like to catch up though. Later this afternoon, if you can. Alone.' Annie's voice sounded constricted, as if she had something caught in her throat.

'Sure. I'll send Mark out on an errand.'

'No, don't do that. Don't say anything to him. Not yet.' Annie wouldn't meet Catherine's eyes. 'Let's meet somewhere private.'

'Where?'

'The pickers' hut. No one's been there for years.'

'The hut?' How strange it would be, to go back there. Catherine wondered if there was anything left in the place, apart from memories. 'Okay. I'll walk back with Angela after her lesson and meet you there.'

'Thanks. Now, I'll let you two get to it.' Annie hugged her daughter with a strange intensity before letting her go. 'See you soon, my darling.'

Catherine led Angela into the lounge room, her head whirling. Annie had been on edge and distracted. What was wrong? She'd find out in little more than an hour.

'Hi, Angela,' Mark said, from the kitchen. During her lessons he pretended to read the paper, but always positioned himself so he could see the two of them from where he sat.

'Hello, Uncle Mark.'

It had been tricky when Angela first started coming for lessons. Mark had been stilted, and Angela shy. But once it was decided that Catherine and Mark could take the place of Annie's estranged family in a way, as an honorary aunt and uncle, their relationship settled into an easy pattern.

Angela took her place at the piano stool as Catherine pulled up a chair beside her. She caught sight of Mark peeking over the top of his newspaper. He warmed her heart in so many ways, and his secret but unwavering devotion to his daughter was one of them. Angela placed her fingers on the keys and began to play the latest piece she'd been practising. The confidence of her technique, her natural aptitude for mood and dynamics, and her extraordinary ear were always a source of wonder to Catherine. Angela was gifted, there was no doubt.

After the lesson, the three of them enjoyed their afternoon tea in the kitchen. While Angela and Mark chattered happily about what she'd got up to at school and the books she was reading, Catherine sipped her tea in silence. She'd made butterfly cakes for Angela today, and as much as she enjoyed watching her tuck into them, her mind was elsewhere. What did Annie want to talk to her about? And why had she looked so wretched?

Annie was already at the pickers' hut when Catherine arrived, pacing nervously on the small porch. 'Thank God you're here,' she said. 'I'm at my wit's end.'

Catherine gave her friend a comforting hug. 'Shall we go inside?'

'I'd rather stay out here in the fresh air. I need to think.'

'I'll get us something to sit on.' Catherine brought out the old chairs, amazed they were still in one piece, and settled herself and Annie. Her thoughts were running in circles. Were Dave and Annie in marital trouble? Was one of the boys in strife? Or was the bank going to foreclose? She knew they were having financial difficulties.

Annie twisted a handkerchief in her hands as she sat on the edge of the chair, nervously tapping her foot. 'It's about Angela.'

A cold sensation hit Catherine in the stomach. 'Is it Lara? Does she want her back?'

Annie shook her head, keeping her eyes downcast. 'It's my mother.'

'What about her?' She knew about the letter and its brutal announcement of Annie's father's death. Before then, Catherine had thought Annie might have exaggerated her descriptions of her mother, but the letter had confirmed them all.

'I went to see her.'

'And what happened?' Catherine had wanted to advise against going, but had held her tongue. She'd seen the light of hope in Annie's eyes and feared for her. Now, it seemed she was right.

'She wants Angela.'

'Pardon?'

'And the truth is, she's right. I can't offer the things she can.' Annie spoke quickly, her words almost garbled. 'Angela is extraordinary. You've been amazed at how fast she picked up the piano. She's always top of her class and reading books way above her age group. She has an endless curiosity and sometimes I wonder if her golden eyes can see things others can't.'

'She's very talented, I agree. But what does that have to do with your mother?'

Annie took a shuddering breath. 'She wants Angela to live with her during the week. She's already enrolled her in a private school in Hobart. And you should see the bedroom she's decked out for her, all in various shades of pink, with a four-poster bed fit for a princess and an enormous doll's house taller than Angela.'

Catherine was flabbergasted. Without warning, Annie's mother had demanded her way back into Annie's life only to take away her beloved child. And she'd been so sure of her victory she'd already put all the mechanisms in place. The woman truly was everything Annie had told her, and more. 'And you're considering this?'

Annie met her eyes for the first time. Catherine saw desperation and heartache there. 'If Angela lives with her, she'll lend us the money we need.'

'Oh.' Catherine's heart sank. She thought she knew how hard things were for Annie and Dave, but they must be much worse if Annie was even considering this.

'I have to send her lawyer a copy of the business plan, but Dave and I know it's sound. We've looked at every angle, cost analysis, budgets, markets, and projections for worst- and best-case scenarios. The bank won't touch us, not with our level of debt. I hate that we've ended up here, but my mother is our only hope.'

'And she'll definitely lend you the money?'

'She didn't bat an eyelid when I told her the amount. She's made it a priority. My mother wants Angela at the new school as soon as possible. They won't hold her place forever.'

'And Dave? What does he think?'

Annie's shoulders slumped as she looked out over the paddock where apple trees used to grow. It was filled with rows of shrubby potato bushes that brought even lower returns than apples. 'We've been going in circles. Her money means a new start, a business we know will work, and security for us and our boys. But the price?' Annie pressed the handkerchief to her eyes, dabbing away tears. 'That's why I needed to see you. For another point of view.'

Catherine felt a surge of anger at Annie's mother. Ultimately the decision would be Annie's and all Catherine could do was help her clarify the possible outcomes. 'You say Angela will stay with your mother during the week. If you go through with this, will she come home on weekends?'

'For the time being, but my mother has plans.'

'No. You have to tell her it's non-negotiable. Angela spends every weekend with you. What about school holidays?'

'Some of the time with us and some with her. She wants Angela to have the kind of cultural experiences she can't get here.'

Catherine couldn't fault the idea. If she'd been able to experience more of the world she would have jumped at the chance. 'Tell her for the May and September school holidays Angela will spend the entire time with you. The summer break is longer, half and half would work.'

'I wish I was as strong as you. I don't know if I can stand up to her. I think I used up all my reserves getting this far.'

'You are strong, Annie.' Catherine grasped her friend's hands in her own. 'You've survived through bushfire and hail, through the worst economic disaster this valley has seen, and you've been a tower of strength all the way through for your family. You can do this. You have to, if you decide to go ahead with it. Otherwise your mother might take complete control of Angela's life.'

Annie's face collapsed in anguish. 'Oh God, how can I think of delivering Angela into that house, knowing what awaits her?'

'You grew up in that house and you turned out all right. Angela's had nine good years with you and Dave. She already knows who she is. She's strong, like you. But how does she feel about living with her grandmother?'

'She was intimidated; who wouldn't be? But she liked the housekeeper, Mrs Parkes, and she loved the bedroom. And the doll. You should see it. It walks and talks! There's a lovely piano she's allowed to play. And my mother is going to find a new piano teacher for her as soon as possible.' Annie looked quickly at Catherine. 'I'm sorry you won't be able to teach her any more.'

Catherine's thoughts went back to earlier this afternoon, sitting in the kitchen with Angela and Mark. He was an important factor in this fraught equation. He loved his time with Angela and they'd grown close. It would break his heart to be separated from his daughter again. Whatever Annie chose to do, Mark would need to find a way to maintain contact. If Angela came down every weekend, perhaps she and Mark could drive her back to Hobart and stop along the way to play at a park and eat butterfly cakes. But for now, her attention was on Annie and her agonising decision. 'And what about you? You were always so afraid of losing her and now ...'

'She's growing up. Becoming more independent all the time. I've got better at letting go over the years. I've had to, with school and her friends.' Annie sighed. 'You're right. She knows her own mind. I think if anyone could survive in that house, it would be her.'

'But how do you feel about not seeing her every day?'

'I'll miss her terribly, I know. That's why this is so hard.' The tears welled in her eyes. 'I'm afraid of losing her, but I'm also afraid of losing everything else.'

'You will never lose her. This will always be her home.'

Annie closed her eyes for moment. 'And if I don't go through with this, she may not have a home any more.' There was a note of certainty in her voice that wasn't there before. It was subtle but Catherine could hear it through the tears. Annie had made her decision.

51

July 1976

Catherine

The vault of the sky stretched up forever. It was one of those rare but beautiful winter days without a cloud when the sun reached into every hollow and nook, lighting up the water, the hills, the trees and the paddocks with a sense of hope after weeks of sleet and bitter southerlies. Catherine was pruning around the grafts on the mature trees to get rid of shoots from the old varieties. 'You did us proud once,' she murmured as she snipped. 'But your time is over; now you must make way for the new.' She heard herself and laughed. Stardust was exacting an influence on her in more ways than one. Catherine had already grassed-down her orchard and now she was talking to the trees. What next? The hessian collars Stardust used to trap the codling moth larvae? That woman would do anything to avoid spraying, preferring to spend hours wrapping and unwrapping the hessian from the trunks and giving the larvae that harboured there to her chickens. Catherine was loath to admit it, but the technique was working. She shook her head. Who else but Stardust would invest that level of time and effort when spraying was so much easier? Stardust still sprayed, but she didn't use any of the chemicals most orchardists used, preferring natural solutions of lime, copper and winter oil. Whenever she borrowed the crawler she'd thoroughly clean out the sprayer before filling it with her own concoctions. 'The sprays you use,' she'd said to Catherine one day while cleaning the tank, 'are not good for the trees and they're very bad for you.'

Her words had reminded Catherine of a story an old friend of her father's had told them. It had been a dreadful year for looper grub and the spray to eradicate them was particularly nasty. The old orchardist was sick of the blackbirds eating his raspberries so he put one drop of this spray inside a raspberry and left it for the birds. A blackbird ate it and dropped dead on the spot. Along came a crow, ate the blackbird and it too dropped dead. 'And we all know,' the old man had laughed, 'it takes a lot to kill a crow.' Catherine had been wary of the spray ever since and wore an old rain jacket, sou'wester and gloves to stop the spray drift from settling on her skin. Her father had never taken any such precautions and he was still hale and hearty, working in the job he'd wanted, leaning on a shovel for the Hobart Council. But Stardust's words had resonated with Catherine and she'd revised her spray schedule to use less toxic alternatives where she could.

Catherine's orchard would never look like Stardust's though, where weeds and herbs grew in tangles of spider webs around the trees. Stardust reassured her that the spiders were good predators, feeding on codling moths, mites, aphids and scale. She also encouraged ladybirds and earwigs, lacewings and predatory wasps to keep the pests at bay. The chickens helped, and the sheep ate fallen apples, which also stopped the pest breeding cycle. But Catherine preferred a neat, freshly mown orchard. She was delighted not to have to battle the mud or dust every time she went into the orchard, but Stardust's jungle was a step too far.

The sun warmed the back of her neck and shoulders, easing the knot of tension that always hit when she was pruning. She glanced at her watch. Izzy and Stardust had asked her to drop in this afternoon, and now was as good a time as any. She walked through the open paddock separating their properties. The ridges where the ground had been hilled up to help the apple trees with drainage were still evident. Catherine thought of these ridges as the ghosts of her trees. Not that she had any regrets. It had been tough to grub out half her trees but she'd made the right decision. The remains of the stumps were heaped into piles. Izzy was gradually working her way through them, chainsawing them into firewood to feed the wood oven, the fire pit and the open fire in their new home. Izzy also burnt them down to piles of grey ash to spread around the trees and on their abundant vegetable garden. 'Great source of potassium,' Izzy had said. 'Makes the plants jump out of the ground.'

Catherine climbed through the fence that kept the sheep out of her orchard and made her way up to their house. It always made her smile when the oddly shaped little home came into view through the trees. It was very much a hand-made house with its mismatched windows, high pointed gables and large verandah, but it suited Izzy and Stardust perfectly. Catherine had got to know some of their friends who'd helped with the build. Though their appearance was odd, with their choice of clothing and unkempt hair, she genuinely liked and admired them. Cygnet would be a ghost town without their presence. Most of them were hewing a life for themselves out of the rough bush blocks further down the river and up in the hills where land was dirt cheap. It'd be a tough life.

Stardust stood on the verandah, her arms and apron covered with flour and her hair pinned back with flower-covered clasps. 'Welcome. I've just finished kneading the bread. Izzy's inside working on something new. Come on in.'

As Stardust washed her hands and arms at the enormous sink they'd bought at a clearance sale, Izzy explained what she was doing. 'We try to use every part of the apple but sometimes we're left with so many cores and peel even the chickens can't eat it all. So—' She picked up a large jar with a piece of muslin tied around the top. Catherine peered at what appeared to be apple scraps floating in water. 'Apple cider vinegar,' Izzy said with a crow of triumph. 'I'm amazed we didn't think of it sooner.'

Catherine was amazed they'd thought of it at all. 'Apple cider I understand. But vinegar?'

'The health benefits are amazing, and of course ours is biodynamic. We've already got a stack of people who want to buy it. Money from scraps. I love it.'

Stardust dried her hands and came over to kiss Izzy lightly on the cheek. 'My lover's a genius.'

'But there's more, and that's why we wanted to talk with you.'

'Please, sit down.' Stardust pulled out one of the mismatched chairs clustered around the old door Izzy had fashioned into a table. She poured cups of tea from the pot, which was always filled with herbs and leaves in various combinations. Catherine sniffed at her mug – a blend of mint and something else she couldn't identify.

'Ooh, wait.' Izzy jumped up. 'Stardust has been experimenting with a new recipe. Muesli and apple slice. It'll go down a treat at the market.' She served slabs of the dense-looking slice onto plates.

'Mark tells us you've had a good season,' Stardust said, sipping delicately at her tea.

'It's astounding. Pulling those trees was the best decision I've ever made. Apart from letting you two come and live here.' Catherine smiled at them with genuine warmth.

Izzy lifted her mug in a toast. 'I'll drink to that.'

'I've gone from ten acres of good apples to five acres of the best quality apples I've ever had. We're making more money now than we have for years.'

'We're very happy for you.' Stardust smiled. 'We've had a good year too with our baking and my homespun knitting.'

'So good that we actually need a bit of help around the place.' Izzy leant forward. 'Have you heard of Wwoofers?'

'You're getting a dog?'

Stardust laughed gently. 'No. Wwoofers. Willing workers on organic farms. It began in England and is spreading through the world.'

'We give them somewhere to stay and feed them, and they work in the orchard,' Izzy added.

'What? You don't pay them?' Catherine shook her head in disbelief. Who would work for free?

'Nope. They want to experience living on the land and we let them do just that. Plus they get to live in heaven and eat amazing food.'

'But how do they survive without money?'

Izzy shrugged. 'Some might be on the dole, but they won't be bludging, that's for sure. Others are from overseas, backpacking around the place. We've met a couple of young travellers at the market who are keen. We don't have the space for them to stay with us.' Izzy indicated their house which was little more than one big room. Their double mattress was in one corner on a platform of old apple boxes and covered with multicoloured quilts and blankets.

'We were hoping they could stay in the cottage. We'd pay you rent, of course.'

'They're beautiful people,' Stardust said. 'Old souls.'

'Right,' Catherine said slowly, trying to keep up with the conversation.

'And there's more.' Izzy glanced at Stardust. 'Stardust needs the sheep for their wool, but they've developed a little too much of an appetite for the trees.'

Stardust nodded. 'I talk to them and they agree to leave the trees alone, but then they forget. It's not their fault. They have very short memories.'

'Uh huh.' Catherine took another bite of the slice rather than comment.

'I think if we rotated them out of the orchard, bring them in only after the season is over, they'd be more useful,' Izzy said as she picked up the few remaining crumbs on her plate with her fingers. 'So, we were wondering if we could lease your five acres, now there are no trees on it.'

'We need more sheep,' Stardust said. 'I'm having to buy fleeces at the moment.'

Izzy looked at Catherine eagerly. 'What do you say?'

Catherine took a slow breath in. The cottage wasn't being used at the moment. Her mother, when she came to visit and see Charlie, never stayed the night. The idea of a few sheep grazing on the fallow land was appealing. No need to slash the paddock for a start. She'd toyed with the idea of getting a few head of cattle to run on the five acres, but Mark wasn't keen. Stardust and Izzy, in their own offbeat way, were offering her money for two assets she wasn't using. 'That's a yes to both,' she said. 'As long as the sheep don't get into my orchard.'

'I'll make sure the fence is sheep-proof,' Izzy said. 'Thanks for this. You won't regret it.'

'Now drink some more tea.' Stardust pushed the pot towards Catherine. 'It's good for you and you know who.'

Catherine touched her stomach. 'You know who?' How could Stardust possibly know?

Stardust smiled. 'Your aura is glowing with the light of two.'

'Oh, um.' Catherine stumbled to find the right words and then gave up.

'Have you told Mark?'

Catherine shook her head. She wasn't sure what he'd think. Neither of them had planned for this. They'd never even talked about the possibility, but now nature had decided for her.

'He'll be thrilled. A baby girl is something he's always longed for.'

Catherine gasped at the fluttery feeling in her belly. 'How can you possibly know it's a girl?'

Izzy took hold of Stardust's hand. 'Stardust is amazing in every single way.'

Back home, Catherine rifled through the top drawer of her dressing table. In among the old pots of make-up she never wore, the hair slides she never used and the bottles of scent she always forgot about, she found the small blue velvet box and flipped it open. The ring gleamed back at her, as beautiful as the first time she'd seen it, with the tiny blue sapphires encircling the diamond. That had been four years ago, before Lara's return had created chaos in their lives. Mark had been patient. He'd never asked her again. If she was happy with their current arrangement for the rest of their lives she knew he would be too. But now? With a baby on the way? She slipped the ring on and watched as the diamond sparkled when she moved her hand. It felt right, nestled on her finger, as if it was always supposed to be there. And there was a sky-blue dress she'd never worn, still hanging in her wardrobe. She'd expected some kind of hesitancy or fear but there was none, just a sense of rightness.

She took off the ring and placed it back in the box. Charlie was having a sleepover with Scott and Greg tonight. She and Mark were supposed to be going to a meeting in Huonville about the proposed new fruit marketing system and the freight equalisation scheme. There was no way they were going to make it, not after she told him her news. A baby girl. She was certain Stardust was right. In some ways Stardust had a knowledge that defied understanding. A baby girl Mark could hold and treasure without any fear, secrets or resentment. At first he'd been angry at Annie for making a deal with her mother and using Angela as the collateral, but eventually he'd come to accept that the decision was for the best. Angela was an extraordinary girl with a talent for music that amazed even Mark. Her ability on the piano was breathtaking from the first. In Hobart she had every opportunity to foster her talent and discover where her gift could take her. And he still got to see her every Sunday afternoon when they drove her back to Hobart, and during the school holidays when Angela would come over and they'd play music together. Catherine knew their daughter could never take Angela's place, but in so many ways it felt as though they were being given another chance.

A quick look through the fridge assured her she had all the ingredients for Mark's favourite dinner. He was up in Hobart today buying a new pump for the lower dam. Catherine busied herself in the kitchen, preparing the lamb for roasting, slicing the vegetables, and getting the potatoes on to parboil for the special crunchy roast potatoes Mark loved so much. She'd make dessert as well – a steamed pudding with custard or a roly-poly made with the last of her homemade raspberry jam. In the lounge room she put her favourite album on the turntable. From the very first note of 'I Feel the Earth Move' Catherine was dancing and singing along with Carole King.

As the dinner cooked and the music swirled, Catherine set the table using her grandmother's finest silver, adding three of the candles they kept for power outages in a small candelabra she'd found tucked away in a cupboard. Lastly she put the blue velvet ring box on Mark's plate. He'd proposed to her all those years ago, but a lot had changed since then. She laid her hands gently on her belly. 'Tonight, my darling girl, we'll tell your daddy all about you and I'll ask him to marry me. We'll become a family, along with your brother Charlie.'

The sound of car wheels on the driveway made her heart skip. She waited in the kitchen for his familiar call.

'Hi, honey, I'm home.'

'I'm in the kitchen.'

He came in, his handsome face wreathed in a grin. 'Something smells good.'

She held him close, feeling the chill from the cold winter's evening clinging to his skin and clothes. 'Something is good,' she whispered in his ear.

52

February 1985
Angela's eighteenth birthday

Annie

Annie and Dave waved the boys and their families goodbye. Michael and Eric tooted their horns, spinning their wheels in the gravel for show.

Dave shook his head and chuckled. 'Grown men with children of their own and still acting like kids.' Both sons had delighted them by becoming parents, Michael three times and Eric once with another one on the way. Annie loved having a house full of children again after so many years, and equally loved waving them goodbye when they left.

Angela stood beside them on the verandah as the cars disappeared and the last of the dust settled. She gave Annie a hug. 'Thanks, Mum. That was the best birthday lunch ever.'

Annie smiled, a little smugly, but deservedly so. Angela had enjoyed an indulgent eighteenth birthday party at the Sandy Bay house, with

411

expensive presents, all the right guests and pricey catering, but still her daughter had preferred a humble family get-together, with a home-cooked roast and her favourite chocolate cake.

It was wonderful to have a day off with all her children and grandchildren, even if it had been a busy one for her. There were still several weeks left of the picking season and life had been hectic, as usual. At first she'd found it hard to adjust to the harvest ending almost at the same time as the apple picking season would've begun but now it was second nature to her. The decision to get into cherries nine years ago had been difficult initially – the outgoings were enormous. The cherry orchard was finally profitable, but they still owed money to her mother. She and Dave had done the sums though, and were now in a position to obtain a loan from the bank to pay her out. The timing couldn't be better. More than ever it was crucial to be free of any hold Cynthia might have on their family.

Angela was an adult now and their boys all grown. Michael was a successful mechanic in Hobart with his own business. Eric had followed in his footsteps and worked alongside his older brother. Annie was pleased to see that the rivalry between them had mellowed over the years. Paul and Greg were living in the house on the property Dave had bought from the Fletchers. Paul was twenty-four now and keen to take over the running of the orchard when the time came. She and Dave were grateful for how hard they worked in the orchard, but hoped they'd stop partying just as hard one day. Much to their surprise, their youngest son Scott had taken advantage of a free tertiary education and was studying to become a lawyer. Perhaps it was Annie's family's genes that had prompted him to pursue a career so different from his brothers. Dave and Annie were proud of all their children, but there would always be a place in Annie's heart devoted only to Angela.

Her daughter had graduated from the Collegiate School at the end of last year, top of her class in many subjects including English Literature and French, but it was her skill at the piano that attracted attention. Angela had a natural aptitude that, coupled with hours of practice, had seen her become a stunning pianist. She also possessed a beautiful singing voice and had begun writing her own songs at the age of thirteen. The Conservatorium of Music would be a natural next step for her, her grandmother was sure of it, but Angela was more drawn to the Victorian College of the Arts jazz program where her piano and vocal skills would meld more easily. Cynthia would prefer her to stay in Hobart, living under her roof. Angela had grown into a beautiful, elegant and celebrated young woman. Her grandmother loved to bask in the glory while claiming credit for passing on her genetic ability. That mightn't be possible after today.

Annie's heart was racing. The world was about to become an uncertain place once more. Would Angela hate her for what she'd done? Would she denounce her and run off to Lara and her glamorous life in Europe? And what would happen once she knew Mark was her father? Annie knew this had to be done, but dreaded it.

She called Angela into the lounge room. The box with the golden snake bracelet sat on the table beside her chair. Dave joined them, sitting beside his wife in their armchairs while Angela perched on the old couch.

'We have one last present for you, my darling girl.' Annie tried to control the tremble in her voice.

Angela smiled. 'You've already given me so much, I feel thoroughly spoilt.'

'You're an adult now,' Dave said. 'Soon you'll be leaving Tasmania to study in Melbourne. The world is opening up for you, and you need to know the truth.'

'Goodness, that sounds rather dramatic.'

Annie folded her hands in her lap, trying to disguise her nervousness. 'It is. There's something we need to tell you. We both love you very much. Very much indeed.'

'I know. I realise it was hard for you when I went to live with Grandmother. Mind you, it was no picnic for me either.'

Annie raised a knowing eyebrow. 'Yes, we all know what a force of nature she can be. But this isn't about her. It's about a night many years ago. Eighteen years ago to be precise.'

'When I was born?'

'Yes.'

'What do you mean?'

Now it was time to say the words, she didn't know if she could. Her devotion to her daughter had been all-encompassing for so many years. The ties had been stretched while Angela lived with her grandmother, but they were as strong as spiderweb, holding firm through the years and the distance. What she was about to do could sever them forever, leaving her drifting helplessly in the wind. Annie glanced at her husband for support. Dave nodded, his face gentle but firm. She picked up the box and handed it to Angela. 'Do you remember this?'

Angela looked puzzled as she opened the lid then her face lit up with surprise as she saw the golden snake bracelet with the emerald eyes. 'I remember a big black car, a tall woman with amazing eyes, and this. She was wearing it.'

'You remember her eyes?'

'Like a tiger's. Brown and gold.'

'Like yours.'

Angela nodded. 'I guess. Is she a relative?'

'Yes. And she sent you this bracelet many years ago. It's time for you to have it.'

'It's beautiful.' Angela slipped the bracelet onto her wrist, admiring it briefly before turning back to her parents. 'How is she related to me?'

Annie hesitated. Was it best to come right out with it or lead up to the critical fact? 'Eighteen years ago she was staying here at the orchard. I was ... unwell.' The pain of that time was still very real but she pressed on. 'You see, I'd just lost a baby. A girl.'

Angela frowned. 'Really? I didn't know that.'

'She was premature,' Dave said gently. 'Stillborn.'

'Oh, Mum. I'm so sorry.'

'I was inconsolable. I loved your brothers, but I longed for a girl. The woman who owned that bracelet was pregnant as well. Our due dates were only a month apart. She'd had a boy but hadn't taken to motherhood and was afraid she couldn't raise one child, let alone two.'

'Mum? Dad?' Angela looked at them both with concern.

'It's okay,' Dave said. 'Let your mother continue.'

'She came to me one night with her newborn baby in her arms. Told me straight out that she couldn't look after her. She said the baby was always meant to be mine. Then she disappeared. Years later we found out she was dead.'

'Oh my God.' Angela covered her mouth with her hands.

'We honestly thought we'd be looking after her baby for a few days, a week at most,' Dave said. 'But she never came back.'

'Until the day when she turned up in the big black car.' Annie spoke slowly, letting Angela take it in.

'But I thought you said she'd died.'

'It was a mistake. There'd been a car accident and the body wasn't found for some time. The police thought it was her, but it wasn't.'

'That's dreadful.' Angela's eyes were huge.

'I know. It was a shock, for all of us.'

415

Angela touched the golden snake. 'So, who is she to me?'

Annie took a breath. 'She's your birth mother.'

'Oh.' Angela nibbled on her thumbnail, an old habit when she was upset. 'I'm adopted?'

'In a way. After she disappeared your birth was registered with your dad and I as your parents. It was what she wanted. Legally you've always been our child.' Annie looked at her hands still folded in her lap, unable to meet either Dave's or Angela's eyes. She'd always felt it was the right thing, but it seemed different, explaining it now.

'What are you telling me? Dad, did you get that woman pregnant? And, Mum, you took on the baby as your own?' Angela's voice held a tremor of anger.

'That's not how it was. Remember I had just lost my baby. Your dad and I were inconsolable. She gave you to us as an amazing gift, one that brought everything we'd wanted and thought we'd lost into our lives.' Annie leant towards her daughter. 'You healed me and you saved us both.'

'But, Dad, you had an affair?'

'No, darling.' Dave's voice was calm. 'I've always been faithful to your mum.'

Angela threw her hands in the air. 'Then I don't understand. I'm adopted but I'm not. You're not my real mother and father – what are you?'

'We're your parents. Your mum and dad. Since the day you were born, eighteen years ago, we have cherished you.' Tears pricked at the corners of Annie's eyes.

'Yeah, okay, I get it. And I love you too. Adoption isn't the big thing it used to be. I'm amazed you've kept it a secret for this long. But who are my biological parents?'

Annie took another steadying breath. So far Angela was taking this well. In some ways it wasn't surprising. Her daughter might've lived in luxury in Hobart and been to Europe with her grandmother to practise her French, but she still loved the orchard, and had managed to keep her feet firmly planted on the ground. But would she continue to be this calm? The hardest part was yet to come. 'Her name is Lara. She lives in England with her husband. Her second husband.'

'Lara? I've heard her name mentioned. Why?'

Dave cleared his throat. 'Her first husband lives here in Wattle Grove. He stayed here to be close to you. He's always loved you, but entrusted you to our care. It was against his wishes at first, but he came to see it was for the best. If he could've taken care of you he would've. Even though it broke his heart, he knew you'd always be loved by us.'

'And we did. I couldn't bear to be apart from you, my little angel.'

'My father lives here? In Wattle Grove?'

Annie nodded, unable to speak.

Comprehension hit Angela's face. 'Uncle Mark.'

Dave leant in. 'We let him know we were going to tell you this today. He'd love to talk if you want to. He said he'll understand, whatever you decide.'

'Mark Davis is my father.' Angela spoke as if trying out the words.

'Are you okay, darling?' Annie searched her daughter's face. 'I know it's a lot to take in.'

'It kind of makes sense. The afternoons at his place after piano lessons with Catherine. Them always giving me a lift back to Hobart after my weekends here. I used to find it strange because you'd want to spend every possible minute with me, Mum, but then you'd always be too busy to drive me back to Hobart. I liked it though because Mark and Catherine would spoil me rotten on the way home.' She shook her head. 'He never said a word about this. Never let anything slip.'

'He's a good man,' Dave said. 'Honourable. He made a promise and stuck to it, even though he found it hard. He wanted the best for you, always.'

'Mark Davis. That's kind of cool. He was a bit famous when he was younger. Those bands, the hit songs.' Angela's eyes widened. 'So that's where I get it from.'

'I guess so.' Annie stifled her annoyance. Angela's delight in having Mark as a father rankled. All he'd done was get Lara pregnant. Dave had been there for her entire life.

Angela appeared to pick up on Annie's irritation. She turned to Dave. 'You'll always be my dad, Dad. You know that, don't you?'

Dave smiled. 'I've always loved you as my own.'

'And Mum, I love you too, and always will. I've always felt like the most precious daughter in the world.'

'You are.'

'But I also have biological parents.' Angela ran her fingers across the golden bracelet. 'Lara. Hah! She's married to a rock star. She's famous in her own right. The things she gets up to.'

'Yes, well.' Annie frowned.

'She only came back that one time though?'

Annie dared not open her mouth to speak. She wouldn't be able to stop herself from saying what she really thought of Lara.

'That'd be right. She doesn't seem the maternal type.' Angela's eyes flashed. 'I just realised. Oh my God. Charlie Davis is my brother. I had a bit of a crush on him when I was younger. How embarrassing. Glad it never went anywhere. Come to think of it, Auntie Catherine picked up on it pretty early and did all she could to discourage me. Just as well.'

'I know this is a bit overwhelming,' Dave said.

'It's amazing,' Angela said. Her expression was one more of delight than concern.

Annie was torn. Part of her was glad Angela was taking this so well, but part of her hated it too. Lara and Mark were much more exciting, dramatic and interesting than she and Dave with their boring days of hard toil in the orchard. Sure, Mark was little more than an orchardist these days himself, but he'd been famous and was a musician, like Angela. She could see the appeal. Of course Angela was going to want to spend time with him. How many precious hours would she lose Angela to him before she left for Melbourne and in the future? 'Do you want to see him, now you know?'

'Yeah, I do. But not yet. I need to think first and get to grips with it. It's kind of weird. My whole life has changed in some ways, but not at all in others.'

'Take as long as you need. And we'll leave it up to you who you tell. As far as we're concerned this is your business. Mark and Catherine know, of course, and Lara. But nobody else.'

'Grandmother?'

Annie huffed. 'No. But if you want to tell her you can. It might be hard for you to keep this a secret.'

'I think Grandmother would be happier not to know. I can't imagine how her bridge club would react. It'd all be too much.'

Annie sighed with relief. She'd hoped Angela would see the sense in keeping Cynthia in the dark.

'But what about Charlie? Does he realise I'm his sister?'

'We're leaving that up to Mark. And you.' Annie knew there'd come a time when the whole valley would know, and she'd be the topic of gossip for the rest of her life. Hadn't she been the focus of gossip when she'd first arrived in the valley, pregnant and on the arm of one of the most eligible local bachelors? She'd put many a nose out of joint. She'd survived that, and worse. It'd been worth it.

53

February 1985

Mark

It was a simple life at Wattle Grove, but one of contentment. Charlie was working with him and Catherine in the orchard, while making grand plans. Although the orchard was making a profit, just, Charlie's ideas might turn it around. Mark was grateful for the small amount of money that trickled in from his song royalties. The Glen Carter track was still on rotation around the world all these years later, and two of his other tunes had been covered by other artists and been moderately successful. Their daughter, Sarah, would be eight years old in a few months, the same age as Angela when she'd started coming for piano lessons. Catherine was teaching Sarah piano now, and so the world turned, the seasons came and went. The dramas of the past resolved themselves or faded into distant memory. But now his oldest daughter was walking towards him. They'd agreed to meet here, on the small sandy arc of Petcheys Bay, away from any interruptions. He took in the stretch of water before him and the bridge of sky above. If this proved too hard he'd take his strength from the eternal presence of nature. He smiled. Stardust was influencing him more every year.

'Hi.' Angela's wave was shy. Her eyes searched his, the golden highlights caught by the sun's rays.

'Hi,' he answered. 'Thanks for meeting me.' He pointed to a log under a large eucalypt. 'Shall we sit?'

'Sure.'

It was a good strategy. They could both look out across the river instead of having to face each other. It would make this easier.

'How are you feeling?' he asked.

'Still kind of weird, you know. But in a way it all makes sense.'

Mark nodded. 'Yeah. It was weird for me too. Really tough. I'm glad you finally know the truth.'

'Do you ever have any contact with my mother?'

'Nah. Lara was always good at burning bridges.'

'Oh.' Her shoulders slumped.

'I'm sorry. I didn't mean that the way it sounded. She did what she thought was best for you.' Mark didn't want Angela to know that Lara had never wanted her. What would be the point? He wasn't here to condemn Lara. He was here to connect with his daughter. 'Lara didn't think it would be good for you to know about her. Too confusing.'

'And you? What did you want?'

'Just to be your dad. But it wasn't possible. Lara was gone, I had Charlie to look after. You were so tiny, and so helpless. Annie told you what had happened?'

'Yeah, Mum told me everything, about losing her own baby and then Lara coming along with me. It sounds intense.'

'Losing the baby was tough on Annie, and Dave too. When he asked me to step aside, well, I wanted to do it for him. And you.'

'And Mum?'

'Annie knew what needed to be done. She never faltered.' He swallowed the last residual piece of bitterness. It had rankled for so long that Annie had gone behind both his and Dave's backs to register Angela's birth, but that was a long time ago. Angela was with him now, with the full knowledge that he was her father.

'And Auntie Catherine knew?'

'Not at first. It was hard when she found out. She sent me packing, actually. She hates lies. Not that I lied to her. I just didn't tell her the truth. But I'd made a promise to Dave. It was tricky.'

'Yeah, sounds it.' Angela dug her feet into the sand. 'What happens now?'

'Whatever you want. I'm here for you, whatever you decide. I'm not going to say we have a lot of catching up to do because we've spent time together every week for ten years, and before that I was always hanging around watching you grow. I've been lucky.'

'So, you were my guardian angel in a way.' She kept her head down but looked at him from under her lashes.

He chuckled. 'A pretty useless one, but yeah, I guess so.'

'And Charlie? Does he know he's my brother?'

'I thought I'd talk to you first.'

'I think he needs to know, don't you?' Angela nibbled her thumbnail.

'I think that'd be great. But it's your call.'

'Where is he?'

'In the orchard.'

'Well, let's go tell him.' She smiled at him for the first time.

Mark relaxed a little. This was going better than he'd hoped.

As they walked up the hill towards the orchard Angela turned to him. 'You know, I think it's cool you're my father. Dad will always be Dad, but my love of music clearly comes from you not him – he's tone deaf.' She laughed lightly. 'Mum tells me she used to play the piano, but with so many kids she never had time. None of the boys are musical. I was always the odd one out.'

'Catherine was astounded how quickly you picked up the piano. You're a natural.'

'Which must have come from you.'

'I can't claim the credit. Maybe there's a musical gene in there somewhere, but your talent far exceeds mine. You could make a real go of it. But it's not an easy life, no matter what you might read in magazines or see on TV.'

'I want to know all about it. The bands you were in, the records you made. You were famous.'

Mark shrugged. 'Not really, but yeah, I had my moments. My old band went on to be pretty big overseas and my other band did well in Australia. But they were different times.'

'True, but I'm hoping you can give me some pointers. You've been where I want to be.'

'I reckon you can go further than I ever did. It'll be tough, but you've got the talent to take on the world, if that's what you want.'

'Big call!' She dipped her head. He'd embarrassed her but he couldn't help feeling immensely proud of his daughter.

Catherine was waiting for them on the verandah. 'Hey, Angela. Are you okay?'

'Yeah, actually. A lot of things make sense now. And I'm grateful, you know. I've been looked out for in so many ways.'

Mark's heart swelled with love. Angela had not only taken this in her stride, she'd embraced it.

'I'm glad. If you're looking for Charlie, he's in the middle block thinning the Granny Smiths. Then come back to the house and we'll have some afternoon tea.'

'Just like usual.' Angela smiled.

Catherine threw Mark a questioning look and he nodded. She smiled as she went inside.

Mark took Angela's arm in his as they walked and it felt right.

'Charlie!' Angela called out as soon as they spotted him among the apple trees.

Charlie turned. He was taller than his dad now, his dark hair tousled and shoulder length. Mark teased him, saying he'd have been right at home in the seventies.

'Hey, Angela. What brings you into the orchard?'

'You.'

He squinted at them. 'Have I done something wrong?'

Mark shook his head. 'Nope. We've got something we need to tell you.'

'You and Angela? Now you're freaking me out.'

'God, no. Nothing like that. There's been a secret in this family for a long time. It involves the Pearsons as well.'

'This is getting weirder by the second. You and Angela, and the Pearsons?'

'You have more than one sister, Charlie,' Angela said. 'And I have yet another brother. Lucky me.'

'What? You're not making sense. Who's this other sister?'

'Me. Your dad is my real father and your mother is my real mother. I was adopted, kind of, when I was born, by my mum and dad.'

'That's crazy.' Charlie stepped back, as if needing distance.

'It's true.' Mark put a hand on his son's shoulder. 'Angela is your sister. I couldn't tell you until now. Annie and Dave decided it was time she knew the truth.'

'My dad is your dad.' Charlie spoke slowly. 'And Lara's your mother too?' His expression changed. 'Bloody hell, we both copped a lucky break then.'

'What do you mean?'

'Lara was never good with kids. I was lucky Cat came along when she did. She felt like a mum even before she became my real mum. And Mrs Pearson? It was clear to everyone how much she adored you.'

'Yeah, you're right. And I'm *so* lucky to have yet another big brother to boss me around.' She lightly punched his arm.

'As if I would ever dare.' He smiled at her, comfortable already.

Mark watched them as they joked around, testing the waters of their new relationship. It had always astounded him that no one had noticed the similarities between them while they were growing up. To him the likeness was clear, but others only saw Angela's eyes and they were pure Lara. Charlie looked more like him. He smiled as his son put a brotherly arm around Angela.

'Well, little sister,' Charlie said. 'That explains why Cat made butterfly cakes today. You've always loved them.'

Angela laughed. 'You like them too. Or do you always have to force yourself to scoff most of them?'

Charlie threw up his hands in mock horror. 'Who, me?'

'I'm sure there are plenty for all of us.' Mark chuckled. 'Let's head down to the house and have some afternoon tea.'

Angela's face grew serious. 'Does Sarah know? Does she know I'm her sister?'

Mark and Catherine had discussed the best way forward, depending on Angela's response today. 'Catherine is explaining everything to her now, in a way she'll understand. It might take Sarah a while to get her head around it, but we decided we didn't want any more secrets.'

'Another brother and a little sister.' Angela's smile was back. 'What a day!'

Mark let their chatter wash over him as he walked with his children back to the house. What a day indeed. A heaviness lifted from him to be replaced with a gentle sense of peace. No more secrets. His family was completed.

54

Spring, Present day

Catherine

It was the scent of the blossom wafting through the window that woke her. The spring evenings still had a frosty edge, but Catherine loved to sleep with the bedroom window open so she could wake with the rising sun and the sound of birdsong. Even on such glorious mornings she was sleeping a little later. Perhaps her body was letting her rest after all those years of early starts. Her days were free now from the backbreaking work of picking, pruning, spraying and mowing. After all the struggles, failures and successes she'd been happy to let it all go. Her orchard thrived under another's care. Her father wouldn't recognise the tight rows of trees grown so close together instead of the spacious plantings of his day. Growing techniques had changed along with pruning, grading and packing. Computers did much of what she'd done when she was young. She stretched and slowly got out of bed, made herself a cup of tea and took it out to the verandah. She'd done the right thing in getting most of it glassed

427

in. She was able to enjoy the view all year round now, but how that view had changed. Where once there was an ocean of apple blossom on both sides of the Huon River, now there were only paddocks of green where cattle grazed, or the tiled roofs of new homes built on the old subdivided orchards – 'lifestyle acreage', as the real estate agents called it. During the Tree Pull Scheme nearly 700 orchardists had left the industry, halving the production of apples and pears, but it still hadn't been enough. Now there were fewer than thirty orchards remaining in the whole of Tasmania. She was glad hers was one of them, greatly changed though it was.

The bleating of the telephone urged her to rise from her pleasant sunny spot. She knew who it would be before she answered it. Annie was forgetful these days, and even though she still had two of her sons nearby to take care of her, she still liked the reassurance of hearing Catherine's voice.

'What time is it happening?' Annie asked. Her voice had little of the waver of a woman her age.

'Two pm. Hardly a decent hour to start drinking but it means people can stay for as long, or as little, as they like. Some are staying in Cygnet or Wattle Grove, but others will want to head back to Hobart.'

'Let's hope they don't get breathalysed. Paul's going to drive me over. Not like the old days when we used to walk to each other's place. It was so easy back then.'

Catherine had to agree. She still walked around the orchard on a regular basis, but these days she did it slowly, and usually with a stop at Izzy and Stardust's for a cup of herbal tea and a rest before she made her way back home. 'How's the crop looking?'

'Marvellous,' Annie said, her voice brightening. 'Another bumper year. I can't believe the amount of money Paul and Greg are raking in. If only my mother was alive to see it. Not because she'd be happy about it. More like livid with jealousy.'

Through the years Annie and Dave's cherry orchard had become spectacularly successful. All of their land plus the Fletchers' old orchard was now blanketed with white netting covering their precious crop. Tasmania's fruit fly–free status had seen their cherries command premium export prices and the domestic orders were phenomenal. One year, when the rain had fallen at the wrong time threatening to ruin the cherries, they'd paid for a fleet of helicopters to hover over their orchard and drive off the water. Charlie had been gobsmacked. 'Do you know how much it costs to hire even one helicopter?' he'd asked Catherine. She'd had no idea. 'A shitload, that's what.' When Catherine had asked Annie about it she'd shrugged. 'If you have to spend half a million dollars to save a five-million-dollar crop then it's an easy decision.'

Catherine was genuinely pleased for Annie and Dave when their hard work finally paid off, and glad Dave had lived long enough to see it happen. Annie was still lost without him, but her sons kept her close. 'Well, we'll see you this afternoon at about two then.'

'I wouldn't miss it for quids.'

After a breakfast of Izzy and Stardust's muesli, Catherine showered and dressed. She left the little cottage, which she felt completely at home in now she was a grandmother herself, to take her daily pilgrimage to the walnut tree. She never visited Peter's grave at the cemetery. To her he was always here. The walnuts were used in the cafe to make cakes and slices, another little touch the tourists loved, but for Catherine it was a symbol of enduring love. She had made peace with the past and with his death. She'd kept her promise. The proof was in the trees that blossomed around them.

It was another death that caused her to weep at the most inopportune moments. She hoped for Charlie's sake that this afternoon wasn't one of them. Beside the walnut tree grew a young apple tree – Mark's favourite variety of Cox's Orange Pippin.

'Hello, my darling.' Catherine touched the leaves of the tree. It was covered with the creamy white and delicate pink blush that made apple blossom so beautiful. 'It's a big day today. Everyone will be here, even Angela. Or should I say, especially Angela.'

She knelt down beside the tree, her knees complaining with the effort. 'Charlie's launching his vodka this afternoon. It comes in three flavours – cherry, pear and yes, apple. Who knew vodka would become so popular? People are making it out of all kinds of things these days, even sheep's whey. It really isn't my cup of tea. I am fond of his cider though, as you know, but even one glass makes me rather giddy. I'd better pace myself this afternoon.' She eased her legs to sit on the ground. 'Izzy and Stardust will be there, and Annie. A bunch of old biddies with not a man between us, not that it ever worried Izzy and Stardust. They miss you too. Everybody does.' She swallowed hard. 'I know you were tired, my darling. I know you had to go. But if I could, I'd have kept you here with me forever. Selfish of me, I know, when you were in so much pain.' Catherine laid her hand on the ground next to the apple tree's slender trunk. 'You are always with me. In the ground beneath my feet, in the air I breathe, in the music I listen to because of you.' A faint smile touched her lips. She still had the turntable he'd given her and all the albums they'd bought. Every day she would carefully slip a disc of vinyl from its sleeve. Sometimes she'd move slowly to the music, imagining Mark there with her. The days were long without him, but the memories kept her company.

Catherine wiped her eyes with the handkerchief she always tucked up her sleeve when she visited this place; one tree old and strong, the other young and full of promise. The irony was not lost on her. She cleared her throat. 'Sarah and Scott will be here. Can you believe we're about to become great-grandparents?' Mark and Catherine's daughter, Sarah, had delighted both her parents and Annie and Dave when she and Scott married. 'Our families are united forever,' Annie had said at the time. Scott was a good ten years older than Sarah, but Annie insisted boys took longer to mature than girls and the age difference made them a good match. Sarah worked as a teacher, as her mother had, and Scott had a small but successful legal practice in Hobart. Catherine had always been proud of her godson and couldn't imagine a better match for Sarah. Lucy, the couple's oldest, was expecting her first baby. 'Great-grandparents,' Catherine sighed. 'Hard to believe.'

She struggled to her feet with the noise old people make when they exert themselves. 'I can hear you laughing, you know,' she said to the tree. 'But let's face it, I *am* old.' She touched the leaves one more time. 'Goodbye, my love, I'll see you tomorrow. And we'll raise a glass to you this afternoon. You're always in our thoughts.'

Later in the day Catherine walked down from her cottage towards the cafe. It was a sprawling affair built to look like an old packing shed, except this shed had a state-of-the-art kitchen, an espresso machine, air conditioning and heating, and a massive deck with big gas outdoor heaters for the crisper weather. Behind the cafe was another building Catherine referred to as Charlie's laboratory. It was where he concocted the brews that kept the orchard alive. More than that, the orchard was thriving because of the changes he'd made, including incorporating a lot of Stardust's techniques. A few years ago, before prices had gone crazy, he'd bought land on the other side of the gully to plant more of the cider apples that were so unfamiliar to Catherine. His cider was an award-winning brew stocked in bottle shops, pubs and restaurants all over the country. Catherine had cried when he'd told her what he'd decided to call his cider. Cat and Mouse. 'I'll never forget how wonderful you were to me all those years ago,' he'd said. 'I began to laugh, to really enjoy life, because of you.'

The cafe was bustling with activity. The waitstaff in their freshly ironed uniforms and long black aprons always looked so professional. The star of the afternoon was Charlie's new range of vodka, the bottles displayed on a table set up on a small stage, with a spotlight shining on them, no less. A huge banner announcing their launch hung across the rear wall and speakers on slim silver stands flanked the stage. It made sense, Catherine supposed. Once people had a few drinks the noise level would increase, and for the speeches a microphone would be a necessity.

Catherine hovered on the deck keeping an eye out for Angela. Her home was in Sydney now, when she wasn't in her flat in Paris or her apartment in New York. Catherine was glad Annie had made the decision to tell Angela the truth before she became famous. As soon as she'd begun to attract world attention, Lara had swooped in like a bejewelled vulture, claiming her for her own via a media blitz, of course. Some claimed Angela would never have made it to such stratospheric heights without the publicity it garnered – Lara being married to rock royalty and Angela her long-missed daughter. Those with any discernment knew differently. The combination of Lara's stunning beauty and Mark's musical talent had created the perfect package. Angela was always going to be a major star. The fact that she'd been adopted under unusual circumstances certainly added an extra fillip of intrigue, but ultimately ended up reflecting badly on Lara.

In interviews Angela was always gracious about being adopted, saying yes, she was surprised when her parents had told her, but grateful they'd given her such a marvellous upbringing on an orchard in Tasmania. The international press in particular loved that fact – to them a Tasmanian orchard was somehow exotic. Angela always mentioned Mark with pride and as a result his songs had seen a resurgence on the Hits and Memories radio stations.

As her music career began to take off, Angela had decided she would be known to the world only as 'Angela'. It wasn't done to shun the parents who'd brought her up, or to shut out her biological father, it was done out of respect to the village that had born and raised her, nurtured and inspired her.

A sleek deep-blue Lexus pulled into one of the reserved parking spaces in front of the cafe. Catherine recognised Angela's glossy dark hair immediately but wondered about the silver-haired man in the driver's seat. Angela unfurled her long legs and stood beside the car, stretching. She was as slender as ever, clad in tight black trousers and a slinky scarlet top. She reached into the car and slipped a soft black leather jacket over her shoulders. Angela was in her fifties now, but still looked every bit the star in her expensive clothes and large sunglasses. The man opened the boot and extracted a long black case. Angela waved at Catherine and took the man's spare hand in her own as they walked towards her.

Catherine enveloped Angela in a lingering hug.

Angela leant back, both hands on Catherine's shoulders. 'You look wonderful.'

'That's very kind and you, of course, are as beautiful as ever.' She turned to the silver-haired man. 'And who's this?'

Angela slipped an arm around the man's waist. 'This is the fabulous Richard. He's my producer. We worked together years ago when I was too young to appreciate him fully, but we hooked up again for my latest project and ... hooked up.' Her laugh was too polished to be spontaneous. Catherine knew she'd used the line before.

Richard took Catherine's hand and kissed it. 'A pleasure to meet you, Catherine. I've heard so much about you and of course your—'

'Shh.' Angela laid a manicured finger on his lips. 'It's a surprise, remember?'

'Ah, yes,' he said. 'Where should I put this?' He indicated the black case.

'We need to find Charlie.' Angela slid her sunglasses up to the top of her head. As always, Catherine was hypnotised by those golden eyes.

'He'll be inside somewhere,' Catherine said. 'Shall we?' She led the way into the cafe. One of the young waitresses gasped and clutched at her chest as if she'd been kicked by a horse when she caught sight of Angela. For those who didn't know her, it was sometimes a shock to encounter someone so famous in everyday life.

Charlie came over and gave Angela a big hug. 'How ya goin', sis?'

'Bonza, mate,' she replied. It was their standard greeting.

Charlie shook hands with Richard and suggested he put the case behind a black curtain beside the stage. 'Just set it up there. There's power and leads.'

'Did you get me a stool?' Angela asked in a whisper.

'Of course, sis. It's all taken care of. Hey, and thanks.'

She grazed his cheek with her lips in a brief kiss. 'No, big brother, thank *you*.'

Catherine watched with curiosity. They were up to something.

'You can freshen up at the house if you want to. You'll have the place to yourself. Melissa is in her studio and Jack's cooking up a storm here in the cafe.' Charlie had met Melissa when she was in the valley sourcing specimens for her art. In the years since they'd married she'd become a renowned botanical artist. Many of her prints of apple and pear blossom decorated the walls of the cafe, along with beautiful depictions of the Tasmanian native flora. Catherine knew she was in her studio putting the final touches on a present for Angela. When their son was born, Catherine's parents had been delighted when Charlie told them they were naming him after Catherine's father. Her mother became close to her great-grandson, as she had done with Charlie, and the hours they spent together in the kitchen baking had inspired Jack to become a chef. Usually he worked in Melbourne, but he'd come down especially for this event to create delicious morsels for the guests.

Angela left the cafe with Richard beside her, causing a ripple of nervous energy from the staff. Catherine raised a questioning eyebrow at Charlie, but all he did was smile. 'Bit busy, lots to do. Oh, look, here's Annie and Paul.' He waved in their direction and, once she was distracted, scooted off.

The crowd grew steadily until the cafe was packed. Luckily Catherine and Annie had nabbed a table as well as saving seats for Izzy and Stardust when they finally arrived, and for Melissa. Paul and Scott made sure they were all kept fed and watered as Catherine caught up on the latest in Sarah's life, the happenings in Annie's orchard, Melissa's art and the latest shenanigans of Stardust's sheep. Catherine was astounded at the number of photographers present. The Huon's Cider Trail and the valley's reputation as a foodie haven had grown exponentially in recent years. That might explain the number of people taking photos of the vodka, the cider, the food and the cafe itself, not only with their mobile phones but with professional cameras. There was also a television crew and one of the local presenters. Since when was the launch of a new vodka so newsworthy? She was pleased for Charlie, but it seemed like overkill.

Charlie climbed onto the stage, his face flushed with excitement, and made a beautiful speech about how much the orchard meant to him and how growing up in such a beautiful part of the world had shaped his work and his aesthetic. He extolled the virtues of the clean air and water helping to make his cider and vodka the best it could possibly be. He proposed a toast to the Huon Valley and the crowd cheered mightily as they tossed back more alcohol. Charlie nodded to a couple of waiters hovering nearby who quickly dismantled the set-up on stage, leaving the space clear.

'Thank you all once again for coming.' Charlie beamed at the crowd. 'I have a big surprise for you today.' As he spoke, Richard appeared with another of the staff members carrying a keyboard between them. They set it up on the stage beside Charlie along with a piano stool. The news crew and photographers rushed to the front of the stage. 'As most of you are aware, Angela is my little sister.' A gasp rustled through the hushed crowd. 'And she has something she'd like to share with you today.'

Angela emerged wearing a silky dress of the deepest purple with a pattern of apple blossom twisting along its length. The only jewellery she wore was the golden snake bracelet with the emerald eyes. The single spotlight glinted on her lustrous hair and highlighted her magical eyes. The photographers went crazy in a flurry of shutters as the crowd roared its approval. Catherine and Annie stood to get a better view, clutching each other's hands in solidarity and support.

Angela thanked Charlie, made a quip about his delicious vodka, and then turned her magnetic personality on the crowd. A hush descended on the cafe. 'As you all know, I grew up right here in Wattle Grove. My mother is here. Hi, Mum.' She waved in Annie's direction and Catherine felt the hand in hers grip more tightly. It was from joy, and pride. 'And both my fathers are here in spirit.' Catherine leant closer to Annie, sharing their losses. 'I also acknowledge my birth mother with this bracelet she gave me.' Angela stretched one toned arm up to display the golden snake.

'She didn't actually give it to her,' Annie muttered in Catherine's ear. 'She sent it in the post without a card or a letter.'

'I know, and so does Angela,' Catherine whispered to her friend. 'And that's what matters.'

'I'm here today to thank them all for the different ways in which they shaped my life,' Angela continued. 'But there's someone else here today who you might not be aware of. This was originally her orchard. She was the only female orchardist here in the valley for many years, and she held on through everything nature and the economy threw at her to remain one of the very few orchards left in the Apple Isle. I wasn't aware of any of this when I was a kid, but I did know she was the first person to demonstrate the beauty and the power of the piano and encourage me to explore it for myself. She was my first piano teacher and to this day I still think she was the best.'

Catherine swayed slightly. Why was Angela talking about her? She remembered the young child, barely three years old, playing along with her on the piano at Dave's birthday party, and coming to the house for lessons from when she was eight. Angela's talent was apparent from the very beginning. It had been thrilling to watch it blossom.

'She was the most inspirational teacher I ever had,' Angela continued. 'I know my father found her inspiring too. That's one of the reasons I decided to record an album of my father's songs. Some of them are famous and others are just favourites of mine. I also wanted to honour my father and the magnificent songwriter and musician he was. A man who gave it all up, not once but twice, for the sake of those he loved. It's an acoustic album, mainly only me and my piano, produced by my marvellous producer, Richard.'

She nodded at the handsome silver-haired man standing beside the stage. 'And today, along with some delicious vodka, you are getting the very first taste of my new album.'

The cheer that erupted was deafening. Catherine and Annie clung to each other in the heaving sea of excitement and enthusiasm. The room shifted and swayed around Catherine as the memories came flooding back; Mark and her playing songs on the tiny porch of the pickers' hut, dancing in the lounge room to their favourite records, and the songs he'd hummed in her ear for only her to hear. He was here with her now, in her heart and in every cell of her body.

Angela took the microphone over to the keyboard and slotted it into the stand. She played a few notes and, once happy with the sound, turned back to the crowd who immediately became silent. 'This is the title track of the album, and my father's most famous song though he never recorded a version of it himself. You might notice a few little changes, including the title, but I've recorded it the way my father originally wrote it.'

Catherine didn't bother to stop the tears from falling. Annie stood close to her on one side and Sarah on the other, her arm tight around her mother, with Izzy and Stardust behind her.

Angela looked right at her with those golden eyes. 'She was Miss Turner, then Mrs Davis, and Auntie Catherine to me for many years, but she was always her own woman. An inspiration indeed, in many ways. Ladies and gentlemen, I give you "Catherine's Song".'

AUTHOR'S NOTE

I grew up in Tasmania, but not on an apple orchard – not even in the country. I'm a girl from the suburbs of Hobart. Before writing this novel, the only time I'd spent in orchards was during primary school excursions and a trip to the north of the state to stay with friends of the family when I was a child. But I do remember the bushfires. I was six years old and a student at Sandy Bay Infant School where *The Last of the Apple Blossom* begins. I remember the frightening sky, the huge alien sun, and lying on the linoleum of the classroom floor in my underwear alongside my classmates, trying to keep cool. I remember arriving home to our house at the bottom of Mount Nelson and the lounge room being full of children whose fathers were up the hill trying to save their homes. I also remember going on Sunday drives with my family and seeing, even years later, the decaying chimneys of houses that had been burnt and abandoned. The legacy of that day lingered on for decades.

Ironically it was a very rainy day when the idea for this story landed inside my heart. I had interviewed Monica McInerney for a literary event in the morning, and in the course of the interview we talked about grief and how it informed her writing. That afternoon the premise for this novel revealed itself to me. I found the idea terrifying. It was too big, too daunting and so very sad.

I emailed Monica the next day to tell her about the idea and added, 'It's your fault. It was all that talk about grief.' She very generously replied that she could take none of the credit and that I must write the book even though it terrified me. In a wonderful turn of events, after I had overcome my fear and written many drafts, Monica became my mentor and guided me through the final drafts before I submitted to publishers.

When I began the research for *The Last of the Apple Blossom* I realised I was right. The job before me was daunting. The events and aftermath of the fires were horrific and the drawn-out demise of the apple industry in the Huon Valley heartbreaking. I knew I needed to be respectful as many people were still traumatised by the fires that roared through Tasmania over fifty years ago. I also needed to do justice to the struggles of the orchardists, many of whom, despite being the ones who created the Apple Isle, considered that they'd worked their entire lives for nothing.

With the fiftieth anniversary of the fires in 2017 there were many resources available for research purposes. *The Mercury* newspaper published a five-part magazine series, *Black Tuesday 50th Anniversary*, featuring archival images, retrospective articles and interviews with people who lived through the disaster. Libraries Tasmania, through the records of the Tasmanian Archive and Heritage Office, collated police reports, photographs, film and handwritten accounts for a website called The Fire of '67. And '67 Bushfires Storymap was a commemorative project by the Bushfire-Ready Neighbourhoods of Tasmania Fire Service. As part of the storymap, Hugo Connor's story

'Country Week Let's Bat On!', about how he made it from Hobart to Cygnet on the afternoon of 7 February, inspired Catherine and Tim's dash to Wattle Grove. Trove and ABC Hobart were also valuable sources of information, as was *Burn: The Epic Story of Bushfire in Australia* by Paul Collins (2009).

However, when it came to the finer details of fire relief efforts, the long-term consequences on the community and the ongoing efforts to recover, I was stymied. After a long search I finally found the missing piece, *Bushfire Disaster: an Australian Community in Crisis* by RL Wettenhall (1975). The book, which uses the 1967 fires as a case study, was long out of print and hard to get hold of. I paid handsomely, but happily, for a copy. The detail in Wettenhall's book on matters of insurance, politics, policies, tourism and even the restructuring of the apple industry is extraordinary. On the back cover there is a frightening quote from one of Australia's leading fire experts at the time, AG Macarthur: 'The energy release at the height of conflagration far exceeded the energy of several atomic explosions.'

While researching apple growing in Tasmania I drew on many resources. The National Library of Australia's Apples and Pears Oral History Project is a rich source of history and knowledge in this area. To hear the orchardists, many since passed away, talk about their personal experiences of working their orchards through the seasons and the years, and the battles they encountered, brought the history of the Huon Valley to life for me. Nathalie Norris's account was inspirational, as she was the only female orchardist of her time. In Brian Clark's interview he praised his daughter's effort to keep the family orchard afloat. It was only after spending time with Naomie Clark-Port, my Apple Angel, that I realised she was the daughter he'd admired so much. He died a few years ago and Naomie wasn't aware that he'd recorded the interview. I have thanked Naomie in the acknowledgements. This novel would have been lacking in many respects without her generosity and her introductions to old orchardists from the area.

ABC Radio National made an evocative radio documentary for Hindsight in 2006, *Huon Valley Apple: a short trip down the periscope of history*, produced by Trish Fox. It's on the ABC website if you'd like to step into the shoes of those who lived and worked on the orchards.

Other material that I pored over, underlined, highlighted and wrote notes on, included 'Apples of the Huon' by Beth Hall (*Tasmanian Geographic*, 2014), *Full and Plenty: an oral history of apple growing in the Huon Valley* by Catherine Watson (1987), *The History and Heritage of the Tasmanian Apple Industry*, a profile by Anne McConnell and Nathalie Servant (1999) and *The Australian Apple Recipe Book* (1982), which not only has recipes, many of which I've made, but also includes an orchard calendar, photographs of orchards in the Huon Valley and details on apple varieties.

In the Hobart Reading Room at the State Library of Tasmania (Libraries Tasmania) I read the *Apple and Pear Growers Association submission to the Senate Review of Australia's Quarantine Function* which includes a history of the Tasmanian industry, *Shaping the Apple Industry: report of the Apple and Pear Marketing Advisory Committee* by A Hocking and others (1978) and *The Tasmanian Apple and Pear Industry 1966–81: a study for the Interim Primary Products Marketing Council and the Tasmanian Apple and Pear Marketing Authority* by A Hocking (1982). For an overview of the changing times and major events of the era *The Tasmanian Year Book* from 1967 onwards provided salient details. The Department of Veterans' Affairs Anzac Portal was my main source for information on the Vietnam War, along with newspaper and magazine accounts. I also studied the Tree Pull Scheme using correspondence and reports from the Department of Agriculture, the Rural Reconstruction Board, the Apple and Pear Growers Federation of Tasmania, the Agricultural Bank, newspaper articles, and letters from the growers themselves. Many of them told a heartbreaking story.

As I researched the book I realised how hard it would be to find any kind of happy ending for my characters. But I felt driven to do the best I could for those who'd worked so hard on the land to eke out a living despite everything nature and bureaucracy threw at them. I knew I wanted to include the hippies or the 'new settlers' who came to the Huon Valley in the 1970s. As such, I needed Catherine's orchard to be close to Cygnet, which was a magnet for many who wanted to live on the land and get back to nature – a strange concept for those who'd lived on the land and with nature all of their lives. I thought if I was going to have any chance of a happy ending the hippies would need to be involved somehow. *A Brief History of Cygnet* by Jean Cockerill (1987), *Mary Street, Cygnet: a history of life on the main road in a Tasmanian country town* by David Coad (2016) and the Cygnet Area School journal helped me understand more about the town. At the Living History Museum at Cygnet, I found transcripts of interviews with orchardists, locals and the new arrivals. The accounts provided by the hippies were fascinating to read and the photographs of their dwellings and lifestyle were illuminating. *The Core of the Matter: Organic Apple Growing in Tasmania* by Chris and Paula Steenholdt (1998) provided the inspiration for many of Stardust's techniques. In the end though, Stardust, Izzy and their friends were only part of the happy ending I came up with while on a silent ten-day meditation retreat. It was the ingenuity and sheer hard work of Catherine, Annie, Dave and Mark that saved their orchards and their livelihoods.

I hope I have done the growers of the Huon Valley justice, those who worked hard all their lives through disasters and hardships so severe it would make most of us give up in despair. I have an enormous respect for them and enormous gratitude. Their grit and tenacity has touched my life deeply and I'm honoured to have been given this story to share with you.

ACKNOWLEDGEMENTS

Just as with an orchard, it takes time and work to create a book, and many hands to nurture it, prune it and make it productive. I am deeply grateful to all of those who assisted in shaping *The Last of the Apple Blossom*, and to those who helped it bloom.

My heartfelt thanks to Naomie Clark-Port, my Apple Angel. Naomie is an orchardist in the Huon Valley, tending the orchard that has been in her family for many generations. I called her, out of the blue, with three pages of questions about apple growing. Even though I was a complete stranger to her, she responded with overwhelming warmth and generosity right from the start. Her helpfulness extended to a private tour of her orchard, cool room and old packing shed, and a guided drive through the Huon Valley. Naomie also set up interviews with some of the orchardists from the area who lived through the times described in this novel. And to top it all off, she agreed to read and fact check a draft of *The Last of the Apple Blossom*. (Any mistakes are my own and certainly not Naomie's.) If you're in the Huon Valley make sure to drop in to

MARY-LOU STEPHENS

Frank's Cider House and Cafe in Franklin and try some of Naomie's award-winning cider.

A soul-felt thank you to Monica McInerney, who mentored me through many drafts of *The Last of the Apple Blossom* as part of the ASA's Mentorship Program. Monica was a hard taskmistress but a loving one, and a constant source of wisdom, warmth and support. Thank you, Monica, this novel would not be the book it is without you. I will never forget your kindness.

Thank you to the orchardists who allowed me to pick their brains over cups of tea and cake: John Marshall at Ranelagh, and Phil Cawthorne and Frank Clark (no relation to Naomie) at Wattle Grove. Their stories were always fascinating, often funny and sometimes heartbreaking.

My husband and I got chatting with Tony Evans at the Summer Kitchen Bakery in Ranelagh. When we discovered he knew a lot about apples, we invited Tony to our Airbnb (a converted apple shed no less) for dinner. Tony regaled us with tales of working on his family's orchard as well as the larger orchards in the Huon Valley.

Moya Fyfe wrote a haunting essay for the *Griffith Review*, 'When the Apple Cart Tipped', about her childhood growing up on an orchard and her memories of the orchard being bulldozed into the ground as part of the Tree Pull Scheme. Moya met with me to expand on those memories and painted a vivid picture of what it was like being a kid during those times.

A cheeky thanks to Tony Rice whose description of being a nine-year-old boy at the time of the fires gave me an insight into how Annie's boys would have reacted. He also gave me the delicious detail of the apple trucks wiping out every guidepost along the Huon Highway.

Max and Dawn Oates's memories of surviving the 1967 bushfires in the Huon Valley gave me goosebumps. My sister, Katy, and her husband, Tony, introduced me to Max and Dawn in Crabtree and

446

also to Tony Rice. Thank you, my darling sister, for the introductions and for lending me your car when I needed to make yet another dash down the Huon Valley.

The Living History Museum in Cygnet is a treasure trove of information about the area, the apple industry and the locals. Thank you to the volunteers who keep it running. The information on the 'new settlers' was especially fascinating and useful.

To Associate Professor Anne-Marie Williams, Tasmanian School of Medicine, Forensic Anthropologist, thank you for your expert advice on the limits of pathology in the late 1960s.

A big thank you to the librarians in the Hobart Reading Room at the State Library of Tasmania, for your enthusiasm, patience and helpfulness. I loved the hours I spent there poring over Tree Pull Scheme applications, Cygnet school records, Apple and Pear Marketing Authority reports, Department of Agriculture information and Rural Reconstruction Board correspondence.

The idea for this novel was niggling away at me for some time before it finally took root, watered by tears and fertilised with determination, at a Writing in Paradise retreat led by the dynamic Shelley Kenigsberg and ably assisted by David Leser. Some of those first handwritten words made it into the finished book. Thank you for bringing them into the light.

I couldn't have spent as much time in Tasmania or the Huon Valley without the generosity of my beautiful friend Penny McDonald. Thank you for all that you did for me, Penny. This novel would have been a lot harder to research without your support. My thanks also to Vicky McDonald for her hospitality.

There are two women who've aided and abetted my writing ambitions since 2008. Together we have laughed, cried, sworn and celebrated our writing and our lives. This journey would be a lot lonelier and a lot less fun without Sue Goldstiver and Jodie Miller travelling alongside me. And an extra special hug (I know you love them, really) to Sue, for a sterling edit along the way.

To my darling Christine Evans, thank you for your unwavering belief in this novel and for your informed and thoughtful writerly advice. You have always been a true friend and a spectacularly talented writer. And thank you to Rachel Baily, another talented writer, for synopsis advice and for holding my hand when the offers came in.

Thank you to Fiona McIntosh for her excellent fiction writing Masterclass. The ongoing support and camaraderie from Fiona and the entire Masterclass community has been a blessing.

The 2020 RWA Conference organisers did a mighty job creating a virtual conference during the ever-changing conditions of that year. Much gratitude to the volunteers who organised it and to those who facilitated the online pitches. It was because of my pitch to Nicola Robinson from Harlequin that you hold this book in your hands.

Which brings me to a massive acknowledgment to Nicola Robinson herself. Thank you for believing in *The Last of the Apple Blossom* and for your thorough structural edit. I do love research, but the book is so much better without all the 'bog'. Annabel Blay took charge of the manuscript for the next edits and in her kind and generous hands the novel was polished to a beautiful shine. Thank you for your heartfelt and encouraging comments, Annabel, you are a joy to work with. And a grateful thanks to Annabel Adair for her eagle-eyed proofreading skills.

The beautiful cover was designed by the talented Christine Armstrong. The image is the perfect blend of warmth and wistfulness, while the ghostly apple blossom reminds me of the days long gone when the Huon Valley was covered in a blanket of pink and white.

Thank you to everyone at Harlequin and HarperCollins, especially Jo Munroe for her marketing panache and Natika Palka for her fabulous publicity prowess.

Deep gratitude and love to my husband, Ken, who learnt almost as much about apple orchards as I did during the research process. Thank you for your support, your patience and for making me smile when times were tough.

talk about it

Let's talk about books.

Join the conversation:

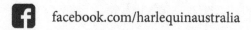 facebook.com/harlequinaustralia

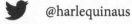 @harlequinaus

 @harlequinaus

harpercollins.com.au/hq

If you love reading and want to know about our
authors and titles, then let's talk about it.